DESERT ROSES

ROSEY DOW
JANET LEE BARTON
RHONDA GIBSON

ISBN 978-1-60260-407-0

All scripture quotations are taken from the King James Version of the Bible.

Cover model photography: Jim Celuch, Celuch Creative Imaging

Published by Barbour Publishing, Inc., P.O. Box 719, Uhrichsville, Ohio 44683, www.barbourbooks.com

Our mission is to publish and distribute inspirational products offering exceptional value and biblical encouragement to the masses.

Printed in the United States of America.

STIRRING UP ROMANCE

Dedication

To My Lord and Savior for showing me the way. And to the family He has blessed me with for your unfailing encouragement and love. I love you all.

Chapter 1

Denver, Colorado, late summer 1899

While Elise prepared afternoon tea, her mother-in-law, Frieda Morgan, reread the letter she'd brought in from the post office earlier that afternoon. As Elise turned to bring the tea tray to the kitchen table, her mother-in-law looked up from the pages she held.

"Elise, dear, I think it's time I take Derrick up on his invitation to come live with him."

Elise almost dropped the full tray, but she steadied herself just before she reached the table. She set the tray down as quickly as she could while her mind screamed, *No, Mama. Please don't go.*

She took a seat at the table and busied herself pouring their tea while she fought to sound calm. "Mama, are you sure this is what you want to do?"

"Elise, I do not want to leave you. But Derrick has been asking me to come live with him down in Farmington for several years. It sounds as though he could use my help with the harvest this year. He says his orchard will produce a record crop if the weather holds. I know I could help him out by cooking for those who come to help pick the apples."

"But, Mama, you haven't been feeling at all well these last few months. I'm not sure you're up to the trip, not to mention the work once you get there." Elise went through the motions of stirring cream and sugar into her tea, but her heart was breaking at the thought that her husband's mother might move away. She'd come to love her as her own mother. With her husband, Carl, and both of her parents gone now, Elise's only remaining relative was Frieda Morgan.

"It will take a few weeks to get ready. I'm sure I'll feel better by the time we get all the arrangements made." Frieda paused and took a sip of tea. "You will help me with all that, won't you, dear?"

Hard as it would be to see her go, Elise loved her mother-in-law enough that she wanted her to be happy. "Of course I will, if it's what you want. But only if you promise to come visit me."

"Oh, dear Elise, you are my daughter. Of course I will. Perhaps I'll stay part of the year with Derrick and part of the year with you. But I just feel that Derrick needs me right now."

Elise felt somewhat better knowing that Frieda wasn't deserting her. She took a sip from her cup of tea. Besides, it would be selfish of her to try to talk her mother-in-law out of going to her son. She sighed. "I'll get the train schedule for you tomorrow so you can start planning your trip."

Frieda reached across the table and patted her hand. "Thank you, dear. I knew you would understand."

"I do. I just hate to see you go."

"I know. And I hate to leave you behind. You and Carl were so kind to invite me into your home after Papa died. And then for you to ask me to stay when Carl passed away. . . You're a wonderful daughter to me, Elise. I could ask for no better."

"Oh, Mama, don't be talking like that. You'll have me bawling like a newborn babe. I'll check into everything for you. But I won't let you get on a train by yourself if you aren't feeling much better than you've been the past few weeks."

"I'm going to be fine, dear. You'll see. But I'd be more than happy for you to accompany me to Farmington."

Elise was quiet for a few moments. She wouldn't have to worry about Frieda if she did go with her, and there was really no reason not to go. Carl had left her with a modest inheritance. The home she and her mother-in-law lived in was paid for, there was a tidy sum in the bank, and Elise had her sewing and cooking skills to fall back on, should she ever need to work.

"Perhaps I'll go with you to make sure you're all right once you get to Farmington. I'd feel better helping you settle in."

"Oh, that would be wonderful, dear! It was just what I was hoping you would say."

"All right, then," Elise said. "I'll get all the information we need so that we can plan our itinerary, and you can write Derrick and let him know we're coming and what day we'll be arriving."

Frieda smiled and nodded. "I'll write him as soon as we have it all planned." She sighed. "It will be so good to see my youngest son again."

Elise sent up a silent prayer asking forgiveness for being so selfish. It was only natural that her mother-in-law would want to be around her only surviving son. She'd been blessed that Frieda had stayed with her this long. And as much as she knew Frieda loved her, most probably she'd delayed moving only to help Elise with the grief they both shared when Carl had died so suddenly from apoplexy. Elise didn't know what she would have done without her.

But now it was time to quit being so selfish and let Frieda do what she wanted—and to do that, she needed help. She prayed silently, *Please, dear Lord, help me to be as giving to Frieda as she has been to me. Please help me not to show how heartsick I am over her decision. In Jesus' name I pray. Amen.*

STIRRING UP ROMANCE

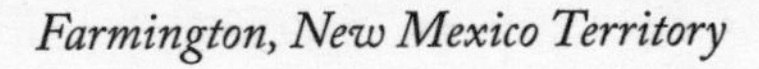

Farmington, New Mexico Territory

After unloading the wagon of supplies he'd bought in Farmington that day, Derrick Morgan unhitched his team from the wagon and put them out to pasture. After he put up the supplies he'd left sitting on the kitchen table, he warmed up the strong coffee left over from that morning and made himself a supper of bacon and eggs. He took his plate out to his front porch and sat on the steps to eat.

Looking out over his apple orchard, he nodded and grinned. Barring bad weather, it looked as if this was going to be the best harvest he'd ever had. His trees were loaded with apples. In another month or so, he'd have people swarming over the place, helping him pick his fruit. They'd begin with the Jonathans, go on to the Delicious, then finally pick the Winesaps. It was going to be a very busy time of year, but he looked forward to it. He needed to look into getting someone to help feed the workers, but he wouldn't complain. The Lord had blessed him with a good crop, and he'd be thankful for it.

Derrick took his dishes back inside and put them in the sink along with the dishes from that morning. He poured himself another cup of coffee before lighting the lamp on the kitchen table. It was then that he pulled the letter from his mother out of his back pocket. He'd been waiting all day to open it. He'd been trying to get her to agree to move down from Denver ever since his brother, Carl, had passed away, but to no avail. He wrote her faithfully each week and looked forward to her replies even though she kept saying she needed to stay in Denver with Elise.

Elise. He sighed and shook off the thought of her. It did no good to think of her now. Derrick opened the letter and pulled the lamp closer as he began to read:

My dear son,

From your last letter, it sounds as though you could use some help with your harvest. And I have been longing to see you. In light of that, I have decided to come and help with the feeding of the workers who will be picking your apples. I will be leaving here in two weeks to come to Farmington. I have included our itinerary for you. Please meet the train in Durango on the first day of September. I am counting the days until I see you again.

Your loving mother

At first, pure joy that his mother was coming at long last flooded over Derrick. Then he read the letter again, and worry replaced joy. *Our* itinerary? That meant someone was coming with her. Surely if Elise was accompanying her, she would have said so. Yet who else could it be? His heart began to hammer in his chest. Would he see her again after all these years?

But what if it wasn't Elise? Maybe he should travel up there and bring his mother back. Only now wasn't a good time for him to be away for any extended time. It had to be Elise who was coming with her; surely she wouldn't let his mother travel with just anyone!

Derrick got up and paced the room. He looked at the calendar hanging by the back door. With mail being what it was here, over a week had passed since his mother had mailed this letter. She would be here in five days. There was no time to get a letter back to her. Maybe he could send a telegram to tell her he would come get her.

No. Derrick shook his head and sighed. His mother would not be pleased if he even implied that he didn't trust her to take care of herself. She'd been doing it for a long while without his help—but still. . .he didn't like the fact that he didn't know who she was traveling with! And if he asked about Elise—well, he didn't feel comfortable asking if she was coming. He'd managed to hide his feelings about her for a very long time; he certainly didn't want to raise any suspicions that he might still care.

Happiness that he would soon be seeing his mother sneaked around the worry as Derrick read the letter one more time. She really was coming. She'd see how well he'd done for himself here in Farmington. He was proud of his orchard and his home. He couldn't wait for her to see them.

He looked around his kitchen. What a mess it was! Dirty dishes filled the sink, the floor needed to be swept and mopped—there was no way his home would pass his mother's inspection for cleanliness. No way at all. He went to the sink and began running water into it. There was much to do to get ready for his mother. . . and he had less than a week to do it.

It hadn't been an easy trip coming down from Denver, and Elise was afraid the altitude change had been hard on her mother-in-law. They'd left Denver before dawn the day before, and at first it was exciting to watch the scenery go by. But most of it was pretty much the same in the mountains. She was getting eager to see what the country around Farmington, New Mexico Territory, was like.

They'd stopped for the noon meal at a nice hotel in Pueblo, and even by then it was a relief to get out, stretch their legs, and have a break. But the respite was over all too soon, and they boarded the train once more for the rest of what was becoming a very long day. Even though they had first-class seats, it was an extremely tiring ride as they sped along the rails.

Elise could see the weariness in her mother-in-law's eyes until finally she drifted off to sleep. She knew Frieda must be exhausted to be able to sleep with the rocking and weaving of the train car. She wished she could do the same. Instead, her mind seemed to flit from one thought to another. It was going to be so very lonely when she got back to Denver without her dear mother-in-law. Would Frieda like Farmington? How was she going to manage all alone in Denver? She wondered what Derrick would think about her traveling with his mother. Had he changed much since he'd left for New Mexico Territory over five years ago? On and on her scattered thoughts went, jumping from one subject to another.

A bend in the tracks sent Elise sliding toward the window with Frieda sliding against her, waking the older woman up.

"Oh! I must have dozed off," Frieda said. "I guess I ate too much lunch. I just could not keep my eyes open. I'm sorry, dear. I haven't been much company today."

Elise smiled at her. "I'm glad you were able to get some sleep."

"I wish you could have. How far away are we from Durango? Do you know?"

Elise shook her head. "I think we're about an hour or two out now."

Frieda looked out the window. "Look, Elise, the scenery isn't a lot different than that in Denver, is it?"

Elise shook her head. "No. But I expect it will change when we travel from Durango to where Derrick lives tomorrow."

Frieda's eyes regained a little of their natural sparkle in anticipation of seeing her son once more. "I hope Derrick received my letter telling him when to meet us."

"I'm sure he did. He'll be there. But if not, we'll just get a room at a hotel and send him a telegram."

"Oh, thank you, Elise. I'm so glad you came with me. I would probably panic if I were by myself. I haven't traveled this far in years."

"You'd do fine, Mama. But I'm glad I came, too. I'd only have worried myself sick if I hadn't."

"Now, you know what the Good Book says about worry, Elise."

"Yes, ma'am, I do. I try not to. I try to leave everything in the Lord's hands. I truly do. But I just couldn't bear the thought of you traveling this far by yourself." Elise didn't like the thought of traveling back to Denver without her, either. But she didn't say so. She didn't want Frieda to worry about her.

"Well," Frieda said, "I should take a little of my own advice. I know what the Bible says very well, yet here I am worrying about Derrick being there."

"We're a pair, aren't we?" Elise teased.

"We are that." Frieda smiled and looked out the window once again. "I'll be glad when we get to Durango. Surely we'll be there soon."

Elise did hope the trip hadn't been too much for her mother-in-law. Frieda claimed she was feeling better, but Elise had her doubts about that. She just didn't seem to have the energy she'd had a few months ago. She could only hope that her mother-in-law would perk up once they got to Farmington and were in her son's company.

Chapter 2

While Derrick was thrilled that his mother was at long last coming, her timing wasn't the best. Harvesttime would be upon them soon after her arrival. He'd be too busy to show her around very much or help her get used to her new surroundings once harvest got under way.

He hoped she wouldn't mind too much. He'd been very busy the past week, checking his orchards, lining up help for harvest, and cleaning his house in preparation for his mother's arrival—and possibly that of Elise, too. He had tried to keep hope from building that he might see her again, but he wasn't doing a very good job of it. Fact of the matter was, he would love to see Elise again. He couldn't help but wonder what kind of woman she'd become.

He traveled by stage to Durango on the day before he was to meet his mother there. He booked rooms at the Strater Hotel. His mother was bound to be worn out after the train trip from Denver, and the trip on to Farmington the next day would be even more tiring for her. He couldn't wait to see her. He was eager to find out who was traveling with her and knew he would be disappointed if it wasn't Elise. Either way, from her letter, it sounded as if an extra room would be needed. If not, he could always give it up.

He spent most of the next day seeing the sights of Durango and looking at his pocket watch. Still, the day seemed to drag for him until it was time to go to the train station.

Derrick stood with a cluster of people anxiously awaiting the train. Once they heard the whistle blow, he, along with the others, craned his neck to get the first glimpse of the locomotive as it rounded the bend and chugged into Durango.

He tried to see if he could see his mother's sweet face in one of the windows as the train slowed and came to a stop, but it was getting on toward sunset and he couldn't make out anything. Everyone on the train platform hurried forward as the conductors let down the steps of each passenger car.

Derrick's gaze went back and forth until he spotted his mother preparing to leave one of the cars. She stood there, looking all around, but he could tell she didn't see him. He hurried forward to greet her.

She spotted him just as he reached her. "Derrick! Oh, my son!"

"Mama, it is so good to see you!" His mother had aged since he'd last seen her, and she looked exhausted to him. Sudden tears sprang to the back of his eyes. To keep her from seeing how much it pained him to see her looking so frail, he hugged her to him and rocked her back and forth.

"It is so very wonderful to see you!"

His mother didn't bother to hide her tears, and Derrick hugged her again. It was only when he looked over her shoulder that he recognized the woman standing just a few feet away from them. "Elise? Is it you?"

The corners of her mouth turned up into a small smile. "Hello, Derrick. I traveled with Mama. I hope it's all right that I'm here."

"Of course it is," he answered. How could it not be all right? It was what he'd been hoping for. She was even lovelier than he remembered. Her eyes reminded him of the pond on his property, deep blue with a hint of green, and her hair appeared more red than brown in the late afternoon sunlight. She seemed a little wary, and he wondered if it was because of the trip or because of seeing him again.

"I'm sure it was a long journey getting here, and we have a ways to go by stagecoach tomorrow. I've reserved rooms for us all at the Strater. We'll have a nice dinner, and hopefully a good night's rest will ready you both for the trip home."

"A good night's rest without all that rocking and swaying over the tracks sounds wonderful," his mother said. "I still feel like I'm moving."

"If you aren't up to it tomorrow, we can wait another day, Mama," Derrick said. He hated to be away any longer than necessary, but his mother looked totally worn out, and he didn't want to tire her even more.

"I'm sure I'll be fine tomorrow, dear. I'm so eager to see your orchards. I plan on cooking for the people who help you harvest your apples."

"Mama, I didn't ask you to come live with me just so I could put you to work. Don't you worry about—"

"I know you didn't, son. But I intend to help you out as much as I can."

Derrick bent to pick up their valises. "We'll see how you feel when we get there. In the meantime, let's get you to the hotel. You can rest awhile, and then we'll get a warm meal into you."

"I certainly won't argue with that," his mother said as she and Elise followed him to the depot, where he made arrangements to have their trunks sent to the stagecoach office across the street. Then they headed down the boardwalk to the hotel.

When they reached the Strater, Derrick got their room keys from the desk clerk, and Elise and his mother followed him upstairs. Stopping at the first room, Derrick unlocked the door and glanced at Elise, who'd been very quiet on the way over. "This is your room, Elise. Mother's is right next door."

"I could stay with Mama, Derrick. There's no need for you to spend more money—"

"Of course there isn't, Derrick. Elise and I can share the same room," his mother said.

"It's all right. I didn't know for sure who was traveling with Mama, and I reserved the extra room because of that. Since I did, you might as well make use of it."

"I'll pay you—"

"I'll not hear of that, Elise," Derrick said. He knew it came out a little gruff but he hadn't meant for it to. He tried to soften his tone. "I was going to do it for a complete stranger, but I'm much happier to be doing it for you."

She gave a small smile and nodded her head. "Then I thank you."

"You're welcome." Derrick moved to the next door and unlocked it for his mother. He set her valise inside before turning back to the two women. "I'm in the room just across from you, should you need me. I've made reservations in the dining room for six o'clock. Will that be enough time for you two to freshen up?"

"That will be plenty," his mother answered.

He glanced at Elise, and she nodded. "Yes, it will be enough time."

"Good. I'll be back to escort you downstairs then." He turned to his mother and kissed her cheek. "I'm so glad you're here, Mama. Try to rest for a little while, all right? I'm going to the stage company to check on our departure time tomorrow and make sure they have your trunks." He left them both with a wave and headed back downstairs.

Elise followed Frieda into her room and saw there was a connecting door to hers. "Oh, look, Mama. I can leave the door ajar in case you need me."

"That's good, Elise, dear. You may have to come wake me in about an hour. I think I'll lie down for a little while."

"I know this trip has been tiring for you. Would you like me to ask Derrick to postpone our trip to Farmington for a day or so? I'm sure he would be glad to do that for you. He's already offered."

Frieda shook her head as she sat in a chair by the window and began to unlace her shoes. "No, dear, I can't do that. He's been away from his place long enough. I'm sure he's anxious to get home with harvest coming so soon."

"All right, I'll let you rest, then." Elise was concerned about her mother-in-law. She did look exhausted. Hopefully a night of good sleep would help her. "I'll check on you in a little while." She plumped the pillows on the bed and kissed Frieda's cheek before going to her room.

She was tempted to take a nap herself but was afraid they'd both oversleep and not be ready when Derrick came to get them. So she sat in the chair and looked out over the street instead. She'd been a little taken aback by her reaction to seeing Derrick. For some reason her heart seemed to have taken wings and fluttered against her ribs, and she wasn't sure why.

He'd aged some since she'd seen him last, just as she had. But the lines around his eyes served to make him seem more mature than his age, and Elise thought he was even better looking than she'd remembered. He and Carl had never looked much alike—Carl had looked more like his mother, while Derrick took after his father. Carl's hair had been sandy and his eyes brown. Derrick's hair was almost black, now with a few silver strands beginning to show, and his eyes were deep blue. He was taller than Carl had been, too. So her reaction to him wasn't because he reminded her of Carl, and that fact discomfited Elise most of all.

She hadn't been able to tell how he felt about her being here. He'd been very cordial to her, but Frieda had taught her sons good manners, and she knew Derrick wouldn't let her know if he was upset about her arrival. She should have asked Frieda why she hadn't told Derrick whom she was traveling with, but she'd forgotten to when they were alone, and she guessed it really didn't matter now. She wouldn't be here long anyway—only long enough to see that her mother-in-law was settled in.

Elise spent the next half hour straightening her valise and freshening up. She took her hair down, brushed it until it shone, and then pulled it up and back into a knot on the top of her head. She looked at the small pendant watch pinned to her lapel and saw that it was time to wake Frieda.

She knocked lightly on the connecting door and was a little surprised when Frieda opened the door with a hairbrush in her hand. "Did you not get any rest, Mama?"

"I tried but was too excited, I suppose." Frieda continued to brush her hair as she spoke. "So I just got up and freshened up for dinner. I'm sure I'll sleep quite well tonight. The bed is good."

Elise hoped Frieda would sleep well, because even through her excitement about being here, she looked very tired. "You just look weary, Mama. I do hope this trip hasn't been too much for you."

"It hasn't. I'll retire early tonight and be fine tomorrow. You'll see," Frieda assured her once more.

Elise sent up a silent prayer that her mother-in-law was right. They still had a long way to go tomorrow, and the stage would be much more uncomfortable than the train had been. "I hope so."

Elise took the brush from Frieda. "Let me do your hair. You know you love to have it brushed."

"Thank you, dear. You have such a nice touch with my hair. I'll certainly miss you dressing it for me when you go back to Denver."

Elise would miss it, too. She brushed her mother-in-law's long silver hair and then dressed it much the same as she had her own. She pulled it up and back and twisted it into a loose knot at the top of Frieda's head. "There. You look lovely. Are you hungry?"

"I am. And I'm looking forward to seeing my son again. He's changed a great deal in the last few years, don't you think?"

"He does seem more—"

"Mature," Frieda said, nodding as she finished Elise's sentence. "I think he's come into his own as a man."

There came a knock on the door, and Frieda crossed the room, opening it to her son. Elise's heart did a little jig as she saw Derrick standing there looking even more handsome than he had that afternoon. He was clean shaven, his hair was neatly parted just slightly left of center, and his coat looked as if he'd just brushed it.

His face lit up in a smile for his mother. "Are you hungry? My stomach is growling at the aromas drifting up the staircase."

Frieda stuck her head out into the hall. "Something smells quite good. And yes, I believe I could eat a bite. Elise, dear, are you ready?"

"I am." She followed her mother-in-law out into the hall. The aromas wafting up the staircase did indeed smell wonderful.

"Well, let's go down. Derrick, you always did have a good appetite."

Derrick crooked an elbow for his mother to take, and Elise followed the two of them down the staircase. Tired as she must be, Frieda looked very happy to be with her son, and Elise couldn't help but be glad she'd come.

They were shown to a table in front of a window overlooking the street, and Elise felt quite comfortable listening to mother and son catch up with each other while they waited for their meal to be served. They weren't disappointed in it. Their supper was every bit as tasty as they'd hoped it would be. The fried chicken was crisp and tender. It was served with mashed potatoes, gravy, and fluffy biscuits. For dessert they had their choice of chocolate cake or cherry pie.

Throughout the meal, Derrick described his orchard and told them of his hopes for the future. "I have one of the larger orchards in the area," he said with a hint of pride in his voice. "The trees are full of apples, and that means I need a lot of help picking them during harvest. Then they're packed and shipped by overland freight here to Durango and then out by rail. I've been working hard to line up buyers for my apples over the last few years. By the time the railroad line finally makes it to Farmington, I hope to have Morgan Orchards firmly established. Shipping by train will make things much easier, and the apples will get to market much earlier. The ground here is so fertile, I think Farmington is going to be a major farming community in the future. And I'm hoping to be a large part of it."

"I am so very proud of you, son," Frieda said. "Your papa would be, too.

I can't wait to see your place."

Elise found that she couldn't wait, either.

Derrick couldn't help but notice that Elise watched his mother as closely as he did while the stage jostled its passengers this way and that on its journey to Farmington. It seemed that with each passing mile, his mother looked paler and more exhausted.

He couldn't have been more relieved when they stopped for a meal at the halfway station. Maybe the brief break from all the jostling would help his mother. Derrick helped her down from the stage, then gave Elise a hand down while steadying his mother with his free arm until she could get used to solid ground once more.

The meal wasn't great, but Derrick was proud that Elise and his mother ate it as if it were, while others at the table groused about the quality of the food. Finally the driver told the grumblers that they could wait outside if the food wasn't up to their standards. That quieted them right down.

By the time they boarded the stage once more, Derrick was just glad that the next stop would be Farmington. He sat beside his mother, hoping that if she were able to get a nap, she would feel comfortable leaning her head against his shoulder. The meal must have helped some, or maybe it was the boredom of seeing mile after mile of the same scenery pass by that had his mother falling asleep only a few miles out from the way station. Derrick eased an arm around her to help steady her in her slumber and could have kicked himself for not staying one more night in Durango.

He glanced across at Elise and found that her attention was on his mother. When she shifted her gaze and saw him looking at her, she smiled. He wanted to ask Elise about his mother's health. He had gone to her door first last evening, hoping to have a talk with her, but she'd been in his mother's room. It wouldn't have seemed proper to knock on her door after his mother retired for the evening. And there was no time this morning, as they were rushing around to catch the stage on time.

There was not even a chance to talk now, with the stage full of passengers and his mother asleep on his shoulder. Conversation with Elise would have to wait until they could have a moment alone.

Chapter 3

By the time the stage reached Farmington, it was almost suppertime. Derrick took his mother and Elise to one of the hotel restaurants to eat before heading home. There was no way he would expect either of them to prepare a meal as tired as they both looked. After they ate, he left them in the lobby to rest while he went to the stage company and loaded his mother's trunks and the rest of their bags onto the buckboard he'd left in town.

He went back to pick them up, and as he headed for home, even though his orchard was only a few miles out of town, Derrick suspected it felt like a hundred to the two women. The sun was just setting when he turned onto the road that led to his place. Derrick could tell just by looking at the two women that they were exhausted. But they were troupers and tried not to show it, exclaiming over the beautiful sunset and the size of his orchard as he pulled the wagon up in front of his house. It was a two-story white frame house that gleamed in the last rays of sunlight.

"Oh, son, what a wonderful place you have here," his mother said as he jumped down and turned to lift her to the ground.

"Thank you, Mama." He gave Elise a hand down and led them to the front porch. "Come on inside. I'll show you around the house, then bring in your things."

He unlocked the door and stood aside so that both women could enter the parlor. As Derrick led them through the dining room and into the kitchen, he was rewarded by the oohs and aahs he heard as they followed him though the house.

"I'll put the kettle on for some tea for you, Mama."

"Thank you, son," she said, nodding as she looked around the room. He could tell she liked it, but he couldn't take a lot of credit for the home's furnishings. The previous owner had sold it to him furnished. She had told him she'd ordered the newest range from Sears & Roebuck just six months before selling the place. Nothing in the house was very old, and he had a feeling she'd furnished the whole house by ordering out of the catalog. He was glad his mother and Elise seemed to like it all.

"Oh, Derrick, I don't know what I expected, but this is all even nicer than I'd thought it would be." His mother turned to him and chuckled as she watched him fill the teakettle. "And I *never* expected that you'd have running water in the kitchen! That will make cooking for your extra hands much easier during harvest."

Derrick couldn't wait to see her reaction to the biggest surprise he had for her. "I'm glad you like it, Mama," he said, kissing her on the cheek. "While we're waiting for the water to boil, let me show you upstairs if you're up to it. Then I'll bring in your things while you and Elise relax with a cup of tea."

"Of course I'm up to it. Lead the way," his mother said with a smile.

Derrick explained more about his home as they went upstairs. "I've done a few things to the place, but I have to admit it was in pretty good shape when I bought it."

"Why would anyone want to sell it?"

"Well, the owner was a widow, and after her husband died, she wanted to take her children back east. I just heard about it at the right time. She was selling it completely furnished so that she didn't have to ship everything back all that way. I made her a fair offer, and she took it. So I had a lot to work with."

"That was the Lord working for you, son."

Derrick felt a twinge of guilt at the reminder of all the Lord had provided for him since he'd moved to New Mexico Territory. He hadn't acknowledged it often enough. "I'm sure you're right, Mama."

He reached the landing and walked down the hall to the room facing the front of his property. "This room will be yours, Mama. I hope you like it."

It had been furnished with a matching bedstead, washstand, and dresser of solid oak. The cream-colored wallpaper was covered with pink and red rosebud vines. The bed coverings looked as if they'd been made to match.

"Oh, Derrick, this is lovely. I love the colors."

"I remembered that red is one of your favorites. You can have any room in the house for your own, but I thought this just fit you."

"It's perfect, dear."

Derrick led the way back out into the hall and opened the door across the way. "I hope this room will be all right for you, Elise. They had several daughters, so both rooms were decorated with girls in mind."

This room also had matching furniture but was decorated in soft yellows. "This is very nice, Derrick. I'm sure I'll be quite comfortable here until I go back to Denver. Thank you."

That was the first mention of her returning to Denver, and Derrick wasn't sure how he felt about it. Seeing the expression on his mother's face, he wasn't sure how she felt about it, either.

"Where is your room, dear?" his mother asked.

"It's at the other end of the hallway. It's done in blue and white. Come and see." Derrick led the way to his room and opened the door, glad that he had made his own bed before leaving for Durango.

"Oh, I like this, too. And I can see why you chose it." Frieda chuckled. "No flowers."

"I'm sure she decorated it with her husband in mind," Derrick said. "I like flowers, but the striped paper suits my taste much better."

"What is this room?" Elise asked as they turned back into the hall.

"Open it and see," Derrick said. "I saved the best for last."

"Ohhh, a bathroom—with running water," his mother said. "We can take real baths, Elise!"

Derrick had been watching Elise's reaction closely, all the while trying not to show how much it mattered to him. He breathed an inward sigh of relief when a huge smile spread across her face.

"This is very nice. And it's very big. Was this here when you bought the house, Derrick?" Elise asked.

"No. Getting running water to the house was my job." And he was very proud of it. He'd worked hard the year before to get the windmill running and then get running water up to the house installed. Now, as he saw the expressions on the two women's faces, Derrick was doubly glad that he could at least offer them a private place with a tub to bathe in.

"This was an extra room, probably meant as a nursery, although the owner had a sewing machine set up in it. Her husband had bought the fixtures and had planned on doing it all. I couldn't see not going on with it."

"Well, you'll be glad to know that we appreciate your hard work very much. We'll be making good use of it, son!"

Derrick laughed. "I figured you might." The teakettle began to sing from downstairs. "Let's get you some tea, and I'll bring in your things so you can get settled in."

Elise followed Derrick and Frieda back to the kitchen. His home was really lovely, and when she left she'd feel better knowing that Frieda had all the modern conveniences she'd become accustomed to in Denver. She hadn't expected it to be this nice. Oh, it needed a few personal touches here and there—although all the furnishings were very nice, it needed the smell of home-cooked meals, the sound of laughter, and the closeness of family to make it feel warm and welcoming. But it was a house that would be a joy to make into a home, and she was sure Frieda would enjoy going about doing just that—once she rested.

Derrick pulled a teapot out of his cupboard. "I'll let you two make your tea the way you like it while I bring in your things."

Frieda started to pull down cups from the cupboard, but Elise gently turned her away. "Mama, let me do this. You go sit at the table and I'll bring it to you."

"Thank you, dear," Frieda said with a sigh.

Elise and Derrick exchanged looks before he went to get their bags. If either of them had needed any convincing as to how tired Frieda was, her words and her shuffle over to the table told it all.

Elise had been watching Frieda carefully over the past few days. She wasn't sure how her mother-in-law could be much help to Derrick during harvest if she didn't get to feeling better. Elise didn't think she could go back to Denver with Frieda so worn out.

She made the tea and sweetened Frieda's just as she liked it before taking it over to place it in front of her. "I'm afraid this trip has tired you more than we thought it would, Mama."

"I'll be fine, dear. I just need a bath and a good night's sleep, then I'll be back to normal. You'll see."

She'd said much the same thing the night before. But Elise had her doubts as she saw her mother-in-law's hand shake slightly when she brought her cup to her mouth. She didn't voice them, however. Instead, she said, "I hope so. I'll run you a bath after you finish your tea and unpack your nightgown and robe."

"That sounds wonderful, dear. I can't wait to try out that nice feather bed upstairs. I am so happy for Derrick. His papa and Carl would be so proud of him."

"That they would," Elise agreed, suddenly feeling a twinge of guilt when she realized she hadn't thought of Carl once since she'd been here at Derrick's home. And it was the day before that she'd been thinking about how different they looked. . . .

She could hear Derrick's footsteps on the stairs as he took up their baggage, and in only moments he was back down in the kitchen. "I've put everything in your rooms. If you need anything, just let me know, all right?" He sat down at the table and grinned at his mother. "I still can't believe you're here, Mama. But I'm afraid the trip has worn you out. Please sleep in and rest up tomorrow."

Frieda looked from Derrick to Elise and shook her head at the two of them. "Don't worry about me. I'll admit that I am a little tired. I'm not as young as I used to be, after all. But a night or two of good sleep will fix me up and I'll be fine." She took a sip of tea and then chuckled. "I'm just glad I don't have to get back on that train or on that stagecoach tomorrow."

"If I had to pick one, it would have to be the train," Elise offered. "I only *thought* it was uncomfortable, but it was nothing like the stage!"

"I hate that you'll have to ride it again, Elise, dear."

"Oh, I'll be fine, Mama. And the train will be on the last leg of the trip." But she didn't want to think about leaving just yet. It was going to be awfully lonely back in Denver with no one but herself for company.

"Well, there's certainly no hurry for you to leave. You both need to rest after your journey here," Derrick said. "I've got to tend to some things out in the barn, so I'll tell you good night now. I hope you both sleep well."

"I'm sure we will, son."

Derrick kissed his mother on the cheek. "See you tomorrow. Good night, Mama. Good night, Elise."

After Derrick left, Elise ran up to lay out Frieda's nightclothes and run her bathwater. Once she had the older woman upstairs and soaking in the tub, she went back down to straighten up the kitchen. She rinsed out the teakettle and washed the teapot, cups, and saucers. Even if Frieda was up in the morning, Elise planned to be down to help her fix breakfast for Derrick. It was the least she could do to repay his hospitality.

She looked in the pantry beside the back porch to find it well stocked with staples. She found the coffee and went back upstairs feeling confident that she could put together a meal for him.

Frieda had just come back from the bathroom, and Elise turned down her bed for her. "I certainly hope you feel better in the morning, Mama. But don't worry about breakfast for Derrick. I'll make it for him if you aren't up to it."

"Thank you, dear. I'm sure I will be. It is so good to finally be here. You aren't going back right away, are you, Elise?"

"I won't be going anywhere until I know you've recovered from the trip, Mama."

Frieda yawned as she sat down on the bed and slipped under the covers. "Thank you so much for coming with me, dear. The trip would have been much harder if you hadn't." Her eyes were closed as soon as her head hit the pillow. " 'Night, dear."

Elise kissed her on the cheek. "Good night, Mama."

She turned out the lamp on the bedside table and went to take her own bath. She couldn't wait to sink into her own bed.

As Elise ran her water, she couldn't help but be touched by Derrick's thoughtfulness to his mother. He'd provided bath salts and soft Turkish toweling for her comfort. There were other towels in the linen closet. Elise doubted that Derrick used the softer ones, figuring he'd bought them for his mother. She felt selfish all over again for keeping Frieda to herself for so long.

As she soaked in the warm water and let the travel weariness ease away, she wondered why Derrick had never married. He was handsome and obviously could provide well. Surely there were women in the area who would be honored to be his wife. Of course there were. But for some reason that thought didn't really sit well with Elise, and she didn't want to delve into why. She hurriedly finished her bath, then drained the tub. It really wasn't any of her business why he'd never married anyway.

Elise straightened up the bathroom and peeked in on Frieda. She was snoring lightly, so Elise went to her room, relieved that her mother-in-law seemed to be sleeping soundly. She went to the window and looked out. Evidently Derrick was still in the barn. She could see a dim light shining from inside. He was probably staying out there so as not to run into the two of them getting ready for bed. She hoped he really didn't mind that she'd come with his mother. Family was one thing, but she was really only related to him by marriage, and they'd not been around each other much after she and Carl married. Derrick had moved away a few months later.

She remembered him from before Carl began courting her. At one time, Elise had hoped Derrick would be the one to ask to court her. But it was his brother instead, and she'd never regretted marrying Carl. He had been a wonderful husband, and she missed him. She missed being married and having someone to care for. Elise sighed. She'd been blessed to have him for the time she did, and she certainly didn't need to start feeling sorry for herself now.

She went to the bed and knelt down to say her prayers. "Dear Lord, I thank You for seeing Mama and me safely here. Please let her sleep well tonight and feel rested tomorrow. Please help me to know what to do, whether to stay here awhile to help out or go back to Denver. It's going to be so very lonely there, Father. Please help me not to show how badly I'm dreading going back by myself. It's Derrick's turn to have his mother with him. I'm sure he's been lonely all these years without family nearby. Please help me to remember that. Thank You for all my many blessings, Father. And thank You most of all for Your precious Son and our Savior, Jesus Christ. In His name I pray. Amen."

She plumped her pillow and got into bed, sighing with relief as her body felt the softness of the mattress.

Derrick put up his wagon, then took care of his horses, feeding them and putting them up for the night. He checked on his barn animals, thankful for his neighbor, Jed Barrister, who'd milked his cow while he was gone. They took turns looking after each other's places when they were away—which wasn't very often—and would help each other with their harvests.

He was a little unsettled about how good it felt to see Elise and his mother in his kitchen. Well, not about seeing his mother there, but Elise. When he'd first moved into the house, he'd dreamed of Elise there in that very kitchen, but she was his brother's wife. Through the years he'd forced thoughts of her to the back of his mind. Only now, his brother was no longer here and Elise was. It was difficult not to think of her when she was there in his house—the setting of many a dream about her. It was also impossible to ignore the pounding of his heart when she smiled at him. But he had to try. She was his brother's widow, after all.

He busied himself for over an hour so that his mother and Elise would have some privacy while they got ready for bed. By the time he finally headed back to the house, he was pretty sure they had turned in for the night. There was only a light shining from the kitchen window and none upstairs. He hoped they both slept well.

He still hadn't talked to Elise about his mother. He'd have to find a way tomorrow. Elise needed her rest, too. She'd looked almost as tired as his mother tonight. Hopefully that meant it was only the travel that had his mother looking so frail and she would be better after a little rest.

He hoped Elise would stay awhile, telling himself it would make it easier on his mother. He could tell she would miss Elise a great deal. Maybe he'd been wrong to insist that she come and live with him instead of with his brother's wife.

As he stepped into the kitchen from his porch, he realized the room had a different feel to it tonight. The kitchen might be empty, but the house wasn't. Suddenly Derrick realized how very lonely he'd been the last few years. He loved his place and the work he did, but at night when he had no one to share it all with, the solitude could be hard to take. He sent up a silent prayer, thanking the Lord above for seeing his mother and Elise safely to his home.

Chapter 4

Derrick awakened early, dressed quickly, and hurried into the bathroom as quietly as he could to wash his face and shave. Had his mother and Elise not been there, the shaving might have waited another day, but having women in the house necessitated sprucing up a bit, and he wanted to do it before they needed to get in the bathroom. He really didn't mind. It was nice to have a reason to do so.

He went downstairs as quietly as he could, so as not to awaken the women, and went out to the barn to milk old Bessie. He loved this quiet time of morning when the sun was coming up over the horizon. He took the warm pail of milk and the fresh eggs he'd collected to the kitchen, and then went back out to feed his chickens and take care of the other farm animals.

When he came back to the house, the smell of brewing coffee and frying bacon wafted out to greet him. His mother must have slept well, or not at all, to be up already. He certainly hoped she was up so early because she'd slept well.

He took the back steps two at a time, entering the kitchen expecting to see his mother standing at the stove. Instead, it was Elise who turned to him with a smile. His heart thudded against his chest, and his pulse began to race. He nearly pinched himself to make sure he was awake.

"Good morning, Derrick. I wanted to get down here before Mama tried to. I hope it's all right that I made myself at home in your kitchen?"

It was more than all right. It was something right out of his dreams. "Of course it is. It's been a very long time since I've had anyone cook breakfast for me—and never here."

She took the last of the bacon out of the skillet and cracked a couple of eggs into a bowl. "How do you want your eggs cooked?"

"Over easy, if it's not too much trouble." He still couldn't quite accept that Elise was here, in his kitchen, cooking for him. "Is Mama all right this morning?"

"I think so. She seemed to be sleeping soundly when I checked on her, and I didn't want to disturb her. So I just let her sleep." Elise slid the eggs into the frying pan she'd just taken the last of the bacon from.

Derrick nodded and poured himself a cup of the coffee he was sure was much better than what he made. "I'm glad she's resting. I'm sure she can use the sleep. She seemed so very tired last night. I've wanted to ask you about her health. I must admit I didn't expect her to look quite so frail."

"She'd been feeling a little poorly for a few months before she decided to come here, but she seemed to perk up as we got ready for the trip. I have a feeling she was only acting as if she felt better, though, knowing I didn't want her to travel until she was up to it. That's why I came with her. I couldn't bear the thought of her traveling by herself." She turned the eggs over and then bent to take a pan of biscuits out of the oven.

"Thank you, Elise. I appreciate your care of her more than I can say. And I know she's going to miss you very much when you do return to Denver."

"Not nearly as much as I will miss her."

"Is there anything pressing that you need to get back to Denver for?" Derrick asked. He thought his brother had left her well off enough that she didn't have to worry about income. He hoped so, anyway.

Elise shook her head as she flipped the two eggs onto a plate and added a good portion of bacon to the side along with a couple of hot biscuits. "No."

Derrick's mouth began to water at the aroma drifting up from the plate he took from her. "Would you consider staying on until we're sure Mama's health improves?"

"Of course I will. And thank you for asking me to stay on until then. I would be miserable worrying about her if I went home with her still feeling poorly." She put a biscuit and a few pieces of bacon on a plate and joined him at the table. "Would you say the blessing, please?"

Derrick was thankful he hadn't already popped half a biscuit into his mouth. Praying before meals wasn't something he was used to doing, living by himself. Thankful he hadn't embarrassed himself, he nodded and bowed his head. "Dear Lord, thank You for safe travel for Mama and Elise. Please help Mama to feel better soon. Thank You for all of our blessings. And thank You for this food we are about to eat. In Jesus' name I pray. Amen."

"Thank you," Elise said as she buttered her biscuit.

By the time she broke off a piece and put it in her mouth, Derrick had eaten a whole biscuit. She was every bit as good a cook as his mother was.

"There you two are," Derrick's mother said as she entered the kitchen, looking a little more rested than she had the day before. "Elise, dear, you should have awakened me."

"You needed the rest, Mama," Elise said, jumping up to make a plate for his mother. "Sit down at the table. I'll fix yours."

"I am perfectly capable of waiting on myself, dear."

"I know you are. But when I go back to Denver, I won't be able to do this for you, so please. . .let me wait on you now." She cracked an egg into the skillet and quickly scrambled it for his mother.

"Just for today," Frieda said as she took a seat at the table. "I can't let you spoil me too much. Harvest will be here, and I need to be in top form to be of help to Derrick."

"Mama, I can hire someone to cook for the hands. It's what I would do if you hadn't come." Derrick was afraid all the extra work would be much too hard for her.

"I'll be fine. When is harvest?"

"In a few weeks, but—"

"Why, that's lots of time. I'll be up to the task by then. I don't want you paying someone for what I can easily do."

Elise brought his mother's plate and a cup of coffee to her. Derrick's glance met hers across the top of his mother's head, but neither of them said what they were thinking. Derrick only knew what he was hoping—that his mother would get better, but that Elise would stay on even after she did.

His mother broke into his thoughts. "What time is church tomorrow, son?"

Derrick had to think. He hadn't been going like he should, but he knew what time it started because the preacher had ridden out to see him several weeks before to remind him of it. "Ten o'clock. That's to give those who live out a ways time to get into town."

"We'll need to press a few things before then. You do have an iron, don't you, son?"

"Yes, ma'am, I do. It's in the pantry."

"I saw it earlier," Elise said. "I'll get everything pressed as soon as we finish up breakfast. And I'll help you unpack your trunk later today, Mama."

"Thank you, dear. There's no hurry to unpack everything, though. We just need to make sure we have things ready for tomorrow. Do you have a good preacher here, Derrick?"

The way his mother was quizzing him, Derrick couldn't help but wonder if she knew he hadn't been attending like he should have. He had heard reports from friends and neighbors on the preacher, though, and could honestly say, "Everyone around here thinks so."

"I look forward to hearing him. . .and to meeting your friends and neighbors."

"After breakfast, I'm going to run to the farm across the way and thank my neighbor for taking care of things while I was in Durango. Would you two like to ride with me?" Derrick asked his mother.

"I'd love to. Elise, you'll come along, too, won't you?"

Elise didn't know what to say. She was already feeling much too comfortable here. She would have to go back to Denver at some point, and the more she came to feel settled here, the more she might hate going back. Besides, Derrick and his mother had not had any time alone.

"I think I'll stay here, thanks. I'll use the time to press our clothes and clean up the kitchen."

"I'll help clean up—"

Elise shook her head. "No, Mama. You and Derrick need some time together, and these will be your new neighbors, too. You need to get to know them. You two go on and have a lovely day."

"But—"

"Mama, I'll hitch up the wagon after I finish this cup of coffee and be back to pick you up," Derrick said, ending any argument his mother might have had.

Elise was grateful. She was having enough problems trying to figure out her confused feelings about being in Derrick's home as it was. She couldn't see how spending more time in his company would help her sort them out.

Derrick got up from the table and took his dishes to the sink. "Thank you for breakfast, Elise. I don't normally eat that well."

"You're welcome. I'm glad you enjoyed it. Your kitchen is a pleasure to cook in."

"Thank you. I didn't show you the root cellar last night, but it's right under the pantry. Just raise the door in the pantry floor and use the handrail on the stairs. There's a hook at the bottom to hang a lantern. I'll be going into Farmington for supplies on Monday. If there's anything you and Mama think I need, just make a list. You're both welcome to go with me into town."

"I'll check it out while you're gone. If you have any salt pork and beans, I can put some of those on for supper. I can make some gravy to go with the leftover biscuits for dinner, too."

"Anything you want to do is fine with me," Derrick said on his way out the door.

"I'll help you when we get back, Elise, dear," Frieda said. "I'm just anxious to see Derrick's place and see what this country looks like. It's far different than Denver, that's for sure."

"It is. I love the mountains in Colorado, but there are so many trees, the views of the sunsets and sunrises are sometimes blocked," Elise said. "This part of the country is so wide open—just the high mesas here and there and not many trees to block the views. I don't think I've ever seen a more beautiful sunrise than the one this morning. And you can see the river from upstairs. I know you're going to love it here. You go and enjoy your time with Derrick, Mama. Get to know your new neighbors."

Frieda smiled and brought her plate to the sink, where Elise had begun to wash dishes. "I think I will."

It didn't take long before Derrick was back to pick up his mother. Elise breathed a sigh of relief when the wagon pulled away. She needed a little time to herself, if for no other reason than to sort out her feelings. Part of her wanted to resent Derrick for pulling Frieda away from Denver. The other part of her felt bad that it'd been so long since Frieda and her son had seen each other. And he was so obviously happy to have his mother here.

When Derrick first entered the kitchen and smiled at her this morning, Elise was sure he'd been expecting to see his mother, so the smile had probably been for her. But it had lit up his whole face and stayed there even after he'd found her, not his mother, at the stove.

Her heart had fluttered like a caged bird in her chest at that smile. She wasn't sure what that was all about, nor did she want to think about it now. She wanted to be happy for Derrick and his mother's reunion—and she was. It was only the thought of going back to Denver alone that put a damper on her joy for them.

She was thankful for the extra time Derrick had extended to her in his request for her to stay until Frieda was her old self again. Yet in the long run, Elise had a feeling it would only make it more difficult to say good-bye.

After another of Elise's breakfasts—this one of ham and gravy and biscuits—Derrick took his mother and Elise to church the next morning. He hoped no one would mention how long it had been since they'd last seen him there, because it had been quite a while. When he first moved to Farmington, he'd meant to come regularly. Instead, he had only attended sporadically the last several years, and he had a feeling his mother was about to find that out.

Several church members he'd never met came up to welcome them and introduce themselves.

Then one of his neighbors came up to him. "Good to see you here, Derrick," Eli Johnson said to him. "It's been awhile."

Derrick cringed inside but only replied, "Good to see you, too, Eli."

After several others had come up and told him how glad they were to see him, Derrick had a feeling from the look his mother shot him that he'd be hearing a word or two when services were over.

But as the service got under way, Derrick realized that he'd missed coming. Peacefulness settled inside him as he sat between his mother and Elise, and it was only then that he came to realize that maybe he'd been a little angry with the Lord over letting Carl win the woman he'd wanted for himself.

Harold Burton preached a good sermon on forgiveness, and Derrick knew the message was meant for him. As he joined in the closing song with the rest of the congregation, he sent up a silent prayer. He asked the Lord to help him forgive Carl once and for all and to forgive *him* for his anger at a brother who was no longer here. He also asked the Lord to forgive him for not making more of an effort to come to church and be part of the body as he knew he should have.

When the service was over, more people came up to him, his mother, and Elise on the way out of the building. Now he was certain he'd be doing a lot of explaining to his mother.

Preacher Burton was standing at the door, along with his wife, Rachel. Derrick didn't think they were much older than he was, but they seemed wise beyond their years. The two men shook hands.

"Derrick, it's good to see you here. We've missed you. Who are these two lovely ladies you have with you?"

Derrick made the introductions. "This is my mother, Frieda Morgan, and my sister-in-law, Elise Morgan. Mother, Elise, this is our preacher, Harold Burton, and his wife, Rachel Burton."

"I enjoyed your lesson a great deal," his mother said.

"Thank you. It's always nice to hear that," Harold replied

"It's very nice to have you with us today," Rachel said. "Will you be staying long?"

"Mama is moving here to live with me."

"And Elise came to help me get settled in," his mother added.

"How wonderful! It's always good to have more women in town. I hope we'll see more of you in the weeks to come."

"Oh yes," his mother said. "We'll be here next week."

"Good." Rachel smiled and nodded at Frieda.

After a little more small talk, Derrick escorted his mother and Elise to the wagon, then helped them up onto the seats. As he turned the wagon, heading it for home, he half expected his mother to say something about his not going to church like he should.

But all she said was, "It's a nice church, and the people are very friendly. I look forward to going next week."

"Yes, it seems a good congregation. And the singing was beautiful," Elise added.

As the two women got into a discussion about the church service, Derrick breathed a sigh of relief. He knew how his mother felt about attending church, and she was right. He deserved whatever she might have to say. But it wasn't until he went with her and Elise this morning that he realized why he'd stopped attending.

Elise and he were the same age, and she had made his heart beat faster for at least a year before his older brother began courting her. It was his own fault that Carl won her heart. He should have acted faster. But he hadn't, and when Elise had accepted Carl's marriage proposal, it had hurt badly. But what had hurt the most was that Carl had never shown an interest in Elise until he found out that Derrick was attracted to her. It had felt like a betrayal to Derrick.

But all that was in the past, Derrick told himself. He needed to keep it there. Carl was gone and Elise was his widow. There was no good in harboring resentment toward a man who wasn't here to defend himself—especially when the man was his brother.

But Derrick knew he could get very accustomed to seeing Elise in his kitchen each morning. He was even more attracted to her now than he had been in Denver. She'd gone from a pretty young girl to a lovely woman, and from the care she showed his mother, he knew she'd kept the sweetness about her.

He was still attracted to her. There was no doubt about that. And the biggest problem with having her here was that he didn't know how he was going to be able to live in the same house with his mother and Elise without giving away how he felt. But even more troublesome—when it was time for her to return to Denver, how was he going to be able to handle losing her once more?

Chapter 5

The next morning when Derrick came down for breakfast, Elise was at the range frying bacon as usual, but her normally smooth brow was slightly furrowed.

"What's wrong, Elise? You look worried. Is Mama all right?"

"She developed a slight cough overnight," Elise said as she poured a cup of coffee and handed it to him. "Is there a doctor in town she could see? It sounds much like the cough she had in Denver when she felt so bad, and I am a little concerned."

"There's Doc Bedslow. I'm sure he will see her. I was planning on going into town for supplies today anyway. I'll take her along if she's up to it. If not, I'll get him to come out here."

He heard his mother cough on her way down the stairs, and he didn't like the sound of it any better than Elise did.

Elise brought a cup of coffee with cream and sugar to the table for her.

"Thank you, dear," his mother said just before she coughed again.

"Mama, I'm going into town, and I want you to ride with me if you're up to it. I want you to let Doc Bedslow listen to your chest."

"No," Frieda protested, "I'll be fine. I've had this before, and—"

"And I'm afraid you never quite got over it, Mama. You need to see a doctor," Elise said.

"If it's nothing, you can scold me, Mama," Derrick said. "I'd like to think that you could just still be tired from the trip. But neither of us like the sound of that cough, and I know I'd find it hard to forgive myself for not getting you to a doctor if you have some underlying illness that needs to be taken care of."

"I feel the same way, Mama," Elise added.

"You need to see the doctor, Mama," Derrick insisted. "If you don't feel like riding into town, I'll have the doctor come out here."

His mother sighed deeply and shook her head. "No, that won't be necessary. I'll go into town with you."

Elise helped his mother get ready to go after they finished breakfast, and she rode along with them. Derrick wasn't sure if it was for his mother's sake or his own, but he was certainly glad she was there.

They didn't have to wait too long for Dr. Bedslow to see her. After listening to her chest and checking her out, he told them that it appeared she had a slight case of pneumonia. "After talking to your mother, Derrick, I'm pretty sure she's had a relapse. She said she'd been feeling poorly before she came down here from Denver. Her resistance hadn't been up enough for the trip, and it probably set her back a week or so. *If* she takes her medicine, rests, and lets herself heal, she should be back to normal in a few weeks."

"We'll see that she does that. Thanks, Doc."

They were relieved that Frieda could regain her health and strength. But both Derrick and Elise took turns blaming themselves as they all left the doctor's office with a prescription for his mother's cough.

"I should have gotten you to the doctor up in Denver, Mama. I am so sorry."

"You tried to get me to go, Elise, dear. I stubbornly refused."

"Well, I shouldn't have kept insisting you make that long trip down here," Derrick said. "Or at the very least, I should have insisted you stop along the way and spend a night in a hotel. It might have taken longer for you to get here, but you wouldn't have been so worn out."

"Derrick, dear, it isn't your fault, either. I have a mind of my own and I wanted to come when I did. I truly thought I was better, and I didn't realize how tiring the trip would be for me. I'll take it easy and regain my strength. I promise. After all, I'm not much good if I can't help you out."

"Mother! You don't have to do anything around the house. I just wanted you here. I didn't ask you to come so that I would have a cook or a maid!"

Frieda nodded. "I know that, dear. I didn't mean that the way it sounded. I just want to help you out."

"You're helping me more than you know just by being here. Don't ever doubt that. Now, let me buy you two dinner and then we'll go get our supplies. But when we get home, Mama, you must take a nap."

He waited for an argument from her, and even Elise looked as if she were holding her breath waiting for the same thing, but none was forthcoming. Instead, all his mother said was, "Yes, dear."

During the next few days, Elise took it on herself to unpack her mother-in-law's trunks. With Frieda's instructions on where to put things, Derrick's house began to look like home. Her mother-in-law had brought family pictures and favorite knickknacks she'd had packed away since moving in with Elise and Carl. Elise arranged them here and there in the parlor and other rooms in the house and hung some of the pictures along the wall next to the staircase. Frieda's tea service seemed meant for the sideboard in the dining room. Derrick seemed pleased with the additions to his home, noticing each new thing that was put out.

They'd settled into somewhat of a routine, with Elise up early and preparing breakfast before Derrick went out to check his orchards and do chores. For the first few days after they saw the doctor, Frieda stayed in bed, and Elise or Derrick took meals up to her. But it didn't take long for her to tire of being in bed all day, so Elise and Derrick agreed that she could come down after her afternoon nap and stay until after supper if she felt like it.

In between meals and before starting supper, Elise would dust and straighten up. Frieda claimed she was feeling better, and Elise knew she wanted to be. But Elise still wasn't sure her mother-in-law was up to the task of all she wanted to do for Derrick—not if he started harvesting those apples anytime soon.

Elise had come to love the smell of Derrick's orchards. There was a big apple tree just outside the back door of the kitchen, and she loved to sit under it at times throughout the day, coffee or tea in hand, and just enjoy the beauty and aroma of this new place.

On this day, Elise decided to surprise Frieda and Derrick. Taking her cup inside, she grabbed a basket and went back out to the tree. She picked just enough of the ripest-looking apples from the lower branches to make a pie for dessert.

After Elise put on a beef stew for supper, she peeled the apples and added sugar, cinnamon, and a teaspoon of flour in the bowl with them to bring out the juices. Then she let the mixture set while she made the crust. She'd almost forgotten how nice it was to cook for a man with a good appetite. Cooking for Derrick was very rewarding, and he'd never failed to tell her how much he enjoyed it. She looked forward to serving him a slice of warm apple pie for dessert.

"Oh, that smells delicious, dear," Frieda said as she entered the kitchen a little later, looking somewhat refreshed from her nap. "You made a pie, didn't you?"

"I did. I couldn't resist picking some apples any longer."

"I can't wait to taste it."

"Neither can I," Derrick said as he came in the back door. He crossed the room to kiss his mother on the cheek. "How are you feeling this afternoon?"

"A little better, I believe. I haven't coughed as much today."

"Is that right?" Derrick looked at Elise for confirmation.

"I don't think she has. Hopefully the medicine Dr. Bedslow gave her is beginning to do some good."

"I sure hope so." He sniffed appreciatively. "My kitchen has never smelled as good as it has since you came."

"What did you eat before we got here, son?"

Derrick grinned and shrugged. "Oh, I ate a lot of bacon and eggs—not nearly as good as what you and Elise can make, though." He chuckled. "Oh, and beans—I ate lots of beans. Occasionally neighbors would take pity on me and have me over. They usually sent some leftovers home with me."

Poor man, no wonder he's so complimentary about my cooking, Elise thought as she stirred up some cornmeal, flour, salt, milk, and eggs for corn bread to go with the stew. She checked on her pie to find it golden brown and bubbling. Pulling it out of the oven, she placed it in the pie safe to cool a bit. Then she melted some lard in a skillet, poured the corn bread mixture into it, and slid it into the still-hot oven.

"I'm sorry, son. I should have taught you to cook more than beans and eggs before you left home," Frieda said.

"Mama, I learned a lot from you," Derrick said. "Cooking just isn't something I enjoy doing very much." He turned to leave the kitchen. "I'm going up to clean up before supper. If I stay here, I'll be cutting into that pie before it's cooled enough."

"We'll be near ready to eat when you come back down," Elise said. "It won't take long for the corn bread to finish baking."

"I'll hurry, then."

Elise helped Frieda set out dishes, then ladled the stew into a large soup tureen and brought it to the table. She set it beside Frieda's place so she could serve it. Then Elise brought out the butter and poured Derrick a glass of the cold milk he liked with meals. She put a fresh pot of coffee on so it would be ready to have with the pie. Derrick came back downstairs just as she took the corn bread out of the oven.

No one had to ask Derrick to say the blessing by now, and when he was finished, Frieda ladled the stew into bowls while Elise cut and served the corn bread.

"How are the apples coming along, son?"

"I think we're going to get started with the picking this coming Monday. I'm going into town tomorrow to see about getting someone in to cook for the hands."

"Derrick, there's no need for that. I can cook for them," Elise said. "I've been planning on doing that anyway."

"I don't expect you to do that, Elise. I can hire someone to come do it. There's no need for you to—"

"Helping you at harvest is the least I can do to thank you for your hospitality, Derrick."

"I don't want payment—"

"I wish I was able to do it. I am a little better. Surely I can help," Frieda said, looking from one to the other.

"No!" Elise and Derrick both said at the same time.

"I want you to rest and get your strength back, Mama," Derrick continued. "You can protest all you want, but Elise and I know you aren't back to your normal health yet. You must let yourself rest."

"Mama, I know you want to help Derrick out. And you'll have plenty of time for that after you regain your strength. But you aren't up to it for this harvest." Elise turned back to Derrick. "Unless you don't think I can handle it, Derrick, I would like to cook for your harvest. Please."

Derrick looked from his mother to his sister-in-law and shook his head. "You two are a pair. I have no doubt at all that you can handle it, Elise. I accept your offer, and I thank you for it."

"I'll do the best I can. Just let me know what you want me to cook and for how many. I'll do some planning and be ready to go on Monday. Do you serve breakfast and dinner?"

"No, I just provide the midday meal. There will be about twenty people, and they'll work for the whole week—picking first, then packing. We all come back to the yard at noontime. Usually there will be beans or stew or something like that. I think the cook I hired last year made rolls or corn bread. For dessert, there was cake or cobbler, too. But he wasn't the cook you are. I hired him for the week from one of the local ranches. I'll get the supplies for whatever you'd like to make. Just give me a list tomorrow, and I'll go into town."

"Well, you have plenty of apples around. I can make apple cobblers or pies. Fried pies might be good. What do you think, Mama?" Elise asked his mother.

"Why, that's a good idea, Elise. You could make the pies and cobblers up ahead of time, but the fried pies would be easier to serve."

Elise nodded. "That's what I thought. And it's still warm in the middle of the day. . . . Maybe I could make bread this weekend and bake a ham and make sandwiches for them?"

"That would be easy to serve, too," his mother said. "I think both of those are good ideas. What do you think, son?"

Seeing how Elise included his mother in the decision making, even though she couldn't do any of the cooking, made him think even more highly of her. "I think anything you two decide is fine. But the sandwiches and fried pies would sure make it much easier to serve."

"You could even take it all out into the orchard to wherever they're working so they don't have to come back to the house. That would save some time, wouldn't it?" his mother asked.

"It certainly would. I could load up the wagon and take it out to them."

Elise was nodding. "Maybe I could vary the sandwiches between the ham and a roast? I don't think they'd get tired of the fried pies."

"No, I don't either. I'll pick apples for you whenever you're ready for them. I can help peel them, too," Derrick offered.

"I think even I can help do that," his mother said. "See, son, there's no reason to hire anyone. I'm sure your help will be thrilled with whatever Elise comes up with."

"I'll have a list for you in the morning." Elise got up to get a pencil and a piece of paper.

Derrick had a feeling his helpers were going to wish they could work another week after tasting Elise's cooking.

Elise did the wash the next day to get it out of the way, and then on Saturday she made bread while Derrick picked apples. On Sunday afternoon she put a ham in the oven while he and his mother peeled the apples. She cooked them down with cinnamon and sugar, and then after supper that evening she finished making up the individual pies and fried them.

That all started a week that was one of the busiest Elise could ever remember. She was up at sunrise to make breakfast for Derrick, and then she began preparations for dinner. Derrick had sliced the ham for her the night before, and now she only had to lay out the bread and put the sandwiches together. By the time she was through, Frieda had made her way downstairs and helped stack them in a box Derrick had provided. The fried pies were placed in another box. Once he picked up the boxes and took them to the orchard, Elise put a roast on for the next day's meal.

They would have some of it for supper that night, and then she'd make sandwiches out of the rest of the roast the next day. She stirred up another batch of bread and set it to rise. While Frieda took her afternoon nap, Elise made more fried pies, then punched down the bread dough and kneaded it once more. After shaping it and placing it in loaf pans, she set it to rise again. She'd bake the loaves after she took the roast out of the oven.

By the time her head hit the pillow that night, she was totally exhausted. But she was happy that she was able to pay Derrick back for his hospitality—even though he wanted no pay.

She stayed so busy the rest of the week, the days passed in a blur.

Derrick was out in the orchard with his help, working hard, but he had a feeling it was nowhere near as hard as Elise was working. For days she'd been up at dawn and stayed up late making bread, frying pies, or baking cookies, making sure there was plenty of food to go around. And it was excellent. The friends and neighbors who'd come to help him with his harvest went on and on about how good the food was. She had a way of seasoning everything that made it all taste wonderful. But then, that shouldn't surprise him. Everything she cooked was tasty. She never complained, but by the end of the week, she was looking pretty tired.

"After the freight company picks up my apple crates this afternoon, why don't I take you and Mama into town for supper tonight, Elise? You certainly deserve it," Derrick said when he came to pick up the boxes of food on Friday.

She shook her head. "There's no need. I'm not sure Mama should be out in the night air just yet. I'll just put on a pot of soup to simmer this afternoon. We have bread left."

Derrick could see the exhaustion in her eyes. He had a feeling she would be too tired to go anywhere that evening anyway. "All right, but I do the dishes tonight. And tomorrow we go into town for dinner."

"We'll see how Mama feels tomorrow. As for the dishes, you can dry, but I'll wash."

Her plan sounded even better than his had. "It's a deal."

By the time he came in after seeing his apples off to market, he found his mother, instead of Elise, in the kitchen, setting the table for two.

"What happened? Is Elise all right?"

"She's fine. But I convinced her to take a nap this afternoon and she's still sleeping. She's worked so hard this week. I couldn't bring myself to wake her. The soup she made is done, and there's fresh bread to have with it. I'm still capable of dishing it up, and together we can surely do the dishes."

"I was afraid the week would take a toll on her," Derrick said. He took a couple of bowls from the cupboard and brought them to his mother.

"She handled it all just fine. But it was a busy week, and I think she just relaxed knowing the pace would slow down after today." She ladled the soup into the two bowls and handed them back to Derrick to take to the table. "I'm glad she stepped in, however. After watching her this week, I can admit that I don't think I could have handled it."

"Well, she made a name for herself around here. No one else in the area has ever gotten as many compliments on the food served during harvest week as I did."

"You be sure and tell her."

"I will." He'd wanted to tell her tonight and was disappointed she wasn't here. As wonderful as it was to share supper with his mother, and as happy as he was that she seemed to be getting better, something was missing at the table. And he knew exactly what it was—or rather *who* it was. He missed Elise.

Chapter 6

Elise woke long before dawn, appalled that she had slept clear through the night. What must Derrick think of her? She'd left him and Mama to fend for themselves last night! And Mama—was she all right? Elise threw off her covers, dressed quickly, and hurried across the hall to check on her.

Frieda was snoring lightly and seemed to be resting easy. Elise breathed a sigh of relief as she tiptoed out of the room and headed downstairs as quietly as she could. It was still dark outside, but there was a hint of light to the east. Elise lit the stove, put on a pot of coffee, then slipped out the back door to inhale the sweet morning smell and watch the sunrise. She'd come to love it here in New Mexico Territory. She never tired of looking at Derrick's orchard or out at the high mesas and the surrounding farmland dotting the landscape. Even though the view was better from upstairs, Elise found that she could get glimpses of the Animas River from the end of the back porch, and that was where she went now, to wait until the rising sun glinted on its waters.

She really should start thinking about returning to Denver once Frieda was better. But returning to her empty cottage held no appeal for her at all. And she felt sorrowful for that. It was her and Carl's home from the beginning of their marriage, and it held many happy memories. . .but it no longer held him. In fact, if it weren't for the few pictures she had of him, she wasn't sure she could pull his face into her memory. Thoughts of Carl seemed to come farther apart these days.

Maybe it was because she'd been so busy lately. Taking care of Frieda and feeding the workers for Derrick this week had filled her days and nights. There hadn't been much time to think about anything else—or so she told herself. She returned to the kitchen just in time to rescue the coffee before it boiled over. She'd better quit woolgathering and concentrate on what she planned to do today.

She needed to catch up on the wash, but she'd wait until Monday to do that. The apples on the tree out back needed picking for Derrick and Mama's own use. Perhaps she could make some apple jelly and apple butter out of some of them.

Elise took the leftover ham from the icebox and began to slice several pieces off it, saving what was on the bone to put into some pinto beans for supper that evening. She heard Derrick's heavier tread upstairs, alerting her that he would be down soon. Elise began to heat the ham in a frying pan, trying to ignore the fluttery beat of her heart.

Derrick woke from a restless sleep. He'd been out of sorts when he went to bed the night before, and he wasn't in a much better mood when he woke up. Elise had never come downstairs last night, and his mother had retired right after she'd helped him clean up after supper. He'd tried to get her to just sit and talk to him, but Mama wasn't one to let a man do a job she thought belonged to a woman. It didn't seem to matter that he'd been doing all of that before she came.

After she'd gone upstairs, the night had seemed longer than usual in the overly quiet house—even though that's how it had always been before his mother and Elise had arrived. He didn't much like the feel of it now, so he'd headed out to the barn, where he spent the next several hours cleaning equipment and taking care of his animals.

It was the smell of coffee and frying ham drifting up the stairs that finally brightened his mood. Derrick doubted his mother was down yet, so that meant Elise was in the kitchen. Throwing the covers off his bed, he hurried to dress and shave so he could get downstairs and see her.

She looked rested when she turned from the range to greet him. "Good morning, Derrick. I am so sorry I left you and Mama on your own last night. I didn't realize how tired I was, I guess."

Derrick poured himself a cup of coffee. "Well, you were up before dawn and awake until very late at night all week; it's no wonder you couldn't wake up! I can't thank you enough for all you did this week, Elise. You've become quite famous among my neighbors and friends for your tasty sandwiches and fried pies. They couldn't get enough. I think they hated to see the week come to an end."

"I'm glad they liked everything," Elise said, forking the ham slices onto a plate. "We had some leftover ham from the last one I baked. I thought it would be good for breakfast. I'm making biscuits and gravy to go with it."

"You won't hear me complaining," Derrick said.

"Nor me," Frieda said from the kitchen doorway.

"What are you doing here, Mama? You're supposed to—"

"I'm feeling better this morning," his mother said as she took a seat at the table. "Don't worry. I'm not going to start cleaning house or cooking. But I'm just plain tired of staying upstairs, away from everything. If I get weary, I'll take a nap. Otherwise, I can at least peel potatoes or snap beans or fold clothes from right here."

Derrick looked at Elise and grinned. "She's sounding a little grouchy this morning. I think she's on the mend."

"Now what do you mean by that? You'd be grouchy, too, if you had to stay in your room most of the day."

"Yes, ma'am, I would." Derrick crossed the room and gave his mother a hug before sitting down at the table. "I'm just glad to see you finally feeling a little better."

"So am I, Mama," Elise said, crossing the room to bring his mother a cup of coffee. "I've missed your company."

"Well, I figured I could do a lot just sitting here. And none of it should tax me too much. Derrick, I'm sure you have some things that need mending. If you bring them down, I can work on some of that while I keep Elise company this morning."

"I'd sure like having you down here with me," Elise assured her as she popped a pan of biscuits into the oven and stirred the gravy she'd begun.

"I have a pile of things in need of mending, Mama. I'll go get them after breakfast." He'd sewn on a button here and there, but anything else was beyond what he was willing to tackle. "Just don't feel you have to hurry. They've waited this long. It won't hurt them to wait a little longer."

Derrick wasn't used to having females around from morning to night. At first he wasn't sure how he felt about it, but he was quickly realizing what he'd been missing. The deep loneliness he hadn't realized he'd been living with—until his mother and Elise came—had eased in all kinds of ways. He liked coming in from his orchards knowing someone was there to ask him how his day was going or if he was hungry—knowing there was someone just to talk to.

Elise turned from stirring the gravy. "When do you think we could get the apple tree out back picked? I'd be glad to help—"

"I realized last night I should have done that when I had all that help. I'll do it today. I'm going to be helping Jed with his harvest all next week. I think I can get them all picked today, but if you want to, you could pick some from the lower branches. I don't want you climbing the ladder or up in the tree."

"No," Frieda said and shook her head. "The last thing we need is for you to fall and break something, Elise."

"I'll pick the lower branches, then. I thought I could make some jelly and apple butter for you to have this winter."

"I love apple jelly," Derrick said. "And if I remember right, Mama loves apple butter."

"Mmm, I do."

"Well, there are canning supplies down in the root cellar. I'll get them out and clean them this weekend, too." Elise poured the gravy into a bowl and brought it to the table. Then she took the biscuits out of the oven, plopped them into a napkin-lined basket, and brought them and the ham to the table.

Derrick waited for her to freshen up her cup of coffee and bring it to the table before saying the blessing. "Dear Lord, we thank You for this day. Thank You for letting Mama feel better. Thank You for the outstanding crop of apples this year. Thank You for this wonderful food Elise has prepared for us to eat. Please help us to live this day to Your glory, dear Lord. We thank You most of all for Your precious Son and our Savior and Your plan for our salvation through Him. In Jesus' name I pray. Amen."

He took a bite of gravy and biscuit and sent up a silent addition. *And thank You, Lord, for letting Mama decide to come to Farmington and for bringing Elise with her.*

Derrick brought down his mending before he headed out to do his morning chores. While Frieda got started on that, Elise cleaned up the kitchen and then went upstairs to make beds and straighten up so that she would be ready to help Derrick pick apples when he was back.

"Is it warm enough for me to sit outside while you two are picking, do you think?" Frieda asked her.

"I think so. I can get your shawl, though, just in case you get cool. The fresh air might do you some good."

"I don't see how it could hurt. I'm feeling kind of cooped up in here."

"Then we'll get you out there for a while," Elise said. "I'll go down to the root cellar later and bring up the canning supplies so I can wash them. I'll just put them in the pantry until I'm ready for them. I figure next week I'll stay busy putting up apples."

"I can peel them for you," Frieda offered as she mended one of Derrick's shirts.

"That will be a great help, Mama." Elise was thrilled that her mother-in-law seemed to be recovering, but she didn't want to tax her. "Just don't feel you have to overdo things."

"I won't."

Derrick opened the back door and peeked inside. "You ready to start picking apples, Elise?"

"I'll be right out. Your mother wants to come out and watch, I think."

Derrick looked over at his mother. "Are you feeling up to that, Mama?"

"Yes, I am."

"All right, I'll bring a chair out for you." He crossed the room to grab a kitchen chair while his mother brought the shirt she'd been working on and followed him outside.

Elise followed them both. Derrick handed her a burlap sack with straps that tied over the shoulder. He helped her put it on and tie it so that the strap rested on the opposite shoulder from the side the bag hung on. "Don't let it get too heavy for you. I have more sacks."

Elise caught her breath at his nearness and could only nod in response.

Derrick put on his own sack and went over to make sure the ladder was secure. "I'm going to start up high. Just be careful to work on the side opposite me so that if I drop an apple, it doesn't fall on you."

It was only after Derrick moved away that Elise seemed to find her voice again. "I'll watch out."

She made her way around the lower branches, picking all she could reach on each one and, after Derrick dropped his first apple, trying to keep clear of the area he was working in.

"Oops, look out, Elise!"

Elise dodged one more falling apple. "I'm not sure there is a safe place to work with you up there, Derrick," Elise teased.

"I'm sorry. I was trying to grab two at a time."

"Trying to show off, huh?"

The teasing banter that ensued between them had Frieda chuckling from the porch.

Elise was nearly through picking from the lower limbs when Derrick yelled, "Elise! Watch out!"

Two more apples fell only a foot away. She could feel the whoosh as they flew by her. Hands on her hips, she looked up to see Derrick peering down at her, concern on his face. "Now what?" she asked laughingly. "Were you trying to grab three this time?"

"I am so sorry. Please—go sit with Mama. You'll be safer there."

"You'd better come on up here," Frieda called. "My son seems to have slippery hands today."

"I think I have most of them. I can pick the rest after you're through."

"I think that would be best," Derrick said with what sounded like relief in his voice. "We've had too many near misses today. I sure don't want you ending up with a concussion."

"No, neither do I."

"I need to come down and get a new sack and move the ladder around. I'll help you get your bag off."

But as Elise turned to move out from under the branches and Derrick started down the ladder, she heard an ominous whoosh as another apple fell. She moved just in time to avoid it hitting her in the head, but the apple struck her upper right arm with surprising force.

"Oh!" She stood rubbing the spot and had a feeling her arm would be bruised soon.

"Elise, did it hit you? I am so sorry. It fell out of the sack—" Derrick broke off midsentence, and the next thing Elise knew, he was standing beside her. He reached out to touch her arm, and she winced.

He quickly pulled his hand away from her arm. "Oh, Elise, I am so very sorry. It's already bruising."

"It wasn't your fault, Derrick. It was an accident."

"I'll go pick some ice off the block and wrap it in cloth to put on Elise's shoulder," Frieda said.

Derrick untied Elise's sack and helped her remove it from her left shoulder. He dropped it to the ground. "I'll bring it in later. Right now, let's just get you comfortable."

"I'm fine, Derrick. It's not broken or anything like that."

"I know it hurts, though." He helped her up to the porch and into the chair his mother had vacated. Frieda came out of the kitchen with a dishcloth-wrapped pack of picked ice. Elise shivered as she put the cold pack on her arm.

"I know it's cold, but it will keep the swelling down," Derrick said.

The pain did begin to ease, and Elise nodded. "It's feeling better. I'm going to be fine. You go on back to work."

Derrick nodded.

Elise insisted Frieda take the chair again, and she sat down on the top step, watching Derrick go back to work. . .until she began to get nervous watching him reach higher than he should and lean out on the ladder farther than she was comfortable with. "I'm going to go in and start dinner."

"I'll come and help," Frieda said.

"No, you stay and watch. It's not going to take long to warm up the soup left from last evening. I'll go ahead and put the beans on for supper, too."

"You sure you're up to it?"

Elise raised her arm so her mother-in-law could see that she could move it. It did hurt, but she grinned to try to hide the grimace that was behind it.

"I'm up to it."

"You're probably going to be even sorer tomorrow," her mother-in-law said with concern in her eyes.

Elise truly hoped not. She made her way to the kitchen and went about heating the soup for dinner.

Soon everything was ready, so she called Frieda and Derrick in to eat. Derrick watched her closely throughout the meal, even though she continued to assure him that she was fine.

"Is there anything I can do before I go back out?" he asked.

"You might bring the canning things up from the root cellar for her," Frieda said. "She wanted to get it all washed."

"I can do that before I finish picking apples," Derrick said.

Elise wasn't going to object. Washing them was one thing; carrying them up from the cellar with her arm still throbbing was another matter. She was glad for the offer. "Thank you. I appreciate it."

"I'll put some of the apples in the pantry and the rest down in the cellar. Will that be all right?"

"That will be fine."

"Don't feel you have to take care of all the apples right away. They stay well in the root cellar," Derrick said.

"I know. I'll do a little at a time. I'll get everything ready and start making jelly next week."

He brought up the canning utensils and empty jars while Elise cleaned up after dinner and got the beans started for supper.

Frieda insisted on drying the dishes and then finally admitted to being tired. "I guess all the excitement of the apple picking wore me out. I think I'll take a nap. Then maybe I can help with supper."

"Don't worry about helping with supper, Mama. You just rest. It was good to have you down here this morning. I'm sorry I gave you such a scare."

"I'm just glad you're all right," Frieda said as she moved toward the stairs.

Derrick brought up the last of the jars and placed them in the kitchen for Elise to wash. "Did Mama finally decide to take a rest?"

"Yes. I think watching you swing from the tree and seeing me get hurt was too much for her."

Derrick looked into Elise's eyes. "Seeing you get injured was almost too much for me. How is your arm? It looks really bad."

Elise looked down and could see that the bruise on her arm was turning blue-black. "It looks worse than it feels."

"I doubt that, but I have a feeling you aren't going to tell me how bad it really hurts." He reached up and tucked an escaping tendril of hair behind her ear. "I really am sorry, Elise. Please call me if you need to lift anything heavy or if you need anything at all."

His nearness had her breath catching in her throat once more. All she could manage was a nod as she turned to the sink and began to wash pots, jars, and lids.

Chapter 7

Derrick went back to picking apples feeling torn. He wanted to stay in the kitchen and help Elise. Much as she tried to hide it, he could tell that her arm was hurting her. He was glad she'd gotten a good night's sleep last night, because he had a feeling she wouldn't be sleeping well at all tonight. He was sure that arm was going to be hurting even worse the next day.

That Elise had worked to the point of exhaustion just to help him out this week and then got hurt helping him pick apples was very eye-opening for Derrick. He'd been attracted to her long ago when she only held the promise of the woman she had become. She was a special lady, and he was realizing that what he'd thought he felt for her years ago was nothing compared to what he was beginning to feel for her now.

Elise pitched in wherever needed. She'd come through with the cooking for all the hands, and she'd been waiting on his mother for the past few weeks. The house was always neat and tidy. Clothes were always clean and pressed. And she never complained.

It'd become pure joy to have this pretty, joyful woman, whom he'd cared about for years, in his house—making it a home. The house had never smelled as good as it did from the mouth-watering aromas of fresh bread, roasted chicken, or beef stew—and especially those apple pies Elise made. He'd always gotten by on his own cooking, but he fully appreciated the difference now.

Derrick sighed as he plucked two more apples off the tree and put them in his sack. Life as he knew it had changed—and he didn't want to go back to the way it had been. With his mother and Elise here, loneliness was a thing of the past. He was very happy to have his mother here—he'd missed being around family very much—but it was Elise who had him sprucing up first thing in the morning and before supper at night. It was she who had his heart thudding when she smiled at him each morning, and his pulse taking off at a gallop when his fingers had grazed her cheek as he'd tucked that tendril of hair behind her ear earlier. It was Elise who had him cringing at the bruise from the apple and wishing he could hurt for her.

He wasn't sure what to do about the attraction he felt for her. He didn't know whether to pursue her or not. She was a widow and free to marry again. But she was his *brother's* widow, and she'd obviously loved Carl. Derrick wasn't sure that he could compete with his brother's memory, and for the sake of family relationships, he didn't know if he should even try. His mother and Elise were close, and he knew they loved each other. If his desire to court Elise became evident and made her feel uncomfortable being in his home, he wasn't sure what it might do to her and his mother's relationship. He didn't want to harm it. Elise was the daughter his mother had never had.

She was in his thoughts more often than not, and while he fought to force his thinking on other things, he just didn't know how to keep her out of his dreams at night. She'd been a frequent visitor to them for a very long time—and he had a feeling she always would be.

While Derrick finished picking apples and Frieda was napping, Elise made another packet of ice with a dish towel and wrapped it around her throbbing arm just long enough to ease the pain for a bit. After she washed the rest of the canning utensils, she peeled and sliced potatoes. She'd just put them on to fry when Derrick brought in a sack of apples.

"I'll put these in the pantry so you can get to them easily. The rest I'll put in the root cellar until you want them. Just let me know, and I'll bring up what you need."

"Thank you, Derrick."

It didn't take long before he had all the apples brought in and stored away. He came back into the kitchen and asked, "How is your arm feeling?"

Elise was glad she could answer honestly, since she'd used the ice packet, "It's better."

"I'm glad. I'll go feed the horses and check on the rest of the animals and then come help you with supper."

Elise wasn't used to a man helping in the kitchen. "You don't have to do that."

"I know. But it was my fault you got hurt today. Helping with supper is the least I can do for you, Elise." Derrick paused for a moment, his gaze meeting hers from across the room.

There was something about the look in his eyes that had Elise's heart beating against her ribs as she waited for him to continue.

"My brother was a very lucky man to have you as his wife." With that said, Derrick turned and headed back outside.

It was a good thing he left just then, because Elise couldn't find her voice and didn't know what to say if she could have. She felt as if the breath had been knocked plumb out of her, and it was all she could do not to read anything into his words. Just because she was attracted to him didn't mean. . . Or did it?

"Elise," Frieda said, coming in from her nap, "I'm sorry I slept so long."

Elise blew out a deep breath and turned to her mother-in-law. "Don't worry about it, Mama. You were up longer than usual today."

"What do you need me to do?"

Help me to stop daydreaming about Derrick, was on the tip of her tongue, but Elise caught herself just before the words left her lips. She pulled her attention to the question Frieda had asked her and thought for a moment. The beans were about done; the potatoes were frying. "You can cut up some onion for me to put in the potatoes."

While Frieda chopped the onion, Elise mixed up a pan of corn bread to go with the beans and popped it into the oven. Then she checked the potatoes; they were brown and crisp on the bottom, so she carefully turned them over, adding the onions Frieda had cut up. This was one of their favorite meals, and she hoped Derrick liked it, too.

Frieda was just finishing setting the table when Derrick came back inside. "Oh, that smells wonderful, Elise. Is there anything you need me to do?"

"No. It's all about ready," Elise said, trying to ignore the way her pulse raced when he entered the room. She couldn't help but notice that he'd washed up outside before coming inside. "We're just waiting for the corn bread and the potatoes to finish cooking."

He crossed the room to kiss his mother on the cheek. "And how are you feeling, Mama? Did you have a good nap?"

"Yes, I slept hard. Must have been that fresh air outside—or the stress from watching Elise get hurt and you weaving all over those tree limbs to pick the apples."

Derrick chuckled. "Hopefully it was just the fresh air."

Elise slipped a tray of fried pies, left from the day before, onto the back of the range to heat up while they ate. She began to ladle the beans into individual bowls.

"I can at least take these to the table," Derrick said.

"Yes, you can do that." Elise smiled at him. It was nice that he wanted to help. While he took the bowls and set them in the middle of the dinner plates Frieda had set the table with, Elise pulled the corn bread out of the oven and set it to the side. She dished up the potatoes into a large bowl and handed it to Derrick to take to the table.

She cut the corn bread into slices, but before she could lift the pan, Derrick had grabbed it. "That's too heavy with your arm hurting. I'll take it to the table."

Elise followed with the butter and then started back to get the water pitcher.

"I'll get that. Please, Elise, just go sit down," Derrick said.

Carl was a good husband, but he hadn't been one to help in the house much. Elise wasn't quite sure what to make of the fact that Derrick was a more-than-willing helper.

Once everything was on the table, Derrick bowed his head. "Dear Father, thank You for our many blessings. Thank You that Elise wasn't hurt any worse than she was today. Please let her arm heal quickly, and please let Mama continue to regain her strength. Thank You for this food we are about to eat. In Jesus' name I pray. Amen."

Frieda served the potatoes and corn bread, and after a few bites, Derrick was lavish in his compliments on the meal.

Suppertime was quickly becoming one of Elise's favorite times of the day.

Elise's arm did hurt more the next day, but she tried not to let on as she went about making breakfast so that they could get to church on time. Going to church on Sunday was Frieda's only outing of the week, and while it did tire her, Elise knew there was no way she was going to miss church. The members had made them feel very welcome, and Elise would have hated to miss going, too.

The preacher's wife, Rachel, had made a special effort to talk to them and introduce them to others of the church family. Today she came up to them as soon as they sat down. "How are you settling in, Mrs. Morgan?"

"It's beginning to feel like home, and I like it here a lot." Frieda smiled at the younger woman. "But I'll feel more at home if you call me Frieda instead of Mrs. Morgan."

"Frieda it is, then. I'm glad you're settling in." Rachel turned to Elise. "And how do you like Farmington, Elise?"

"I like it—what I have seen of it. I certainly love the countryside."

"Are you thinking of staying, then?"

"Oh, I'll need to get back to Denver before too long. It's where my home is," Elise said. And then she wondered how her house was going to feel like home when she was settling in here so easily. And how empty was the house going to feel when the others who'd made it home for her were no longer there? She pushed those thoughts to the back of her mind. She didn't want to think about going home yet. Frieda still needed her, and as long as that was the case, she didn't have to think about returning to Colorado.

"Well, I'm sure you could sell your home up there and relocate down here in New Mexico Territory."

Elise wasn't sure how to reply, and she was relieved when Rachel hurried off to speak to someone else who'd just arrived. Elise couldn't help but admit to herself that Rachel's idea was one she'd thought of herself. But she couldn't live with Mama and Derrick forever. It was one thing while she was needed; it would be something else entirely to just expect to stay. She put her attention on the church service, where it should be, instead of weaving daydreams on what-ifs and maybes.

Harold Burton's sermon was a good reminder about putting one's trust in the Lord and looking to Him for guidance. Elise wasn't sure she always gave things over to Him, but she was going to strive to do so from now on. When the service was over, she stood with a renewed determination to let the Lord lead her as she followed Derrick and Frieda down the aisle.

"Let's go over to the Grand Hotel for Sunday dinner," Derrick suggested as they left the church after telling Harold what a good sermon he'd given.

"I can make something at home, Derrick."

"I know you can. But that arm is bound to be bothering you today. And besides, I think Mama would like to enjoy her outing a little longer."

"I wouldn't mind," Frieda agreed, "especially as it's such a nice day."

"I'll drive you both around to see some of the area after we eat," Derrick said.

Elise wasn't going to turn down the offer. Frieda had commented on feeling all cooped up lately, and she wouldn't mind seeing more of the countryside herself.

Elise enjoyed the meal at the hotel very much. The dining room was nicely decorated, and on Sundays they served everything family style.

"This is good," Derrick said after taking his first bite of fried chicken. "But it doesn't hold a candle to yours, Elise."

"Why, thank you, Derrick. I was thinking it was better than mine."

"No, it's not," Frieda assured her, "but I know how you feel. Sometimes it's just good to eat someone else's cooking."

Elise guessed she was right, because everything tasted great to her.

After dinner, Derrick showed them around the town, passing the drugstore where they'd taken Frieda's prescription to be filled and the newspaper office and one of the cafés.

"What is that, son?" Frieda asked as they passed an adobe building.

"It's an Indian trading post, Mama."

"Oh? Is that like a general store or mercantile?"

"I guess you could consider it that way. You can find warm blankets there, and pottery and baskets, among other things. They make wonderful fry bread."

"There are a lot of Indians in this area?" Elise asked.

"Yes. There are Navajo, Jicarilla Apache, and Ute tribes in this area. They were here long before Farmington became the town it is now."

From there, Derrick took them out to see some of his neighbors' orchards and farms. "The soil in this area is very rich, and with the Animas, San Juan, and La Plata rivers all converging, it makes it easy to grow just about anything."

Elise could see how it was likely to become a major farming community in the years to come. Derrick had been very smart to settle here.

By the time they arrived back home, she knew she could be happy living in this area for the rest of her life. But it wasn't likely that was going to happen. She really needed to try to look forward to returning to Colorado, but Elise had a feeling that was going to be very hard to do.

~

The next morning, it was Derrick's turn to help a neighbor with his harvest, and Elise got up earlier than usual to make breakfast for him before he left. His smile, when he entered the kitchen and found her at the stove, made it worth the effort.

"I thought I must be imagining that smell of bacon frying. You didn't have to do this, Elise. I would have grabbed a couple of cold biscuits and eaten them on the way over to Jed's."

"That's not a good way to start the day," she said as she dished up the bacon onto a plate. She cracked three eggs into the skillet and cooked them over-easy for him. "And don't worry about milking Bessie. I'll do it after you leave."

"Elise, I can't let you do that," Derrick said as he poured himself a cup of coffee.

"Derrick, I know how to milk a cow. I grew up on a farm just like you did."

"I know, but—"

"I'm sure Jed needs you over there as soon as possible. You were glad for those who showed up early here." She took a pan of biscuits out of the oven.

"I was."

"Well then, I can milk Bessie and gather the eggs and feed the chickens while you're helping others out."

"Elise, your arm—"

"Feels better today." Elise handed him a plate filled with bacon and eggs and biscuits. "It looks worse than it feels."

She fixed her own plate and brought it to the table. She bowed her head while Derrick said the blessing, and then she looked up to find his gaze on her.

He shook his head. "You are some woman, Elise. I'm not going to let you milk Bessie. I'll do that. But you can gather the eggs and feed the chickens, if you will."

From the look in his eyes, Elise had a feeling there would be no sense in arguing with him. She nodded. "All right."

~

The end of September and first part of October seemed to fly by as they settled into a routine of sorts. Derrick milked Bessie while Elise made his breakfast. After he left to help with other harvests, she fed the chickens and brought in the eggs. Then when Frieda came down, she made breakfast for her.

She stayed busy during the day—making apple butter and jelly, doing the washing and the ironing. She baked bread and churned butter, cleaned house and helped Frieda with the mending. And she looked forward to the minute Derrick would walk in the back door and sniff appreciatively of anything she had cooking.

Frieda was better but still not up to taking care of Derrick and his home by herself. For the time being, Elise was happy to push thoughts of returning to Denver to the back of her mind.

But as the days went by, Elise found that her thoughts of Carl had all but disappeared. The fact that she could no longer readily recall his sweet face brought her deep guilt. Instead, and hard as she tried to avoid it, she found herself thinking of Derrick more and more each day. Was it because he was the only man she'd been around for any length of time since Carl's death? She sighed and shook her head. She didn't know. All she did know was that Derrick wasn't only in her thoughts during the day; he'd come to occupy her dreams at night, and was the first person she thought about when she woke.

His smile, when he came into the kitchen after milking the cow each morning and found her dishing up his breakfast, had her heart doing little somersaults. She never tired of the compliments he showered on her over her cooking or of his appreciation for all she did for him and his mother.

It was while she sat under the apple tree out back, taking a break one afternoon, that she realized she could no longer deny that her feelings for Derrick were growing with each passing day. But she had no business feeling this way about her husband's brother. While the very thought of leaving here broke her heart. . .maybe it was time to make plans to return to Denver.

Derrick found himself looking forward to coming home each evening. It was getting dark by the time he returned, and his house was lit with light. He always felt welcomed into his own home as he walked into the kitchen to find Elise cooking supper and his mother setting the table. Life was good.

Tonight he fed his horse and washed up before going inside. But as he started to open the back door and enter the kitchen, he heard his mother exclaim, "No, Elise, you can't go home now! Why, I need you and Derrick needs you."

Derrick felt as if the breath had been knocked right out of him as he waited to hear what Elise had to say.

"Mama, don't worry. I won't leave until you've recovered. But it's something I need to be thinking about once you're well. I've already been gone a long time."

It was only when Derrick heard Elise say she wasn't leaving just yet that he realized he'd been holding his breath. He let it out with a whoosh, not sure whether to be relieved that she was staying for the time being or devastated that she was planning to leave at sometime in the future. His heart grew heavy in his chest at the thought of her going back to Denver. He loved Elise—had always loved her. And he was falling more in love with her with each passing day. All he could think to do was pray.

Dear Lord, please don't let me lose Elise again.

Chapter 8

"What's this? You're thinking of leaving us? Are we working you too hard, Elise?"

Elise turned swiftly to find that Derrick had entered the kitchen. His brow was furrowed as he waited for her answer. She rubbed her suddenly pounding temple. She hadn't meant to cause such a stir. "Of course you aren't working me too hard, Derrick. And I wouldn't think of leaving until Mama is fully recovered."

"What's this all about, then? Are you homesick?"

Elise knew him well enough by now to know that the expression in his eyes was one of concern. But she couldn't tell him that the very last thing she wanted to do was return to Denver. Or that she was fast losing her heart to him—or that she felt guilty that she was having trouble remembering what his brother looked like without the aid of a picture. But she wasn't homesick, so she could answer his second question truthfully. "No, I'm not homesick."

"Elise, have I done anything to make you feel unwelcome?"

"No, of course you haven't! You've made me feel right at home." *Too much so,* she thought. But she couldn't say that, either.

"Is there anything you need to go back to Denver to take care of?"

Grasping at anything she could answer truthfully, she said, "Eventually I'll need to check on my home, Derrick. I wasn't planning on staying for an extended period when I left."

"Is there a neighbor you could send a letter or telegram to asking him or her to check on things for you?"

"Mrs. Nordstrom knows where you are, Elise," Frieda said. "You could send her a key and ask her to check on things."

Elise wasn't really worried about the house, but she grasped at any excuse to get out of the conversation. "I could do that. I could send her your key. I probably should have contacted her before now. That's a good idea, Mama. I'll write her tonight."

"Good. Then you can stop worrying about things in Colorado," her mother-in-law said.

"I have to pass the post office on my way to Ed Holly's place tomorrow. I'll be glad to send it off for you."

"Thank you, Derrick." Elise was more confused than ever. She was both relieved and apprehensive—relieved that she didn't have to go home just yet and apprehensive because she knew that staying longer would more than likely make it heart wrenching for her when she did return to Denver. She already felt sick inside at the very thought of leaving.

During supper, no more mention was made about her going back to Colorado. But as she finished cleaning up the kitchen after the meal, Elise turned to find Derrick bringing in a box containing Frieda's writing supplies.

"Mama asked me to bring these to you. She said you might need them to write to your neighbor."

"She's right. I didn't bring letter-writing materials with me. Thank you, Derrick."

"It's no problem." He put the things down on the kitchen table. "I'm glad to do it for you. If I haven't said so lately, I'm very thankful that you came with Mama and have been willing to stay. I know you do have a life in Denver and we've taken up a lot of your—"

"Derrick, I'm not in that big of a hurry to go home. I just was mentioning to Mama that I probably needed to think about returning. She does seem to be getting better, and even though I know she's not fully back to normal yet, I'm sure you didn't think I would be here this long when you asked me to stay until she was better."

"Neither of us did. But, Elise, even if Mama was completely well, I want you to know that you are always welcome here. . .for as long as you want to stay. You are part of this family, and you always will be."

"Thank you, Derrick." Elise felt a sudden urge to cry at his sweet words and turned to hang up the dish towel with which she'd just dried the last dish. Derrick was a wonderful man, and knowing she would always be welcome in his home meant a great deal to her. But she couldn't keep from wondering if he'd still be so hospitable to her if he knew how much she'd come to care for him. Not as Carl's brother—but as the man who could make her heart turn to mush with just the hint of his smile or the sound of his laughter.

Derrick wasn't sure what to say next. Hearing Elise talk about going back to Denver had thrown him into a panic, and all he'd wanted to do was take her in his arms and tell her that he never wanted her to leave his home. And it was what he still wanted to do.

But he was afraid that action might send her running right out the door. She was his brother's widow, and Derrick had no reason at all to believe that she felt the same way—or ever would. To her, he was probably just Carl's brother and Frieda's younger son.

Elise wasn't aware that he'd cared about her for a very long time, and he had no idea how to—or even if he should—let her know how he felt about her. He certainly didn't want to say or do anything that would have her catching the next stage out of town.

"Would you like a cup of coffee?" Elise asked, easing the uncomfortable moment for him. "There's some apple pie left, if you'd like some of that."

"Thank you, I would. But I can get it. You go ahead and write your letter." He would feel much better once she sent that letter off to her neighbor. Maybe then she wouldn't worry about getting back to her house.

She sat down at the table and pulled the ink jar and writing paper toward her. Derrick poured himself a cup of coffee and cut a piece of pie from the one sitting in the pie safe, listening to the scratch of pen against paper. He breathed a sigh of relief that she was writing the letter. He sat down at the table across from her to eat his pie while she finished her correspondence.

It didn't take long before she put the pen down and reread the letter. She nodded, seeming to be satisfied. "Now I just need to get the key from Mama."

"Oh, she gave it to me as she was going upstairs." He stood and dug into his pocket, pulling out Frieda's key to the house in Denver.

"That's all I need." Elise took the key from him and sighed. "Surely I can trust Mrs. Nordstrom with it. I've known her for many years."

"I'm sure you can, Elise. Mama is a good judge of character. She wouldn't have suggested her if she didn't think your neighbor could be trusted."

"That's true. And they were pretty good friends even though Mrs. Nordstrom is younger than Mama." Elise slipped the key into the envelope with the letter and sealed it with Frieda's wax. Then she handed the envelope to Derrick.

"I'll be sure to get it mailed tomorrow." He certainly hoped that would settle her mind about the house and that there'd be no more talk about leaving. Not for a long time.

Before Elise knew it, Thanksgiving was almost upon them. October had passed swiftly with Derrick helping his neighbors and friends. Harvest was over now, and she thought Derrick's workload would slow down, but he kept very busy. He planted more apple trees of varying kinds and took care of all sorts of things in the barn—cleaning it and the other outbuildings, fixing broken equipment, and getting everything in good working order. He took care of the livestock and tried to do all the things he didn't have time for during growing season.

The weather had changed quickly, with the mornings and evenings turning much colder. Derrick always had the stove lit and a fire in the fireplace by the time Elise came down in the morning. He kept wood chopped and stacked out by the back door, but he always made sure there was plenty of wood right inside so that Elise didn't have to bring it in.

Derrick was the most considerate man she'd ever known—even more so than his brother had been. He brought up potatoes and apples from the root cellar to the pantry so they would be easy for Elise to get to. He put up a lean-to over the wash kettle to keep the wind from making it colder than usual to do the wash.

Because he was right there, Derrick was in and out a lot during the day. Elise didn't mind at all—except for the fact that it was becoming very difficult for her to hide her growing feelings for him. She could feel the telltale color creep up her neck each time Derrick popped into the kitchen to see what was cooking or when he complimented her on the meal he'd just eaten.

She could tell when he walked up behind her just from the tickly feeling along the back of her neck. He was very thoughtful. He always seemed to know when she needed help hanging clothes on the line, and before they went to church on Sunday, he'd warm several large stones and put them in the wagon for his mother and Elise to prop their feet on.

Going to church was still Frieda's biggest outing, and she enjoyed it immensely. The people of the church they attended had gone out of their way to make them all feel at home. They'd been asked to join several different families for Sunday dinner during the last month, and Frieda was happily getting to know their neighbors. Several of the ladies had come out to have afternoon tea with them. The days seemed to speed by.

This afternoon was no different. Elise found herself on the back porch, sipping her coffee and looking down toward the river, easier to see now that the leaves were gone from the trees. The river sparkled in the sunlight, and the winter landscape was as beautiful, in its own way, as it had been in late summer. She was sure it would be beautiful in the spring with all the apple trees in bloom. But now she was looking forward to the first snow.

Farmington was a place where she could be happy living for the rest of her life. In fact, she never wanted to leave. But that presented a problem in itself. She didn't know how she could stay—falling in love with Derrick as she was.

She closed her eyes and sent up a silent prayer. *Dear Lord, I don't know what to do. Should I stay or go? Mama seems a little better, but she's not up to keeping house for Derrick or cooking three meals a day. I know he would help her, but I want to be the one cooking for the two of them. I want to be the one taking care of the house. I don't want to go back to Denver. There's nothing there for me to go home to. Lord, please help me to know what to do. I'm afraid if I stay too much longer, it will be even harder to leave. And yet the last thing I want to do is go now—or ever. Please help me, Father. Show me what You would have me do. In Jesus' name I pray. Amen.*

"Elise! Are you out back?" Derrick called out the kitchen door. It wasn't like her not to be in the kitchen this time of day.

"I'm out here, Derrick." Elise hurried around the corner of the porch. "I've been enjoying the crisp air this afternoon. What's wrong?"

He opened the door wide as she came inside. "Nothing is wrong. I just wanted to ask you something and I didn't know where you were."

"Did you need something?"

He looked at her for a moment without saying anything. How did he tell her that he needed to know where she was at all times, that he loved seeing her at the stove, in his house, doing anything around there? He just needed to see *her*. "Not really. I just. . . Do you need anything from town for the Thanksgiving meal? I thought I would go in tomorrow or the next day."

"Oh. It's nearly upon us, isn't it?"

"It is. And I was wondering. . ." He paused.

"What?" she prodded.

Derrick sighed. He didn't think she'd mind, but he wouldn't know for sure until he asked. "For the past several years, I've gone to Jed Barrister's for Thanksgiving. He and his wife Caroline have had me over to their house for dinner. But she's expecting a baby anytime now, and Jed's mentioned a time or two that she tires real easy. I thought maybe—"

"Oh yes, of course. You'd like to have them over here?" She smiled and tilted her head to the side as she waited for his answer.

"Yes, if it's all right with you. Mama said it was fine with her."

"I think that would be wonderful! With just the three of us, there will be way too much to eat anyway, if I make everything Mama says you'd like."

Derrick chuckled. "Mama is just trying to make up for all those Thanksgivings we were apart."

"Well, I think it's very nice that you want to invite Jed and Caroline over. Please do. I know Mama will love having company."

"You're sure? I'll help in any way you need me to."

"I'm sure. I'll start a list of things we need tonight."

"Thank you, Elise."

"You're welcome. But you really didn't need to ask me. This is *your* home, Derrick."

He shook his head. "You're the one who will be doing all the work."

"Oh, don't worry. I'll be putting you to work, too."

"Good." He could think of nothing better than working alongside Elise.

Over the next few days, they did just that. Jed and Caroline eagerly accepted his invitation to Thanksgiving dinner, and Derrick didn't know who seemed more excited about it—them or his mother and Elise. He had to admit that he was looking forward to having company over, too. He knew his home would be gleaming from top to bottom from the cleaning Elise had started that morning. It would be nice to welcome his friends into what had become a warm and hospitable home.

Elise and his mother had gone over their list one last time before he headed off to town for supplies, and when he returned that afternoon, he found them both in the kitchen. Mama was polishing the silverware that'd been stored in the dining room, and Elise was washing the china he'd bought with the house. He put up the supplies in the pantry and came back to help.

"My, I didn't realize I owned such beautiful things," Derrick said, picking up a plate and drying it.

"I still can't believe you bought this house completely furnished, son. We're going to set a beautiful table in that dining room we've never eaten in."

"We can eat right here in the kitchen, Mama. You two don't need to go to all this trouble."

"Oh, don't say that, Derrick. Mama has wanted to eat in there ever since we got here."

"If you can't eat in there for Thanksgiving, then what's the purpose of having a room like that?" his mother asked.

"If you two wanted to eat in there, then why haven't we?"

His mother and Elise looked at each other and shrugged. Elise grinned and shook her head. "The table just seemed kind of big for the three of us for everyday use. And we didn't want you to think we were putting on airs."

Derrick laughed. He couldn't imagine his mother or Elise "putting on airs." "How about if we start out slow. We can use it for holidays, and if you two want to, we could eat Sunday dinners in there, too."

"Well, I think we should," his mother said. "It's a shame not to use a room like that."

"Good. It's settled, then. Sunday dinners and holidays we'll eat in the dining room." They both looked so pleased. Derrick wished he'd known how much they wanted to eat in the formal room. He'd have suggested it long ago.

The next two days were full of activity. While he shelled pecans, Mama chopped them up. Then Elise baked pecan and pumpkin pies and a three-layer chocolate cake thickly iced with chocolate frosting and decorated with pecans. On the day before Thanksgiving, Elise made corn bread for dressing and put Derrick to work chopping onions and celery. His mother set the table in the dining room with the linens she'd found in the large sideboard.

On Thanksgiving morning, Derrick got up and went to light the stove only to find that Elise was already bustling around the kitchen, humming to herself. She'd lit the oven herself and put the turkey in to roast.

"I should have known you'd be up with the chickens this morning," he said.

"I was too excited to sleep," Elise replied, pouring him a cup of coffee and handing it to him.

"You really enjoy all this cooking, don't you?"

"I do. I'm looking forward to the day."

He was, too. It was the first Thanksgiving he'd enjoyed thinking about in years. He just wished he could tell her that she was the one who was making it so very special for him.

When Jed and Caroline arrived, Elise joined him in welcoming them into his home, and his mother took the young woman under her wing, giving her a baby bonnet she'd managed to crochet in the last few days. Caroline seemed to thrive with the attention his mother and Elise gave her, and Jed beamed seeing his wife enjoy herself so much.

After everyone was seated around the table in the dining room, and before they began to eat the delicious meal Elise had prepared, Derrick bowed his head and prayed. "Dear Lord, we thank You for this day and for all of the many blessings You've bestowed on us. We thank You for friends and family to share this day with, and we thank You for this wonderful meal we are about to eat. Most of all, we thank You for Your Son and our Savior, Jesus Christ. It is in His name we pray. Amen."

Derrick couldn't remember when he'd enjoyed a day more. His house had become a real home thanks to his mother and Elise, and he was happy he'd been able to ask Jed and Caroline over.

That evening, after the Barristers had gone home, he helped his mother and Elise with the cleanup. As they talked over the day, Derrick knew his joy had been complete because he had the two women he loved the most here to share it with. It was a day he would never forget—and one he prayed would not be the last of its kind.

Chapter 9

Thanksgiving had been a blessing for Elise. . .if for no other reason than it seemed to have perked Frieda up considerably. The last few Thanksgivings, after Carl passed away, had been very hard on both of them. But this one was different and special because they were able to share it with Derrick, who hadn't been around family in so long. It did her heart good to see him so happy.

Frieda seemed to have regained some of her energy and began helping Elise in the kitchen a little more often. Elise watched and learned as her mother-in-law made her chicken fricassee—one of Derrick's favorite dishes. Carl hadn't liked it much, so there had been no reason for Elise to learn to make it before now. But after seeing Derrick's expression when he took his first bite of the dish, Elise was determined to learn what some of his other favorites were.

"I think you must like chicken better than Carl did. He preferred beef."

"I like beef, too," Derrick said. "But there aren't many ways you can cook a chicken that I don't like."

"Carl was just a little pickier than Derrick," Frieda said. "But they both ate what was put before them. Derrick just enjoyed more of it than Carl did."

"And so Mama began to make more of what Carl liked."

"Son, I didn't play favorites. You know that."

Derrick chuckled. "I do. I'm just teasing you."

Elise couldn't help but wonder if he'd been right, though. It probably had been easier to make what Carl wanted since Derrick liked it all.

That night, after she'd cleaned the kitchen, Elise looked through the *Fannie Farmer Cookbook* that Frieda had brought with her. There were several chicken dishes she thought she might try. She flipped the pages looking for more.

Derrick came in a little later. "Would you like some cocoa? Mama said she would, and I have a hankering for it, too."

"That sounds good." Elise shut the cookbook. "I'll—"

"No, you sit. I know how to make it. It's one thing I make really well."

"I'd love a cup, then," Elise said, watching him gather the cocoa, sugar, and milk. He pulled out a battered old pan she rarely used and put it on top of the range.

"Mama taught me how long ago. I love it this time of year—makes me sleep better."

Frieda came into the kitchen with her crochet bag. She'd found something to keep her hands busy in quiet moments. She loved to crochet, and after meeting Caroline, she was busily crocheting a complete layette for the baby-to-come. Her hands seemed to be flying across the piece she was working on as Derrick went about making the cocoa.

He moved the teakettle over so that the water would boil, and he put milk in the pan to scald it. Elise watched him mix the cocoa and sugar. He added a pinch of salt and mixed it in. Elise thought he added something else, but she couldn't see what it was. Once he decided that the milk was ready, he poured boiling water into the dry mixture and stirred it into a paste. Then he added it all to the milk and stirred it again, bringing it to a near boil.

The kitchen smelled delicious. Elise felt as though she should be helping, but it was Derrick's kitchen after all, and he seemed to want to do this for them. He filled three cups with the aromatic liquid, then brought Elise and his mother a cup. Then he brought his own over and joined them at the table.

Elise lifted the cup to her mouth and blew on it. "Mmm. It smells wonderful, Derrick." She took a small sip. "This is delicious."

"Thank you."

"I think it's better than mine," his mother said. "What did you add to it, Derrick?"

"Just a hint of cinnamon."

"Ah." Elise nodded. "That's what it is. It's very good."

"Thank you. I'm glad I can make something for the two of you."

It quickly became a family custom for Derrick to make them cocoa before bedtime. It was a time of day Elise found herself looking forward to. Frieda and Derrick shared memories that she'd never heard before, and with each passing day she felt she knew Derrick better.

By the first week of December, Derrick's mother was making great progress with the layette. She began on the tiny booties one evening while Elise was finishing up another batch of jelly and Derrick was reading the newspaper. He loved this time of day with them. He would read them tidbits from the paper from time to time. Even if there wasn't much talking going on, there was always a cozy feeling in his kitchen that he couldn't seem to get enough of.

"Derrick, I so enjoyed having the Barristers over for Thanksgiving," his mother said as she crocheted. "It made me think of the family custom we used to have—up until you and Carl became adults. Then your papa and I continued it on a smaller scale. Do you remember what it was?"

"Of course I do. I don't think a Christmas goes by that I don't think about it. We used to take candy and baked goods to neighbors and friends the day before Christmas Eve."

"I truly enjoyed doing that at Christmastime."

"Well, Mama, I have to admit it's not a family custom I've kept up. Before you and Elise got here, I was doing good just to cook for myself."

Frieda chuckled. "Son, I sure didn't expect you to keep up with it. Elise and I did it on a smaller scale in Denver. We usually made cookies for the neighbors on each side of us. But that was about it."

"I remember that Carl and I always went with you and Papa to deliver everything when we were young. And you bade us to mind our manners."

"Which you always did. You were both good boys." She sighed and looked thoughtful. "It would be nice to start the tradition back up here. I don't want to put it all onto Elise, but I think I'm feeling up to making some candy and cookies. What do you two think? Could we do it?"

Derrick exchanged a glance with Elise. He hadn't heard his mother sound so enthused about anything in a long time. But even though she seemed to be doing better, he knew most of the work would fall to Elise.

"I don't see why not," Elise said.

"I can help shell pecans and chop them. . .and whatever else you need me to do," he hurried to assure her. No wonder he was falling in love with Elise. She was perfectly aware that she'd be doing most of the work, but because his mother wanted to do it, she readily agreed.

"Well, we need to do first things first. Derrick, you need to make us a list of your neighbors and friends—anyone you'd like to give to. Just make sure you include them all. We don't want to have any of them feeling slighted. Then we can figure out what to make and how much of it."

It was wonderful, if a bit surprising, to see his mother take control of the planning, and he and Elise were quick to agree with her. "I'll start making a list tonight, Mama," Derrick said.

"I'll check the pantry to see what we have on hand after I clean up here," Elise said as she put the lid on the last jar of jelly.

"You two don't have to do it all tonight." Frieda paused in crocheting another round of tiny stitches. "Tomorrow will be soon enough."

"You know, we could ask Harold about the needy around here that I don't know personally," Derrick said. "I'm sure there are some people around here who could really use a helping hand this Christmas. I've been very blessed with a bumper crop of apples. I'd like to do something to help the less fortunate."

"That's a wonderful suggestion, Derrick." Elise took several jars of apple jelly to the pantry.

"Yes, it is. I like that idea a lot, son," his mother said. "Please do check with Preacher Burton."

Derrick got up to begin making cocoa. "I will. I'll go into town tomorrow and ask him about it."

"We could make a list of the things you enjoyed giving out, if you'd like, Mama," Elise said as she came out of the pantry.

"All right. I think I can remember most of it."

"I'll get some paper so I can write it down. Then after Derrick finds out how many people we're talking about, we can decide what might work best."

Elise got the paper and a pencil and sat back down just as Derrick served their cocoa. Elise took a sip before asking, "What were your favorite things to give out?"

"Everyone liked my sugar cookies. And I took gingerbread. I made fudge and fondant, too. What were your favorites, Derrick?"

He brought his cup to the table and sat down. "I thought we made up some popcorn balls some years."

"We did," his mother said, nodding. "What else?"

"You made molasses cookies, didn't you?"

"Yes, I did! They were a particular favorite of the Wilsons." His mother smiled at the memory. "This is going to be so much fun. I'll look through my cookbook tomorrow and see what else I can come up with."

She went back to her crocheting, and he and Elise exchanged a smile. He had a feeling they both were of one mind. Whatever they could do to keep his mother this happy and active, they would strive to do.

"Son?"

Derrick pulled his gaze away from Elise to find his mother's glance going back and forth between the two of them. "Yes, ma'am?"

"When you go into town tomorrow to talk to the preacher, would you see if you can get ahold of some of this white yarn? I can cut you off a piece so it will be easy for you to match."

"I'll try to find you some."

"Good. That baby will need a blanket, too."

Harold Burton did indeed know of a couple of families who were struggling to get by this year. He wrote down the names and ages of the children in each family and handed the slip of paper to Derrick. "This is a good thing you're doing, Derrick. I know the Ballards and the Hansons will be more than a little appreciative."

"Well, the Lord has blessed me greatly this year. I feel I should be giving to others."

"I'm sure the Lord will continue to bless you with that attitude, son."

Derrick began to shake his head. That wasn't why he was doing this.

"I know you aren't doing it to get anything back, Derrick," Harold said as if he knew what Derrick was thinking. "We both understand that we can't work our way to heaven. Still, we're to do the work the Lord puts before us, and He certainly knows a good deed when He sees it."

"It makes me feel good to be able to give to those less fortunate. But I suspect that most of them would just as soon not need the help."

"That's true. Most people would rather be in a position to give." Harold nodded and stood up to shake hands as Derrick stood and stuffed the list into his pocket. "God bless you, son. We'll see you on Sunday."

"See you then."

Derrick had a feeling his mother and Elise were both going to be even more excited once they knew they could help make Christmas special for the Ballard and Hanson families. As for him, he felt more blessed than ever knowing that he didn't have to spend this Christmas alone. It had been so long since he'd spent the holiday with family.

He stopped at the mercantile to see if he could find the yarn his mother wanted and was glad to find that they had several skeins in stock. He bought two of them to take home to her. The shopkeeper was getting in new items for Christmas, and just seeing him put a doll in the window made Derrick feel like a child again. He found that his mother and Elise wouldn't be the only ones getting excited about helping these families out. If he wasn't mistaken, there was a little girl on his list who would probably love that doll.

He checked to make sure and then asked for a doll just like the one on display. One gift bought and many more to go. As he tied the packages onto his horse, Derrick realized that he probably should have waited and asked the women in his home about the doll. He certainly didn't want them to miss out on the fun, but he was afraid the dolls would all be gone before he got back into town. As Derrick headed home with his purchases, he couldn't wait to tell them about how their plans to give goodies had grown into something much bigger.

When he rode up to his house, he was pleasantly surprised to find Jed's horse and wagon tied to his hitching rail out front. Derrick forgot his packages for the moment and hurried inside to find Jed and Caroline sitting at the kitchen table visiting with his mother and Elise.

"Here is Derrick now," his mother said as he entered the kitchen. "Look who has come to see us."

"Jed, Caroline, it's good to see you. How are you feeling, Caroline?"

"Like a whale," she said, laughing good-naturedly.

Derrick knew enough not to comment about that and was glad that Jed did, too.

"You look beautiful to me," Jed told his wife. He looked at Derrick and grinned. "Doc says we may have our baby anytime now. Caroline wanted to check with your mother and Elise to see if they had any advice for us for when it's time. Doc said he would be coming out the next few days to check on her, but what if things start to happen in the middle of the night? I need to know what to do."

"I've told him to bring her here at the first sign of labor, Derrick. That way you could go for the doctor and he could stay with Caroline. Also, Elise and I would be here to help."

Derrick wasn't quite sure how he felt about that until he looked at Jed. He could see that the man was concerned about having to leave Caroline alone. He'd feel the same way if it were his wife. "That sounds like a good plan to me, Jed."

The younger man let his breath out in one giant whoosh. "Thank you, Derrick. Caroline has taken to your mother and Elise, and with no women relatives around. . . Well, it makes us both feel better to know we have someone nearby who knows about these things."

Derrick nodded. He could understand that. "I'm glad we're here, too. And glad Mama and Elise are here to know what to do—if needed. It's for sure that I don't."

Elise and his mother convinced the young couple to stay for supper, and Caroline pitched in and helped finish it up while Jed went out to help Derrick with his evening chores.

"I can't tell you how much it means to Caroline and me to have you all to turn to," Jed said as he took the bridle off Derrick's horse for him. "She's been missin' her mama something awful. But ever since Thanksgiving, she's felt better. It kind of felt like being with family to be over here with you all."

"We enjoyed having you two with us, Jed. And I'm glad that my mama and Elise have made a difference to Caroline."

"I'll sure be glad when this baby gets here. I can tell you, I'm plumb nervous about it all."

Derrick's heart went out to the younger man. "I'd be just as anxious as you," he assured Jed. "And I doubt there's a man out there who wouldn't feel the same way."

"You think so?"

"I do."

Jed only nodded, but he seemed to relax just a bit. By the time they went back to the house, supper was ready. Derrick brought his packages in and put them in the pantry for the time being.

He half expected that they'd eat in the dining room. Instead, they all gathered around the kitchen table, and after he said the blessing, they shared a meal of beef stew and Elise's fluffy biscuits.

"This tastes so good to me," Caroline said. "I guess I'm just getting tired of my own cooking."

"You're probably just plain tired, dear," Derrick's mother said.

"Well, whatever it is, it sure is nice to taste someone else's cooking. I'll repay you after the baby gets here."

"We'd love to come over for supper one night after you have the baby, but not until you're up to it."

Caroline nodded. "Soon as I am, though."

"We'd be glad to come then," Elise assured her.

They sat and talked for a while after supper, but even Derrick could tell Caroline was tiring fast when Jed suggested that they leave.

"You be sure and bring her over here first sign of that baby coming, Jed, you hear?" Frieda said.

"Oh yes, ma'am. You don't have to worry about that." Jed chuckled.

As they waved the young couple good-bye, Derrick had a feeling they'd see them again in a day or two—if not sooner. "Do you think she's going to have the baby soon, Mama?"

"Oh, I think so. It wouldn't surprise me a bit if we saw them again tonight. We probably should have had them just stay here until the baby comes."

"Do you want me to go after them?"

"No. It'll be better for them to decide what to do, son." She turned to go back into the house.

Derrick looked at Elise. He wasn't sure his mother was making sense.

"They'll grow closer as a couple through all this if they're the ones deciding when they need help and when they don't," Elise explained.

Derrick nodded. He thought he understood now, and as he followed Elise inside, a sudden wave of longing washed over him. . .for his deepest dreams to come true. But he'd been dreaming the same thing for a very long time. It would be only with the Lord's help that he had any hope of it coming true. But it sure seemed to be taking Him a long time to show Derrick what to do.

Chapter 10

With all the excitement over Caroline and Jed's baby coming soon, it was the next morning before Elise thought to ask Derrick about his trip to town. "What did you find out from the preacher, Derrick?" she asked as she dished up breakfast.

"He gave me the names of two families who could use some help this year. I'm not sure I know them." He took his plate and his mother's and brought them to the table. "Have either of you met the Ballard or Hanson families?"

His mother shook her head. "I don't believe so. What about you, Elise? Do those names sound familiar?"

Elise joined them at the table with her own plate and the coffeepot. "I think I might have met the Ballards. I seem to recall a couple who had three children coming up to me a few weeks ago at church. I believe their last name was Ballard. I can't remember their first names, though. I'm terrible at that."

Derrick looked at the list of names while Elise warmed up his coffee. "That might have been them. The Ballards have three children—Anna, who is six; Benjamin, nine; and Luke, twelve."

Elise took her seat and nodded. "I think it was two boys and a little girl. They were very well mannered. The little girl had a really sweet smile."

Derrick suddenly jumped up from the table and hurried into the pantry. He came back with two packages wrapped in brown paper. "I almost forgot these. Mama, here is your yarn. They have a few more skeins of white if you need it. And they have a lot of other colors in stock."

"Thank you, son," his mother said, taking the yarn from him. "I just ran out of what I had yesterday. I can finish the blanket now. What's that other package you have there?"

"Well, ordinarily I wouldn't have bought this without talking to the two of you first, but the shopkeeper was just putting them out, and I didn't want to take the chance that he might sell out before I got back in there." He carefully unwrapped the doll and held it up. It had blue eyes and blond hair and rosy cheeks. "Do you think this is something young Anna might like?"

"Oh, Derrick, it's perfect." Elise took it from him and turned it this way and that before handing it to his mother. "Nearly every little girl dreams of getting a doll just like this for Christmas."

"It's lovely, son. I'm glad you went ahead and bought it. As pretty as it is, it might have been taken. Now tell us what you want to do for these families."

Derrick sat back down at the table and took a sip of coffee before answering. "Well, I'd love to make this a wonderful Christmas for them. But I'd like to help them get through some tough times, too. It can't be easy to raise a family when hard times are on you. I need to give more thought to what I might do there, but in the meantime, I think we need to plan on buying presents for the children and maybe providing the makings for Christmas dinner."

"That sounds great. But that's mostly buying things. What about the baked goods and candy we'd planned on giving out?" his mother asked.

"Oh, I want us to take that to them, as well. . .and to the neighbors around here, too."

"Good, good." Frieda nodded her head. "Well then, we need to start listing ideas for gifts and what we want to buy for their Christmas dinner, and then decide what all we'll be cooking to give out."

"We need your list of neighbors and friends, too, Derrick," Elise reminded him.

"I'll make up that list today. Oh, and another thing—I'd kind of like the help we give the families to be anonymous. I don't want them feeling beholden to us."

Elise's heart turned to pure mush. Derrick was a wonderful man. The more she got to know him, the more deeply she cared for him. "I love that idea. Maybe you could give the things we get to Preacher Burton and he could see that they get them? Then the parents could put the gifts under the tree and the children wouldn't have to know that they couldn't afford to get them on their own."

Derrick grinned at her, sending her pulse racing. "That's what I was thinking, too. I'm glad you agree."

Elise looked over at Frieda and found her gaze going back and forth between Derrick and her. Her mother-in-law smiled at the two of them. "You two think an awful lot alike. I think that's the right thing to do, too. The pleasure comes from the giving and knowing it was put to good use, not from making people feel they owe you."

They'd just finished eating breakfast and had begun to make their lists when a loud pounding came at the back door. "Derrick!"

"That's Jed's voice!" Derrick said, hurrying to the door.

Elise jumped to her feet and was by his side when he opened it to find Jed standing there holding up his wife, who was obviously in labor.

"I've got to go get Doc! The baby is coming, and you said to bring Caroline over first thing."

"Yes, we did," Derrick said, moving away from the door so that Jed could bring his wife inside.

Elise quickly decided what to do. "I'll go up and turn my bed down. Can you carry her up, Jed?"

"I can." He swept his wife up into his arms and followed Elise up the stairs. She'd barely pulled the covers down when he laid his wife down as gently as possible. "I'm going after the doc, Caroline."

"No," Derrick said from the doorway, where he stood with his mother. "You stay with your wife, and I'll go get Doc."

"Are you sure?" Jed asked.

Elise could see from the grip that Caroline had on her husband's hand that she didn't want him to go anywhere. So, evidently, could Derrick.

"I'm sure. I think Caroline would much rather have you by her side right now than me."

"Thank you, Derrick."

Derrick nodded and turned quickly to go back downstairs.

"I'll go get some water on to boil and get some fresh linens and bring them up," Elise told Frieda.

Her mother-in-law nodded. "Jed and I will try to make Caroline as comfortable as possible." She leaned over and whispered, "Tell Derrick to hurry."

Elise nodded and hurried downstairs just as Derrick grabbed his jacket from a hook beside the door and pulled it on. "Mama said to tell you to hurry."

"I will. I'm hoping I'll run into Doc on his way to their place. Tell them I'll get him back here soon as I can. And pray that I don't miss him."

"I will," Elise said as she saw him out the door.

Then she put the teakettle and a big pot of water on to boil. She hurried back upstairs and gathered some clean towels and linens and took them to her room. Jed was on one side of the bed and Frieda was on the other. Caroline's color was a bit better, and she seemed to be in between labor pains at the moment.

"Thank you for letting me use your room, Elise," Caroline said, sounding a little breathless.

"You're quite welcome. Derrick said to tell you that he would hurry to get Doc back here."

"Good." Caroline began to breathe shallowly, and Elise could tell another pain was on its way.

The pains seemed to come more often and last longer as the clock ticked the minutes away. Hard as she tried to keep from showing it, Elise couldn't help but be apprehensive. Her labor had been similar to Caroline's, only her child had been stillborn. Memories sent tears flooding to her eyes, and Elise blinked quickly, trying to keep them from falling. She turned toward the door. "I'm going to see about the water."

"Yes, dear," Frieda said softly and nodded. "I'll call if we need you."

Elise hurried out of the room. This was a joyous time for Jed and Caroline, and she didn't want to put a damper on it with her painful memories. There were other things she should be doing. She dropped to her knees at one of the chairs and prayed. *Dear Lord, please watch over Caroline and the baby. Please let Doc get here soon, and please, please, dear Lord, let the baby be all right. In Jesus' name I pray. Amen.*

The teakettle began to whistle, and Elise hurried to push it to the back of the stove. Just then the back door opened and Derrick and Doc entered.

"I found Doc," Derrick said. "He was on his way to Jed's."

"Oh, I am so glad. I think it's about time," Elise said.

"I'll show him the way up," Derrick said, leading the doctor through the house and up the stairs.

Elise sent up a prayer of thanksgiving that Derrick had been able to find the doctor. "And please let this baby be born soon and be healthy, and please let Caroline be all right, dear Lord," she whispered.

Derrick came back downstairs to find Elise making a pot of tea. She looked as if she'd been about to cry when he and Doc had come into the room, and he couldn't help but wonder why. He crossed the room to stand behind her. "Elise, are you all right?"

"I'm fine." She didn't turn around, and he was pretty sure he heard a sniffle.

Derrick put his hands on her arms and gently turned her to face him, but she wouldn't look at him. "What is it? What can I do?"

She shook her head, and Derrick reached out to tip her chin so he could see her face. Her eyes were swimming with unshed tears. "Please tell me. Let me help."

Suddenly her face was burrowed in his shoulder and she was sobbing. "I just pray everything is all right with the baby and Caroline."

"I'm sure it will be. Doc is here now, and he'll take care of things," Derrick said, rubbing her back. He didn't know what to do. He just wanted her to quit crying. He could feel her nod, but she didn't lift her head.

"Elise, this is more than just concern. Please tell me what's wrong. Please."

She took a deep breath and brushed at the tears that began to stream down her face. She shook her head. "I'm just a little. . .worried. I thought everything. . . was fine when it was time for mine. . .and Carl's baby to be born."

She choked up, and Derrick felt as if the breath had been knocked clean out of him. How could he have forgotten that Elise and Carl had lost their baby? "I'm so sorry, Elise. This must be very stressful for you."

"I just want them both to be all right. I don't want Caroline and Jed to have to go through that kind of pain."

She began to cry again, and he pulled her closer into his arms, rocking her back and forth. "I'm sure they'll be fine, Elise. Doc is here, and—"

The sound of a baby's cry could be heard from the top of the stairs. Elise pulled back, and the smile on her face was one Derrick knew he would never forget.

"The baby is here. And it's. . .crying. It's all right!" Elise turned and rushed to the stairs. Derrick hurried up right behind her. But outside the door she paused and wiped at her tears with her apron while Derrick knocked to make sure it was all right for them to enter.

"Come on in," Jed called.

Elise took a deep breath before opening the door to her room.

Mother and baby were indeed fine. They entered the room to find Caroline propped up on several pillows, holding her brand-new baby. Jed was sitting on the bed beside her, the baby's tiny fist in his hand.

Standing right behind Elise, Derrick put his hand on her shoulder and gave it a squeeze. She reached up and patted it as if she knew that he was trying to comfort her in the only way he could at the moment.

"Come see, Elise," his mother said, motioning Elise on into the room. "Doc says baby Jonathan is beautiful and very healthy."

Derrick was pretty sure his mother was aware of what Elise had been going through downstairs.

Elise moved away from him and over to the side of the bed. He couldn't see her face, but he could hear her voice.

"Oh, Caroline. . .he's gorgeous," Elise said.

The next week was a bevy of activity at Derrick's house. His mother and Elise insisted that Jed, Caroline, and the baby stay with them until Caroline had regained her strength. After his mother and Elise assured him that they didn't mind sleeping in the same room until the young couple went home, Derrick readily agreed.

Elise was sure he didn't mind, but he seemed a little unsettled that their normal routine had changed. He never griped about it, though. After breakfast each day, Jed would go to his place and take care of things there while Derrick did the same at home, leaving the house to the women and the newborn baby most of the day.

When Derrick did come inside, he never complained if a meal was a little late getting to the table or if he had to come upstairs to find them. Elise was a little concerned that all the going up and down stairs and the busier pace of the days might take their toll on her mother-in-law, but Frieda assured her that she loved every minute of it.

And Elise had no doubt that she meant every word. More often than not, when Caroline was napping, Frieda could be found humming a tune and rocking the baby in the rocking chair in the corner of the room. What a wonderful grandmother she would have made had her and Carl's baby lived. Then Elise fought off the sorrowful memories and went back downstairs without disturbing the two.

Her own workload had doubled, but she didn't mind. She liked taking care of people, and, especially right now, it gave her less time to think about her crying episode the day the baby was born.

Elise had felt a little uncomfortable around Derrick ever since that day, but it wasn't because of Derrick's treatment of her. It was because she couldn't forget how wonderful it had felt to be held in his arms.

Now, as he entered the kitchen, her heart seemed to do a funny little dip and flip. She tried to will it to beat as normal, but that had become nearly impossible when Derrick was around.

"It's awfully quiet this time of day. Are Caroline and the baby napping?" he asked as he poured himself a cup of coffee.

"I think so. They were a little while ago."

"Where's Mama?"

Elise chuckled. "She may be napping, too, by now. But last I saw her she was humming to a sleeping baby."

"She's enjoying herself, isn't she?"

"Yes, she is." Elise nodded. "I think she's going to miss all the hustle and bustle when they go back home."

"I'm afraid of that, too. But with Christmas coming, and all the plans we need to finish making, maybe she won't miss them too much. We'll just have to keep her interest up in everything else." Derrick finished his coffee. "Do you need me to bring anything in from the pantry or root cellar before I go back out?"

It warmed Elise's heart that Derrick asked her if there was something he could do for her at least once a day. "You could bring in potatoes if you would."

He went to get them right away and placed them on the worktable.

"Thank you."

"No. Thank *you*, Elise. You've been working tirelessly these past few days. I thank you for all you do for us all."

She could feel the color rush up her neck and into her cheeks at his words. "You're welcome, but it's something I enjoy doing."

"That makes it even better. I'm going to be working close by. If you need anything, just yell."

"I will. Thank you."

It was several minutes after he left the room before her heartbeat slowed back to normal. She should be getting used to its erratic behavior by now, but it never failed to surprise her. Elise had never thought she'd feel like this again. She'd never thought she could care about anyone other than Carl. But it seemed she was wrong. She was falling more deeply in love with his brother with each passing day.

Later that night, when Jed and Caroline announced that they would be going back to their place the next day, Derrick couldn't say he was disappointed. They'd been there well-nigh a week.

"Are you sure you're up to going home?" his mother asked Caroline.

"I think so. You and Elise have helped me so very much. And, Derrick, Jed and I appreciate you welcoming us into your home like you did. I can't begin to tell you all how much it's meant to us." The tears in the young woman's eyes told them even more than her words.

"I can't thank you enough for taking care of Caroline and the baby like you have," Jed said. "Not to mention that you've fed us all and. . . Well, if you ever need us for anything at all, just know that we will be there."

"You've become family to us, and we just love you all," Caroline added.

"You've become like family to us, too, you know," Elise said.

"And that baby of yours. . . Well, we feel we have a claim on little Jonathan now, you know?" Derrick's mother said. "It's going to be real lonely around here with you gone."

"You come over anytime, Miss Frieda."

"What about Christmas? You'll spend it here with us, won't you?" Frieda asked.

"Why, that is so wonderful of you. We would love to—"

"But I'm afraid we won't be able to," Jed said, interrupting his wife's acceptance.

"Jed—"

Jed smiled at his wife. "I was saving this for a surprise, Caroline. But I can tell I'd better let you know about it now. Remember I telegraphed your mama and papa about the baby?"

Caroline nodded. "Yes."

"Well, I went into town today and we had an answer back from them. They're coming out here for Christmas. They can't wait to see you and their grandson."

Caroline caught her breath just before she began to cry. "They're coming here? Mama and Papa?" she asked through her tears.

Jed nodded, looking confused. "I thought you'd be happy about it."

"Oh, Jed. I *am* happy! I just never thought my parents would make the long trip out here." Caroline cuddled her son to her breast and dropped a kiss on his head. "I can't wait for them to see the baby and our place."

Derrick smile at the young couple. They were happy to be going home, and he would be glad for things to get back to normal. He'd been missing the routine he and Elise and his mother had developed. But he was glad they'd been able to help the young couple.

Chapter 11

Both Elise and his mother seemed a bit lost right after Jed bundled his wife and son up and took them back to their place. Elise reclaimed her room and spent most of the afternoon getting it back to normal while his mother pulled out her crochet work, wanting to get finished with the blanket she'd barely started for little Jonathan.

Even Derrick had to admit that the house seemed more than a little quiet after Jed and Caroline and the baby went home, but he wasn't complaining. It wasn't until that evening, though, when Elise was making supper and his mother set the table for three, that things seemed to be returning to normal.

"Your workload should be a little easier now," Derrick said to Elise as she fried potatoes to go with the beans she'd put on earlier.

"Yes, it will be," Elise said, carefully turning the potatoes. "But it's going to seem a little lonely without that sweet baby."

"Yes, it is. And I do miss them already, I admit it," his mother added. "But Jed and Caroline need to be in their own place and leaning on each other. Besides, they don't live that far away. I can get you to take me over there if I get to missing that baby too much, can't I, son?"

"I'll be glad to take you over anytime, Mama. I know you both miss the hustle and bustle of having houseguests, and especially the baby. But I have to tell you, I'm kind of glad things are getting back to normal."

"Why, son, I never knew you were missing our company so," his mother said, patting him on the back.

"Well, I was." Derrick couldn't believe he'd let those word escape his lips. But they were true. He'd missed his mother's and Elise's company. They'd been so busy taking care of their guests, he'd barely had a conversation with them the last few days. "I guess you've spoiled me."

"Well, you can have our undivided attention tonight, can't he, Elise?"

Derrick watched the delicate color flood Elise's face. His mother had kind of put her on the spot, and for a moment he thought she wasn't going to answer. Then she smiled and said, "Only if he makes cocoa for us."

"Consider it done," Derrick said, agreeing to the terms.

The next morning, his mother and Elise still seemed a little down until Derrick reminded them they had some unfinished business to take care of. "You know we're a little behind on our Christmas plans. I know that our guests had to take precedence while they were here, but it's time we get back to planning what we're going to do."

Elise looked at the calendar. "You're right. We've only got a little over two weeks until Christmas!"

"My, I didn't realize we were that far into December," his mother said. "Let's get those lists made up."

Derrick pulled out the names the preacher had given him, and Elise got some paper and pencils and brought them to the table.

"We have the doll for Anna. I was thinking maybe a slingshot for Benjamin, but I'm not sure what to get Luke," he said.

"Wouldn't they both like a slingshot?" his mother asked. "You and Carl liked them at twelve."

"We did, didn't we? That would make it easier. And then I thought maybe some books?"

"I've heard that *The Red Badge of Courage* by Stephen Crane is very good. The boys might enjoy it," Elise said. "And maybe Anna would enjoy *Black Beauty* by Anna Sewell. If she can't read yet, I'm sure someone in the family will enjoy reading it out loud to her."

"Yes, those are good suggestions, Elise. Thank you." Derrick wrote them down.

"What about clothes—do they need those, Derrick?"

Derrick sighed and shook his head. "Mama, I didn't think to ask. I'll check with Harold next time I go into town. He'll know. Now, what about the Hanson family? They have two girls—one fifteen and one sixteen. I'm not sure what they might like."

Elise looked thoughtful before she answered. "At that age, most likely, clothes, even if they don't need them. Or I'm sure they'd like a parasol, a reticule, or maybe a pretty shawl for winter."

Derrick's mother nodded. "Those are all good suggestions, Elise. I wish I had your sewing machine right now. I could sure put it to good use here."

"I wish we had it, too, Mama," Elise said.

Derrick suddenly knew what he was getting his mother for Christmas. He hoped the mercantile carried sewing machines. If not, he could order one from the Sears & Roebuck catalog, but he wasn't sure he could get it on time. Maybe Elise could go into town with him and show him what to buy.

"Will you be getting anything for the parents, Derrick?" his mother asked.

"Well, I'd like to help them out monetarily, but I'm not sure how to go about that."

"Could you put some cash in an envelope? Or maybe pay for a line of credit at the mercantile?" Elise suggested.

"Oh, that's an excellent suggestion, Elise. I'll definitely look into the line of credit. If it's possible, I think I'll have Harold take care of it so that no one knows."

"I'm sure he'd be glad to help you out in that way," his mother said.

Derrick nodded, pleased with the way their plans were coming along. "I'm sure he will."

"We still need that list from you of neighbors and friends."

"I can start making that now."

Elise slid him a sheet of paper and handed him a pencil and then got up to get his mother's cookbook. "Here, Mama. Look through this and see if there are any new recipes you want us to try out. I'll go take stock of what we have in the panty."

Derrick smiled as he worked on his list. Finally, things were really getting back to normal.

Elise was just finishing her inventory when Derrick came into the pantry. Her heart skittered at his nearness.

"How's your list going?" he asked.

"It's a big one that will probably get longer once I talk to Mama and see what she's come up with to try out."

"Would you go into town with me today or tomorrow to make sure I get everything and help me pick out some presents?" His voice changed to a whisper. "I particularly need you to help me with Mama's present. I know what I want to get her, but I'd like your advice about it."

Elise peeked into the kitchen to see Frieda going over the cookbook. "What are you thinking of buying her?"

"I want to get her a sewing machine."

"Oh, Derrick, she's going to love that! I'll be glad to go with you. But what if she wants to come along?"

"Then we can just take her with us and plan another outing to get her present then."

"Does the mercantile carry sewing machines?"

"I don't know. If not, I'll order from the catalog and just wrap up a picture for her if it doesn't get here in time."

Elise chuckled. "That would work."

"I just don't want to wait too long. I'd like to make sure I get the things on our list for the Hansons and the Ballards while there's still a good selection."

"I can go either day—whichever one is best for you."

"Let's go see how far along Mama is with her list."

As Elise followed Derrick back into the kitchen, she found she was looking forward to the outing very much. She needed to do a little shopping herself. With all their talk of lists, she thought Derrick might enjoy a book to read in the evenings this winter. And she had a feeling his mother would be happy with a lot of yarn and maybe a few new crochet pattern books.

"Mama, do you have your list finished? I thought Elise and I might go into town and buy the staples and other supplies you two will need for your baking and candy making. And I thought I'd go ahead and get some of those presents on our list. You can come along, too, of course."

"No, I don't think I'm quite up to a trip to town after all that's been going on lately. I'll let the two of you go. I'll be fine here."

"Are you sure?"

"Yes. I want to finish the blanket for little Jonathan. You can pick me up some more yarn, though. I'd like several skeins of black, and some of red, if they have them."

"They did last time I was in. We'll get them for you."

Frieda handed her list to Elise. "These are some ingredients we'll need for a few new recipes I found. I didn't know if we had them or not."

Elise glanced over the list. "Some of them we do, but I'll pick up the rest today. We can start trying some of the new recipes out tonight or tomorrow."

"Oh, one other thing I've been thinking of. Derrick, I don't suppose you've put up a Christmas tree since you've been here?"

"No, Mama, I haven't."

"Well, we can make popcorn garlands and that kind of thing, but you might look at decorations if you plan on cutting a tree this year."

"I'll see what's available." Derrick poured himself a fresh cup of coffee and turned to Elise. "How long do you think it will take to get ready?"

"What about dinner for you, Mama? Should we wait until afternoon to go?"

Frieda shook her head. "I'm perfectly capable to see to my own dinner. We have beans I can heat up from last night, and there are biscuits from this morning. You two go on and have dinner in town somewhere. I'll be fine."

"You're sure?"

"I'm certain. Go. Have a good time shopping."

Elise looked at Derrick. "I just need to freshen up. That won't take but a few minutes."

"I'll go get the wagon and bring it over, then."

Elise ran up the stairs feeling almost like a schoolgirl. She hurriedly freshened up, straightened her hair, and went back down the stairs as fast as she could.

Derrick had just entered the kitchen. "Are you ready?"

"I am. I just need to grab my cloak."

"You'd better take mine, dear. It's a mite heavier than what you brought down from Denver."

"Thank you, Mama. It will be much warmer than mine." She really hadn't planned on staying this long and didn't have the wardrobe for wintertime. But she'd been making do. She could do so awhile longer. This past week had shown that Mama was getting back to her old self, and Elise knew she needed to get back to Denver. She didn't want to think about it now—in fact, she didn't want to think about it at all. She was aware that she wasn't going to be able to put it off for much longer, but she wasn't going to think about it today. She was going to enjoy this outing with Derrick. It might never happen again.

Derrick couldn't believe Elise had agreed to go into town with him. Ever since the day she'd cried in his arms, he had a feeling she was uncomfortable around him. He'd tried to act as normal as possible, but he didn't know how much longer he was going to be able to hide how he felt about her.

It'd been all he could do today, when they were both in the pantry and standing so near each other, not to pull her into his arms and tell her he loved her. But with her acting so skittish around him, he wasn't sure at all what her reaction would be. She might decide to head back to Denver right away.

That was the last thing he wanted, and it was fear of losing her that had him trying to be patient. Part of him just wanted things to go on like they were, with Elise growing to love him one day. But being around Jed and Caroline had made him long for a loving relationship like theirs, and he was getting impatient to have a family of his own. Waiting on the Lord to show him what to do was getting harder all the time.

"Where are we going first?" Elise asked as he helped her into the wagon.

"I think we should pay the preacher a visit and then have some dinner," he said, making sure she had the lap robe pulled up. He hurried around and took his seat beside her and flipped the reins. "We can do our shopping after that. How does that sound to you?"

"It sounds fine," Elise said. She took a deep breath of cold air and blew it back out, giggling when she saw the vapor it left.

She watched the scenery go by with interest, and Derrick could tell she was enjoying the ride. He felt bad that he hadn't taken her on more outings.

Between taking care of his mother, the house, and then Jed and Caroline, there hadn't been much free time for her. He'd have to see what he could do about that in the future.

When they arrived at the Burton house, Harold and Rachel welcomed them into their home and kitchen.

"What brings you two out today?" Rachel asked as she poured them both a cup of coffee.

"Well, I talked to Harold a week or so ago about doing something for a few of the families around, and we came for more information and to ask a favor," Derrick said.

"What do you need to know, Derrick?" the preacher asked.

After Derrick explained what they were doing and what he wanted to do to help in a monetary way, Rachel had tears in her eyes. "The children are going to love the things you want to get them. As for the line of credit at the mercantile, well, that's just a wonderful idea."

"That was Elise's suggestion," Derrick said.

Elise shook her head. "Derrick wanted his gift to be anonymous, and that just seemed an answer to how he could keep it that way."

"We all agreed that we don't want them to know where the gifts come from. If I could have kept it from you two, I would have," Derrick said, grinning at the preacher before continuing, "but I need your help in getting the presents to them. And, Harold. . .I would like it if I could give you the money and you could pay for the line of credit at the mercantile. You could let them know that they have it, but that way the families wouldn't feel they had to pay it back or have to feel beholden to anyone."

The preacher and his wife exchanged glances. "We've just come from visiting the Barristers," Harold said. "They told us you opened your home to them, Derrick, and they mentioned how much your mother and Elise here helped Caroline. It's a blessing to see Christian values put into action. We'd be glad to help you out with your plans for Christmas. Be more than happy to."

The Burtons asked them to stay for dinner, but Derrick wanted to treat Elise to a meal at the hotel dining room. She'd seemed to enjoy it when he'd taken her and his mother before.

"Thank you, but we have shopping to do yet, and we don't want to leave Mama alone too long."

They said their good-byes, then Derrick helped Elise back onto the wagon seat. "We're off to have dinner at the Grand Hotel, and then we'll get to our shopping."

"Derrick, we could have eaten with the Burtons. It would have saved you some money."

"I know—and I'm sure we would have enjoyed it—but I want to take you out for something special. You deserve it."

Elise was more than a little pleased that Derrick wanted to take her to dinner at the hotel. She'd enjoyed it a lot when they'd gone there before. It did have a special feeling to her. Maybe it was because she could order whatever she wanted and have it brought to her. And she didn't have to worry about cleaning up.

She was sure the meal at the Burtons' would have been very good. But they'd just dropped in on the couple, and Elise was sure they hadn't planned to have company for dinner if they'd just returned from Jed and Caroline's. She hadn't wanted Rachel to go out of her way. Besides, she would have felt the need to help in the kitchen, and that would have held them up with the shopping they needed to do. It would have been fine, but she was very pleased that Derrick had kept to his original plans.

Derrick pulled the wagon near a hitching post close to the hotel and hooked the reins around the post. He helped Elise down and pulled her hand through his arm as they made their way to the hotel dining room. It was nothing any of the other gentlemen escorting ladies into the room weren't doing, but it made Elise's pulse race once more. As they were seated across from one another, her heart was pounding so hard, she could hear it. She was thankful of conversations going on in the room so that Derrick couldn't.

The special of the day was stuffed pork chops with lyonnaise potatoes, served with hot rolls and a choice of dessert—peach cobbler or apple dumplings. The meal was truly good and not just because she got tired of her own cooking from time to time.

"This is all wonderful," she said as she cut another piece of her apple dumpling—her choice for dessert.

"The Grand Hotel started out as a boardinghouse," Derrick said. "Through the past few years they've gained a reputation for serving fine food."

"I can certainly see why. Everything is delicious. Thank you for bringing me."

"You're more than welcome. Thank you for accompanying me. I ate here often before you and Mama came. But it was never quite so enjoyable as today."

"I'm sure there are several single women in the area who would be more than glad to have dinner with you, Derrick. I'm curious as to why you never married." Elise inhaled quickly. She couldn't believe those words had actually left her mouth.

"Are you sure you want to know?"

"I'm sorry, Derrick. It's really none of my business," she apologized.

Derrick smiled across the table at her. "Perhaps not. But maybe it's time you know. There's only one woman I ever thought seriously about courting."

"Oh?"

"Yes. I was attracted to her for a very long time. But I didn't act fast enough."

"What happened?"

"She married my brother."

Elise could feel the color flood her cheeks as she realized she was the woman he was talking about. "Oh! Derrick, I don't know what to say. I never knew about your feelings for me."

"As I said, I wasn't fast enough. Carl was."

"I—"

"It's all right, Elise. You were happy with Carl, and I know he had to be a happy man—married to you. I didn't mean to upset you. You asked about it, and I just thought it was time you knew."

"I—thank you for telling me." Elise's heart was pounding against her ribs so hard it almost hurt. Should she tell him that she'd hoped he would ask to court her long before Carl did? No. That seemed too disloyal to Carl. And yet. . .he'd been honest with her. To keep herself from acting before thinking things over, she forced herself to take another bite of her dumpling. She was relieved when Derrick seemed to sense her discomfort and changed the subject.

"Do you really think Mama will be happy with a sewing machine?"

He smiled at her, and Elise felt herself relax. "Oh, I'm certain of it."

"I'm glad you came with me today. I don't know a thing about sewing machines, and I need your advice."

"I'm glad to give it to you. There are several different kinds out there. I have a Singer and I love it, but there are others that are good, too. Sears & Roebuck carries other brands. We'll just see what we can find. Mama is going to be thrilled—whether she gets it Christmas morning or has to wait a little while if you have to order it. She's wanted one of her own for a long time. She's a very good seamstress, but having a sewing machine will make it so much easier for her."

"Good. I'm glad she seems to be doing better. Having Jed and Caroline and the baby really did perk her up. She seems to be doing well now."

"Yes, she does. I pray she continues to." Elise held her breath, waiting to see if Derrick was going to suggest that she could feel free to go back to Denver, but he didn't. She knew she should bring it up, but she couldn't bring herself to do so. Surely all of that could wait until after Christmas. Surely it could.

Chapter 12

As they finished their meal and left to go shopping, Derrick was glad he'd finally let Elise know he'd wanted to court her before his brother beat him to it. It was something he'd lived with for so long, and somehow, when she'd given him an opening, he felt it was the right time to tell her. He could only pray he was right. Maybe it was the expression in her eyes when he'd told her, but he had hope that maybe now she would begin to think of him as more than just Carl's brother.

Derrick couldn't remember when he'd ever had such fun shopping. With Elise at his side, the day was more enjoyable than any he'd had in a long while. They had to go to both mercantile stores in town to find the right sewing machine for his mother.

He'd never have been able to decide if Elise hadn't been with him. They all looked the same to him, but Elise knew what she was looking for. Neither store had any Singer sewing machines in stock, but Elise looked closely at what they did carry and found one she thought would be just as good.

She convinced the storekeeper to let her try it out, and when all was said and done, she'd found one she thought his mother would love.

"Its stitching is every bit as good as my machine—maybe better because it's newer. It's very nicely made and easy to thread. I've heard the Minnesota is a very good machine, and it appears to be. Sears & Roebuck carries it, too. I think your mother is going to love the walnut cabinet with all those drawers. It's beautiful."

"I ordered this machine in from Sears & Roebuck," the storekeeper said. "With Christmas coming, I always sell several."

"Do you think I should wait and try to get a Singer?" Derrick asked.

"No," Elise said, standing firm in her choice. "I think this machine is as good as my own. I know I'd be happy with it."

That was all it took to convince Derrick. He asked the shopkeeper to box it up for him and went to the counter to pay. "I'll bring my wagon back in a little while."

Elise looked around while he paid for the sewing machine, which gave Derrick a chance to buy her present, too. "Do you have that wool cloak there in the display window in a size that would fit the young woman who helped me with the machine?" he asked.

The shopkeeper looked over at Elise and nodded. "I'm sure I do. If it doesn't fit, you can bring it back."

"But it's a Christmas present, so it'd be after then before I'd bring it back if it's the wrong size."

"Doesn't matter. I'll take it back or get you another one if it doesn't fit."

"Good. Add it to the sewing machine, then. I may make more purchases later, but I'll pay for those two items now." Elise was coming his way, so he quickly paid the man. "I'll pick them up in an hour or so."

The man nodded as he took the cash from Derrick and handed him a receipt. "See you in a while."

Derrick met Elise halfway up the aisle and asked, "Did you find anything else on our list?"

She nodded. "I found a few things. But I think we need to go back to the other store. I saw several items there for the children and the older girls. And I think they have the books we wanted to get."

"Let's go." Derrick felt good about getting presents for the two most important women in his life. He'd never looked forward to Christmas quite so much in his life.

At the other store, they handed their list of staples and goods they needed for all the cooking to a salesclerk. Then they went to look for presents while he was filling the order.

This store did have what they wanted for the Hansons and the Ballards. For the Hanson girls they bought the reticules Elise had suggested—one in black trimmed in gold for Margaret, and one in gold trimmed in black for Jennifer. They even found matching parasols to go with them.

"Oh, look at this, Derrick," Elise said, showing him a bag of marbles. "Do you think the boys would like these?"

"I'm sure they would. I wanted to get them something besides just the slingshots. Let's add those to our purchases."

By the time they got through, they'd bought most everything on their lists. They had the books they'd talked about for the children, although Derrick wouldn't have minded buying one for himself. He liked to read.

They'd picked up a few more items for the families when Elise remembered to look for the ornaments his mother had requested. She found some pretty glass ones that Derrick was sure his mother would like. He'd have to go out and look for a tree to cut soon.

Elise also remembered to pick up some tissue paper and ribbon to wrap the presents in, and the yarn she wanted to give his mother for Christmas—plus the red and black yarn his mother wanted now. When they thought they had it all, Derrick went to get the wagon and took it to the first store to load the sewing machine. Then he came back for all the other things they'd purchased. The sun was setting when they headed back home.

Elise couldn't remember when she'd enjoyed a day more. Derrick had a little-boy side she'd never seen until today. He'd had fun looking over all the toys for the boys and even those for the girls. He was very excited about the sewing machine he'd bought for his mother. But it was his admission that he'd once wanted to court her that had made the day most special for Elise.

He stopped the wagon at the house. "I'll bring everything in except the sewing machine. I'll keep that out in the barn until Christmas Eve. Then I'll bring it inside after she goes to sleep." He grinned. "I can't wait."

Elise laughed. His excitement was contagious. "Neither can I."

She helped him bring some of the packages in. Once they were inside, they were met by the wonderful aroma of vegetable soup simmering on the back of the stove.

"Oh, Mama, that smells delicious. I was wondering what to cook for supper," Elise said.

"I thought you might be getting hungry and be a little tired from your shopping trip." Frieda turned from stirring the soup. "How did it go? Were you able to get everything on our lists?"

"We were," Derrick answered his mother. "I'll let Elise tell you about it while I put up the wagon."

Elise took off Frieda's cloak and hung it on a hook in the pantry. "We got more than was on our list, but it was so much fun, Mama! Do you want me to show you everything now or wait until after supper?"

"After supper will be fine, dear. Now, just tell me what all you bought."

"Oh my, we bought a lot." She filled Frieda in on their purchases while she put the staples and other items away in the pantry. "I think they will like everything."

"I'm sure they will."

"How did you do today? Did you get finished with your blanket?"

Frieda popped the corn bread she'd mixed up into the oven. "Almost. I just have the last round to do and the fringe to put on it."

Elise hurried back into the pantry. "I almost forgot. We got the yarn you wanted."

"Wonderful!" Frieda took it and put it in her crochet bag.

Derrick came in the back door. "It's getting nippy out. If that soup tastes as good as it smells, it's going to be great, Mama."

"Thank you, son. I'm kind of out of practice, but I think it will be pretty good."

Elise set the table and ladled soup into the bowls before Derrick took them to the table. Once the corn bread was done, they all took their places and Derrick said the blessing.

"It sounds like our families will have a good Christmas," Frieda said. "I forgot to ask Elise what the preacher thought about your idea to give them a line of credit at the mercantile."

"He's more than willing to help me. I'll give him the money and he'll procure the line of credit for them. They won't ever know who paid for it."

"Sounds like all we have to do now is decide what we're making and when to deliver it all, then." Frieda said.

"We can get started trying some new recipes anytime you want, Mama," Elise said. "Some of the items can be made ahead, so we should be able to start our Christmas baking and candy making by the end of next week, don't you think?"

"I think that will be time enough to get it all done. Since Christmas falls on Monday, maybe we should distribute our gifts on Saturday?"

"I think that would be good. With Christmas Eve on Sunday this year, it will probably be better to make our deliveries earlier. We don't know what plans everyone might have. Besides, we'll be busy cooking and getting ready for Christmas ourselves," Elise suggested.

"We could even do it Friday. I'll get the things to Harold and Rachel by then so that they can get things to the Ballard and Hanson families well before Christmas," Derrick said.

"This is all so exciting. I think this is going to be the best Christmas we've had in a long time," his mother said.

"I know it's going to be the best one I've had in years," Derrick said. "Much as I like all we've planned to do, the best part for me is that I won't be alone."

Elise's heart went out to him, and she had a pretty good idea that his mother's was breaking at his honest statement. It must have been terribly lonely for him the past few years with no family around. Even if he ate a meal with Jed and Caroline, it wasn't the same as being part of all the preparations and having loved ones around.

It became even more important than ever that they have a good Christmas all together. She didn't know if she would be with Frieda and Derrick next year, for like it or not, she was going to have to go back to Denver. This day had meant too much to her—the man sitting across the table from her meant everything. Derrick had let her know that he'd once cared a great deal for her, but he didn't say that he still did. And because of that, she needed to go back to Denver. If she didn't leave soon, she'd never be able to hide how much she'd come to love Derrick. And just admitting that to herself filled her with guilt that she couldn't remember Carl's face anymore or even recall what their life had been like together—even less now that all of her waking thoughts seemed centered on Derrick and his admission that he'd once wanted to court her.

She had to leave. But she couldn't bring herself to do that before Christmas. She just couldn't. Not after hearing how much it meant to Derrick to have family around. And he and Frieda might do just fine by themselves, but she wouldn't. She couldn't force herself to leave until after the New Year. So until then—and especially for this Christmas—she was going to strive to do her part to make it the best she could for Derrick's sake, for his mother's sake, and even for her own.

The next day was Sunday, and the three of them were eager for Harold or Rachel to point out the Hanson and Ballard families to them. It would make it more fun to know who it was they were getting so excited about surprising.

Elise had been right about the Ballards. They were who she thought they were. Derrick was doubly pleased he'd bought the doll after seeing Anna. The doll even resembled the child with her blue eyes and blond hair. He was pretty sure the boys would like the presents they'd chosen, too.

As for the Hansons, their girls were beautiful young ladies who seemed very considerate of their parents. He hoped they liked the gifts they'd chosen for them. Their clothes were clean, if a little worn, and he felt good knowing they would be able to get something new or buy the dry goods to make something after Christmas. He was glad that he could help these families out, and he could hardly wait for Christmas to arrive.

That evening after supper, Elise and his mother decided to try out a new candy recipe. He volunteered to be their taste tester. He'd never had a praline before, but his mouth was watering even before the rich candy was cool enough to eat. It became an instant favorite along with the chocolate fudge thick with pecans that his mother always made.

"That's a definite winner. I'd say those should go out to everyone," he said after he finished the second one.

"Fudge and pralines—I think that's good for the candies, unless you want to make some fondant, Mama. You always have liked that," Elise said.

"We might. I do love a good fondant," his mother said. "We need to decide on the cookies or breads, too."

"Why don't you work on those tomorrow? I don't think I can test any more sweets tonight," Derrick said. Suddenly he wished he'd settled for only one praline. "I don't think I'm even up to hot cocoa tonight. But I can make some for you two."

Elise shook her head. "None for me, thank you. I've been nibbling here and there, too."

"I don't need any either, son. One of those candies goes a long way. Maybe we'd better put a warning on them."

During the next few days, Elise's guilt over her growing feelings for Derrick began to take away some of the joy she felt with their Christmas preparations. Finally, she decided she was going to have to start preparing Frieda for her eventual move back to Denver. If she told her, maybe, just maybe, she could start preparing herself.

They were trying out a new molasses cookie the next afternoon when Elise broached the subject with her mother-in-law. She waited until the cookies were out of the oven and they took an afternoon tea break to taste test them.

"Mama, after Christmas I'm going to have to make plans to go home to Denver," Elise said.

"Oh, Elise, I've been praying you would see that there's no need for you—"

"I can't stay here forever, Mama," Elise interrupted. "This is Derrick's home—and yours now—but it isn't mine." No matter how much she would like it to be.

"Elise, you know you're welcome to stay as long as you want."

Elise sighed heavily. "Mama, I know that. But. . .I—" She broke off the sentence and shook her head. It was time to be truthful with her mother-in-law. "I can't stay here. I'm beginning to care too much for Derrick, and I feel I'm being unfaithful to Carl's memory."

"Why, child, I know you loved Carl. But he's been gone over two years now. There's nothing wrong with you caring about Derrick the way you do. In fact, it's most likely because you and Carl had such a good marriage that you're able to fall in love with someone else and think of marriage again."

"Oh, Mama, I'm not sure. . ."

"Elise, dear, there's nothing I'd like better than to keep you in this family always. You are much too young to stay a widow forever. I know Carl would want you to go on with your life and be happy."

"I just don't know. I feel so bad that I can't even remember what Carl looked like without seeing his picture, Mama. And I feel guilty that it's Derrick who is in my thoughts so much."

Frieda reached out and patted her hand. "Elise, what you are going through is perfectly natural. You are young. You need a husband and a family to take care of."

"Maybe I do. But I don't know that Derrick wants that. And even if he did, I don't know that it would be me he'd want it with. The longer I stay, the harder it's going to be for me to leave."

"Elise, dear, I can only tell you to take these concerns to the Lord. Ask Him to show you what to do. I don't want you to leave. I think you should stay right here. But I know you have to make that decision yourself. Please just pray about it. And I will do the same. The Lord will answer us in His time."

"I will pray, Mama." And she would. She needed the Lord's guidance as she'd never needed it before. She sent up a silent prayer just then, asking for Him to help her sort it all out and show her what to do, and—if it be His will—soon.

Chapter 13

As it turned colder, Derrick spent less time in the barn in the evening and took to spending time in the parlor reading the Good Book before going to bed. Hearing footsteps coming down the stairs one night, he looked up from reading and was surprised to see his mother coming back downstairs. Once she went up for the night, she rarely came back down.

"Mama, are you all right?" he asked as she shuffled into the room, wrapped in her warm robe.

"That depends." She seemed a woman on a mission as she crossed the room and took a seat on the sofa.

"What do you mean? Are you feeling poorly?"

"I'm feeling all right, I suppose." She sighed deeply, and he could see that something was bothering her. "I'm just sad."

"What are you sad about? Have I done anything to upset you?" He couldn't imagine what, but he did sometimes put his foot in his mouth.

"No, son. You haven't done anything. It's Elise—she's talking about going home to Denver again. She says she's going to make plans after Christmas."

Derrick felt as if a vise was squeezing his heart tighter and tighter until it took the breath right out of him. He could only manage to shake his head. When he could finally breathe again, he managed to get out, "No! She can't go, Mama. We can't let her."

"I don't see how we can stop her if she decides it's what she has to do, son."

"But I—*you* still need her here. You aren't up to—"

"Son, I'm doing better each day. But I don't want her to go any more than you do. Still, she feels she should be leaving. I've told her she's welcome—"

"So have I." Derrick got up and began pacing the room. Elise couldn't leave. He couldn't let her. "I've told her she can stay as long as she wants to. I guess she doesn't want to anymore."

"I don't think that's it, Derrick. I think she—"

"Have I done anything to upset her?"

"No, son, I don't believe you have. She's just. . ." His mother just sighed and shook her head.

Derrick needed some advice. It was time to open up to his mother. "Mama, what am I going to do? I love Elise. I don't want her to go!"

His mother nodded. "If that's the case—and I suspected it might be—why haven't you told Elise how you feel, Derrick?"

He dropped back down into his chair. "Mama, I've loved Elise for years. I've cared for her since even before Carl started courting her."

"Did she know?"

"No, not then." Derrick shook his head. "Carl started wooing her and. . . Well, when she accepted his proposal of marriage, I thought my heart would surely break. That's why I left Colorado in the first place."

"I see. I never knew, although I did wonder about it."

"There was no point in telling you, Mama. It would only have upset you. But Carl knew how I felt about Elise before he ever decided to try to court her, and I can tell you now that I was unhappy with my brother for a good long time. Still, it really was my fault. I should have acted before he had a chance to."

"I see."

He wasn't sure she did. Even he didn't know why he hadn't pursued Elise before Carl did. He continued explaining, "Once they were married, I knew I couldn't stay in Denver and watch them start a life together. It was just too hard for me. So I began a new one here."

His mother nodded. "Now I understand why you left and moved here. But Carl has passed away, and Elise has come back into your life."

Derrick nodded and put his head in his hands. "I don't know what to do, Mama. I don't want to lose her again. I did let her know that I'd wanted to court her but that Carl beat me to the asking. I felt I had to let her know." He shook his head. "But I still don't know if she'll ever see me as anything but Carl's brother."

"Son, you did the right thing by leaving Denver and coming to New Mexico Territory—feeling about Elise the way you did. And Elise made your brother very happy. But that was then. Carl is gone, and now Elise is alone. It could be all in God's plan for you and Elise to be together now. After all, she had plenty of suitors at our door in Denver before we came down here. But none of them interested her. And none of them had her blushing at their nearness or at their teasing like she does around you, Derrick."

Derrick felt a glimmer of hope begin to grow at his mother's words. He had noticed that there were times when Elise's face flushed with color when they were together. "You think she might care?"

"I believe so. But, Derrick, if you don't want her going back to Denver, you need to take action. Pray on it and let the Lord lead you to find the way to let her know how you feel."

It was what Derrick wanted to do with all his heart, and yet. . . What if Elise didn't return his feelings? What if he could never measure up to his brother? But his mother was right—it was time he took it all to the Lord. "I'll do that, Mama.

It's for sure I don't know what to do on my own."

"He'll guide you. Just be still and listen," his mother said. "I'm going up to bed now. I'll be praying for the Lord to show you what to do, too, Derrick."

"Thank you, Mama. Sleep well."

She kissed his cheek on the way out the door. Derrick felt better after telling her how he felt about Elise, but still, the fact that Elise was thinking about going back to Denver gave him a heavy heart. He didn't want to lose her again.

Derrick went back to his Bible and tried to take up where he'd left off. But thoughts of Elise kept filling his mind. Finally, he bowed his head and began to whisper, "Dear Lord, I need You to help me. Elise is talking about leaving once more. Father, You know I don't want that. You know I love her. Yet I'm afraid to let her know how I feel. I lost her to my brother before—and I could always use that as an excuse for my heartache—but deep down, I know that it was my own inaction that gave Carl the opportunity to win her heart. I can't blame him forever. And it could be that even with Carl gone now, Elise might not ever feel the same about me as I do her." He sighed and rubbed his temple before continuing to open up his heart. "I'm afraid to find out how she feels about me—and I'm afraid not to. Lord, please let me know what to do. Family relationships count on me doing the right thing. While I pray it's Your will that Elise become my wife, I want to do what truly is *Your* will. Please guide me in this, Lord. In Jesus' name I pray. Amen."

Elise slept fitfully that night. She did feel better that Frieda knew how she felt about Derrick, but at the same time, she still didn't know what to do about it all. It wasn't as if she could just walk up to him and tell him she loved him.

No, all she could do was pray that if he cared about her, he would let her know soon. She didn't want to hurt the good relationship they had as in-laws. She wanted to be able to see Frieda again. Hopefully she could talk her into spending part of the year here and part of the year in Denver with her. Yet Elise wasn't sure her mother-in-law was up to that kind of upheaval in her life. Coming down here had taken its toll. Going back and forth—well, that just might be too much for her.

She tried to shake off her forlornness as she came downstairs. Christmas was coming, and they had a lot to do. She'd have to think about it all later. She was surprised to find her mother-in-law already there, standing at the range, making breakfast. "My, you're up early, Mama."

"I just woke up with a hankering for pancakes, dear. I thought I'd see if I still knew how to make them."

Elise looked at the golden rounds on the griddle. "It certainly looks as if you do. Those look perfect. I love your pancakes!"

"I'm glad to hear it." Frieda looked out the window. "I see Derrick coming this way. Will you get the butter and maple syrup out?"

"Certainly." Elise could feel her face flush at the mere mention of Derrick's name, and she knew it was because Frieda was now aware of how Elise felt about her younger son. But Elise trusted that her mother-in-law hadn't told him how she felt, and she didn't mention anything about it now. Frieda had never been one to meddle in her children's affairs of the heart. Elise knew that from experience.

"Good morning!" Derrick said as he entered the kitchen and smiled at her. "It's a beautiful day out. But it's cold. It's feeling a little like Christmas."

Elise's heart was hammering against her ribs as Derrick's gaze never left her face. She forced herself to respond to his comment about the weather. "Do you think it might snow for Christmas?"

"It's always a possibility. We had a white Christmas year before last." Finally, Derrick broke eye contact and hung his coat on the hook, then went to the stove to warm his hands. "Mmm, Mama, those pancakes smell delicious!"

Frieda put the last of the pancakes on the platter and handed it to him. "I hope they are. Take these to the table, please."

She then took the bacon out of the warmer and brought it to the table. "This should get us going. We have a lot to do today."

"I thought I'd go scout out a tree—unless you need me here to help," Derrick said as he forked a couple of pancakes onto his plate, spread them with butter, and poured syrup over them.

"I think we can handle the baking today. You go on and look for a tree," Frieda said as she took her seat. "Will you cut it already?"

"I might. Depends on how far I have to go to find one. I can put it in a bucket of water until we're ready for it next week. But if it's nearby, I'll probably just wait until closer to Christmas."

"I am so excited about starting our family tradition here," Frieda said. "I've missed it so much."

Elise thought back to the past several years and realized they'd done well to celebrate Christmas at all. The first year after Carl died was a bad one. And last year wasn't much better, but she found herself truly looking forward to this year. She'd think about next year. . .well, next year. "I wish I'd known, Mama. We could have done more in Colorado."

"I know. But after Papa passed away and then Carl. . .it took awhile to get over all that heartache."

"I should have come up there. I'm sorry, Mama and Elise," Derrick said. "I shouldn't have let you two go through that heartache alone. Instead, I stayed here and we were all miserable."

"That is the past, son. We must all let go of it and look forward to the future.

We have some cherished—and some fading—memories. But our loved ones are in a better place now, and we must get on with life."

Elise had a feeling her mother-in-law was trying to get her to see that she should treasure her memories of Carl but not worry that they were not as clear as they once were. And that she should feel free to love again. If so, it was what Elise wanted to hear. But even if she could get past the guilt she felt because Derrick had taken up a bigger chunk of her heart than Carl's memory held, she still didn't really know how he felt about her now.

When Derrick came in later in the day, it was to find a whole table full of molasses cookies. "I feel like a kid again just waiting for Mama to get busy so I can grab a cookie and run outside. Carl and I both used to do that." He sniffed appreciatively. "These smell just like I remember them."

His mother laughed. "I knew what you and Carl were up to. But don't you dare snitch one of those. That's the first full batch of cookies we've made. I think we have about twelve dozen, don't we, Elise?"

"Yes. At least I hope so." Elise turned from the stew she was stirring. "We have eleven families, besides us, that we're making goodies for—including the Hansons and the Ballards."

"I didn't realize I'd made so much work for you two. We can make the list shorter."

"And hurt a neighbor's feelings? No, we don't want to do that," his mother said.

"We can handle it. Besides, we're going to put you to work chopping pecans tonight, Derrick. You aren't going to get out of all the work," Elise said in a teasing tone.

"I'll be glad to help. I can't let you girls have all the fun," Derrick bantered back. "Guess what?" he asked while he washed his hands at the sink. "I found a tree. It's beautiful, and it's just over the way past the Jonathan apple trees. Since it's so close, I'll wait until you're ready to put it up to cut it."

She and Frieda hadn't bothered with a tree the past few years, and Elise was excited at the prospect of putting one up. She could see that Mama was, too. "When do you think we should put it up?"

"We used to always put it up on Christmas Eve. But since it's on Sunday this year, and we'll be taking our Christmas baskets out on Saturday, why don't we put it up on Friday?" Frieda said.

"The sooner the better as far as I'm concerned," Elise said as she ladled the stew into bowls.

"I have to admit I'm excited about it going up, too. I haven't had a Christmas tree since I left home." Derrick took the full bowls to the kitchen table.

"We're all agreed, then. We'll put it up on Friday night. We'd better start popping some corn soon. It won't hurt to start stringing it now," Elise said when she and Frieda joined him at the table.

"I'll start popping anytime you say," Derrick said. "I can chop nuts and string popcorn at night."

"That's good, because we're going to keep you busy doing just that," his mother said.

Derrick felt blessed beyond measure that he had his mother and Elise to spend this Christmas with. He didn't know what the future held for him and Elise, but he'd been busy talking to the Lord about it. Now as he said the blessing, he thanked the Lord for all they had and were about to eat, knowing that the Lord also heard the prayer he wasn't voicing at the moment—the one he'd been praying about off and on all day. And Derrick had faith that the Lord would give him an answer. . .in His time.

Chapter 14

The next few days were very busy with cookie baking. They were saving the candy making until the next week. On Saturday morning, they sent Derrick into town for more cookie tins and baskets to place their gifts in.

As the day went on, Elise was a little concerned that her mother-in-law didn't seem as energetic as she had the past few days. But nothing would satisfy Frieda but to be in the kitchen helping.

"Mama, I forgot to ask about the blanket for little Jonathan. Have you been able to finish it?"

"I have. And I'm eager to get it to him. Maybe I'll take it in tomorrow and give it to them at church—if they're there. Or we can wait and I can wrap it up as a Christmas present to add to the basket we're taking them."

"Either way would work."

"I sure would like to see that baby. I'm glad we've been so busy, though. Otherwise, I'd have missed him something terrible."

"I'm sorry Carl and I couldn't make you a grandmother, Mama."

"Oh, I didn't mean for you to feel bad about that, Elise. I know how badly you wanted a child."

The squeak of wagon wheels alerted them to Derrick's arrival back from town just then. Elise hurried out to help him bring in the baskets and tins.

"I'm glad I went today. They were getting low on these," Derrick said, bringing in the last of the baskets. "But I have some news. Guess what?"

"What is it? What's going on in town?"

"I ran into Jed and Caroline and little Jonathan! They were in town to pick up Caroline's parents who've come for Christmas. They're very nice people, and they couldn't wait to get that baby in their arms."

"Oh, I'm glad they're here! How are Caroline and the baby?" his mother asked.

"Caroline was glowing with health, and the baby has filled out and put on some weight from when we saw him last. Caroline says he's growing like a little weed."

"Oh, I would so like to see him," Frieda said.

"You'll get to tomorrow. They all plan on being at church."

"Wonderful! I'm still not sure when to give them the layette I made, but I'll figure it out before tomorrow. I'm anxious to meet Caroline's family."

Elise was pleased that the anticipation of seeing baby Jonathan again seemed to perk her mother-in-law up for the rest of the day.

Excitement over seeing baby Jonathan had Derrick's mother up early, and she was ready long before they needed to leave for church.

"Are you going to give the baby present to them today, Mama?" Elise asked as they ate a breakfast of biscuits and gravy.

"I think I'll wait and give it to them for Christmas. I don't want to take away from their excitement about having her family here and bringing the baby to church. I can't wait to see them all, though."

Derrick took the stones he'd been warming out to the wagon just before they got ready to leave. When they took off, Derrick was glad that the day wasn't quite as cold as the last few had been. Otherwise, he might have had to give Elise her Christmas present early. That cloak of hers wasn't meant for winter weather.

They arrived at church just about the time Jed pulled up with Caroline, the baby, and her parents. After introductions were made, they all hurried inside to keep the baby out of the cool weather.

The Barristers and Caroline's parents, Mr. and Mrs. Walton, sat on the same pew with them, and it didn't take long for little Jonathan to travel from one set of arms to another until he wound up in Derrick's mother's arms. The look on her face was priceless. And there was no mistaking the longing in Elise's eyes as she took her own turn holding the baby. Derrick had a feeling that she wanted a family of her own just as badly as he did. When she looked over and her glance met his, he wondered if she had any inkling at all of how much he wanted her for his wife.

Derrick's heart hammered in his chest at the thought that it might be possible they both wanted the very same thing. Just as the service began, he sent up a silent prayer that the Lord would show them that they did.

When the service was over, Jed and Caroline asked if they would join them for dinner at the hotel. Derrick readily agreed. His mother and Elise could use a break from all the cooking they were doing.

They were seated at a round table, but the three men sat close so they could talk. Somehow, though, Elise ended up sitting next to Derrick, with his mother next to her. Caroline's dad sat between him and Jed, with Caroline on Jed's other side and her mother next to her. Mrs. Walton and Derrick's mother took turns holding the baby during the meal.

Caroline and Jed had already told her parents how much Derrick and his family had done for them, and her parents thanked them over and over for being there for their daughter and son-in-law. By the end of the meal, they all felt like family. When they got back home, Derrick was pleased that his mother seemed very happy, if a little tired.

Elise must have noticed, too, because she put on the teakettle and then turned to his mother, who'd sat down at the table. "Mama, why don't we wait until tomorrow to finish our baking and start the candy making? I'm sure we have time to get it all done, and you've been on your feet an awful lot this week."

"I am a little tired. But, oh, wasn't it good to see the Barristers? And that baby is so adorable! I really like Caroline's parents, too."

"Her papa said they were thinking of moving out here," Derrick said. "Caroline is an only child, and they want little Jonathan to grow up knowing his grandparents."

"I can certainly understand that," his mother said. "I hope they do make the move here. It's good for families to live close to each other."

The next morning, Elise had breakfast on the table before Frieda came downstairs. It seemed to Derrick that his mother was moving a little slower than usual. "Mama, are you feeling all right this morning?"

Frieda sat down at the table. "I'm feeling a little weak for some reason."

"Most probably because you did too much this last week," Elise said. "I was afraid I was letting you overdo things."

"It's not your fault, Elise, dear. All this was my idea, remember?"

"Well, I don't want you wearing yourself out right before Christmas. I know you had your heart set on doing a lot, but it's important to us that you don't overdo. I'd like to do the rest of the baking and candy making—with you supervising, of course—if it's all right with you."

Derrick's heart warmed at the way Elise still tried to make his mother feel needed, even though he was sure she knew quite well what needed to be done.

"I can't let you do it all, Elise."

"Mama, I can help Elise when I get through doing all my chores."

"Are you sure?"

"Of course I am. We'll do fine—as long as you supervise."

His mother sighed and nodded. "All right, then, I'll let you two do all the standing. I can sit here and crochet or string popcorn. I'm sorry I won't be doing my share—with this being my idea and all."

"Mama, it may have been your idea, but Derrick and I are both as excited about it as you are," Elise said, bringing a plate of sausage and eggs to the table. "You eat and rest and get your strength back. The last thing we want is for you to have a relapse of the pneumonia."

"I don't think that's what this is. I'm not coughing and my chest isn't hurting. It's just that my legs are giving me a little trouble, that's all. I'm sure I'll feel better in a day or two."

"Maybe, if you rest. And Elise and I are going to make sure you do," Derrick said as he helped himself to a couple of eggs and some sausage. "I'll get through with the chores as soon as I can and be in to help."

"Thank you, son."

Derrick was looking forward to helping Elise. She was so competent she rarely needed help at all, but with Mama feeling poorly again, Elise wouldn't have much choice in accepting his help. When he came in that afternoon, however, Elise already had several batches of fudge made.

"Mmm, I love coming in the house—especially the last few days. It always smells so good," he said. "Where's Mama?"

"I convinced her to take a nap. I really don't want her getting sick again, but she just doesn't seem to have the energy she did last week."

"Has she been sleeping long?" He took off his coat and hung it on a hook beside the back door.

Elise shook her head. "No, she went up not long before you came in. I told her I'd call her when supper was ready."

"What can I do to help?"

"Why don't you wrap up some of this fudge? The tissue paper is there on the table. You can wrap it like a present or pull the sides up and tie it with ribbon—however you want to do it."

"Uh, all right." Derrick had never been great at wrapping things, but he was willing to try. He washed his hands and went over to the table, where pans of candy were cooled and waiting to be cut.

"How big do you want the pieces to be?"

"Oh, cut them in about two-inch squares. I think that should be about right."

He could do that. Derrick sliced the fudge into nice, neat pieces. But it was when he started wrapping them that he ran into problems. "Uh, Elise?"

She looked up from pouring another pan of fudge. "Yes?"

"I really don't know how to wrap candy—or much of anything else for that matter."

She chuckled and put the empty pot into the sink. "I'll help."

It took several tries before they decided that stacking several pieces of fudge in the middle of the tissue paper and then pulling up all the sides and tying the package with a ribbon worked best and was the easiest way to do it.

"I think I've got it now," Derrick said, looking down at the top of Elise's head while she tied a ribbon around the gathered-up paper he was holding.

She smiled up at him. "Are you sure?"

"I think so." He'd been tempted to tell her no, just so she would stay and help him—not that he needed the help—as he loved the smell of her hair and the nearness of her. He wanted nothing more right at that moment than to claim her lips in a kiss. But she finished the bow and moved away before he could turn his thoughts into action.

"Good. I need to check on the roast I have in the oven for supper. Tonight I'm going to try my hand at making some popcorn balls."

"Now that's something I can help with. Carl and I used to help Mama make them."

"I'm glad to hear it. I can use all the help you want to give. I've never made them before."

Derrick was more than glad to help her. His kitchen had turned into his favorite room in the house, because it was where Elise could most often be found. For the next half hour, they worked together getting the fudge wrapped, and then Derrick set the table while Elise finished up supper.

He was just about to go up and check on his mother when she came through the door.

"There you are! How are you feeling, Mama?"

"A tad better, I think. I heard some laughter down here earlier. You two sounded like you were having a good time."

"I couldn't figure out how to wrap the fudge," Derrick explained. "And then after I thought I knew what to do, Elise had to show me how to make a bow."

His mother looked at the tissue-wrapped candy. "The packages look quite nice to me. They don't have to be perfect."

After supper, Derrick took it on himself to pop the popcorn while Elise cleaned up the supper dishes. He popped two large pans full. Then he turned to his mother. "Okay, it's just the syrup that we add to the corn, right, Mama?"

"No, it's more than that, son. You need to combine one cup of sugar, a cup of syrup, one tablespoon of vinegar, and a teaspoon of salt together and cook that mixture to hardball stage."

"I thought you knew how to do this," Elise teased.

Derrick laughed and looked at her. "Uh. . .I guess Carl and I just got to mix it all together."

"That's what you did, all right," his mother said.

Elise got out a pan and mixed all the ingredients together and put them on to boil. "Once it reaches hardball, Mama, then what do we do?"

"You remove it from the heat and add a tablespoon of butter to it. Oh yes, Derrick, salt the popcorn, too. Next you mix it all together until all the kernels are coated with the syrup. Then you quickly form the coated popcorn into about three-inch balls."

As soon as the mixture was ready, Derrick helped Elise pour it over the popped corn. It wasn't but a minute before they were all laughing as he and Elise tried forming the balls. "I forgot how sticky they are, Mama. Why didn't you remind me that we needed to butter our hands?"

"I couldn't resist seeing the looks on your faces when you tried to get the mixture into a ball and off your hands. I haven't laughed like this in a long time."

"Well, I'm glad you're having such a good time." Derrick grinned at her while he and Elise quickly washed their hands and started over. This time they managed to form the sticky popcorn into nice round balls. Derrick knew that he and Carl had never had quite this much fun as kids. He would cherish the memory always, and he knew he would never eat another popcorn ball without thinking about Elise.

The next few days and evenings were full of fun and work. But by Thursday night, they had everything made and wrapped to be put in boxes or baskets the next day. On Friday, Derrick was going to take the Hansons' and Ballards' presents—along with the money for the line of credit for them—to Harold and Rachel's place. Then he would come back to cut the Christmas tree so they could put it up that evening. He couldn't wait to see how the house looked once they'd put on the glass ornaments and the garland of popcorn they'd all taken a turn at stringing. It was going to be the best Christmas he'd ever had, and he prayed it wouldn't be the last with Elise.

Chapter 15

When Elise went down to start breakfast Friday morning, it was with mixed feelings. She was more excited about their Christmas plans than she'd ever been, but it would soon be over, and once it was, she was going to have to make plans to go home.

The last few days had been wonderful and full of fun, working with Derrick to finish all the Christmas goodies they planned to give out. She would have memories that were bound to be both wonderful and bittersweet throughout the coming years. But Elise just could not continue to stay here any longer only as Carl's widow. She wanted to be a living part of this family—not part of it only because she'd been married to Frieda's son and Derrick's brother.

After spending so much time with Derrick, she was fully aware that she was head over heels in love with him. She could not continue to live in his home, taking care of it and caring about him more each day, without wanting to be his wife. There. She'd admitted it—if only to herself. No. It wasn't just to herself. The Lord knew how she felt.

There'd been a few times in the last few months, and particularly the last few days, when she thought Derrick might care about her in the same way—especially after he'd told her he'd once wanted to court her. But she didn't know if he really did or if it was just wishful thinking on her part. All she did know was that it was going to hurt badly enough to leave here in the next few weeks. If she stayed and fell even deeper in love with him and he didn't return her feelings, it would only create more heartache in the long run. Better to go through it now.

But since Christmas was upon them, Elise pushed sad thoughts away as she forked up the bacon she was frying. She was determined to enjoy the next few days. Memories of them might well be all she had in the coming years.

Derrick entered the kitchen just as his mother came in from upstairs. "Good morning, Mama and Elise. Can you believe it? I'm almost sad because all of the cooking is done."

"Oh, not all of it, son. We still have Christmas dinner to look forward to. How is that turkey doing out in the pen?"

"It's getting fatter by the day." Derrick chuckled. "Are you two ready to decorate the tree tonight?"

"I think so." Elise smiled as she brought the food to the table. "Are we going to put it in the parlor?"

"You know, we spend so much time in the kitchen, I wouldn't mind putting it right here. But wherever you two want it is fine with me. I'll be bringing it up when I get back from town."

After supper, Derrick brought the tree in and set it up in front of the window by the kitchen table. They hung the popcorn garland and then the glass ornaments that Elise had picked out in town. Feeling it needed a bit more color, they strung cranberries while they drank Derrick's hot cocoa. When they put that garland up, they all agreed it was just what the tree needed.

"No matter how many trees I put up in this house, I'll always remember this first one," Derrick said.

"It's lovely," Elise said, standing across the room to take a good look. "I'll always remember it, too."

Later that evening, Elise brought down the prettily wrapped presents she'd bought for Derrick and his mother, only to find several other packages already under the tree, two of them with her name on them. She suddenly felt like a child again, and the hope of the season flooded her. She placed her packages under the tree and sent up a silent prayer, finally asking the Lord outright to let her know soon how Derrick felt about her. And that—if it be His will—she would never have to go back to Denver to stay.

"I think there's going to be a weather change," Derrick's mother said around noon the next day when they were about to eat dinner. "I can feel it in my bones. They're kind of achy."

"It's a mite colder outside now than it was this morning," Derrick said. He'd just come in from doing some chores and was warming his hands over the range.

"Maybe I ought not to go with you two to deliver the baskets this afternoon. All that going in and out in the cold might not be the best thing for me now that I'm feeling better. I sure don't want to feel poorly tomorrow and have to miss church."

"Mama, I hate for you to miss out on the fun since all this was your idea," Derrick said. "I know you've been looking forward to it, but I certainly don't want you to chance getting sick again right now. And I know you want to go to church tomorrow, especially since it's Christmas Eve."

"I hate not to go with you two, but I think you're right. You and Elise can deliver it all. I'm just glad to know we've started the tradition back up. I do want to go to church tomorrow, and I'm afraid that all the up and down, getting in and out of the wagon, and into one house and then another might be a bit tiresome. You two can tell me all about it when you get home."

"I do so hate that you won't be with us, Mama, but I'll try to remember every last detail to share with you when we get back," Elise promised as she fixed their plates and brought them to the table. "I'll put on a pot of soup before we leave, and when we return we can tell you all about our visits over supper."

"I'll have the table set and ready. I can do that much at least," Frieda said. "I also think I'll keep the present for the Barristers here and take it to them tomorrow. But you can take them the cookies and candy."

"I think that's a good idea. That way at least you'll get the joy of giving the baby's gift to them in person," Elise said.

While Elise cleaned up the kitchen and put on the vegetable soup for supper, Derrick began loading the wagon with the baskets they were giving out.

"We can take off whenever you're ready, Elise," he said as he came in from loading the last of the baskets. "Dress as warmly as you can. It's getting colder out."

"Please wear my cloak, Elise, dear. I don't want you getting sick."

"I will borrow it, since you aren't going. I'm going to have to—" Elise suddenly shook her head and turned to go upstairs. "It won't take me long to change."

"Take your time," Derrick said. "I'll heat a rock for your feet." He pulled out one of the rocks they kept in the fire box just for that reason and stuck it inside the range.

Elise had no more than left the kitchen when his mother motioned for him to come close. "Son, if you're going to do anything to stop Elise from going back to Denver, you'd better be planning on doing it soon," she whispered.

Derrick only nodded and turned away. He knew full well he was running out of time. He took the rock from the range and wrapped it in a towel just as Elise came back downstairs. She looked lovely in a green and white striped dress that seemed very Christmassy.

"Oh, how nice you look, Elise," his mother said. "I do feel I've let the two of you down this week. I'm sorry."

"You haven't let us down at all, Mama," Elise said, kissing her on the cheek. "We do wish you were up to coming with us, but better that you're up to going to church tomorrow and enjoying Christmas Day with us."

"Yes, well, I pray you two will have a wonderful time this afternoon."

"Keep an eye on that soup for us, Mama. We'll be back before you know it." Derrick helped Elise slip into his mother's cloak, then they headed out the door.

Outside, Derrick assisted Elise into the wagon, then went around and climbed up on the other side. He looked at the heavy sky. "I think it may snow before Christmas gets here."

"Do you really?" Elise asked, her eyes shining like a child's.

"I do." Derrick flipped the reins and they took off. "Perhaps I can pull out the sleigh."

"You have a sleigh? I haven't ridden in one in years!"

"I do. Actually, it's one more thing that came with this place. I've only had it out a time or two, but it's quite fun." He hoped he'd have a chance to take her for a ride.

As they traveled down the road, Elise turned quiet, watching the scenery, and Derrick sent up one silent prayer after another. He prayed he would have the courage to tell her how much he loved her before this night was over. He prayed that he could convince her not to go back to Denver. He wasn't sure how he was going to go about it exactly, but he had faith that the Lord was going to guide him. He couldn't put it off any longer. If he did, he might lose Elise forever.

Elise was sorry that Frieda couldn't make the trip, but she couldn't say she was disappointed to have this time with Derrick alone. She enjoyed stopping at each neighbor's home and handing out the baskets of baked goods and candies.

At the Millers', the children couldn't wait to try the fudge. And at the Sanders', it was the popcorn balls that garnered the most attention. Without fail, all of Derrick's neighbors were pleased by his gifts to them.

"What a good idea this is. I'd like to do something like this next year," Maude Sanders said when Derrick explained that it was his mother's idea to carry on a family tradition. "I seem to remember my grandparents giving out different kinds of breads at Christmastime. It would be good to get the children involved in something like this."

Derrick exchanged a glance with Elise and chuckled. "I guarantee they'll have a good time. But it isn't just for children. Adults can have just as good a time working together."

Elise could feel the color rise into her cheeks. There was something in Derrick's expression—as his gaze captured hers—that had her heart fluttering in her chest. She didn't quite know what it was, but it had her feeling a bit. . . breathless.

As the afternoon wore on, they were welcomed into each house and offered coffee or tea or hot cocoa. They didn't stay long anywhere, but it was enough time to give her several good stories to tell to Mama when they got back to the house.

It was at the Barristers' where they stayed the longest time, however. Baby Jonathan was wide awake, and Elise couldn't resist holding him awhile. Derrick didn't seem to be in any hurry, as he, Jed, and Caroline's father talked about the weather and farming in this part of the country.

Elise looked down at the baby in her arms. He was adorable. "Oh, Caroline, he's grown just in a week."

"I know. He's filling out and changing so much. It seems there's something new about him each day. I wish Frieda could have come."

"She's been a bit tired this past week, and we all thought it might be best if she stayed in today so that she would feel like going to church tomorrow."

"Oh no, we don't want her getting sick again. I'm glad she'll be at church tomorrow. At least we'll get to see her then," Caroline said.

"Giving out baskets to the neighbors was actually her idea," Elise said. "It was a family tradition that Derrick plans on continuing here."

"This is so nice," Caroline's mother said as she looked into the basket and saw all the goodies they'd made. "We've managed to make a few sweets, but Jonathan takes up a lot of our time. I'll tell her tomorrow, of course, but please let Mrs. Morgan know how thankful we are for all of this."

"I will," Elise promised.

By the time they left the Barristers', it was almost suppertime. This was their last stop, so they headed for home.

Much as she hated the time alone to end, Elise loved seeing the light pouring out of Derrick's windows. The house looked warm and welcoming. Derrick dropped her off at the back door and then went on to the barn.

His mother must have been listening for them, because she was ladling up steaming bowls of soup when Elise came inside.

"It's getting colder out there, Mama! Derrick will be here as soon as he feeds the horse and puts the wagon up," she said, taking off the cloak and hanging it on its customary hook. She hurried across the room. "Here, let me help you."

"Just take these over to the table, dear." Frieda handed her a bowl. "This should warm you both up. How did it go?"

"Oh, Mama, everyone was so appreciative, and they thought your tradition was just wonderful. I think several of the women will try to do something similar next year."

Frieda nodded and smiled. "Good. That's what I hoped would happen. Swapping small gifts and visiting helps to bring neighbors closer together." She took the corn bread she'd made out of the warmer just as Derrick came inside.

"Mmm, that smells delicious!"

"It does," his mother replied. "And I have to admit I'm a bit hungry. I've smelled it all afternoon. You and Elise can tell me all about the afternoon right after you say the blessing, son."

~

Derrick did say the blessing, but he added a silent prayer of his own. *Dear Lord, please help me to tell Elise how I feel about her tonight. I've been on the verge of telling her all day, but I'm running out of time and I need to let her know how I feel. Please give me the words to say, and, Father, please let her feel the same way. In Jesus' name I pray. Amen.*

"Elise tells me that everyone liked our gifts. Did you get to see Caroline and the baby and Jed?"

"We did. I mostly visited with Jed and his father-in-law, while Elise visited with Caroline and her mother. She can tell you about the baby."

"I got to hold Jonathan. Oh, Mama, he's growing so! Caroline was disappointed that you weren't able to come, but she's looking forward to showing him off to you tomorrow."

"I can't wait to see him. Have her parents said if they have decided to stay?"

"Well, her father is looking at property in the area," Derrick said. "That's a good signal that they might be. They really didn't say outright, though."

"Oh, I hope they do. I know that will mean a lot to Caroline and Jed, and her parents, too, for them all to have family close."

After supper, Derrick helped Elise clean up the kitchen, and they both entertained his mother with stories about the Miller and Sanders children and how excited they were about the baskets.

"Oh, and, Mama, Caroline and her mother were so happy to have the cookies and candy," Elise said. "With taking care of Jonathan, they haven't been able to do all the cooking they would have liked to do for Christmas."

"Well, I'm glad everyone liked our gifts. It makes it all worthwhile—although the two of you did most of the work."

"It was your idea, Mama," Derrick said. "I wouldn't have attempted it otherwise. And it's for certain we'd never have gotten those popcorn balls made without you. They were quite a hit with the children especially."

"Well now, that is quite true. I'm not sure what you would have had if you'd just mixed that syrup in with the popcorn," his mother said.

"A gooey mess, most probably." Derrick laughed and made a face.

"It was quite fun, though," Elise added.

His mother laughed just thinking about it again.

"Would either of you like a cup of cocoa?" Derrick asked.

"I was just waiting for you to make it. Then I'm going up. I'm getting sleepy," his mother said.

While Derrick made the tasty drink, he tried to think of ways to talk to Elise after his mother went upstairs. Elise usually went up at the same time, but Derrick was determined to talk to her—to tell her how he felt about her. He had to. As he stirred the ingredients together, he sent up a silent plea. *I know I should have brought it up while we were out today, Lord. But please give me the courage to talk to her tonight. I know that even if she says she could never love me, You will see me through. I finally realize that's exactly what You did when I let my brother win her heart. You saw me through the pain then, and even though I couldn't see it at the time, I see it now. So please just guide me, help me find the right words, and if my heart is broken once more, I'm trusting in You to see me through.*

"Derrick, son! Are you scorching our cocoa?"

He hurriedly took the pot off the stove. "No, I think it's all right, Mama, but I'm glad you got my attention."

"You must have been woolgathering," his mother said with a chuckle.

"Mmm," Derrick said noncommittally. No, what he'd been doing was much more important than daydreaming—much more important.

Chapter 16

Elise helped him take the cups of the frothy drink to the table. Derrick tried to keep his mind on the conversation as his mother and Elise talked over the day again and pondered whether the Ballards and the Hansons were going to like their gifts. But it wasn't easy to do. All he really wanted was for his dear mother to retire for the night and for him to find some way to talk to Elise before she followed his mother up.

They seemed to linger over the steaming cups of cocoa, but finally his mother yawned and said, "I guess it's time I went to bed. I'll help you clean up first, though, Elise."

Suddenly Derrick had his opening. As his mother stood up and picked up her cup to take it to the sink, Derrick quickly took it from her. "I'll put this up, Mama. And I'll help Elise clean up. You go on to bed."

He looked at her intently, hoping she would read his mind as well as she'd seemed to when he was a child.

"Well, all right, son. I'll see you two tomorrow. Be sure not to let me oversleep."

Derrick placed a kiss on her delicate cheek. "We won't. Good night."

Elise turned from the sink she was filling with water. "Good night, Mama. I hope you sleep well."

Derrick brought his and his mother's cups to the sink, turning to make sure she'd left the room. "Uh. . .Elise, I—"

"Look, Derrick!" Elise interrupted him as she peered out the window. "I think I just saw a snowflake."

Derrick looked over her shoulder. "It wouldn't surprise me if we have snow on the ground tomorrow," he said.

"Really?" Elise asked, her eyes shining bright as she turned to him.

They were standing so close she was near to being in his arms. All he would have to do was slide them around her. He looked into her eyes, and something in her expression held his gaze. His heart was hammering hard against his chest. "It's possible," he said to her.

Elise never broke eye contact as she smiled at him, and Derrick felt a flash of hope. He reminded himself that with God all things truly were possible. It was time to step out in faith. He slid his arms around Elise and looked deep into her eyes.

"Elise, I don't want one more day to pass without telling you. . .that. . .I love you." Her eyes widened, and if anything, her smile grew larger, giving him the courage to go on. "I have loved you for years. Do you think you could ever feel the same way about me?"

"Oh, Derrick. . ." She shook her head.

His heart seemed to stop beating as he waited for her to continue. He could see the tears that gathered in her eyes, and he held his breath, waiting for her to break his heart once more.

Elise reached up to touch his cheek. "I already *do* feel the same way about you. I've been in love with you for months now, and I was afraid—"

Derrick didn't let her finish the sentence. His lips claimed hers in a kiss that told her just how long he'd waited to hear her words. Hoping he'd convinced her of how much he cared, he lifted his lips from hers and looked deep into her eyes. "I've dreamed of this moment for so long, Elise."

She smiled at him. "Now might be the time to tell you that you *were* too slow back then. Happy as I was with Carl, and as much as I came to love him, there was a time when it was *you* I was hoping would court me. I've been hoping you still felt the same ever since you told me you'd wanted to do just that."

"I never stopped caring about you, Elise. The love I felt for you has only grown over time." Derrick paused and took a deep breath before continuing. "Will you marry me. . .now, before the year is out? I can think of nothing I'd like more than to start the new year with you as my wife. That's all I want for Christmas—for us to be married."

"Oh yes, Derrick, I will marry you, before the end of the year, if we can get the preacher to do it that soon."

He claimed her lips in another kiss that very effectively promised their love to each other. It was only the sound of a loud whoop from outside the kitchen that broke them apart.

"Mama?" Elise said. They turned to find Frieda barreling into the room, breathing hard.

"Mama, are you all right?" Derrick hurriedly seated her at the table while Elise filled a glass with water. "Maybe I should go for the doctor?"

"No!" his mother finally said. "There's no need for the doctor," she assured them. "I've never been better."

Indeed, her eyes were sparkling as she looked at the two of them and continued. "I heard your proposal to Elise, Derrick—and her acceptance." She put a hand over her chest and sighed. "My prayers have been answered."

Derrick sighed with relief, and he chuckled. "So have mine, Mama."

"And mine," Elise added as Derrick pulled her into the circle of his arms once more.

"I am so thankful," Derrick's mother said. "I don't know how much longer I could have pretended to feel bad, when all I've really been doing is trying to stir up a little romance between the two of you!"

"You haven't been sick?"

"Well, not lately. Since I got over the pneumonia, I've been fine." She grinned at them.

"Mama!" Derrick said. "We've been worried about you."

"Well, I could see the Lord at work, but you two just didn't always open your eyes to what He was showing you. I don't think He minded a little help from me. You both seemed to need all the help you could get! And I figured the more time you spent together, the better."

"Mama!" Elise shook her head and began to giggle.

"It worked, didn't it?"

Derrick looked into Elise's eyes and smiled. "It worked. Thank you, Mama."

He hugged Elise to him and sent up a prayer of thanksgiving. For he knew full well that it was the Lord who'd given him the best Christmas present ever. It certainly didn't bother Derrick that He might have used his mother to help things along.

Light snowflakes were indeed falling the next morning when Derrick went down to light the range so the kitchen would be warm for Elise and his mother. It was more than a little cold when he made his way over to the barn to do his chores and even colder on the way back. He was struck with a sudden idea, and he hurried back inside the house to see what Elise and his mother thought of it.

His bride-to-be was at the stove, an apron covering her Sunday dress. The look in her eyes and the smile she gave him told Derrick all he needed to know—last night was real and Elise did love him. He strode over to her and gathered her in his arms. "Good morning, my love," he whispered before lowering his lips to hers.

The sound of his mother clearing her throat broke them apart. But when he turned to look at her, Derrick could see she wasn't the least bit disturbed to find them kissing in the kitchen. She was grinning from ear to ear.

He smiled and winked at her. "I have an idea."

"Oh? What is it, son?"

"Well, I've waited so very long to have family with me at Christmastime. Do you think it would be all right if we open some presents today—before church?" He turned to Elise. "I've already got what I wanted for Christmas—Elise has promised to be my wife. But, Elise, I'd like for you and Mama to open what I got each of you. Please."

Elise grinned and glanced at his mother. She nodded. "It's all right with me, Mama, if it's all right with you."

"Please, Mama," Derrick implored his mother with a smile. She knew what he'd gotten for Elise, and he hoped she remembered and realized she could use it today.

"Well, if you think we have time." She looked at the clock on the wall. "It appears that we do. Evidently we were all so excited about you two finally admitting your love for one another that we didn't sleep as long as usual."

"I don't think I slept much at all last night," Derrick said, glancing over at Elise. "I couldn't wait for morning so I could see Elise again and make sure it wasn't all a dream."

"I felt the same way," Elise admitted, her cheeks coloring as she returned his smile.

"Well, obviously it was no dream. Or else we were all dreaming the same one," Frieda said with a chuckle. "Let's get breakfast over with, and then we can start unwrapping those presents."

They didn't linger over a second cup of coffee that morning. Instead, while Elise and Frieda cleared the table and did dishes, Derrick headed back out to the barn. Elise knew he was going to get his mother's present, and she could barely contain her excitement at the anticipation of seeing Frieda's reaction when she opened it. She had to giggle at the look on her mother-in-law's face when Derrick brought the crate inside and set it near the tree.

"This is yours, Mama."

"Oh, Derrick, that's very big. I can't imagine what you have in there," Frieda said as she dried her hands and hung the dish towel on a hook.

"Well, don't try. Just come open it."

Elise took off her apron and hurried to watch.

Derrick loosened the top of the crate and stood back as his mother opened her gift. "Oh! Oh, Derrick—a sewing machine!" she exclaimed. "You couldn't have gotten me anything I wanted more—well, besides you and Elise getting together!" She turned and gave Derrick a hug. "Oh, son, thank you!"

Tears gathered in Elise's eyes as she watched Frieda and Derrick. This was the most wonderful Christmas she'd ever had! The man she loved had asked her to marry him, and his mother would still be part of her family. Who could ask for more?

Derrick reached under the tree and handed her a large present. "For my bride-to-be."

Elise's heart felt near bursting with happiness. "You've already given me the present I wished for most, too. I don't need anything else."

"Oh, this you'll be able to use. Please, open it," Derrick said with a grin.

Elise had shaken the package a few times when she'd been in the kitchen with no one else around, but she still didn't have any idea what it was. She laid the box on the kitchen table and carefully unwrapped it. She took the top off the box and caught her breath. Inside was the beautiful wool cloak she'd seen when they were out shopping. She hadn't been aware that Derrick had even noticed her looking at it. "Oh, Derrick," she breathed as she lifted the cloak out of the box and held it up for Frieda to see. "It's lovely—and just the right weight for this winter weather."

"I thought it might come in handy today. It's getting quite cold out," Derrick said.

Elise rushed to hug his neck. "You are so very thoughtful. Thank you so much. I can't wait to wear it." She turned back to the tree, picked up a small package, and handed it to Derrick. "Now it's your turn."

He quickly tore the paper off and smiled at what he saw. "*In His Steps*! Oh, thank you, Elise. I really wanted this book—I've heard it's excellent." He pulled her close and gave her a hug. "I'll treasure it always because it came from you." He reluctantly released her and said, "But that's all we have time for now."

"Are you sure? You've waited a long time—"

Derrick pulled her to his side and shook his head. "No, we really don't have time. We'll wait until tomorrow for the rest. I just wanted you to have the cloak to wear to church today. . . and for Mama to have her sewing machine."

"But—"

Derrick ended her objection by placing a gentle kiss on her lips. He broke it off and looked deep into her eyes. "There's no other present I need—but to settle a date for our wedding. If we get there a little early, maybe we can talk to Harold before services."

Elise wasn't about to argue with that. She couldn't wait to be able to call this wonderful man her husband. She slipped on the first Christmas gift he'd given her, knowing she would cherish it each time she wore it in the coming years. "I'm ready whenever you two are."

Snowflakes were still falling gently as they made their way to church on Christmas Eve, promising a white Christmas for the next day. Derrick and Elise were anxious to talk to Harold and see when he could preside over a wedding, hoping it could be during the next week. But before they had a chance, his mother took charge, pulling the preacher to the side as soon as they got to church. After several nods and grins, Harold came over to them.

"You know, I wanted to thank you for giving me the opportunity to be part of the happiness you made possible for the Hanson and Ballard families. It truly was a joy to see their expressions when I gave them your gifts. And the basket you gave Rachel and me. . . Thank you for your thoughtfulness. Your mother says there might be something I can do for you in return. How would you like to be married today, right after services?"

"Oh, well, yes, of course I'd like to," Derrick said, "but I don't have a ring for Elise yet, and—"

His mother pulled the simple band his father had given her off her finger and handed it to him. "You can use this until you can get her one, son."

"But, Mama, Elise might not—"

Elise rushed to assure him. It was all he wanted for Christmas, after all. "It's fine, Derrick. I don't need a ring to prove we're married. All we need are witnesses and a preacher to marry us. We certainly have that today."

"You're sure? I'll buy you a ring right after Christmas."

Her heart was filled with so much love, Elise felt it might burst. "I'm sure."

"Then yes, Harold," her husband-to-be said, "we'd love to have you to marry us after services today."

"Consider it done."

At first Elise was afraid she wouldn't be able to keep her mind on the sermon Harold brought to them as she sat beside Derrick. But as soon as the preacher began speaking, he had her full attention, for he brought a lovely lesson on God's love to them, reminding them that He brought His only Son to this earth that all might have the hope of salvation through Him. What greater love could there be than that?

That the Lord loved her had never been clearer to Elise than today. He'd provided for her salvation through His precious Son, but He'd also provided for her happiness here on this earth. He'd answered all of her prayers. And He'd answered abundantly.

Oh, she was going back to Denver, but it would be as Derrick's wife and only to pack up her belongings and put her house up for sale. It would be their wedding trip after the first of the year. And her beloved mother-in-law would still be just that. The Lord had shown her over and over again just how much He loved her.

Elise felt surrounded by His love now, as the service ended and Harold asked everyone to remain seated for their wedding. The congregation seemed quite happy to stay a little longer for the simple ceremony.

As Elise stood beside Derrick and they said their vows, she felt overwhelmed by the joy she felt. When Derrick kissed her for the first time as his wife, Elise returned his kiss with a heart full of love.

"I present to you Mr. and Mrs. Derrick Morgan," Harold said as they turned to face the congregation.

They walked down the aisle as husband and wife, and Elise sent up a silent prayer, thanking the Lord above for answering all of her prayers and for giving her a new love, a new home, and a new life. She would be forever grateful.

JANET LEE BARTON

After living all over the south, Janet now lives in Oklahoma where she and her husband and her daughter and son-in-law have bought a house together. They are finding that generational living can be much fun—especially with two granddaughters added to the mix! She and her family are active members in their church, and they feel very blessed to be part of a large, loving church family.

Janet is well-published though Barbour and their Heartsong Presents line, having written twelve Heartsong novels (six historical, six contemporary) in addition to five novellas. She is a member of American Christian Fiction Writers and is president of her local chapter, OCFW.

SHARON TAKES A HAND

Dedication

To Jeanne Dow, my proofreader extraordinaire, my kind mother-in-law, and my dear friend. I love you!

Chapter 1

June 4, 1891

Sharon Hastings shifted an eighth of an inch on the unforgiving leather seat of the dusty stagecoach. For more than an hour, the rotund lady next to her had been droning on about her marvelous grandchildren. Sharon made some kind of reply from time to time, but the woman's voice had faded into a jumble of sounds. The only thing on Sharon's mind today was a single word. It rang and rumbled through her thoughts with steady intensity—a chant, a sonnet, a song: *home.*

More than a thousand nights she'd closed her eyes and pressed her cheek into her boarding school pillow, holding that word close to her heart. She'd spent five years studying the three R's, perfecting her form on the violin, and faithfully adhering to Mrs. Minniver's Rules of Decorum. Headmistress at the school of fifty girls, Mrs. Minniver was a kind of sword-wielding archangel—perfectly groomed, precise, and terrifying.

Two weeks before, Sharon had received tickets for the train and for the stage from her guardian, Rudolph Hastings, with a one-sentence note saying he'd pick her up at the station in Farmington, New Mexico. She'd arrive a week after her eighteenth birthday.

When she was thirteen years old, Sharon's parents and sister had succumbed to cholera while traveling on the Oregon Trail. Soon afterward, her father's brother, Rudolph, had arranged for her boarding school. He'd sent her presents at all the right times and given her a generous allowance for clothes, but he never came to Springfield, Missouri, to see her. She'd never been to the Lazy H ranch. She'd never once met her benefactor.

When she'd sent a letter asking him if she could visit the ranch, he had responded by saying the Lazy H was no place for a young girl like her. She'd had to be content to spend her holidays with her best friend, Candace Matthews, and a dozen other girls who also didn't leave the school for holidays.

Today, none of that mattered. Today, she was coming home.

When the stage reached Farmington, Sharon was the last to disembark. Her trunks were already on the boardwalk when she stepped down. From an old tintype photograph, she knew that Uncle Rudolph looked a lot like her father except shorter. She should be able to recognize him.

The boardwalk creaked under the weight of a dozen people and at least that many trunks. Everyone was chattering, hugging, and gathering their belongings. Everyone except Sharon.

Several minutes passed, and no one had stepped forward to speak to her. Careful to maintain her poise (Rule 1 on Mrs. Minniver's List), she commanded her hands to stop fidgeting with the folds of her gray twill skirt (Rule 2).

For five long years she'd lived by the decalogue of the headmistress and could recite each of its strictures forward and backward:

1. Maintain your poise at all times.
2. Never touch your person or adjust your clothes in public. Fidgeting is forbidden.
3. Always keep the voice modulated and gentle.
4. When in polite company, engage in intelligent conversation. Seek to find common interests that both parties will enjoy.
5. When asked how you are or any polite question that doesn't require a complete answer, say, "Fine," and thank the speaker for asking.
6. Always say thank you for even the smallest kindness.
7. Sit with the spine away from the chair back, with hands folded and ankles crossed.
8. Never laugh aloud in public.
9. When outdoors, always keep your head covered.
10. Always maintain a calm and sedate pace. Never dash about.

The street was hard-packed brown earth. A double row of false-fronted shops stretched out as far as she could see in both directions. Someone nearby was cooking cabbage seasoned with salt pork.

"Miss Hastings?" a deep voice asked from behind her.

She turned to see a giant, dark-haired cowboy—complete with chaps and a cowhide vest. He had a boyish face with a thick jaw and eyes the color of brushed steel. He held a brown Stetson against the side of his leg. Beside him stood a slim, hatless man wearing a blue pinstripe suit, his black hair slicked back from a center part.

"Yes, and you are. . . ?"

The cowboy spoke. His voice was hard and dry. "I'm Jason Riordan, foreman at the Lazy H. This is Edward Kellerman, Rudolph's lawyer."

The attorney smiled into her eyes and made a tiny formal bow. She offered him her gloved hand. "How do you do, gentlemen?" she asked. As an afterthought, she shook hands with the cowboy.

"Where's my uncle?" she asked, looking behind them.

"Miss Hastings," Kellerman said, "would you mind stepping into my office?" His words were precise with no trace of a Western drawl. "We need to speak to you about some private matters. It's only a few steps from here."

She gazed at her trunks piled on the boardwalk.

The foreman said, "I'll have my men load your things on the wagon. A couple of the boys came to town to fetch some oats and cracked corn. They're heading back now." He gave a signal to a lean cowboy who looked as thin and tough as a strip of dried leather.

"What's this about?" she asked, falling in step with the men.

Kellerman's squarish face lit up as he smiled. "How was your trip?"

"It was fine, Mr. Kellerman," she said, remembering Rule 5. "Thank you for asking." Actually, the trip was hot, confining, and—worst of all—intensely boring.

Leaving the stage station behind, they passed a one-story building that called itself a hotel. Next was the Farmington General Store. Wearing black garters over his white shirt-sleeves, a young blond man came out, glanced at Sharon, and nodded before hurrying down the street in the opposite direction.

The cowboy's boots clomped on the boardwalk. He greeted a passing older woman with a brief, "Miss," and a tug on his hat brim.

Edward Kellerman's office was next, a single room over a milliner's shop. Holding her skirts up to clear her feet, Sharon climbed stairs so narrow that her elbows sometimes bumped either wall.

A heavy desk, a bookcase, and two chairs filled Kellerman's office. The room smelled like linseed oil and old leather with a hint of sweet pipe-tobacco smoke clinging to the air. Sharon sat down as Mr. Kellerman moved to his seat behind the desk. The foreman stood near the door.

Taking in the somber expressions of both men, Sharon's throat tightened. "Where is Uncle Rudolph?" she asked again.

"Miss Hastings," Edward Kellerman said, "your uncle had an accident. He went missing six weeks ago."

Sharon's breath left her. Where would she go? Her only other relative was her mother's sister, a widow with eight children to feed.

The lawyer reached into a drawer and removed a long sheaf of papers. "At this point, we all agree that if Rudolph Hastings were living, he would have come home by now."

The foreman cleared his throat. "We've searched and searched until every one of us gave out. Rudolph knew his land so well that if he could, he would have found a way to make himself known to us when we were passing by him." He rubbed his jaw with his calloused fingers. "He must have fallen into a ravine or. . ." He hesitated and glanced at Sharon. "There's wildcats and bears out there, Miss Hastings."

Sharon shivered.

Mr. Kellerman went on, "I have here your uncle's will, Miss Hastings. I know this is a shock to you, but I have to tell you that he left almost everything he owned to you—the ranch, the cattle, everything."

She pulled a handkerchief from the pocket of her gray traveling jacket and touched her nose with it. "Mr. Kellerman," she whispered, "I need a moment to take this in."

He stood. "Certainly. I'll fetch you a glass of water." He hurried out.

Sharon closed her eyes and her head spun. Her breath came in short, shallow gasps.

Mr. Kellerman returned and pressed a glass into her hands. "Here. Sip this. You'll feel better."

"Thank you," she murmured, then drank the cool liquid.

Foreman Riordan spoke from behind her. She had forgotten he was there. His words were friendly, but his voice was strained. "Would you like to stay in town tonight? I can bunk at the livery stable if you want to get a hotel room."

Still trying to regain control, she turned to him. "That won't be necessary, Mr. Riordan."

She handed the glass to Kellerman. "Thank you. That did help." She drew in a slow breath to continue calming herself. "Do you need anything else from me, Mr. Kellerman?"

"Edward," he said, smiling. "At your service." He gave that small bow again. "And no, there is nothing else. If I need you to sign any papers, I'll ride out to the ranch. It isn't so far."

The cowboy said, "An hour on horseback, twice that in the surrey."

"Did you say a surrey?" Sharon asked, turning toward him in surprise.

"Yes, Miss Hastings. Rudolph took real pride in that surrey. He ordered it brought in from Abilene two years ago. Corky keeps it blacked up and polished, so it still looks brand-new. I thought it would be more fittin' for a lady than the buckboard."

An hour later, Jason helped Sharon into the surrey, and they set off. With its flat roof and fringe swaying all around the top, Sharon felt like she was riding in high style. It was a perfect June day. A light breeze carried the faint aroma of sage and cedar. So many thoughts and feelings coursed through Sharon's brain, she felt as if her bonnet were shrinking against her scalp.

The land was rugged and dry, dotted with scrub brush and bits of grass that seemed to stretch to infinity. A gentle breeze cooled her forehead and slowly, gradually settled her mind. For the first time in her life, she had options. She could sell the ranch or stay on and live here. But nothing had to be decided today.

She let out a slow breath and began to relax.

Jason Riordan kept his eyes straight ahead. After a while Sharon began to search her brain for some statement to start a polite conversation (Rule 4). Oh, what could she say? Why didn't *he* say something?

Finally, she blurted, "What's the ranch like?"

He glanced at her.

Was that a surprised expression on his face? Her voice had sounded awfully loud when she'd asked that. Had she broken Rule 3? If only willpower could force her cheeks to cool. The new owner of the Lazy H shouldn't be blushing like a schoolgirl, even if she was one.

Gazing at a spot over the horse's head, he said, "The Lazy H covers two thousand acres, give or take a few hundred. We run steers and horses, and we have the biggest water hole for miles around. The homestead has a bunkhouse, a corral and barn, and Rudolph's house, of course."

"Please, tell me what happened to Uncle Rudolph," she said. "What kind of accident did he have?"

His expression grew troubled. "We don't know what happened, miss. He went out riding one morning and never came back. His horse came in with an empty saddle shortly before dark. There was a lot of blood on it." He rubbed his jaw. "We've all been tore up about it. Can't seem to get settled down."

"Perhaps someone just kidnapped him? Indians or outlaws?"

He started and sent her a disbelieving look. "We don't have Indian trouble hereabouts. And even if we did, what would Indians want with an old sidewinder like Rudolph? He'd be too dangerous for them to keep alive—for anyone to keep alive."

He paused a moment, then went on. "We searched for days from dawn to dark, and never came up with a single track or scrap of cloth or anything to help us. He started out riding for the water hole, but who knows where he went after that. Could have been anywhere, on our land or off it." He took off his hat and wrapped his arm around his forehead to blot the perspiration with his sleeve.

Replacing his Stetson, he said, "It's a puzzle. There are some broken hills north of here where he could have fallen into a ravine, but I can't see Rudolph being so foolish as to get that close to the edge. He'd lived here for years. He knew every square foot of the place."

He leaned forward with his elbows resting on his thighs, both hands gripping the reins. His jaw had the barest hint of a five o'clock shadow.

"Do you think there could have been foul play? Did he have any enemies?"

"Everyone has enemies, Miss Hastings. Rudolph had his share. There were a couple of old grudges and the like, but were they big enough to cause someone to do away with him?" He shook his head. "Nah. If someone was that fiery mad, they'd call him out and try out a fast draw. This is New Mexico, not New York."

Sharon let that seep into her brain for a few minutes. There had to be a plausible reason that Rudolph had disappeared without a trace. Unfortunately, she knew too little about the life here to make any more guesses.

Finally, she said, "Those mountains are beautiful. What are they called?"

"That's the tail end of the Rockies, the Sangre de Cristos. That mountain there," he pointed northeast, "is Taos. It's about ten thousand feet high, from what I understand. Farther south is Santa Fe Mountain. That one goes up to twelve thousand feet."

"Have you ever climbed them?"

He shot her a disbelieving look. "Why would I want to do that? Mountain climbing is for tourists. Out here folks ride most everywhere they go."

She rushed on. "The train came through a long, winding gorge. Those must be the same mountains that we came through." She smiled shyly. "We studied the Rocky Mountains in geography, of course. I can tell you all about them, but I've never lived near them like this." She went on wistfully, "My folks and my little sister died in the Colorado foothills. We never even made it to the first mountain."

He shifted to a more upright position on the seat and glanced in her general direction. "I'm sorry," he said, his voice softening a little. "That must have been real tough."

She didn't know what to say in reply to that, so she let some time pass.

Finally, she asked, "How many hired hands do you have?"

"Two full-timers, besides me and Max, the cook. We'll hire more for roundup." He gave her an edgy look. "Miss Hastings, I can run the ranch for you. I've lived here all my life, and my father was foreman right up until he died."

"I have no doubt that you are capable, Mr. Riordan," she said, moistening her lips. "I'd very much appreciate your help. As you know, I'm at a distinct disadvantage."

He turned to look her full in the face. "You sure did get a sight of book learning at that school, didn't you?"

"What do you mean?" she asked, wondering if she should be offended.

"Miss, you won't get too far with the hands, talking like that. We're plain-speaking folks hereabouts."

Her chin came up a fraction of an inch. "Well, so am I."

He stiffened. Looking away, he ran his thumb and forefinger down either side of his mouth, then looked at her again. "Yes, miss."

"Would you do me a great favor?"

"Of course."

"Don't call me *miss* anymore. I don't like it. Please call me Sharon."

He touched the brim of his hat and nodded. "We don't *mister* much out here, so you can call me Jason." He reached under the seat and picked up a small box. "Here. Open this. It's our supper. Max will have finished putting the food away before we get there, so I picked this up at the hotel restaurant."

The smell of fried chicken was heavenly. Fresh-baked rolls and thick-cut fried potatoes. She was starving.

She poked around inside the pasteboard container. No plates or silverware or napkins. Jason pulled off his gloves and picked up a crusty chicken leg.

Intent on supper, she carefully removed her white cotton gloves and placed them in her handbag. Before long, she was munching chicken and licking her salty fingers, remembering younger days and wishing she could taste her mother's cooking one more time.

At least the food kept them busy for a while. Trying to hold polite conversation with this man was exhausting.

Chapter 2

They rode into the ranch at the edge of dark. Though still fully visible, the yard had shadowy corners. The greens and browns glowed rich and deep, and the scent of horses and straw hung in the air. The lane split into a Y shape, the wide right side heading for the barn and a long, low building beyond it. The narrow left side led to the house. That part of the lane stretched out beside the porch, then circled a giant tree and rejoined the stem of the Y.

A short man a few years past middle age stood on the porch. He had a large face and a round body. His head was completely bald, and he wore a white apron that almost touched the floor.

"Max!" Jason called, a humorous note in his voice. "Meet Miss Hastings—Sharon." He turned to Sharon. "Your cook, Max Martin. He'll take good care of you."

Max bounded down the stairs and helped her from the surrey. "Miss Hastings! It's so good to meet you!"

When she stepped to the ground, she was at least four inches taller than he was. She shook his hand. "It's nice to meet you, Mister Mart—"

"Max!" he said. "Just Max." He turned to Jason still in the surrey. "Wilson brought her trunks from town. We put them in the master bedroom."

Jason nodded. "You having hotcakes for breakfast?" he asked.

"Beef and biscuits, but if you want hotcakes, I'll make hotcakes."

"Another day," Jason said, grinning as he shook the reins.

"Thank you, Jason!" she called to him as the surrey began to move, remembering Rule 6 just in time.

"My pleasure." Without looking directly at her, he touched the brim of his Stetson and set off. The wheels of the surrey made grating sounds on the driveway as he rounded the sharp curve.

"This way, Sharon," Max said, beaming up at her. "I'll show you your room." As he opened the door, he went on, "Rudolph couldn't wait for the day when you'd come." He sobered. "I only wish he was here to welcome you like he dreamed of doing." He stepped aside for her to enter.

In the center of the open room stood a massive stone fireplace with a wide hearth. A long-barreled shotgun hung over it. The fireplace stones were round, smooth, river rock in varying shades of yellow and orange. The hearth stones were flat and gray. Two matching camelback sofas closely flanked the fireplace with two rocking chairs at the outside end. The floor was made of dark planks in various widths with deep cracks between some of them.

Max led her toward the right. "Your room is in the back," he said. "The two doors off the living room lead to the other bedrooms. We have three bedrooms in all. Rudolph built this house for a family, but he never married." He chuckled sadly. "We were both bachelors, he and I. We used to play checkers in the evenings." He shook his head. "I'm sure glad to see you come, Miss Sharon. This place has been like a tomb since he's been gone."

The kitchen filled the entire back half of the house, and Sharon was surprised to see another fireplace, back-to-back with the first one. This one had no hearth, and the firebox was taller and deeper. It had iron pothooks on both sides of the blackened opening.

"That's the old cooking setup," Max said. "Now I have a woodstove with a hot water reservoir." He proudly pointed to the black porcelain Enterprise cookstove on the opposite wall. "We have an inside pitcher pump, too." A red water pump sat on the counter near the back door, its long handle extending well below the edge of the counter for better leverage.

He turned to the bedroom door that opened from the kitchen. "This was your uncle's room, and now it's yours. I left everything mostly as he had it." He led the way inside. "I took out his clothes and put them in one of the spare rooms. You can decide what to do with them later."

Sharon slowly stepped across the threshold. A giant bed dominated the room. It had massive round posts at each corner and was covered with a faded Texas star quilt. A small fireplace faced the end of the bed. Her trunks stood in a row before the fireplace.

"I put water in the pitcher on the dry sink," Max said, stepping back through the door. "If you want anything, I'll be around for another half hour. I'm setting up some sourdough." He reached for the door latch. "I bunk with the hands. If you need me, jangle the triangle on the front porch and I'll come a-running."

"Thank you, Max. I'm sure I'll be fine. Good night." She reached for her bonnet strings.

Twenty minutes later, her traveling gown lay draped over her trunks, and she slipped into a cotton gown. It was barely past dark, but she was exhausted.

The bed was soft. The night was cool. Sinking deep into the feather pillow, Sharon let out a long, weary sigh. She felt like she'd been holding her breath for five years. Closing her eyes, she fell into a deep, dreamless sleep.

∞

When Sharon opened her eyes, a faint gray light came through the room's four windows. She heard pans clanking in the kitchen and gruff voices speaking low.

Throwing off the quilt, she padded to the pitcher and basin on the stand. The morning was pleasantly cool. The air felt thin. It was a welcome relief after the humidity in Missouri.

She came from her room, wearing a wrinkled housedress that she'd found lying near the top in one of her trunks. Shaking and smoothing the fabric had hardly loosened the deep-set creases.

Max stood at the dishpan next to the pitcher pump. "Well, Miss Sharon!" he exclaimed. Drying his hands on his apron, he lifted a clean plate from the stack beside him. "I saved you a steak and some biscuits." He forked them onto the plate. "Care for some milk? I can fetch some from the springhouse."

"That's not necessary," she said. "Do you have any coffee left?"

He chuckled. "We have coffee all day long. It's ranch house tradition." He set her plate on the table.

"I was hoping to meet the hands this morning," she said, looking across the long, bare table beside her. She pulled out the head chair and sat well away from its back.

"We serve breakfast at five o'clock," Max replied, filling two enamel cups with coffee. "The hands are usually on the range by six." He sat down near her.

"Six?" She picked up her fork. There were no napkins in sight, and she was too uncomfortable to ask for one. "I'll have to get up earlier. Would you mind knocking on my door when you come in to make breakfast?"

"At four o'clock in the morning?" he asked, surprised.

"I'd appreciate it, Max." She sipped the coffee. It was strong. "This whole situation makes me feel strange, like I'm walking around in a Dickens novel instead of real life. I came here expecting to meet my uncle. I was so looking forward to getting to know him. And now. . ."

Max nodded. "You're not the only one. We've all been wandering around here like lost boys. Even though we know that Rudolph's not coming back, we still keep waiting. That's the only way I can explain it. We're all still waiting. I wonder if we'll ever stop."

"I wanted to thank him," Sharon said. "For five long years, I've been waiting to thank him in person." She sipped her coffee.

He smiled with his lips and also with his eyes. "The best thanks you could ever give him is to take care of the ranch for him. He loved this place like most men love their wives. It was his whole life."

Setting down her coffee cup, she met his gaze. "That's exactly what I'm going to do." Her chin came up. "And one more thing, if someone hurt Uncle Rudolph, I'm going to find out about that, too."

He grinned. "Your teachers' reports showed you have spunk. Rudolph read them to me, and we chuckled over 'em." He leaned in. "If you need anything,

anything at all, call me and I'll come running."

From the head of the table, she could see into the far right section of the living room. The morning light revealed the dusty corners and the grimy windows.

Max turned to follow her line of sight. "I'm a cook, Miss Sharon, not a housekeeper. Mrs. Riordan used to come in to clean for Rudolph, but she's got arthritis. It got worse last Christmas, and she had to quit. He never got anyone else."

"The foreman's wife?" she asked.

"His mother," Max said. "His pa used to be foreman, and his ma worked in the house up until five years ago when she took sick. That's when I came to cook for him. After that, she came in once a week to clean. About six months ago she had to give that up, too." He shook his head regretfully. "Wonderful woman, Agnes Riordan. It's such a shame."

"Don't worry about the cleaning," Sharon told him, turning her attention to breakfast. "I grew up on a farm in Missouri until I was twelve. I can ride, plant, sew, scrub clothes, and clean. My father got the itch to go west, and that's how my parents and sister caught cholera. I didn't get to boarding school until I was thirteen." She smiled wryly. "I was gangly as a newborn colt when I got there. And I could never keep my hair out of my eyes."

She felt his gaze upon her perfectly coiled blond French twist and stifled the urge to run her hand across it. Poor Miss Rollings, her personal dresser, had worked with her for almost a year before Sharon could manage her hip-length tresses alone.

"What happened to Uncle Rudolph, Max?" she asked, moving the subject away from herself. "What do you think?"

His face darkened. "I haven't the first notion what happened to him. He was canny in the saddle, an old veteran. He'd raised his horse, Star, from a colt, had him for about fifteen years, and rode him almost every day. I can't see Star throwing Rudolph off, or even leaving him if he was hurt. But he did." He tapped his fingers on the table. "None of it makes a lick of sense."

They were silent for a moment, then Max said, "Rudolph used to joke about his Cattleman's Treasure when he was jawing with a group of men. He wouldn't say what it was, and that got some men riled."

"What was it?"

He sipped his coffee. "He never told anyone. That's the frustrating thing. Now, we may never know."

"Could it have been gold or silver, do you think?"

Max set down his cup. "If it was, he would have never admitted it. Remember what happened to poor Sutter in California? He lost everything."

A few minutes later, she set down her fork. "I'm sorry. It's delicious, but I can't finish it all."

He chuckled. "I'm used to feeding big cowboys, miss," he said. "Don't you worry about it." He stood and picked up her plate. "I'd best get started on lunch. I'm going to chip up the beef left from breakfast and make a thick stew."

Sharon took a last sip of coffee and set her cup on top of the enamel plate. "Thank you, Max." She smiled. "That was wonderful."

"You're welcome, miss."

"Sharon," she said, standing. "I'd rather you call me Sharon."

He grinned, showing her a row of thick teeth, then hurried back to his dishpan.

She returned to her room to start the tiresome job of unpacking. The bedroom contained a highboy with six drawers and a small chest with four. On the wall next to the door stood a narrow wardrobe with three more drawers and a fifteen-inch space for hanging clothes. Five pegs behind the door held two old hats and a worn leather gun belt holding a gleaming revolver.

She asked Max where she could find a mop, a broom, and some old rags, then began by giving the entire bedroom a good cleaning. By the time she was finished, the room was filled with light from its four sparkling windows. She threw them all open and let the wispy breeze clear out the last hint of dusty smell. She even swept out the fireplace.

Getting her things out of their trunks was another matter altogether. Uncle Rudolph had been very generous with her clothing allowance. Maybe too generous. She filled the drawers and then jammed her eight dresses and four crinolines into the wardrobe. The massive skirts competed for space and bulged out the front. This was an ironing disaster. Everything in there would stay constantly wrinkled.

Finally, she went back through everything to sort out what she really needed. Where was she going to wear all of this now? When Max jangled the triangle, calling for lunch, she had five gowns lying in a mound on the quilt. She dabbed at her hair with a brush to smooth the stray wisps before she went out. Closing the bedroom door carefully behind her, she joined the men.

Two of the hands were already seated at the table, but they immediately stood when she entered the room. Conversation died.

"Men, meet Miss Sharon Hastings," Jason Riordan said. He held the head chair for her, and she sat down.

Max stepped up, a large pot of stew in his hands. "She's been up since before six," he announced, as though he were proud.

Sharon felt like a prize calf at the county fair. "Please be seated," she said, trying to smile. Her heart was jumping in her throat. "I don't want you to stand on ceremony on my behalf."

"Let's get the names out of the way," Jason said. "This is Corky McCormick and his two boys, Roddy and Mike." The boys were in their early teens, she guessed. They both had dark auburn hair like their father. "They live on the back side of the range. Their third boy, Ian, had to stay at home and help his ma today." Roddy grinned at Sharon. Mike stared at the floor. Somewhere between thirty and forty years old, Corky was of medium height with craggy cheeks and dark, intense eyes. He had a deep crease going up from the bridge of his nose into his forehead.

"Howdy, miss," he said. When he shook Sharon's hand, his palm felt stiff.

Jason held out his hand toward the second cowboy who was taller and leaner than Corky. He was the same one who had brought her trunks home from town. "Wilson Gants," Jason said. "He lives in the bunkhouse with me and Max." Wilson's face was scrawny. He had thinning brown hair and a deep scar that showed through the thick stubble on his right cheek.

"Miss," he said, ducking his head. Quickly, he pressed her hand and glanced at her. He stepped back, then shied away from looking at her again.

The plank table was set for eight with blue enamel plates and coffee mugs, some tin and some enamel. Chairs scraped across the plank floor as they all took their places. The stew smelled meaty and rich.

"Jason," Sharon said, "would you offer thanks for the food?"

He didn't say anything in reply but bowed his head and offered a blessing over the food. His words were smooth and natural sounding, like he was used to saying them.

While they ate, Jason asked, "Will you need anything from me today?"

She set down her spoon. "Not today, Jason. Would you mind showing me over the range tomorrow?"

He hesitated. "You may have forgotten that tomorrow is Sunday," he said.

"Oh, that's right. I'm sorry. I'm all confused from so many days of traveling. Do you attend worship?"

He nodded. "My mother, my sister, and I are members of the Farmington Congregational Church. In weather like this, we usually take a buckboard to town. Too many people for the surrey."

"What time do you leave?"

"I usually leave here at seven o'clock," he said. "I stop by the cabin to fetch Ma and my sister, Lucy. Corky's family comes along."

"Would you mind if I join you?"

He grinned. "Not at all. My sister, Lucy, will be glad to meet you."

"I'm looking forward to meeting her and your mother, too," she said.

"On Monday, we can ride over the ranch if you'd like." His brow twisted and he stammered, "We—don't have a sidesaddle, miss—I mean, Sharon."

She let out a soft laugh. "I can ride, Jason, and I don't need a sidesaddle to do it."

She looked up to see six pairs of male eyes on her. Her cheeks felt like they were on fire. Swallowing a sip of coffee, she went on a bit louder. "So I won't have to repeat this over and over again, I want to tell you all a little about myself and what my plans are at the moment." She gazed at each man in turn. Wilson Gants and young Mike McCormick focused on their empty plates.

She told them where she grew up, then how she came to be an orphan and a ward of Uncle Rudolph. "This has been a shock to all of us, and I'm going to need your help for the next few weeks while I get my mind settled. You're all concerned with the future of the ranch and how my being here is going to affect things. I want to be very fair to all of you. I need some time to sort things out."

Picking up her spoon, Sharon paused. "I do have one request," she said. "Please don't call me *miss* or *ma'am*. While I was at school, we had to call everyone *miss* or *ma'am*—the teachers, the dorm mothers, the aides, and the cleaning ladies. I came to despise the terms. My name is Sharon, and I'd appreciate it if you'd address me that way."

Roddy nudged Mike, and the boys shared a secret smile.

Sharon noticed the move. Jason leaned toward her to whisper, "They think you talk funny. That's what they're grinning about."

"I suppose I must," she murmured. "As I recall, you think so, too."

His lips twitched. The next moment, he turned to speak to Corky on his other side.

On Sunday morning, the breakfast hour was moved back to six o'clock, but Sharon was out of bed well before then.

Wearing a dress of burgundy silk and white lace with a matching hat and parasol, Sharon stepped outside as Jason said, "Whoa," and pulled back on the reins to stop the wagon beside the porch. He wore a black suit with a black felt hat, a great change from his cowboy garb. The two-seater buckboard had wool blankets draped over both seats.

The instant Jason caught sight of her, his expression changed. That instant Sharon knew she had overdressed for the occasion. Why hadn't she worn the dark blue calico? At school, that would have been considered a day dress, but here it would have been perfect for Sunday meeting.

It was too late now. She'd spent more than an hour coaxing the wrinkles from this gown. The calico dress hung limply from a peg, still waiting for her attention.

Jason jumped down and came around to help her up. "Good morning," he said as he rounded the wagon.

Was that disapproval in his voice? She had a sudden urge to run back to her room and bolt the door. At school she'd always known exactly what to do. Here, she felt like a fish on a grassy bank, wriggling and its mouth gaping for water.

When Jason drew closer, his chilly smile disappeared and some other expression stilled his face. His eyes were gray and deep, surrounded by small lines from hours of squinting in the sun. He had a small scar on his left cheekbone. Two seconds and the moment passed. He helped her into the buckboard, and they set off.

"We'll have to stop for Ma and Lucy," he told her as he guided the horses around the curve in the driveway and through the gate. Today was already warmer than yesterday. The sun made the top of her head feel warm beneath her hat. She raised the parasol and let it rest against her shoulder.

"Do they live far from here?" she asked.

"On the eastern corner of the ranch," he replied. "We have a cabin near a stand of trees with a stream running through it. Corky's cabin is within sight of ours."

He went on. "A few years back, Rudolph deeded each family the ten acres surrounding our homes." He gazed at her. "He was a good man, Sharon."

"I wouldn't be here if he wasn't, Jason," she said softly. "He was very kind to me, generous and considerate. I only wish I could have known him, too."

"It would have been good for Rudolph to have met you," he said. "He tried to help a couple of young people and ended up being disappointed." He smiled at her. "But he wouldn't have been disappointed in you."

Chapter 3

Twenty minutes later, the Riordan cabin came into view. It was smaller than Uncle Rudolph's house, but it had a more steeply pitched roof. A stone fireplace almost covered one end of the building.

"When I became foreman two years ago, I moved into the bunkhouse," he told her. "Ma's arthritis flares up every now and then, so I still sleep here some nights to give Lucy a hand." He looped the reins over the whipstand and stepped to the ground.

The cabin door opened to reveal a slim girl wearing a blue gingham dress and a white cotton bonnet. She had dark hair and quick eyes. "Hello, Jason," she said, giving him a brief hug. "Mother is having a bad day. She said for us to go on without her."

Gazing intently through the cabin door, Jason asked, "Is she in bed?"

His sister nodded.

"I'll say hello to her before we go." He hurried inside, and Lucy moved toward the wagon.

Crossing a small field, Roddy and Mike McCormick ran toward the wagon. From their intent faces and long strides, they appeared to be racing.

Looking away from the boys, Sharon smiled at Jason's sister and said, "Good morning."

Lucy paused. "How do you do? I'm afraid Jason left without introducing us. I'm Lucy Riordan."

"It's good to meet you, Lucy. I'm so glad to meet someone my age."

She came closer. "I know. At least Ma and I can keep each other company. You've had to go it alone in the male world over there."

The McCormick boys scrambled in to the back of the buckboard, panting and arguing between breaths about who won. Lucy laughed at them. Sharon laughed, too.

"Have you met Roddy and Mike?" Lucy asked.

Sharon nodded. "Yes. Yesterday."

The next moment Jason dashed out and helped Lucy to the buckboard seat between him and Sharon.

Corky and his missus arrived at a more sedate pace and took the second seat. He introduced Sharon to Mrs. McCormick, a small woman with a shy demeanor. As the buckboard lurched forward, she turned and shushed the boys from their wrangling. Immediately, they went silent.

Lucy was a lively girl with a sparkle in her eye. "What do you do for fun?" she asked Sharon.

"Fun?" Sharon tried to find a quick answer but came up blank.

"What do you like to do? Grow things? Cook? Sew?" Lucy smiled. "I quilt, and I draw." She grimaced. "Not that I'm any kind of an artist." She plucked at Jason's coat sleeve. "My big brother buys me paper."

He grinned at her, a softness on his face and in his eyes.

"I like to paint with watercolors," Sharon announced with great relief. "I have a set of paints. You must come and see them."

"Watercolors!" Lucy gasped. "I've never actually seen a set. Could I come this afternoon?"

Jason sent her a warning look. "Lucy—"

"That would be wonderful," Sharon interrupted before he could squelch the idea. "I'd love for you to come."

Lucy's smile faded. "I may have to stay with Ma. She was hurting something awful this morning. The pain seems to be worse when she's alone."

"I'll stay with her this afternoon," Jason said. "I'll read to her. She likes that."

"You're a dear!" Lucy leaned against him in a kind of sideways hug.

Jason turned to ask Corky a question about the ranch, and Lucy kept Sharon busy with questions about boarding school for the rest of the trip.

The church was a whitewashed stucco structure. Inside was a double column of wooden benches with low backs on them and a platform at the front that rose about a foot from the floor. The pulpit was a square, slanted board on top of a single post attached to the platform.

Sharon sat wedged between Lucy and a blond-haired young man. Lucy briefly introduced him as Timothy Ingles.

"Glad to know you, Miss Hastings," he said. About Sharon's age, he had wide-set blue eyes and a friendly, boyish mouth. "I believe I saw you the day you arrived."

"Do you work at the general store?" Sharon asked. When he nodded, she said, "Yes. I do remember you. You were standing outside the store when I first got here."

He blushed and suddenly seemed about twelve years old.

Looking toward the front, Lucy held her finger to her lips. The song leader had come to the pulpit to begin the service. Everyone in the pews had his or her own copy of the hymnbook. Sharon shared with Lucy.

Rev. Nelson looked like he could have been a cowboy at one time; he was muscular and tall with a full, dark beard. He had a voice that came from deep within his massive chest and a powerful message that came from deep within his soul. Sharon lost track of time. She had received Christ as a child of six. The boarding school was a Christian establishment, but it was Christian only in form and rules. The daily chapel sessions were dry and boring, and church was a time to sit next to her best friend, Candace, and study the clothes of everyone in attendance for later discussion.

This service was much different. There was life in the message and power in the Word like she hadn't felt for years. After the service, she shook the preacher's hand. "Thank you for that message," she said.

He smiled. "Welcome to Farmington, Miss Hastings," he said. "I trust you will find it a blessing."

"It already has been," she told him.

Lucy stayed beside Sharon, making introductions so fast that Sharon's mind reeled.

A man not much more than Sharon's height of five feet six paused near the girls. What he lacked in height, he surpassed in width.

"This is Jim Boswell," Lucy said. "He's the local blacksmith."

The stout man shook her hand and smiled with his pudgy, wet mouth. "I'm delighted to meet you, Miss Hastings." He ended the sentence with a short wheeze. "I blacksmith for the Lazy H from time to time." He had an anxious look on his face. He wheezed again and his thick neck convulsed as he swallowed. "I—I was wondering—if it would be agreeable to you if I were to come and call on you next Saturday."

Sharon blinked. She'd never had a man ask to call on her before. What should she say? Wanting to say no but not sure how, she said, "I would be honored, Mr. Boswell. Would three o'clock be a good time for you?"

His head bobbed. "Thank you, Miss Hastings." He backed away for two steps, then turned and headed for the wagons.

Lucy giggled. "I think you've made a conquest already," she said.

Sharon sent her an alarmed look.

Lucy went on, "Oh, there's my friend, Julia. You've got to meet her." She hurried away. Sharon followed, but at a sedate walk, according to Mrs. Minniver's Rule 10.

By the time they reached the buckboard, Sharon had a throbbing headache. The sun made her dress feel sticky. She found it hard to breathe.

They set off at a brisk pace. The breeze felt so refreshing. Lucy untied her bonnet and took it off to let the wind blow in her dark hair. Sharon wished she could do the same, but she couldn't force herself to ignore Rule 9.

SHARON TAKES A HAND

After saying good-bye to the McCormick family and Jason, Lucy drove the buckboard to the ranch house. What a relief to step out of the sun.

After getting drinks for both of them from the pump in the kitchen, Sharon said, "If you don't mind, I'm going to get out of this hot dress. I'm about to suffocate."

Lucy laughed. "Of course. I don't know how you can take this heat, wearing silk."

Heading for her room, Sharon paused to say, "This will be the last time you see me in anything but cotton for a long time, I promise you."

A few minutes later, she rejoined Lucy at the dining room table. Max had left several bowls of food in the center of the table, covered by a large towel. On Sunday mornings, he cooked all of the food for that day so he could have a half day off. Today, he'd prepared a large pot containing potatoes, green beans, and pork. It didn't look like much, but it tasted great.

After the meal, Sharon brought her paints and sketchbooks to the table. Lucy sat speechless as Sharon showed them to her.

"You are an artist," Lucy breathed, staring wide-eyed at a painting of a puppy playing with an old shoe.

"That's a copy of a painting my teacher set up for us in the art room," Sharon said. "I copied the light and shadows from the other artist, so it's not really that good."

"That may be so, but it looks almost real. You should frame it and hang it up."

Sharon shrugged. "Maybe someday. Right now, I'm still trying to decide if I want to stay on here or sell the ranch to someone who can run it better than I can."

Lucy looked up, horrified. "Sell the ranch?" She reached out to clutch Sharon's hand. "You mustn't, Sharon. You mustn't."

Sharon became alarmed. "Why not, Lucy?"

"If you sell, Jason may lose his job. Who would support me and Ma? And what about Corky and his family? Where would they go?"

"Do you think that would happen?" Sharon asked, dismayed. "Why wouldn't they stay on and work for the new owner?"

"When the Widow Braddock sold her ranch, the new owner brought in his own crew. Everyone down to the cook had to find a new job. They all ended up going to Texas. My best friend, Sally, was the foreman's daughter."

"Lucy, I'm so sorry!" Sharon told her about Candace Matthews and how much she missed her best friend.

"I knew we were kindred spirits," Lucy declared when Sharon had finished. "I knew it right away."

Sharon laughed. "I've been here for two days now, and I haven't been to the barn. Would you mind walking out with me?" she asked. "I want to look at the horses."

"So do I," Lucy said. "When we were kids, Jason and I used to hang around the stables almost every day, but lately I haven't had any time."

They strolled outside and entered the wide barn. It was dim and cool inside with the smell of cattle and straw pervading the massive structure. A long row of stalls ran its length. They were all empty.

Hearing faint mews, Sharon went for a closer look. In a corner of one stall, a black cat lay nursing four medium-size kittens.

"Aren't they cute!" she exclaimed.

"Be careful about touching them," Lucy warned. "Their mother isn't too friendly. She's a barn cat with long claws. I speak from experience." She moved to the half door in the back. "You can see the horses from here."

Sharon left the kittens and joined her.

Ten horses, mostly mustangs, browsed the grass or stood head to tail with a friend, swishing flies off each other.

Lucy named them off, ending with, "Maribell is the little black. She's going to foal any day."

"I can't wait to ride," Sharon told her. "It seems like forever since I've been in a real saddle in the open pasture."

"We should go riding sometime," Lucy said, smiling widely.

"Let me know when you are free and we'll go," Sharon promised.

They lingered for a few more minutes, then Lucy said, "We need to check the time. I can't be away too long with Ma so poorly today."

As they entered the house, the thirty-day clock on the mantel shelf chimed three times.

"I'd best get back to the house," Lucy said regretfully. "I put hot compresses on Ma's knees when she's hurting bad. She may need me."

"How about if I walk home with you? We can talk on the way." Sharon hurried to fetch her cotton sunbonnet and they set off.

As they meandered down the narrow dirt road, Sharon said, "When can you come back for another visit, Lucy?"

"How about if you take Sunday dinner with us next week?"

"Won't that be too much trouble for you?" Sharon asked. "You've got a lot on you, Lucy. I don't want to add to it."

"Oh, no," Lucy said. "I always get up early to cook. Jason usually stays for dinner after church, too." She swung her bonnet against her side. "Besides, Ma has a hankering to meet you. She was the one who made Rudolph give you an allowance, you know."

"She was?"

Lucy nodded, smiling as though she were telling a deep secret. "When Rudolph got word about the deaths in your family and your being orphaned and all, he was in a dither. He had no wife and no one to take care of a little girl. So, he talked to Ma about it. She told him what to do and how much money to send you, too." She laughed, delighted. "Later, Ma told us that she'd picked a number and then doubled it, to be sure you'd be taken care of proper. She couldn't stand to think that a poor little girl would be left with nothing and no one, all alone in a boarding school."

"This is the first I've ever heard of that," Sharon said. "I owe your mother more than I can say. Uncle Rudolph was very generous to me, and I'm so grateful. I wish I could have known him."

"He was a crusty old codger," Lucy said, "but underneath he was pure gold. He truly tried to help people be better than they were."

Sharon let a few paces pass in silence, then said, "Your brother seems kind of sad or troubled, Lucy. Is he always like that?"

She nodded. "He's been that way ever since Pa died." She shrugged. "Well, not all the time. He does laugh sometimes, but it's always with a little bit of sadness in it. You know what I mean? He worries about Ma. Since Rudolph's been gone, Jason's been full of worries. He's been sick with wondering what happened to Rudolph. And now he's got to run the ranch, take care of me and Ma, and wonder what to do if we have to leave the Lazy H. It's too much for a man who's barely twenty-five."

Sharon didn't reply. Watching the path ahead, she put one foot in front of the other. Would the Riordans and McCormicks have to leave? Would she?

Chapter 4

A few minutes later, Sharon said good-bye to Lucy without going inside the Riordan's cabin. If Mrs. Riordan was in that much pain, Sharon didn't want to disturb her.

Still thinking about their conversation, she headed back down the trail. What an interesting girl Lucy was. They were going to be close friends. She knew it.

Jason caught up to Sharon before she reached the edge of the Riordan's yard. "Mind if I walk with you?" he asked, swinging his black broadcloth coat over his shoulder.

"Not at all." She kept her pace the same, not hurrying but moving along at a good clip.

They walked in silence for a while. Jason Riordan was evidently a man of few words. She may as well get used to it.

Finally, Sharon summoned up enough courage to say, "Jason, I want you to know something."

He turned toward her but didn't reply.

Something held her back. She couldn't say what she really wanted to tell him—that she didn't want to do anything that would force his family to leave the ranch. Finally, she went on, "I'm going to need your help, Jason. I want to learn as much as I can about every detail of this place. You're the one to teach me."

He stopped and turned back. She glanced at him, wondering what he was doing.

"The Colorado line is about fifteen miles straight north," he said, pointing. "See the mountains?"

Self-conscious, she turned to gaze at them, jagged and dark in the distance. "I came through them on the train."

In a moment, they continued down the path, and he went on: "East and south are more of the same thing you see here—brush and grass and scattered trees. Five miles beyond our south fence line is the San Juan River."

He pointed west. "Over there's the water hole. Beyond that, the grass turns to scrub brush and the trees disappear. It's the edge of the desert, the home of the Navajo."

"Indians?"

He nodded. "Good people. All they're worried about is growing corn and weaving blankets. Totally different from their Texas cousins."

She breathed deeply of the clear air. "I really like it here," she said. "It's so peaceful."

Scanning the horizon, he murmured, "We all do. . .we all do."

When they reached the house, he dipped his head and tugged the brim of his hat. "Good afternoon, Sharon," he said. "We'll ride out after breakfast." He strode toward the bunkhouse without looking back.

Sharon slowly untied her bonnet strings as she trudged inside. Did he naturally dislike her? No matter what she said or what he replied, she felt like she was on trial. She wished she could have Max take her to see the ranch. He was much nicer than Jason Riordan.

The sky was a faded blue gray when Jason and Sharon mounted up the next morning. Jason had brought her a roan mare named Springtime. The horse was sweet and gentle, the perfect mount for a lady.

Dressed in a wide split skirt that fell in deep folds around her in the saddle, Sharon was thrilled to be on horseback. She gripped the reins and squeezed with her knees. As her horse cantered neck and neck with Jason's gelding, Sharon couldn't stop an exhilarated laugh.

"We'll ride the fence line to start out," he said when they pulled up. "Then I'll take you to the water hole. That's all we'll have time for before lunch."

"Next time, bring me a horse with more spirit," she told him. "I grew up helping my father train horses, and I like them lively." She patted the mare's neck. "Which way?"

He nodded east. "That's the closest boundary to the house. We'll start there."

She didn't wait for him to say more. She urged the mare to a faster pace than before and didn't slow down until silvery barbed wire glinted ahead of her.

Laughing from sheer joy, she tried to catch her breath. Jason was grinning like an impudent schoolboy, but he didn't say anything. He dealt out words like they were silver dollars.

Walking the horses along the fence for a few minutes to let them cool off, Jason and Sharon rode apart. Sharon let her eyes feast on the vastness of the land surrounding her. There wasn't a man-made structure as far as she could see. The wind rustled through a small grove of desert willows. It lifted the brim of her bonnet and cooled her face.

This section of the land was grassy and rolling with small groves of trees here and there. Longhorns grazed in the distance.

"There's a stream up ahead that goes behind Ma's cabin," Jason said. "It's a fork off the big creek that comes down from the north. The main creek continues southwest and just about splits the ranch in half."

The stream was narrow, but its banks were four feet high in some places. Now and then a stretch of bank had been dug down, so cattle could drink from it.

For half an hour they followed the stream northwest until it joined a wider body of water flowing south.

"Our fence line is about three hundred yards north of this fork," Jason told her. "If we followed the fence on around to the west, we'd pass through the edge of the desert. That side meets the Navajo Reservation. Fall is the best time to go over there. It's much too hot and dry this time of year."

"I'm trying to comprehend how big this place is," she said, straining to see far into the distance. "How can three men handle all of this land?"

"We hire extra hands for roundup and the cattle drive, the busiest time of the year," he said. "Otherwise, we're doing maintenance, and three men can handle it. Corky's boys take care of the barn, mucking out the stalls and all."

She studied him. "I've heard of a roundup, but I've never understood how it works."

He spent the next ten minutes explaining the process of gathering the herd, branding the calves, and moving the yearlings to the railroad where they could be sold. "We usually manage to make enough from the cattle drive to finance the rest of the year."

"And if we don't?" Sharon asked.

"Rudolph has a long-standing account at the Farmington National Bank. If we run short, he goes in and adds a little to the mortgage to tide us over. If we have extra, he goes in and pays some of it off. Every once in a while, he'll sell some of the breeding stock and buy new blood to keep the herd strong. We usually make a little extra doing that, too."

"How much is the mortgage?"

He shook his head. "That's something you'll have to find out at the bank. I have no idea."

She said, "He paid for my schooling and sent me a generous allowance even when he was short here? Why would he do that for a child he'd never met?"

Jason's eyes narrowed. "You never met him?"

"He moved to New Mexico before I was born. My parents exchanged letters with him, but I never saw him myself."

"Were he and your father close?"

She nodded. "They were two years apart. Uncle Rudolph was older, and he always took care of my father. A few times he sent us money to help us out of a tough spot. Pa never said much about money, but once I heard him talking to Mama about it after I was in bed.

"Pa practically worshiped Uncle Rudolph. From what Mama said, he was pretty lost when Rudolph decided to go west."

"Why didn't your father come here to join his brother instead of heading to Oregon?"

She slowly shook her head. "I'm not sure, Jason. My folks didn't tell me much about what they had in mind. I was only thirteen at the time."

They topped a rise and an oval-shaped pond came into view. The ground around it was hard packed; there was little grass anywhere around.

"This is the famous Lazy H water hole," he said with a touch of pride in his voice. "It's a little over four feet deep at the center and about fifty feet across. One of the first things Rudolph did when he came to these parts was to dig it out, so it would hold more water and last through the dry months."

"You grew up here, didn't you?"

He nodded. "Do you want to walk a little?"

She swung down with no help from him. Looping the ends of the reins over their pommels, they let the horses drink.

As though the conversation had never paused, Jason said, "My parents were married after my pa had worked here about two years. I grew up running all over this range, like Corky's boys do now. Rudolph was like a second father to me."

"Like an uncle?" she asked.

He glanced at her. "I reckon that's right."

"That's ironic. He was my uncle in blood but your uncle in fact."

"He was a godly man, Sharon. He loved God, and he tried to help people. I think that's why his life was so blessed."

"You're a believer?" she asked.

"I accepted the Lord when I was fifteen." His lips twisted into a wry grin. "I was a bounder before that. It was Rudolph who took me aside and told me I was headed for a bad end." He took off his hat and tapped it against the side of his leg. "He was right."

"I was saved when I was six," Sharon said, "but since my parents died, I haven't thought about it much. The boarding school was a Christian institution run by two sisters: Miss Oliver and Mrs. Minniver. But they didn't emphasize religion much. We had morning prayers and went to church, but that was all. I used to pray before I went to sleep that God would bless Uncle Rudolph and help the days fly past until I could come and live with him here."

"God did bless him," Jason said. "You weren't the only one he helped, either. He set up Timothy Ingles's father, Zach, in the Farmington General Store and helped him run it until Zach got his feet under him." He kicked at a clump of scrub grass. "Ingles had been in trouble with the law sometime back, but Rudolph saw something in the man."

"I wish I could have known my uncle," Sharon murmured. "If not for him, I'd have gone to an orphanage. Now I can't even thank him."

"If he saw how you'd turned out, that would be thanks enough," Jason said. His face still had that guarded expression, but his eyes were alive. "Don't worry about the ranch. I'll carry the load for you, Sharon. I give you my word on that."

She put out her hand to shake his. "Thank you, Jason. I'm going to depend on that."

He seemed to forget that he still held her gloved hand as he stared at the darkening sky. "There's gonna be a gully washer," he said. "They come up fast in these parts. We'd best head for home." He whistled. Both horses lifted their heads and came toward him.

They rushed for their saddles. He held his hands together to give Sharon a leg up, then mounted his own horse.

"Who's your horse trainer?" Sharon called to him. "He knows his business."

"Max."

"Max?"

He chuckled. "When he's not slinging hash, he's in the corral. Didn't he tell you that?" He laughed at her shocked reaction. At that moment, a cold wind swept across the range. The soft, deep sigh of thunder spurred them to a gallop.

Ten minutes later, the first fat drops splattered on the mare's neck. With a whoop, Jason veered onto a wide trail. Sharon kept the mare at full gallop to keep pace with his gelding.

When the torrent broke loose, Jason reined in a little to let her come up beside him. "Do you want to find shelter?" he hollered.

"How far are we from home?" She blinked to see him through the hazy cloud of falling water. Her chin was dripping.

"It's another twenty minutes if we keep moving."

"Let's keep on going!" she called. "Why be miserable longer than we have to be?"

He leaned over the horse's neck and let out another whoop. The gelding raced down the trail. The mare did her best to keep up, but she was no match for Jason's horse.

Sharon tucked her chin down, so the rain would fall away from her face. Cold, damp fingers trickled down her spine. Her shoulders hunched against the chill. She tried not to shiver. Her bonnet brim hung limply before her eyes.

Trusting her mount to find the way home, she simply held on and prayed for the ride to be over.

They heard the call for lunch as they rode into the yard. Jason grabbed her horse's reins and guided the mare to the edge of the porch so Sharon could dismount directly to its high floor.

Max stood near the triangle at the corner of the porch. He hurried toward her. "I'll fetch you some towels!" he called and trotted inside. He met her at the door with five of them.

Peeling off her bonnet, she let it drop to the porch floor and wrapped her head in one of the towels. Blotting her face, she took the other towels and hustled into her room to peel off her sodden clothes.

Was there anything more miserable? How could one be soaking wet and yet feel so filthy?

Shivering, she took a few minutes to sponge off in the basin. Then she loosened her blond hair and combed it out. If she wanted to join the men for lunch, she'd have to go out there with a wet head. There was nothing she could do about it besides have Max bring her a plate in her room. The last thing she wanted was to act like a prima donna before the men.

She stared at herself in the mirror. Did it really matter that much? "Mrs. Minniver is in Springfield, you goose. You're home." Her chin quivered as she spoke. "Stop acting like she's still your headmistress." With shaking hands, she pulled her hair to the front and wove a loose braid that came over her shoulder. She got into a thick dress of blue twill and found some wool socks. It was June, and she'd probably regret the warm clothes ten minutes after putting them on, but she was freezing now, and that's all that mattered.

When Sharon reached the table, the men were already eating.

"Don't get up," she told them, taking her seat. "Max, could I have some hot coffee?"

"You look chilled to the bone, child," he said, handing her a steaming cup. "It's not that cold out, is it? It's pretty warm inside today."

Sipping, she nodded. "I'll be okay once I warm up. We were riding fast and getting wet at the same time. That's what got me chilled." She breathed in the warmth spiraling up from her mug. Sipping again, she felt the hot liquid soothing her inside.

Max filled her plate with stew and placed a biscuit on the rim.

Wilson finished the last of his stew with a large mouthful and stood. "Jason'll need a hand with those ho'ses," he said. Striding to a row of pegs beside the door, he lifted his tattered gray Stetson and ducked out into the weather.

"Where did you ride?" Max asked, taking his seat.

"We went around the fence line behind the cabins and then over to the water hole. When it started pouring, we headed home." She put down her spoon. "I can't get over how big the ranch is. It's enormous."

Corky chuckled. "Pardon my saying so, but you only saw half of it, maybe less."

Sharon looked up to see the third McCormick boy sitting next to his father with his brothers lined up beside him. He was smaller and darker than his brothers. "Hello," she said to the boy. "We haven't met yet, have we?"

He shook his head.

Corky gave him an elbow in the ribs.

"No, miss," the boy said, his cheeks pink.

"This is Ian," Corky said. "He's thirteen."

The boy's freckled face turned brilliant red, and he bent his head down. Roddy snickered.

Corky chuckled.

The door opened, and Jason strode inside wearing a dripping yellow slicker. He hung it on a peg and topped it with his hat. His shirt looked fresh, but his jeans and boots were still wet. He ran his hands along the sides of his head, smoothing his wet hair away from his face.

"Thanks, Max," he said, dropping to a seat as the little man handed him a cup of coffee. "That rain'll chill you clean through." He glanced at Sharon. "Are you all right?"

Sipping coffee, she nodded. "Now I am."

He drank some black coffee, then dug into the stew.

"The boys and I will clean the tack room this afternoon," Corky said.

Chewing a biscuit, Jason nodded, then swallowed. "Knock off whenever there's a break in the rain," he said. "The sky's so dark it may rain all night. If you wake up to rain in the morning, take the day off."

Jason finished his meal without saying anything more to her. After the others had left the table, they still sat in silence.

"Thank you for taking me out today," she said finally.

"That's what I'm here for," he said, glancing in her general direction. "We'll ride south when there's a good day for it. Not as much to see that way, though." He drained his cup and stood. "Max, I think the little mustang mare is going to foal any time."

Max left the dishpan and buried his wet hands in his apron. He turned away for a second to cough. Clearing his throat, he nodded. "I'll come out and take a look at her when I get a chance," he said.

Jason nodded. He gave Sharon a casual two-fingered salute as he headed for the door.

Sharon dragged off to her room. Her riding clothes lay in a puddle on the floor. Throwing her wash water out the window, she gathered the wet clothes into a ball and plopped them into the basin. There would be time to deal with those later. At this moment, she had to get under the quilt and rest her eyes. She pulled off the twill dress and slid into her cotton nightgown.

The sheets welcomed her. The down pillow cradled her head. Yet, strangely, the rest she craved slipped out of her reach. Why had Jason ignored her at lunch? They'd had such a good talk at the water hole.

Jason Riordan was a fine man. She was blessed to have him as foreman. She could see that clearly. But he was so distant, so guarded most of the time. Why didn't he like her?

Outside the house, a big cowboy wearing a yellow slicker stood on the edge of the porch and gazed across the yard. He ought to get to the bunkhouse and change into dry clothes. His mother would have a conniption if she knew he was standing here in wet jeans and soaked boots.

He stood there, unmoving, staring at the silvery curtain surrounding the house. It sometimes moved with the breeze and doused him with spray. He didn't feel the wind or the damp. All he could see were cheeks like fine china, green eyes with a spark like flint on stone, and those soft, quivering lips against the coffee cup. If only she hadn't taken down her blond hair. If she hadn't done that, he would have been all right.

Drawing in a long breath, he adjusted his hat and stepped into the rain.

Chapter 5

Late Friday evening, everyone was on the front porch, enjoying the first cooling breezes of the sweltering day. Sharon and Max sat on the bench, Jason on a chair brought from the kitchen, and Wilson on the step.

"Did you see this?" Wilson asked no one in particular. "The bottom step is loose." He wiggled it with his foot. "Looks like it's fixing to split down the middle." He bent over to tug on it. "We can't have that. I'll have to fix it next chanc't I get."

Jason said, "The parson called on Ma and Lucy this afternoon. They're having a prayer meeting at the church on Saturday night." He looked around. "Anyone else want to go?"

Sharon felt a squeezing in her chest, that awful feeling that she was forgetting something. She knew she had something to do on Saturday. What was it?

"Not me," Wilson drawled. "The Almighty would be shocked to see me after all these years."

"I don't have anything better to do," Max said. "I'll come along."

Jason turned to Sharon.

"What time would we leave?" she asked.

"Five o'clock, I reckon."

Sharon felt a jolt. Jim Boswell was coming to call at three o'clock. She stifled a relieved laugh. That meant he'd only stay for two hours. She could deal with him for that long, surely.

"Is Lucy going to the prayer meeting?" she asked.

"Lucy and Ma, too, as long as she's up to it."

"Good." She turned to Max. "I think I'll bake some molasses cookies in the morning. Jim Boswell is coming out tomorrow afternoon."

Wilson came alert. "Is he now? Maribell has a shoe that needs to be checked."

Jason let out a hoot. "Sorry, Wilson. Blacksmithing is gonna be the last thing on his mind."

Wilson looked confused.

Sharon's face was on fire. She stood, said good night, and made a hasty escape. The laughter of the three men followed her into the house.

~

And their smiling didn't stop there. It lasted through Saturday's breakfast and got worse at lunch.

Clearing the table, Sharon asked Max, "Why is Jim Boswell's visit such a joke?"

Max chuckled. "You really don't know, do you?" When she shook her head, he went on, "You're way above his league, Sharon. Why on earth did you agree to see him?"

Sharon stiffened. "He came up to me after church last Sunday. He was so nervous that I felt sorry for him. I couldn't think of a way to say no without seeming rude." She let out a moan. "How did I get myself into this? We can't go riding because we're going to be leaving for church at five. What are we going to do while he's here?"

Max's thick teeth gleamed. "Feed him cookies. He'll stay as happy as a goose in a corncrib."

As soon as Max had cleared away the lunch dishes, Sharon mixed a triple batch of molasses cookies. Whatever Jim left, the men would clear up in short order.

When Jim arrived, she was wearing a dress of pink gingham and a fresh white apron. Pressed and polished in a white shirt, he had on a black string tie, pressed pants, and gleaming boots. His face glowed from a recent scrubbing.

"Good afternoon, Miss Sharon," he said when she answered the door.

"Hello, Jim. Won't you come in?"

He stood uncertainly just inside the door, his felt hat in his thickly calloused hands.

Sharon smiled in his direction. "May I take your hat?" she asked, then hung it on a peg. "The house is too warm this time of day. I set some chairs outside the back door in the shade." She led the way through the kitchen and down the back step.

The wide limbs of a cottonwood tree made a perfect shady spot for their visit, especially because it was out of range of the prying eyes of the smirking ranch hands.

At least Jim Boswell knew how to hold polite conversation. They talked of local news, that evening's prayer meeting, and Jim's work while he munched cookies and drank buttermilk.

"Have you ever heard of the Cattleman's Treasure?" he asked her.

"I heard someone mention it."

He reached for another cookie. "It's a legend, or a myth, or something in these parts. No one knows what it is, but it's supposed to be on this ranch somewhere."

"As far as I know, Uncle Rudolph never told anyone what it was. We'll probably never know."

Finally, Max came to the back door. "Jason's bringing up the buckboard," he said. He coughed and tapped his chest. "He'll be here in a few minutes."

Sharon tried to hide her relief. "Thank you, Max. We'll be right there."

She walked with Jim through the house to the front porch. The afternoon sun shone into the porch and made her blink. Off to the left, a fly buzzed. Corky's boys played catch under the shade of the giant cottonwood in the front yard.

"Thank you for a pleasant afternoon," Jim said, beaming at her. "I hope I can call again sometime."

"Thank you for coming," Sharon replied, careful not to commit herself this time. She handed him his hat, and he headed down the stairs.

Suddenly, his arms flew out, and his hat went flying. He let out a loud cry and tumbled forward. His shiny boots came up and his shiny face hit the ground. Rolling over twice, he came to a stop in the driveway.

The boys roared with laughter. Ian threw himself on the ground while Roddy and Mike reared their heads and howled.

Her heart pounding, Sharon started down the steps toward Jim until Max cried, "Look out!" and she drew up short.

The bottom step wasn't broken or loose anymore. It was gone.

At that moment, Wilson came out of the barn at a trot with a weathered piece of wood in his hands. He was in such a hurry that he stepped on a kitten's tail. With a snarl, the cat streaked into the safety of the barn.

Sharon raised her skirts a little and stepped gingerly to the ground.

"Jim!" she cried when she finally reached him. "Are you all right?"

Muttering, he slowly got to his feet. His face was the color of an old brick. His eyebrows drew down until his eyes almost disappeared. "Who was the stupid. . ." He let off a string of words that made Sharon gasp.

Wilson reached them as Jim ran out of breath. The cowhand held up the plank in his hands. "I took the step to the barn to add some support," he said, turning it over. On the bottom was a neat strip of new wood across the middle. "I'm sorry, hombre," he said to Jim. He gave the blacksmith a hand up. "No harm done?" He turned toward the still-hooting boys and gave them a sign to cut it out.

Sharon turned to stare at Max. "You just came up those steps, didn't you?"

He held his hands up, palms out. "I stopped to take care of something in the kitchen and plumb forgot to tell him." He looked at Jim. "My apologies, Boswell," he said.

Sharon turned to look Wilson in the eye. The cowhand was all sober-faced concern.

Ignoring them all, Jim turned his attention toward beating his dusty clothes. Finally, he picked up his hat, gave Sharon a nod, and headed for his horse where it was ground-hitched under the tree.

At that moment, Jason and Corky pulled up in the buckboard and Max climbed aboard. Wilson helped Sharon up and stood back as the McCormick boys scrambled over the tailgate. No one spoke a word until Boswell's horse disappeared in a cloud of dust.

Roddy started with a little giggle, followed by Ian's chuckle. The next moment, every male in the wagon was guffawing and slapping each other.

"Did you men cook that up to embarrass me?" she demanded. "What were you thinking of? Jim could have been hurt."

Max took a breath to say, "Only his pride, Sharon. And he's got plenty of that to spare." He slapped his knee and laughed again, ending with a coughing spell.

Sharon tried to squelch her smile, but her lips wouldn't cooperate. Several times after the prayer meeting had ended that evening, she had to chuckle to herself. Those men seemed tough and hard, but they were nothing but big boys.

Shortly after dark, a cool wind came up, followed by a thunderstorm that shook the house. Alone in the house, Sharon stood by the window and watched lightning streak across the black sky, thrilled at the glory of it. She stayed there until it stopped, then went to bed and fell into a dreamless sleep.

The next morning, Sharon came out of her room to find Jason in the kitchen, looking in the cabinets. He'd already built a fire in the cookstove.

He paused when he saw her. "Max's sick," he said. "He's burning up with fever and shaking with chills by spells." He lifted a yellow crockery bowl of day-old biscuits and set it on the counter. "He was up most of the night with Maribell in foal and got soaked to the hide, going back and forth to the barn." Jason's eyes had dark rings around them like he hadn't slept much either.

"It's still raining," he went on. "Lucy usually helps out at times like this, but she can't get here in the rain." He shrugged. "It's just as well. Ma's arthritis is awful bad in this weather. It'll only be you, me, and Wilson to meals. Corky's staying at home today."

Sharon rolled up her sleeves. "I'm not much of a cook," she said, stepping forward, "but I think I can get us through breakfast if we have any eggs."

He turned full circle and spotted a basket of eggs in the corner. "Max keeps ten chickens in a coop out back."

"Max is a marvel," Sharon said, reaching for the basket. "Could you fetch me some milk?"

"The springhouse," he said. He disappeared out the back door and was soon back with a jar of milk. He lifted the lid and sniffed. "It smells a little sour."

"I can still use it."

He stood in the center of the room, arms at his sides, with an uncertain look on his face.

"You don't have to watch over me," she told him, whipping milk into the eggs with a fork. "I can manage."

He looked relieved. "I've got chores in the barn," he said and headed for the door.

Sharon dumped out the old coffee grounds and rinsed the pot. She wasn't sure how much coffee to use, so she guessed. She found some brown paper, dampened it, and wrapped up the hardened biscuits left from yesterday's lunch.

By the time the hands arrived twenty minutes later, the omelets were ready, and the biscuits were soft and warm. The coffee, however, was lukewarm and weak as dishwater. Only Jason drank it.

As the men were leaving, Sharon said, "Jason, is there anything I can do for Max? Maybe we ought to bring him into the house where I can look after him."

"He's too sick to be moved in this rain," Jason replied, standing. "I wish the doc was handy. He's mighty bad."

"I'll go and take a look at him. At least I can make him more comfortable." She pushed back from the table. "Will you take me to him?"

"Of course. Let me go out and make sure he's awake and decent," he said. "I'll come and fetch you when he's ready for you to come in." He shrugged into his slicker and pulled the hood over his Stetson. The next moment he closed the door behind him.

Sharon washed the dishes while she waited. She dug around in the kitchen cabinet next to the back door and found some tonic, powdered mustard, and a small tin of black tea. That was all there was of any medicinal value whatsoever.

Whispering a prayer for guidance, she fetched her wool cape from her room and laid it across the back of the couch where it would be handy when Jason returned.

What would they eat for lunch and supper? How she wished the rain would stop so Lucy could come. Maybe she could ask Max for advice if he wasn't too sick to talk to her.

Spooning tea into a pint jug, she added hot water from the reservoir in the cookstove. At least she could take him some tea. Sick people needed plenty to drink.

She found a sack of rice beneath the counter. If she set on some beef to stew and made a gravy for it, they could eat beef and rice. She could manage that. They might be eating beef and rice for the next two or three days if it kept on raining. She didn't even know how to make johnnycake or biscuits. Bread was out of the question. Why hadn't she stuck closer to Mama in the kitchen instead of running out to the stable to help Pa with the horses?

Jason came in as she was measuring rice into a bowl. Two cups should be enough.

"Can you fetch me some beef?" she asked him. "Where does Max keep it?"

"There's a smokehouse out back," he told her. "I'll get you some." Lifting a metal basin from the counter, he stepped through the back door and returned in five minutes with a shapeless hunk of meat.

Setting it on the counter, he said, "Max says he doesn't want you to worry over him. He said he'll be all right in a couple of days."

"What about you?" she asked. "Do you think he'll be all right in a couple of days?"

He shook his head doubtfully. "I'm no doctor, but he looks bad to me."

"If he's that sick, he won't be able to make too much of a fuss about my coming out to see him then," she said. "If you'll lead the way, I'll come after you." She added two spoonfuls of sugar to the jug and strained the results into another small jar. Lifting a tin cup from a shelf, she turned it upside down over the top of the jar and wrapped the whole thing in a dish towel.

"Is that for him?" Jason asked. When she nodded, he picked it up.

Wrapping herself in the cape, she huddled down and ducked her head to hide under its hood. She followed Jason by watching his boots splashing across the yard.

Finally, he opened a door and let her pass him into the bunkhouse.

She stood dripping just inside the door. A few moments passed before her eyes could adjust to the dim light inside.

"I'll take your cape," Jason said, setting the jar on a ledge. He waited for her to hand the cape to him. "Max's cot is the last one on the left." He hung their wraps on pegs.

The room had cots along both walls, enough for a dozen hands in all. Two lanterns hung from square-headed nails in posts along the walls. The windows were high and small. The room felt drafty and damp. It smelled of coal oil and stale clothes.

Sharon moved down the center aisle and stopped beside Max's bed. Stooping down, she felt his dry, hot forehead. His eyes fluttered open. "Sharon, you shouldn't trouble yourself about me," he rasped. "I'll get over this in a day or so." He coughed weakly.

She knelt beside him. "It's no trouble, Max. I hate to admit it, but I came out to help myself as much as to check on you. I'm not much of a cook, you know." She looked up to meet Jason's worried gaze. "I came to ask a favor."

Max peered at her and tried to moisten his dry lips.

"Would you mind if Jason and Wilson brought you into the house? You could stay in one of the spare rooms. Then I can ask your advice about the meals. I'm afraid the men will starve to death if I don't get some help. Cooking has never been my strong point."

He drew in a labored breath. "I guess that would be all right. I feel terrible about leaving you to do it all."

"I don't mind doing the work," she said. "That's not it at all. I'd feel better if you were nearby."

She tucked the blanket around him. "It's raining too hard for you to come in now. I brought you some tea. Try to drink it for me, will you? Then you can rest until the weather eases off. That'll give me a chance to get your bed ready."

Jason handed her the jar, then helped Max sit up enough to sip from the cup. Max gulped down half of it, then sank back. His eyes drifted closed.

"Could you stay with him and see if he can drink the rest of that cupful?" she asked. "I can get back to the house on my own."

Jason stood and followed her to the door. "When Wilson comes back from the barn, we can bring him in right on that cot," he whispered. "When it quits raining, we'll cover him up and haul him out."

She nodded as she fastened the clasp on her cape. "I only hope we can get him through this," she said. "Is there a doctor in Farmington?"

Jason nodded. "After we get Max inside, I'll send Wilson to fetch him."

Sharon hurried through the rain, dodging puddles and wincing at the sogginess of her shoes.

An hour later, the sun took a peek at them. The men arrived on the porch a few minutes later, Jason at the front and Wilson at the back of the cot. A tarpaulin covered Max from head to toe.

Sharon flung open the door to the front bedroom, and they marched inside. Within five minutes, the little man was in his new bed with a quilt tucked under his chin.

Following Jason out, she pulled the bedroom door closed. Now that she had Max in the house, she wasn't sure what to do with him. She had no medicine and knew precious little about nursing the sick.

"Wilson's going to fetch the doc," Jason told her. "If he's quick, they could be back in two or three hours."

"We'll pray they are," she said.

"Is there anything I can do to help you?" he asked as Wilson hurried away.

"If you have time on your hands, I could use some company in the kitchen," she admitted. "I've been hoping the rain would stop so Lucy could come. We'd have a good time working together."

"She'd like it," Jason said, smiling. "I'll fetch her as soon as it eases off again."

"Let me check on Max first," she said and eased his door open. He was sleeping soundly, a little gurgling rasp at the end of each breath.

Leaving the door ajar, so she could hear him if he called, Sharon joined

Jason in the kitchen and picked up the basin of meat. "I guess I should cut this up into chunks and stew it. We can eat it over rice."

He pulled a knife from a sheath in his boot. "I can help you there," he said.

She stared doubtfully at the gleaming blade. "Where was that used last?" she asked.

He chuckled and ambled to the pitcher pump to wash it. "I guess all you womenfolk think alike. That's exactly what my ma would have said."

Sharon found a knife, and they sat at Max's worktable on the left side of the cooking fireplace. The tabletop was four inches of solid oak, worn and scarred from years of such abuse as they were working on it now.

In case Max was awake, she whispered, "I hope you don't think badly of me for telling Max that I needed his help. I do need advice, but I was really trying to get him to agree to come in without an argument."

Jason nodded. "You handled him like a lynx after a jackrabbit," he replied, his tone matching hers.

She looked up at him. "I'll take that as a compliment."

Still cutting, he grinned. "As intended."

As they worked, she asked a question that had been long on her mind. "Jason, what's the Cattleman's Treasure Uncle Rudolph talked about?"

He chuckled. "It may have been nothing but the good earth on the ranch. Rudolph liked to tease and that was one way he did it. You should have seen the men gathered around the potbelly stove at the general store when he'd start talking about his treasure. He wanted to get a rise out of them, and the Cattleman's Treasure did just that."

"I wish I knew what it was," she said, slicing a large onion.

"Don't we all?" They worked in silence for a few minutes, then Jason let out a soft chuckle.

Sharon glanced at him, surprised.

Softly, as though talking to himself, Jason said, "I sure wish I'd been close enough to get a look at Jim Boswell's face when he realized he'd stepped off into thin air."

Sharon's lips tightened. "You can be glad you didn't hear what Jim said when he hit the ground," she retorted. "I haven't heard that kind of language since I went with Pa to the beef auction in St. Louis when I was ten years old."

His expression brightened. "You don't say." Suddenly, he snapped his fingers into the air.

The move was so sudden that Sharon jumped. She glanced at him from the corner of her eye. Why was he so pleased?

Chapter 6

In thirty minutes the beef was simmering on the stove, and the rice pot, too.

Sharon went to check on Max and found him awake. "Are you in pain, Max?" she asked, feeling his burning forehead.

"My chest hurts when I breathe."

"Wilson went to fetch the doctor. He should be back in an hour or so."

The sick man's eyes closed. "Too much trouble," he wheezed.

She turned to Jason standing in the bedroom doorway and said, "I feel so helpless. I'm afraid he has pneumonia. What would your mother do if she were here?"

"Her cure for everything is a good dose of castor oil and a hot toddy for a chaser." He stepped back. "Let's wait for the doc. He should be here soon."

He arrived twenty minutes later.

A short, wiry man with a long, bony nose, Dr. Lanchester was too old to be young and too young to be considered an old man. The deep creases on his thin face bore witness that he'd seen his share of life.

The moment he stepped inside, Jason ushered him into the sickroom. The doctor shooed everyone out and closed the door. Wilson peeled off his slicker and stood uncertainly at the door, his boots making twin pools on the plank flooring.

"The cookstove is hot," Sharon said. "Why don't you stand over it and get warm?" She hurried to bring him a towel.

"Much obliged, miss," he said.

"Who?" she asked with a small smile.

He grinned and his face went lopsided. "Sharon," he said, burying his grizzled face in the towel.

Sharon pulled a chair for Wilson close to the stove, then returned to the living room to sit on the sofa. "Do you think we should start a fire?" she asked. "It's not really cold, just a chilly dampness. I'm afraid we'll get too warm, but I'm miserable in this chill."

"How about if I start a little bitty one?" Jason asked. "One small log and a few branches. We can always kick it apart if it gets too warm, or open the front door for a spell."

She nodded. "It would chase out the dampness."

He seemed relieved to have something to do.

While Jason was still laying the wood, the doctor came out. His face was drawn.

"How is he, Doctor?" Sharon asked.

Lanchester shook his head. "It's touch and go," he replied. "He'll need someone with him around the clock." He pulled a pad of paper from his pocket and wrote on it. "Here's how to make a mustard plaster." He scribbled for a few seconds. "Keep changing it out every hour. Make him drink plenty—water, tea, anything he'll swallow. That's very important. He's dried out pretty bad."

Sharon took the paper from his hand. "Will you come back tomorrow?"

Shoving the pad of paper into his inner coat pocket, he nodded. "I've got office appointments in the morning, but I'll try to get out in the afternoon. If he should go out of his head with delirium, come and get me right away, day or night."

Jason shook his hand. "Thank you, Doc."

"You're welcome, Jason. How is your mother doing? I haven't seen her for a while."

"She's been having a lot of bad days lately, I'm afraid."

"When I come out tomorrow, I'll stop by the cabin and take a look at her."

"Thank you, Doctor," Sharon said.

"You're welcome, young lady," he said and hurried out.

When the door closed, Sharon gasped in alarm. "What about paying him? Am I supposed to pay him?"

Jason said, "Rudolph used to take him a quarter of beef every spring and that covered his services for the year. We won't owe him anything until next spring, the way I figure it."

She read the slip of paper. "I found some mustard in the kitchen that we can use. I hope it's enough."

He gazed at her. "Are you going to be able to handle all of this? Cooking and nursing besides?"

"I can manage for a day or two. What will your mother do if Lucy comes here? Can Lucy leave her?"

"Corky's wife will take care of Ma. When Lucy has to go somewhere, Corky's wife sends one of the boys to stay with Ma and sends over meals. They're good neighbors." He peered out the misty window. "Rain or no, I'm going to fetch Lucy tomorrow."

But later that day the rain stopped, and Lucy arrived at the ranch house before nightfall. Sharon wanted to cry from relief when her new friend came through the door.

Jason took his sister's coat and hung it up. "I've got to help Wilson with the chores," he told them. "I'll come in afterward." And he left.

"How is Max?" Lucy asked.

"He's in there." Sharon nodded toward the front room. "I've got to change his plaster in ten minutes."

"Show me what you're doing and I'll take over. You look all in."

Sharon tried out a weary smile. "If I could sleep for two hours, I'd be able to sit up with him tonight." She found the doctor's slip of paper. She told Lucy what he had said and showed her the mustard paste warming on the stove.

They changed the next plaster together, then Lucy sent Sharon to bed. Exhausted, Sharon changed into a gown and was asleep seconds after the quilt covered her.

A dim stream of light across her bed woke Sharon up. She rubbed her eyes and wondered if it were dusk or dawn. She splashed water on her face and pulled on a fresh housedress. The smell of biscuits and bacon told her she'd slept longer than she'd intended.

The sick vigil lasted for two more days. Finally, the fever broke, and Max started coughing in earnest. As painful as it was for him, they were all relieved to see him throwing off the infection. The following day, Dr. Lanchester declared him out of the woods.

Lucy stayed one more day after that.

While she was there, the girls had spent every spare moment in the kitchen with Lucy teaching Sharon how to cook. Within a few days, Sharon was well schooled in biscuit making, bread making, and the art of cooking beans. She could throw together a fine johnnycake, too. Sharon worked at cooking like she did everything else—with intense concentration and determination. She never wanted to feel so helpless in her own house again.

While Lucy was sleeping, Sharon dished up beans, beef, and biscuits for Max and poured him some hot tea.

He made a face when he picked up the blue enamel cup. "Don't you have any coffee?" he asked. "This is women's brew."

Sharon grinned at him. "You should be thankful. The last thing you want to drink is my coffee. I'm hoping you can help me make cowboy coffee when you get better. Lucy said she had no idea how you do it."

He savored a bite of a golden biscuit. "You'll be putting me out to pasture," he said after a moment. "These are better than mine."

"Not by a country mile," Sharon told him. She sat near him in the rocking chair. "You've still got a lot to teach me, Max. And I want to learn it all."

He chuckled and ended up coughing. Sipping tea, he drew in a breath and said, "When you first got here, you were so brittle I was afraid you'd break, but underneath all that boarding school polish was a real genuine lady. I only wish your uncle Rudolph could have been here to know you."

She felt a sweet warmth inside that blossomed into a wide smile. That was the kindest thing anyone had said to her since she'd arrived.

At that moment, she looked up to see Jason coming through the cabin doorway. He wasn't smiling at all.

Chapter 7

Jason had never liked or trusted Edward Kellerman. When he saw the lawyer riding into the ranch yard on that June afternoon, Jason wasn't happy. When old Stewart Pitt passed away two years before, Kellerman had appeared in town within a month to take over Pitt's practice. Always fawning over the women and flattering the men, he was altogether too polished for Jason's liking.

What does he want? Jason wondered as he strode forward to meet the man. Riding high on the back of a gleaming black gelding, Kellerman wore a black suit and flat-crowned hat. The lawyer's only tribute to his Western surroundings was his polished black boots.

"Good afternoon," Kellerman said. "I've come to see Miss Hastings."

Jason said, "She's inside. You can tie your horse here at the porch, unless you'd like me to take him to the barn."

"That won't be necessary. I won't be long." He dismounted and unfastened a leather case tied to his blanket roll behind the saddle. "I have a few papers for her to sign, and then I'll be on my way."

Jason led the way to the front door, opened it, and stepped inside.

In the bedroom, Sharon was sitting in the rocking chair beside Max's bed. She was smiling at something Max had said. Through the window, the afternoon sun shone on her and made her flaxen hair gleam like pure sunbeams.

When she saw Jason's scowl, her smile faded. "What is it, Jason?" she asked.

"Mr. Kellerman's here to see you."

Edward Kellerman stepped forward, grinning and bowing like some kind of duke.

Sharon rose to meet him. "How nice to see you again," she said, offering him her hand.

He bowed over it. For a moment, Jason thought the man would kiss it—and her with no glove on, either.

Jason took two steps back and quietly closed the door. Nothing for him to do in there except fight the urge to punch Edward Kellerman's distinguished nose.

~

Edward glanced through Max's open door. "I didn't know you had sickness here. How is he doing?"

"Better, thank the Lord," Sharon said. She hurried to the spare room door. "I'll close this, Max, so you can rest." He already had his eyes closed when she pulled it shut.

She turned to the lawyer. "Please, have a seat." She sat on the edge of the sofa. "What brings you to the ranch, Edward?" she asked when he found a place across from her.

"I have some papers for you to sign," he said, "but I'm in no hurry." He unbuttoned his jacket and leaned back. "How do you like the ranch?"

"It's massive," Sharon said. "Jason took me over part of it on Monday."

"Did you see the famous water hole?"

"Is it famous?"

"You'd be surprised." He picked up the leather case and rested it on his lap. "How are the hands treating you?"

Sharon smiled. "They already feel like family. At first I wasn't sure if I could make it here, but now I really want to try. I've got good people here. Leaving now would break my heart."

He nodded. "I'm glad to hear that." Leaning forward, he said, "Would you mind if I come to call on you sometime?"

Her heart lurched. Her cheeks grew warm. "That would be nice, Edward." How could her voice sound so calm? She swallowed and drew in a long, slow breath.

He unclasped the leather case. "The will has been sent to probate court in Albuquerque. Once it's recorded, the property can be sold. However, in the meanwhile, your uncle's wishes for maintaining the ranch are being carried out. It's going on as before." He paused to look into her eyes. "I want you to know that I'm totally at your service, Sharon. Anything you need—or even want—let me know and I'll take care of it."

"That's very kind," she said, "but there's nothing that I need at the moment."

He pulled some pages from the case and moved to sit beside her. His shoulder brushed hers as he leaned to point out where she should sign. "This is a document transferring the mortgage to your name as the new owner. As you can see there's a debt of $2,061.49 and a yearly payment of $463.32 due on October 1 every year."

Sharon took her time reading through the closely written script. The mortgage payment seemed huge. Just looking at the amount gave her a knot in her stomach. Finally, she said, "Should I pay a visit to the banker?"

"If you'd like to, you can do that, but it's not absolutely necessary. The banker's name is Tom Jenkins. He's a nice chap, a friend of mine."

Sharon looked up. "We'd better move to the table so I can set this down to write on it." She stood and walked five steps to the kitchen table.

Edward moved fast enough to pull out her chair for her. From his case he pulled a small bottle of ink, then filled a fountain pen and handed it to her. When she gave the pen back to him, he pulled a lever on its side to release the ink back into the bottle and wiped the tip with a small cloth. As he tucked the cloth into his case and slid the pen into a slot, he said, "How about next Saturday morning? Around ten o'clock? Not the Saturday coming, I mean, but the one after that."

Sharon stared at him, not sure what he was talking about.

He went on, "Would it be convenient for me to call on you then?"

She couldn't believe that she had already forgotten. "That would be fine," she said. "I'll look forward to it."

He bowed over her hand, said, "Good day," and left in short order.

He had no sooner closed the door when Lucy came from the middle bedroom. Her cheek still showed the marks from where she had been sleeping on the pillow.

Watching Sharon, Lucy giggled. "You may not know it, but you've got a date with the most eligible bachelor in the territory." She plopped into a chair at the table. "I can't believe it. You just got here, and you've already had two callers."

"I'm just a new face, that's all," Sharon replied. To get Lucy off the uncomfortable subject, Sharon hurried on, "Lucy, I have lots of clothes that I don't need. They would fit you perfectly. Would you be offended if I gave them to you? If you don't like any of them, you can give them to someone else."

"Offended?" Lucy demanded. She wrapped her arms around Sharon. "I haven't had a new dress since I was sixteen years old."

"Oh, these aren't new."

"They'll be new to me." She hugged Sharon again.

The girls went into Sharon's room to sort her things. Sharon emptied one of her trunks and happily stuffed it with everything from nightgowns to crinolines to silk dresses. Finally, they jammed the lid shut.

"Mother will think I'm awful for taking all this," Lucy said.

"You're doing me a favor," Sharon insisted. "I feel guilty having so much when you have so little. We'll get Wilson to put it on the wagon when he takes you home tonight."

Before retiring that evening, Sharon went to check on Max. For once, he didn't say anything when she came in.

She picked up his empty pitcher. "Do you need anything else?" she asked.

"Have a seat, Sharon." When she eased into the rocking chair, he went on. "Rudolph had a lot of faith in Stewart Pitt. Stewart was his lawyer for thirty-five years. After Stewart died, this young fellow Kellerman came to town and took up the law office. He's been in Farmington for nigh on two years." He gazed at her.

"The way I hear it, since he came to town he has called on the banker's daughter, the mayor's daughter, and the daughters of four big ranchers."

Sharon laughed. "Don't look so worried. He asked me if he could come to call. He didn't propose." Still laughing, she took his dishes to the kitchen and slid them into the soapy water in the dishpan. Yet even as she laughed, a nagging doubt formed in her mind. Edward Kellerman was handsome and very smooth. Was that what she wanted in a man?

After a week in bed, Max moved back into the bunkhouse. Sharon missed him. It had been nice to have someone else in the house in the evenings after Lucy went home. He was able to return to work on the last day of June.

The weather grew warmer by the day, and no rain came to break the heat. She helped Max set up a summer kitchen in the lean-to behind the house. That did a lot to ease the scorching afternoons.

After another downpour, it didn't rain for the next two weeks and the heat became relentless.

Sharon was scrubbing clothes in a big iron pot on a stand in the backyard when Wilson galloped his horse across the field. Normally, the men kept the horses to a moderate pace, so Sharon watched his arrival with concern. He went to the barn, dropped the reins, and strode inside.

A few minutes later Jason appeared in the barn door and headed for the house. Sharon waved at him and called, "I'm over here! What's wrong?" She had images of one of Corky's boys hurt or maybe a horse down. She dropped the skirt she was rubbing on the washboard and hurried to meet him.

His eyebrows were drawn together, his mouth tense. "Our neighbor to the south, Jared O'Bannon, has run his cattle to our water hole. He had to cut a fence to do it."

"Why would he do something like that?" Sharon asked.

"It hasn't rained for weeks, and things are getting dry farther south." Sharon's dismay must have shown on her face because his expression softened a little, so did his voice. "It's not a catastrophe at this point. There's plenty of water—more than enough for both of our cattle. But I'm going to have to find out why they're trespassing."

He went on, "O'Bannon's spread is called the Double O. He and his men usually keep to themselves. I'm going to ride over there and have a talk with his hands."

"I'm going with you," she said.

He tilted his head. "That's not necessary, Sharon. I can take care of it."

She dried her hands on her apron. "I'm not doubting you, Jason, but I want to go. I *am* going with you."

His face took on that guarded look again. "Suit yourself. I'll saddle the horses."

On her way inside to change, she stopped in the kitchen to talk to Max for a moment. He was kneading bread dough on the counter when she stepped through the back door. He stopped working and turned toward her when she told him of Wilson's news.

"What kind of man is Jared O'Bannon?" she asked. "Has Uncle Rudolph had trouble with him before?"

Max leaned against the counter. His apron was smudged with flour and dabbed with grease. "No trouble," he said, "but O'Bannon can be hotheaded if you get on his wrong side. He almost had a feud going with the Box B a few years back. It was over a fence line, I believe. No shots were fired, but it was tough going for a while there.

"Rudolph fought shy of the man," he went on. "He said a man with a temper is worse than a gun with a hair trigger."

"I hope we don't have any trouble," Sharon said, moving toward her room.

"We?" Max called after her.

"I'm going with Jason to talk to those men," she said. Before he could answer, she latched the door firmly behind her.

She changed into a riding skirt and fresh blouse and re-combed her hair. She had always felt a little out of her depth here, but she had a heavy responsibility to fulfill. Nothing was going to stop her. Not even a hotheaded range lord.

"Don't borrow trouble, girl," she told her image in the shadowy mirror above the washstand. "Wait until you meet the man. He might be all right."

She threw open the windows, glad the room had windows on three sides. Maybe it would cool off a little after dark. As much as she had hated the damp and chill of the June rain, she longed for it now.

She heard the horses outside and hurried to meet Jason. Ignoring his stony face, she led out on Ginger, a high-spirited bay mare. Jason soon came up beside her and they road abreast for a while.

"Let's swing south and check the fence line!" he called. "We need to know what we're dealing with before we meet those hands."

When they reached the fence, Jason got down to take a closer look. Sharon joined him. "See that?" he asked, holding up a strand of loose wire. "This was definitely cut." He threw it down. "Who would be so brainless as to do a fool thing like that? Shooting wars have been started for less. A lot less."

"Well, now we know," she said, heading for her horse. "Let's go see what they have to say."

He swung up. "I doubt O'Bannon will be there himself. He may not even know what they're up to."

A few minutes later, the water hole came into view. Fifty longhorns drank from its rim while fifty more browsed the clumps of grass nearby. Double O brands mixed with the Lazy H cattle.

When the Double O hands caught sight of Jason and Sharon, they sat up straighter and stared. A tall, gangly cowboy on a black stallion rode toward them in a cloud of dust.

"That's Luther Heinburg, O'Bannon's foreman," Jason told Sharon.

Heinburg came close, then had to back away when the stallion reared his head back.

"What do you think you're doing, cutting our fence?" Sharon burst out before Jason could speak. "Do you want to start a shooting war right off or do you want to wait a day or two?"

Heinburg stared at her, then glanced at Jason.

"If you know what's good for you, you'll round them all up and move back to your own property," Sharon went on. "You're lucky I'm in a good mood today. I ought to call the law. There's a legal name for what you did."

O'Bannon's foreman glanced toward the three men behind him, then pinned her with a hard stare. "That's big talk from a girl with only one cowpoke to side her."

She gasped, truly angry now. "Are you threatening me on my own land?" She worked the reins as Ginger sidestepped and pranced. When the horse settled down, she went on. "Do you really think that I'd let all my men stand out here exposed? What's the range on a good rifle with a scope, do you think?"

Scanning the horizon, Heinburg's Adam's apple bobbed. He went on in a more reasonable tone. "Our groundwater is halfway down," he said. "We didn't think—"

"That's right. You didn't think," she said. "I suggest you begin to use your head, starting right now."

With another glance at Jason, Heinburg wheeled his horse and headed back to his men. After a short confab and several glances their way, the hands began the tedious process of separating out their cattle and herding them south.

Sharon noticed that Jason's ears were red. He had his jaw clamped down and didn't look at her.

When the Double O cows started moving, Jason ground out, "We may as well head out. They'll be here most of the day. Wilson and Corky will come back before dark and fix that fence." He wheeled his horse and set off at a leisurely trot.

She followed him until they were out of sight of the Double O hands. Then her hands started shaking like a willow tree in a windstorm. She felt sick to her stomach and a little faint.

She closed her eyes and drew in several calming breaths. At least Mrs. Minniver had taught her how to get control of herself.

Jason continued ahead, gaining distance by the minute.

She urged Ginger to catch up to him. "Hey, wait for me!" she called when she drew closer.

He ignored her, and her temper flared.

"What's the matter?" she demanded, coming up beside him. "They backed down."

He kept his face straight ahead. "Right. That's just what they did." He leaned forward and kicked his horse to a gallop. Sharon let him go. If he was that bad-tempered, she didn't want to talk to him anyway.

When she reached the ranch yard, Jason and Wilson were in a close conversation outside the barn door. Jason wore a scowl as Wilson spoke rapidly.

When Jason came to the house for dinner a few minutes later, a hint of that scowl remained.

"What happened out there?" Max asked when they began to eat. "What did O'Bannon say?"

"He wasn't there. It was his foreman," Sharon replied, scooping potatoes onto her plate. "I told him to gather up his cows and leave, and that's what he did." She set the bowl down and picked up a dish of peas.

"Jason?" Max prodded.

He drank coffee and didn't answer right away. Setting his cup down, he said, "Heinburg didn't know what to do when he had a woman facing him down. He couldn't pull a gun on her, could he?"

Chuckling, Max turned to Sharon. "You faced him down? Good for you."

She smiled at Max, then noticed that Wilson's lips were turned down, and Jason was glaring at his steak.

Sharon ignored them and focused her attention on her food. When she looked up, Jason was gone, finished before anyone else. Wilson left soon afterward.

"What did I do wrong?" she asked Max. "I went out there to protect my property. And that's what I did. Why is Jason so angry?"

The little man worked his lips left, then right, considering. "It's not what you did," he said. "It's what you did with Jason looking on. This is a man's world, Sharon. Jason was shamed because you took charge of the situation."

Her eyes flashed. "I may be a woman, but I'm also the owner of this ranch."

"And a good one," he told her. "You did fine, Sharon. Give the men a chance to simmer down, and they'll be all right."

After helping Max clear the table, she retired early. She had a sick feeling in her stomach and a distinct urge to cry.

Lying awake long after dark, she tried to figure out what had gone wrong that afternoon. The answer: nothing. Whatever the problem was, it was in the male mind of Jason Riordan.

She turned over and closed her eyes, willing herself to sleep. Tomorrow was Saturday. Edward would be coming to call in the morning, and she wanted to be up early. She had a lot to do. Press a dress, wash her hair. . . .

Jason Riordan lay back on his bunk and stared at the pine boards on the ceiling. He flung his hands up to settle them behind his head. His thoughts wandered to Sharon's set-to with Luther Heinburg. Jason had seen red when she took over and faced Heinburg down herself. But now that he'd had time to cool off, he had to admire her nerve.

He chuckled softly. What a girl. Eighteen years old, on the range for no more than a month, and she was ready to take them all on. O'Bannon included. He'd never met a female like her in all his life.

Bringing one arm forward to cover his eyes, he fell asleep with the hint of a smile still on his face.

Chapter 8

A few minutes after ten o'clock, Edward arrived on his black gelding. Sharon went out to meet him. She had chosen a navy dress in soft calico with a tiny strip of lace around the neck.

"Good morning," he said, ground-hitching his horse in the grass under the big tree in the front yard. "All right if I leave Midnight here?"

"Will he be happier there or in the barn?" she asked.

"He's in the shade, and there's plenty of grass. He'll be fine."

She paused beside the door, waiting for him to reach her. "Would you like some coffee?"

"In this heat? A cool glass of water sounds more like it." He removed his hat as he crossed the threshold and followed Sharon into the kitchen.

She pumped the handle of the pitcher pump four times to prime it, and water gushed out into the metal pitcher standing there.

"Max is in the corral, training a yearling," she said, pouring water into a glass. "Would you like to watch him for a while?" She handed it to Edward.

He took a long drink, then said, "Actually, I'd like to sit on the porch for a spell, if you don't mind. We can enjoy the breeze and talk."

"That sounds wonderful," she said. Actually, she'd rather go to the corral, but she could do that any time.

Sitting close together on the short bench, they talked about the need for rain while they watched Midnight leisurely cropping grass. When conversation ran thin, Sharon said, "Would you like to go for ride? It's cooler out by the water hole."

He made his little bow. "Your wish is my command."

She stood. "Would you ask Wilson to saddle Ginger for me? It'll take a minute for me to change." She hurried to her room and got into her riding clothes, which were waiting on the peg behind the door.

When she reached the barn, the black barn cat and her kittens were sunning themselves at the edge of the doorway. "Hello, kitties," Sharon said, wishing she could pet them. The next litter, she'd be there to tame the kittens before they got so big and wild.

Inside, she found Edward watching Wilson tightening the cinch strap around Ginger, a tall bay mare with a black tail and a white blaze on her face.

Wilson looked up when Sharon approached, concern on his grizzled face.

"Are you sure you want Ginger?" he asked. "She can be tetchy."

"I rode her yesterday," Sharon replied. "We'll get along fine." She stroked the mare's neck. "Won't we, Ginger?" The mare nickered and nuzzled Sharon's blouse.

Wilson slipped the bit into the horse's mouth and fit the headstall over her head. "If you say so," he said doubtfully. He glanced at Edward, then continued speaking to Sharon. "I reckon you'll have help if you need it."

Sharon gathered the reins and led the horse to the mounting block. "We're only going to the water hole and back. We should be gone an hour or two at the most."

Wilson nodded but didn't reply.

Edward said, "I'll fetch Midnight," and strode out the open double doors.

As Sharon slid into the saddle, Jason ambled in through the door leading to the corral. His chin came up an inch or two when he caught sight of Edward's back going through the barn door. "Going riding?" he asked when he reached Sharon.

"I thought we'd ride to the water hole. I want to see how the Double O people left it. Besides, it's cooler out there." Why did she feel defensive?

His lips twisted. "What brought Kellerman out here so soon? More papers to sign?"

Looking down at him, she didn't like the way his eyebrows slanted as he waited for her reply.

Not answering him was a direct violation of Rule 4. With her face muscles under strict control, her gaze toward the distance, she nudged Ginger. The mare's hoofbeats echoed and reverberated through the posts and beams of the massive structure. Sitting astride Midnight, Edward met her at the door, and they set off at a canter.

Riding at that pace made conversation impossible. She savored the sage-scented air and focused on the movements of the horse beneath her, the lazy looping of a hawk overhead, and the feeling of the wind on her face.

When they stopped to give the horses a rest, Sharon told Edward about the Double O hands and their cattle at the water hole. Intent on her words, he drew his horse closer. His face had smooth planes. His eyes were wide-set and dark. He was the most handsome man Sharon had ever known.

"So, you let them turn around and go home? That's it?" he asked.

Her eyes narrowed. "What are you trying to say?"

He drew back a little. "I wonder if you shouldn't let the sheriff know what's going on. For your own protection, Sharon. In a situation like this, things can get out of hand in a heartbeat."

"I'll think about that," she told him. "I don't want to make the situation worse by calling in the law. Max said he thinks they were trying to see how far I can be pushed, being the new owner and new to the area. I'm hoping he's right and they won't try anything again."

"As long as it rains before too long, you'll be all right," Edward replied. "If this drought gets worse, all bets are off."

Tired of the conversation, she squeezed her knees into the mare's sides and Ginger lurched ahead. Both woman and horse enjoyed a good run. Sharon let the mare have her head for a few minutes, then reined her in.

Edward caught up to them in seconds. He was grinning. "That horse has a lot of pep," he said. "Wilson was right."

"I can handle her." Sharon leaned over to speak to the horse. "Good girl, Ginger. You and I are going to be best friends."

"Let's walk awhile," Edward suggested a few minutes later.

"The water hole is over there," Sharon told him, urging Ginger ahead.

They soon reached the water's edge, and Edward helped her down—not that she really needed help. His hands lingered in hers. Uncomfortable, she turned away to walk along the bank.

The next moment, she drew up, alarmed. The water level was about a foot lower than its original depth. "Look how low it is!" she cried. "What will we do if it dries up?"

"Say, that sounds like you're borrowing grief that will most likely never happen." He took her hand and placed it inside his elbow. "Let's forget about the drought and walk for a while."

The gentle breeze was cooler here than at the ranch. Sharon had a sudden urge to bring a bedroll and bunk down here instead of on that sweltering straw tick that Rudolph had called a bed.

"So tell me," Edward said as they strolled along the bank, "what are your plans?"

"Plans?" She tried to think. "Well, tomorrow I'm taking Sunday dinner at Lucy's house. I was supposed to go long ago, but then Max got sick and other things got in the way. Finally, I'm going to be able to go. After that, I'm not sure."

"Would you ever consider selling the ranch? If you had a good offer?"

She laughed. "Do you know anyone with a million dollars? That's my best price."

He chuckled. "Not offhand. I'll let you know if I come across anyone though."

"Be sure you do."

At that moment the faint cry of an animal came from a nearby stand of mesquite. "Is that a sheep?" Sharon asked.

Edward turned around. "Where?"

The cry came again.

Sharon pointed toward the brush. "Over there. It sounds like a sheep." Pulling away from him, she crossed twenty yards of hard-packed earth. When she reached the mesquite, she gasped. Before her lay a mother goat that had been torn by some animal. Beside the dead mother stood a small she-kid about a month or two old. The baby backed away from Sharon but stayed nearby.

"I wonder if she's weaned," Sharon said, stooping down and watching the kid. It had a black body with a black face and tiny white hooves.

"It must have been a bobcat or a coyote," Edward said, still looking at the mother goat. "It's strange that whatever it was got the mother and left the kid."

"The kid may have been sleeping under some brush."

"Did Rudolph keep goats?" Edward asked.

"Max has two nannies that he milks," Sharon said. "I don't know of any others. I'll have to ask." The kid took two steps toward its mother. Its little pointed chin quivered when it bawled.

"We can't leave the baby here for another wild animal to find," Sharon said. "I couldn't sleep knowing it was out here."

Edward stared down at his pressed black suit and glanced at the bawling kid.

"It should be easy to catch her," Sharon told him. "Circle around and move in. The kid will forget about me and run for her mother. I'll get her when she gets close enough."

And that's exactly how it worked. The problem was figuring out what to do with a wriggling baby goat once you caught it.

"I was going to hold it and carry it home," Sharon said, arching her head back as she clutched the thrashing kid, "but it will annoy the horse with all this kicking."

Edward said, "How about if we wrap it in a saddle blanket? I always carry one for emergencies."

"Hurry! I'm losing my grip!"

He pulled loose the two rawhide thongs holding the wool blanket roll behind his saddle and flipped the blanket open. Holding it with his arms apart, he came to Sharon and wrapped his arms around the kid. Sharon had trouble pulling her arms away with Edward holding the kid so tightly. Their cheeks touched, and she felt the roughness of his sideburn against her face.

Finally, she was able to take a step back.

"Wrap the blanket around her a few times," he said, "so she can't move."

Sharon wrapped her up in short order. Only her black ears and glistening black eyes were able to move. Sharon took the rawhide strings from Edward's hand and tied the blanket around the kid's hind feet and front feet, making her sharp hooves harmless.

"Put her across my saddle," she said. "I'll carry her home."

Once the horse began to move, the kid settled down. Sharon kept her hand against the blanket roll, so she wouldn't slip off the saddle. "What are we going to name you?" she asked the tiny bundle. "Emily? Sarah?"

"Did you say something?" Edward called.

"I'm trying to figure out what to call her," Sharon told him. "Any suggestions?"

He didn't answer.

"Sophie!" she cried. Stroking the kid's ears, she cooed, "Your name is Sophie. Little Sophie, baby girl."

By the time they reached the house, Max was setting lunch on the table. "What in the world?" he exclaimed when he saw the bundle in Sharon's arms.

"It's a baby goat," Sharon told him. "Something got her mother. We found her by the water hole."

"Bring her back to the nanny pen, and we'll see if one of them will feed her. If not. . ." He shook his head.

Edward spoke from the doorway. "Sharon, I've got to be going. I'll see you tomorrow in church."

Sharon jerked around. She'd forgotten Edward. Where were her manners? "Edward, I'm so sorry! I'm afraid I've spoiled your morning."

"Not at all. I have an appointment this afternoon, and I must be on my way."

Still holding Sophie, she called, "Thanks for coming!"

He turned away from the door, and she rushed to follow Max. The poor baby had to be roasting in that blanket. She had to get her unwound right away.

The nanny pen was fifty feet from the back door, a room-sized area with a small structure at the back for protection from the elements. Inside its shade, two gray goats with small curved horns lay resting. Farther back in the yard, another pen held five or six more goats.

"Give me the bundle," Max said holding out his arms. He took the baby inside and shut the gate behind him. He set the kid down and pulled loose the raw-hide strings. Soon, the baby stood swaying and crying in the center of the yard. Immediately both nannies stood up and started bawling. One nanny came close, raised her nose, and sniffed the air, then turned away. The other nanny came up to the kid and nuzzled her. The kid trotted around and began to nurse.

Max beamed. "That one lost a kid a couple of months back. Rubbing his bald head, he let himself out of the pen. "I wasn't sure it would work. You never know."

"Her name is Sophie," Sharon said. "She's the first thing on this ranch that's really mine."

Max came to stand beside her. He leaned his arms against the top fence rail to watch the new baby. "What was it like living at that boarding school?" he asked.

A sudden rush of a deep sadness made it hard for Sharon to speak. "I cried for Mama every night for the first year. After that, all I thought about was coming here."

Max moved closer to her. Together, they watched the baby and its adopted mother for a few more minutes.

Finally, Max said, "The men will be coming up for lunch. I'd best put food on the table."

"I need to wash up," Sharon said, falling into step with him.

"Your gentleman friend took out for home, I guess."

"He said he had an appointment," Sharon said.

"He must be dedicated. First lawyer I ever heard of that keeps hours on Saturday afternoon." Max stomped up the two steps to the back door. He pumped water into a basin, so she could wash her hands.

Jason and Wilson arrived a few minutes later.

"We found an orphan kid at the water hole," Sharon told Jason, lifting a towel from a nail nearby. "A bobcat or maybe a wolf got its mother. I brought it home, and Max put it in the nanny pen."

"How did a goat and a kid get there?" He turned to Wilson behind him. "Do we have any goats on the range?"

Wilson had a creaky voice with a hint of whine in it. "It could have wandered over here from the reservation. There's no way of telling really. . .unless the Double O has taken to branding everything that moves."

The men chuckled at that and took their seats, anxious to dig into thick beef sandwiches and hearty vegetable soup.

"Didn't your boyfriend stay for lunch?" Jason joked to Sharon.

"First of all, he's my lawyer," she shot back. "And second, he had business to attend to." She made a point of turning toward Max. "I'm going to eat with the Riordan family tomorrow after church, so it'll only be you and Wilson for lunch," she said.

Max glanced toward Wilson. "It's not often you get to call the menu," he told the cowhand. "Now's your chance. Give it your best shot."

Sharon spent most of the afternoon hovering around the nanny pen. When Max came out to milk the goats that evening, he said, "Why don't you come inside with me? They won't hurt you."

The nursing nanny was standing on the opposite side of the pen with Sophie beside her. The second nanny stood in the lean-to.

Sharon said, "When I was about six, a goat knocked me down. I've been wary of them ever since."

"These girls are harmless," he said, swinging the gate open for her to enter ahead of him. He set down the stool and bucket he was carrying. Gripping the collar of the non-nursing goat, he led her to a short rope hanging from the fence and tied her there. "I'll leave the other one to nurse your baby," he said. "From the size of that kid, she should be weaned in a couple of weeks."

Sharon edged up to the kid and held out her hand for Sophie to sniff. To her delight, the kid let Sharon stroke her head. "Sophie," she crooned. "You're a sweetie." The next thing she knew, Max was gone, and she was in the pen alone.

She stayed until the triangle jangled for dinnertime.

Chapter 9

The next morning, Sharon was up at first light. She threw on an old housedress and hurried to the nanny pen to check on Sophie. Today, Sharon would stay at the Riordans' cabin after church, so she wouldn't see Sophie again until late afternoon.

The baby goat was lying contentedly next to her new mama. Satisfied that she was okay, Sharon went to the cooking lean-to to give Max a hand. She pulled an apron from a peg and tied it around her waist. "Jason will be delighted to see hotcakes for breakfast," she told him. "Do you want me to fry the bacon?"

"How are you at turning hotcakes?" he asked. "I never have cottoned to that part of it. I always feel like every hotcake is a personal test, and I can't pass every time."

"I can't promise that I will, either," Sharon told him with a small laugh. "But I love a challenge."

He handed her the wide spatula and moved aside. A long iron grill covered two burners on the hot stove. The yellow crockery bowl stood nearby, full of yellow frothy batter and a small ladle. Max moved to the other side of the stove and filled a hot skillet with thick-cut bacon. On the short counter behind them lay a large bowl of peeled potatoes in water, and beside it a head of cabbage and a bowl of string beans.

After breakfast Sharon's cheeks were still rosy from the heat as she went to change for church. She'd only worn the navy calico dress for a few minutes yesterday, so she'd wear it again this morning. She spent extra time on her hair to form a deep wave over the right side of her forehead. Her arms ached before she was satisfied, but she finally got it right.

Jason was already on the porch when she stepped outside. He helped her into the buckboard and set off at a nice clip.

"I wish this wagon had a roof like the surrey," she said. "If it's this hot now, what will it be like after church?"

"Just wait until we get inside the building," Jason remarked dryly. "I hope the parson is as hot and anxious to get outside as the rest of us."

Rev. Nelson, however, was oblivious to the weather and kept them until a few minutes to one. Sharon could hardly wait to get to the cabin. Even with a cotton dress, she was much too warm.

"Ma can hardly wait to meet you," Lucy said when they set off from the church. "She's been talking about it all week."

The Riordan cabin was basically one large room. The fireplace covered the east wall. A settee, two chairs, and a heavily padded rocking chair stood in a semicircle before it. On the rear wall were two narrow doors.

On the other side of the room, the kitchen area resembled the one at the main ranch house, except it was half the size of Max's domain. A staircase at the back of the kitchen told that there was a second floor under the eaves of the roof. The house smelled of coal oil and liniment. The floor was worn in places and the covering on the settee was frayed, but it felt like a house filled with happy memories, strong faith, and lots of love.

When they came in, Mrs. Riordan was sitting in the rocking chair beside the cold fireplace. Her face was thin and deeply etched from years of constant pain. In her younger days, she must have been a beauty like Lucy. Now her hair was white, her eyes two dark hollows in her pale face.

Lucy bent over to kiss her mother's cheek. "Ma, meet Sharon Hastings."

Sharon drew near and gently clasped the woman's gnarled hand. She knelt to be at eye level with her. "Mrs. Riordan, I've been looking forward to meeting you. I have so much to thank you for. If not for Uncle Rudolph's generosity and your kindness, I don't know what would have happened to me."

As she gazed into the older woman's eyes, Sharon had the urge to cry. If there was ever a loving mother, this was her.

Resting her hand on Sharon's head, Mrs. Riordan said, "Give thanks to God, child. He's the One who gives perfect gifts." She opened her arms and drew Sharon to her breast.

Tears flowed down Sharon's cheeks. She felt embarrassed, but she couldn't stop them. Her broken heart had yearned for this moment ever since she had lost her mother.

When she drew back, Mrs. Riordan's cheeks were wet, too.

Jason pulled a chair closer, and Sharon sank into it. She took out her handkerchief and tried to dry her streaming eyes.

"Tell me about your parents," Mrs. Riordan said, dabbing at her own cheeks.

Sharon swallowed and forced her voice to work. "Mama was the best cook in our neighborhood when we lived in Missouri." She sniffed and pressed her handkerchief against her nose. "I didn't appreciate it back then, but after I got to boarding school. . ." Her throat closed up, and she couldn't speak for a moment.

Finally, she drew in a quavering breath. "She loved planting flowers. She took a dozen cuttings with her on the Oregon Trail." She talked on without stopping until Lucy called them to the table. It felt so good to be able to talk about those she loved. She hadn't been able to until now.

"I'm sorry, Mrs. Riordan," Sharon said as they stood. "I've been rattling on and on and boring you unmercifully."

"Not in the least, my dear," the older woman said as Jason helped her move to the table. "I've been waiting for five long years to get to know you. I expect you to come and talk to me regularly."

"I will," Sharon said. How could she stay away?

After Jason prayed, Lucy passed Sharon a platter of fried chicken and told her mother, "Sharon has a new baby, an orphan she found yesterday."

"You don't say," Mrs. Riordan said with a feeble smile. "And what kind of baby is it, Sharon?"

"It's a tiny black goat about six weeks old. Its mother was killed by a wild animal. I couldn't bear to leave her to die, so I brought her home and named her Sophie. One of our milking nannies has adopted her. She's doing quite well."

"You named her?" Jason asked, amused.

"And why not? She's the first thing on the Lazy H that's really mine, and I intend to treat her special."

Jason laughed. "The men will enjoy that," he said. He slanted his eyes at his sister. "Life is going to be different with a lady running things around there. I can see that right now."

"I, for one, am glad," Lucy declared, smiling at Sharon.

Sharon turned to Jason. "In all the excitement yesterday, I forgot to tell you that the water hole is a foot down."

He laid down his fork. "I know. I was out there two days ago. I can't imagine what the ranchers south of here must be dealing with." He looked at his mother. "We need to have special prayer for rain, Ma. Things are getting critical."

"I have been praying, son," she said. "The Good Lord knows what He's doing. Even if we can't figure Him out."

After the meal, Mrs. Riordan announced that she must lie down, and Lucy went to help her. Feeling that it was time to give them privacy, Sharon said good-bye to both ladies.

"I can walk home if you want to stay awhile," she told Jason when they were alone.

"No reason for that," he said shortly. "I've got some things to see to this afternoon. I was planning to go back to the ranch anyway."

He held the door for her and then helped her into the buckboard.

As they jostled down the trail, Sharon said, "I'd like to go into town sometime this week. I need a few things."

"Talk to Max," he said. "I know he'd be glad to go along. He's always needing something for the kitchen." He leaned toward her with a conspiratorial air.

"Tell him to get some of that fine sugar to dust on doughnuts. We haven't had them for coon's age."

She let her mouth fall open for a second. "Jason Riordan, you have a sweet tooth!"

He chuckled. "That being my only weakness, I think I'm doing all right."

She laughed aloud.

Not wanting to lose the moment, she asked, "Have you always wanted to be foreman of the Lazy H? Didn't you ever dream of doing something else?"

He shifted his legs and found a more comfortable position on the seat. Tilting his head back, he thought about that. "I can't say I ever did. I started mucking out the stalls when I was eleven or twelve years old. After that, there was always something to keep me busy. I never had a lot of time to think of leaving or doing something else. Everything I wanted was here."

He glanced in her direction. "That must seem pretty tame to you. You've been over half the country and back again."

"Not that it did me much good," she replied. "Believe me, there's nothing out there that you don't have right here."

Though he didn't move an inch, his look became somehow closer and more intent. "Now that you're here," he murmured, "I reckon that's true."

Chapter 10

Monday morning, while helping Max in the kitchen, Sharon said, "I'd like to go into town sometime this week. Do you think you could find time to go with me?"

He stopped pinching off biscuits. Covered in clumps of flour, his hands hovered over the baking pan. "That's a grand idea. I need some things."

She grinned. "Jason told me you'd say that." She told him Jason's request for sugar-sprinkled doughnuts.

"Ha! I'm not surprised." He pinched off an egg-sized lump of dough and dropped it onto the baking pan. "That boy would eat sweets the livelong day." He finished the last bit of dough and rubbed his hands over the bowl to clear them off. "How about tomorrow?" he asked.

"Let's eat at a restaurant. My treat."

With Max driving the surrey, they set off for town around nine o'clock on Tuesday morning. She had chosen the pink gingham dress today because it was cooler than most of her others. Its bonnet was of matching gingham lined with white muslin. She carried her white cotton gloves in her purse until they reached town. No sense soiling them on the ride in.

Wearing a cream-colored Stetson and a blue chambray shirt with a black string tie, Max looked fine. He had to sit on the edge of the seat to reach the brake.

"Are you from Farmington originally?" Sharon asked him.

"I was born in Santa Fe. I had a good business there when I was only twenty-one years old. I had almost two hundred people under me."

Sharon gasped. "And you gave it up to be a cook?"

He laughed, too tickled to answer right away. "I—I mowed a graveyard."

It took a moment for her to understand. Then she laughed. "Max, you are too much."

"Seriously, I came north to run cows in the early seventies. I stayed in this corner of the territory, working for one rancher or another. I was in Farmington between jobs when I got the word that the Lazy H was looking for a cook. I've always been a hand in the kitchen, so I came out and took the job. Breaking horses is a hobby. No one ever told me I had to do it. I just do."

"I'm glad you're at the ranch, Max. You've made things so much easier for me."

He patted her hand. "Same here, my dear. I don't know what would have become of me if you hadn't been there while I was sick." He sighed. "It's such a shame about Rudolph. I can't get over it. He wasn't a young man, but he was still in his prime, full of life with plans for the future."

He glanced at her. "You were a big part of those plans, Sharon. He talked about you coming and what he wanted to do when you got here." He gazed into the distance. "Then one day, nothing. He was gone."

"I'm sorry I missed the funeral," she said.

"Funeral? There wasn't one. A few days before you came, we had a little private service at the house in his memory. The parson came, and we gathered in the living room. He read some verses and prayed. That was it."

He wiped his face with his handkerchief. Sharon did the same with hers. The heat was almost unbearable. Even in the shade of the surrey's roof, the top of her head felt the ruthless rays of the blistering sun.

When they reached town, Sharon pulled on her gloves and said, "Let's go to the bank first. I want to meet Tom Jenkins."

Max nodded. "I know him. Good man. Rudolph liked him." He angled the wagon to the edge of the street and jumped down. Moving quickly, he looped the reins around the hitching rail, then came to help her down.

The Farmington National Bank was an unpainted structure in the center of the main street. It had double front doors with nine glass panes in each one. A bell jangled when they let themselves in.

Before them, a short counter had iron bars from its wooden top to the ceiling. A short, round man with black hair and a gray beard stood behind the counter.

"May I help you folks?" he asked.

Sharon said, "I'd like to see Tom Jenkins, if I may."

"Yes, miss. I'll tell him you're here." He disappeared through the door behind him for an instant. "He'll be right with you."

A minute later, the banker stepped out and came through a hinged half door at the end of the counter. He was built like a bear from his shape and size to his brown hair and dark eyes. When he saw Max, he beamed. "Well, Max Martin. It's good to see you."

"Tom, this is Sharon Hastings. Rudolph's niece."

She offered him her hand. "It's good to meet you, Mr. Jenkins. I've come to talk about the mortgage on the ranch."

Jenkins stood aside and held the half door open. "Please come into my office."

Max hesitated. "If it's all right with you, Sharon, I've got some things to attend to in town."

"Of course," Sharon replied. "I'll meet you at the general store."

Max trundled away.

Turning toward the banker, Sharon said, "I don't know what we would do without Max."

Jenkins smiled down at her. "A man of many talents, to be sure."

The banker's office was much like Edward Kellerman's except it was triple in size and smelled of nasty cigars. The large open window behind the desk showed a dusty backyard with a cactus garden in one corner. The grass was brown and parched. The breeze coming through the window felt hot and dry.

Jenkins held the padded back of a leather chair until she took a seat, then sat down and waited for her to begin.

"There's no problem," she began. "I came to learn more about the terms of our mortgage and what's required of me as the new owner."

Jenkins leaned back, one elbow resting on the leather-covered chair arm. "I sent the paperwork over to Edward Kellerman," he said.

"Yes, he brought it to me to sign. Unfortunately, I didn't understand the terms. I was wondering if you could explain them to me."

"It's pretty straightforward. We financed the ranch fifteen years ago for six thousand dollars at 2 percent interest. Since that time, Rudolph Hastings has refinanced several times. At this date the full amount. . ." He leaned forward to open a huge volume. It was about half the size of that bottom step Wilson had repaired and twice as thick.

Running his finger down a long column of tiny writing, he paused, then said, "Is $2,061.49 with a single payment of $463.32 due once annually."

"Mr. Jenkins, what if we can't make that mortgage payment in October? If the drought continues much longer, we may not have any cattle to sell."

He nodded, his face grave. "Every other rancher in this area has the same question on his mind, Miss Hastings. We understand that." He closed the book and shoved it farther back on the wide desk. "If you come up short, let me know, and we'll refinance for $2,524.81. Your new payment will be a few dollars more the following year, but that's unavoidable."

"I see." It was a short-term fix that left her with a bigger long-term problem.

"Is there anything else I can help you with?" he asked.

"No. That answered my question. Thank you." She stood and offered him her hand. "It's been a pleasure meeting you, Mr. Jenkins."

He gently squeezed her hand and let it fall. "The pleasure is mine, Miss Hastings. Feel free to stop in any time." He walked with her to the office doorway, and the teller opened the half door to let her out.

Closing the jangling bank door behind her, Sharon paused on the boardwalk, blinking in the brilliant glare. She waited for a wagon to pass, then crossed the street to the general store.

The store had both doors open like the mouth of an enormous barrel with its contents spilling out over the boardwalk—small kegs of nails and screws, a table piled high with hand tools and neatly wound lengths of rope, and a bare wooden table that the young clerk, Timothy Ingles, was filling with stacks of enamel dishes.

When he saw Sharon, he grinned and his whole face lit up. He had a wide smile and twinkling blue eyes, a boyish pug nose with a few freckles scattered across it.

"We had vegetables on here earlier," he told Sharon, "but we had to take them in. The sun is too hot, you know."

"It is too hot," Sharon agreed. "For people as well."

She noticed a ripe tomato on the windowsill and pointed to it. "You forgot one."

He shook his head. "That's for good luck," he said, still stacking plates. "A tomato on the windowsill keeps out bad luck. Didn't you know that?" He grinned again.

Setting the last stack of bowls on the table, he picked up the empty crate and followed her into the store.

"What can I get for you today?" he asked.

"I have a list here." She drew it out of her purse and gave it to him. "While you're filling that, I'd like to look around, if I may. This is my first time in the store."

"That's fine, Sharon," he said. "Take your time."

She spent the next half hour in the tiny shop. It had a narrow counter that wound around the three inner walls. Beneath the counter, more shelves contained everything from building tools to canned goods, eggbeaters, and coffee grinders. Wooden shelves lined the walls behind the counters, as well—from dress goods to ready-made shirts, ammunition, and so much more.

The front of the store had a wide variety of leather products for horses—two saddles, several bridles, quirts, and horse blankets—all in neat rows.

She picked up a pair of riding gloves and met Timothy at the counter. Handing the gloves to him, she said, "Max Martin, our cook, will be here soon. He'll have a list of things as well. Could you wrap up all of this and have it ready in about an hour?"

"Why, sure thing, Sharon," he said. He paused. "Uh, Sharon, would you mind if I ask you something?"

She waited, smiling softly to encourage him.

"Would you like to go riding with me up to Chimney Rock? The view up there will take your breath away."

"Why, that's a fine idea," she said, delighted at a chance to go on a riding excursion. "I'd love to see it."

"I have Saturday off. I'll come to fetch you."

"I'll pack a picnic lunch," she said, pleased.

At that moment, Max arrived, red-faced and puffing. He glanced from Sharon's smile to Timothy's delighted grin. "Sorry I'm late," he panted. "I went down to the livery stable to check on something and lost track of time."

"I'm in no hurry," Sharon told him. "Do you need to go anywhere else?"

He shook his head. Digging into his shirt pocket, he handed Timothy a short list.

A portly, middle-aged man with heavy jowls came through the back door. "Hello, Zach," Max said. "Have you met Rudolph's niece, Sharon Hastings?" He turned to Sharon. "This is Zach Ingles, the owner of the store. Timothy's father."

Zach Ingles smiled, and the shape of his face changed. "I'm proud to know you, Miss Hastings," he said, coming to shake her hand. "I hope you'll be happy in these parts."

"Why, thank you, Mr. Ingles," she said. "I'm sure I will."

Max and the storekeeper discussed the weather and the danger of drought to the cattlemen. Finally, the men said good-bye. Max and Sharon headed for the boardwalk.

"Let's eat lunch," Sharon said when they reached the doorway.

Max mopped his streaming face. "I'm all for that."

"Lead the way," she told him. "I've no idea where we are going." She waved to Timothy who had moved to a ladder some distance away.

When they reached the boardwalk, Max said, "Did you know that Rudolph used to have partial ownership in that store?"

"Jason mentioned that Uncle Rudolph had helped him get started. He didn't tell me he was a partial owner."

Max's large head bobbed. "He sold out to Ingles a few months back."

"Was there some kind of trouble?"

He shrugged. "Rudolph never discussed his business dealings. I have no idea what happened. You'd have to ask Zach Ingles about that."

The hotel was four doors down the street, a two-story structure that looked more like a large home than a public building. It had whitewashed siding and a large, wraparound porch that was half-filled with hungry patrons sitting at long, narrow tables.

The restaurant was bustling inside as well. People filled six more tables, and two young girls rushed around serving them. A small blond girl paused long enough to tell them, "We can serve you if you don't mind sitting on the porch.

Today's meal is on there." She pointed to a blackboard nailed to the wall beside the door and hurried away.

Scrawled in white chalk was the following menu: ROAST BEEF, MASHED POTATOES, CARROTS, AND CORN: FIFTY CENTS.

When she passed their way again, Max raised two fingers toward the waitress. She nodded and dashed toward the kitchen.

On their way outside, they passed two cowboys going in.

"Is it always this busy here?" Sharon asked.

He nodded. "Evenings it's worse, especially when the stage is in."

Sinking onto a bench she said, "I'm glad we can sit out here. It's stifling inside."

"Kitchen heat," he said. "I don't know how the cook stands it all day. I may know how to cook, but working in that setup isn't my idea of a good life."

They sat in silence for a few minutes, nodding to people passing in or out.

Finally, Max said, "Did I hear you making a date with Zach Ingles' boy?"

She laughed. "It's not a date. We're going to ride up to Chimney Rock and see the view."

He chuckled. "That's not a date? Chimney Rock is one of the favorite haunts of the young people hereabouts."

She acted offended. "Well, this time it's not romance. I love to ride, and he offered to show me a new place, that's all."

"Maybe to you it is," Max said sagely as their food arrived.

Two days passed and still no rain. By Thursday, the thought on everyone's mind was rain. The constant topic of conversation was rain. The prayer at every meal and every quiet moment was for rain.

Sharon's concern grew by the hour. What if the water hole dried up?

Max became conservative with the pump water in the kitchen. "If the water table is that low," he told her, "we could lose the prime on this pump and then we'll be carrying water from the pump in the yard—as long as that one holds up." He rubbed his shiny head. "The first year I was here, we had a terrible bad drought. I wouldn't want to live through that again."

Chapter 11

Sharon found peace in her time with Sophie. Soon the kid was coming to the gate whenever Sharon arrived. She found a piece of red grosgrain ribbon and tied it around Sophie's neck. It was soft, so it wouldn't chafe her skin, yet strong enough so that it wouldn't break. The ribbon collar gave Sharon a handhold when she needed to control the kid.

Sophie was a lively baby. She bounced around the nanny pen from morning 'til night, only stopping to nurse or to nuzzle Sharon. By standing at the corner of her bedroom window, wedged against the headboard, Sharon could see the pen and watch Sophie's antics.

On Saturday morning Timothy Ingles rode in shortly after breakfast. He was at the door before Sharon realized he had arrived. She was sweeping out the doorway when he stepped onto the porch.

"Come in," she said, smiling.

He stared at her broom.

She eyed it to see what was wrong with it. Nothing she could tell.

"You should sweep *into* the house," he said. "Sweeping out is bad luck."

Moving to the porch, she swept the dirt off the edge, then turned to him. "I was about to check on Sophie, my goat. Would you like to come along?"

He nodded. "I brought along my pup. I hope you don't mind. He goes with me almost everywhere."

"Did you really? I've half a mind to bring Sophie along, too. She follows me all over. I know she'll spend the day bawling until I get back." She led him through the house to the back door.

When they reached the pen, Sophie came to the gate, and Sharon laughed. "See what I mean?" She stroked the kid's black head.

Timothy said, "My pup grew up around all kinds of animals—goats, sheep, chickens, you name it. Let's see how they get along. Maybe you can bring her."

Sharon moved down the fence and untied a length of rope. "I've been keeping her on this when she's out, so I can bring her back to the pen when I'm ready. Otherwise, she'll run and run and run, and I'll have to wait until she gets hungry before I can put her back in." She leaned over to talk directly to Sophie. "You need to learn some manners, don't you, baby?" She tied the rope to the ribbon around the kid's neck and opened the gate.

Sophie bounded out. Sharon wound the end of the rope around her hand to keep it from slipping out of her grasp.

Timothy laughed. "She must be half jackrabbit."

"I don't know where she gets so much energy." Sharon's arm waved back and forth from Sophie's pulling. "She wears me out in half an hour, but she can keep doing this all day long."

They worked their way around the house. Timothy's mount was a golden-haired pony. He had his nose deep into the water trough when Sharon first saw him. A long-haired sheepdog lay nearby. When Timothy came around the corner, the dog stood up and wagged his feathery tail.

The young man patted his pant leg. "Here, Bandit."

The dog trotted over. He raised his nose to sniff Sophie, then politely ignored her.

"See what I mean?" he asked. "I think they'll be all right. Go ahead and bring her along."

"If she gets tired before we get back, I'll put her across the saddle and carry her." Sharon tugged at the dancing rope. "I need to fetch my bonnet and our lunch basket. I'll be just a minute." She quickly tied Sophie's rope to the porch post and hurried inside.

When she came back, Corky had Ginger at the door, and they set off with Bandit roaming the countryside along the trail and Sophie bounding beside the horse.

"It's cooler in the mountains," Timothy said. "Once you get up there, you won't want to come back, I promise you."

"That I can believe," Sharon said. "I don't think I've ever seen a place so hot and dry in my life."

He pulled his horse up so they could ride side by side. "Where are you from?" he asked. "Back East?"

"Well, farther east than here. Missouri." She told him about her family and the boarding school.

"Tough luck for a kid," he said. "My ma died four years ago when I was twenty. That was hard enough. I can't imagine what it must have been like for you, losing your family at such a young age."

"I had friends at school. And I had Uncle Rudolph."

The trail stretched out long and flat before them. Ginger bobbed her head and Sharon laughed. "She wants to run." She patted the mare's neck. "Save it, girl. You'll get plenty of action before this day is out." She turned to Timothy. "I understand that my uncle and your father were partners at one time."

He nodded. "Rudolph was like a part of our family. He put up the first stake for Pa to start the store. He kept the books until I got old enough to learn it."

"Why did he sell his share? It seems strange when the store is doing so well."

"I'm not really sure. He said that he had enough on his mind with his ranching and he wanted out." He shrugged. "Maybe he needed the money. I don't really know."

She nodded. "One thing I've learned about Uncle Rudolph. He never discussed business."

The land began to slope upward. It was hard going, and Sharon stopped to put Sophie over the saddle ahead of her. The goat fought being picked up at first, then snuggled next to Sharon and quieted down.

"That kid thinks you're her mama," Timothy commented. "We had that happen once with some baby geese. Ma bought some eggs from the neighbor lady and put them under one of our setting hens. Ma was so anxious to see them hatch out that she kept going to check on them. Next thing you know, six baby geese were following Ma everywhere she went—to the clothesline, to the outhouse, everywhere. She had to run inside the house to get away from them." He chuckled. "That's the last time she did that."

Sharon stroked Sophie's soft head.

It was close to noon when they topped a rise and drew up to let the horses blow. Before them lay rolling hills that swept toward the horizon like giant waves. A breeze covered the riders with luxurious, cooling gusts.

"I wonder why no one lives here," Sharon murmured. "It's so beautiful."

"See what I meant? One of these days I'm going to have the first house in these parts." He turned his pony north. "But this isn't the greatest. Let's keep going."

They moved ahead without speaking for another thirty minutes. Finally, the sound of a trickling stream and the cooling fingers of a soft wind over water reached them.

Ginger quickened her pace. Sophie pricked up her ears.

"Over here!" Timothy called, leading them down a small slope to a winding stream full of rounded stones.

When they stopped, Timothy dismounted first. Then Sharon lifted Sophie, handed her down to Timothy, and slid from the saddle. Holding the goat's rope, she let her drink at the stream's edge. Ginger sank her front legs into the stream. She drank, tossed her head, and drank some more.

"Watch out!" Timothy called. "She'll end up with a bellyache."

"She's all right," Sharon replied. "She didn't get winded at all. She could have run most of the way." She knelt and wet her hands to wipe her face.

"Let's leave the horses and the kid here, and hike the rest of the way," he said. "It's not much farther."

"I don't think I could pull Ginger away from this water if I tried. She's having a marvelous time." She gazed at the swirling stream. "I'm tempted to dive in myself," she whispered, drying her face with her handkerchief.

With Timothy carrying the picnic basket, they continued their climb. Bandit raced ahead and fell back by turns, nose to the ground, tail high. Behind them, Sophie baaed loud and long.

"I hate to leave her behind," Sharon said.

He pulled in a corner of his mouth as he grinned at her. "She's got plenty of grass and water. She'll be fine for an hour or so." He laughed. "I think Sophie's not the only one who thinks you're her mama."

"*Touché*," she said.

"What?"

"That's French. It means 'you got me.'"

He was impressed. "You speak French?"

She shook her head. "I studied French. There's a big difference." She stopped to catch her breath.

"It's not much farther," he said, offering her his hand. "You can lean on me, if you want to."

She ignored his hand and forced her shaking limbs to climb. At this height, the trees thinned out and tall, spiky evergreens populated the hillside. The air was cooler, only she was sweating too much from exertion to appreciate it.

Then she stepped out of the trees and onto a wide, flat rock.

Ahead of her, Timothy watched her expression. He waited without speaking.

She turned north and gasped. The view was magnificent. Greens and browns rippled into a blue distance. The breeze was constant. It lifted her bonnet and loosened the pins in her hair. It plastered her skirts around her knees. It was glorious.

She stood there for several minutes just staring and breathing.

Timothy's delighted laugh brought her out of the trance. "You'll have to help me get this tablecloth down!" he called. "It won't stay put!"

Every time he tried to flip it out, the wind turned the red-checked square into a sail. Exasperated, Timothy stood with his boots holding down two corners while Sharon set the picnic basket on a third corner and a large stone on the fourth. He waited while she found two more stones to replace his feet.

Finally, they were able to plop down in the center.

"No problem with ants at this picnic," he said. "They'd blow clean off the edge."

She opened the picnic basket and offered it to him. "We'd better eat right out of the basket," she told him. "We'll be diving for our lunch if we don't."

Munching chicken, they sat together and enjoyed the view.

She leaned back on one hand and said, "I wish we could stay all day, Timothy."

"Wouldn't you like to live up here?" he asked.

"The view would be great, but how would I get anything done? I'd be sitting on my front porch all day long." She reached into the basket for a biscuit.

He lay back and stared at the sky. "And what's wrong with that? Sounds like my kind of life."

"You'd get bored in a couple of days. You know you would."

He sat up. "How do you like ranch life?" he asked. "Are you going to stay here?"

"Except for the drought, I like it fine. Love it, actually."

"Oh, yeah. I forgot about Sophie."

"Don't forget Ginger," she said with a smile. "Now that I've settled in, I can't imagine living anywhere else." She watched a hawk circling at eye level before her. Wings spread, it looped and dove. Not a care in the world.

"That's me," he said, nodding at the bird. "Free as the wind."

They spent another hour, then reluctantly captured the tablecloth and headed down the mountain.

"This is the nicest day I've had in a very long time," she told him as they neared the ranch yard. "Thank you for inviting me."

He grinned. "The pleasure was all mine. We'll have to do it again."

"I can hardly wait," she said.

At that moment, a black barn cat dashed across the lane and disappeared into the corral on the right. Timothy yanked on the reins, and his pony reared. Before Sharon could fully grasp what had happened, the young man lay in a dusty heap beside Ginger.

Sharon caught a movement some distance down the fence. Just a flutter and then it was gone. Had she imagined it?

She swung down and helped Timothy to his feet. "What happened?" she asked.

Timothy stood and stared at the fence line, the corral, the barn in the distance. "Did you recognize that cat?" he asked.

"I think it's one of our barn cats," she said, puzzled. "Why?"

He grabbed his pony's reins. "I'm sorry, but I have to get home. Do you mind if I don't see you to the door?" He scrambled into the saddle and waved. "Thank you for a pleasant day!" he called, then disappeared down the trail with Bandit following close behind.

Corky's boys must have been playing ball somewhere behind the barn. She heard them shouting and laughing, but she couldn't see them in the field.

She took her time leading Ginger to the barn. Wilson was there to take the horse from her when she arrived. He avoided looking at Sharon and took Ginger directly to her stall.

Sharon openly stared at him. She'd never seen Wilson looking so pleased since she'd come to the Lazy H. But it was no use questioning him. She'd learned that much by now.

Troubled, she made her way to the house.

When Jason came to the house later that afternoon, she was waiting for him at the door.

"Something's going on, and I want to know what it is," she told him, stepping aside so he could enter.

"What kind of something?" he asked.

"Every time I have a guest, something embarrassing happens to him. I want to know why."

His head came up a fraction, his jaw clamped tight, and a little pink showed around his ears. "That would be hard to say, Sharon," he said slowly.

"Not hard to say. Hard to admit." She faced him square on, a determined glint in her eyes.

His expression changed, and he stepped closer. "A girl who's had so much schooling should have all the answers, don't you think? Open your eyes, Sharon. You are a wealthy woman. What exactly do you think has been going on? Do you think those Romeos never thought about getting their hands on the Lazy H?"

He moved so close that she could see the tiny brown mole beside his mouth. His gaze burned into hers. "Which would you rather have, an opportunist who wants to use you to get what Rudolph worked so hard to build, or someone who cares for you because you're sweet and spunky and smart?"

When she didn't answer, he turned around and strode out the door, closing it firmly behind him.

She stared at the wood grain on the oak door. Was that all she was to Jim and Timothy? And Edward? She turned and ran to her room. It was too humiliating for words. And what about Jason? Who did he think he was, talking to her like that?

Jason strode to the corral behind the barn and paused to lean his folded arms over the top rail. He told himself that he was only protecting the ranch from the greedy paws of a couple of counterfeit suitors who only wanted to pad their pockets with the rewards of Rudolph's hard work. Yet, even as he tried to rationalize his actions away, a silent voice told Jason that he was kidding himself.

On Thursday, Wilson rode in from the south and came straight to the porch where Max and Sharon were shelling beans.

"I just talked to one of O'Bannon's men," he rasped. "South of our fence line, the stream is about played out."

Max asked, "Did he say what O'Bannon has in mind?"

"He said he had no idea, but it doesn't look good." Wilson took off his hat and blotted his forehead with his shirtsleeve. "I'm afraid they might cut the fence again."

Sharon swallowed to ease the growing knot in her throat. She needed advice, but from whom?

Chapter 12

On Sunday morning, Jason had just come to take Sharon to church when Wilson came to the house. "There's about a hundred head of Double O cattle stomping through the water hole," he said.

Jason turned to Sharon. "What do you say, boss lady?" he asked. "What now?"

"I don't know." Her heart was thumping in her throat. "What would Uncle Rudolph do?"

Jason hesitated.

Wilson scratched his stubbled jaw. "Miss Sharon, Rudolph kept the peace because of who he was, not what he did."

"I need some time to think," she burst out. "I'm afraid this will end up in gunplay. We don't want that, do we?"

Neither of them answered. Helping Sharon aboard, Jason climbed up on the other side and shook the reins. The buckboard rumbled down the trail.

"Don't you have anything to say that would help me?" she demanded of Jason after a few minutes. "I thought you promised to take care of things for me."

"What do you want me to do?" he flung back. "Grab some rifles and run them off? If we do that, we're burning bridges that will never be mended with the Double O. Someone may be killed, maybe Corky or Wilson." He turned to her. "How would you feel about that?"

When she didn't answer he went on, "On the other hand, let's say we do nothing. We'll end up in the same shape as O'Bannon—our cattle bawling for water and maybe dying."

Jason's mother was feeling too ill to come out, and Lucy decided to stay with her. As soon as the McCormick family climbed into the back of the buckboard, they were on their way.

For the rest of the ride into town Sharon sat silent. When they reached the church, she spotted Edward Kellerman's horse tied with the rest. She met his gaze when she stepped through the door, and he came to meet her.

"What is it?" he asked. "You look like you've got something on your mind."

Without answering, she turned back through the door and kept walking until they were some distance from the closest listener. "O'Bannon's men drove some cattle onto our land. They're stomping through the water hole. As low as it is, soon it will be pure sludge." She gripped his arm. "What am I going to do?

I'm afraid there will be shooting."

His face stiffened. "This is a wild country, Sharon. Sometimes you have to protect what's yours with guns. It's not easy, but it's necessary." He placed his hand over hers. "Send your hands over there and drive those cows back—the Double O cowboys, too. Do you want your own cattle to die of thirst? That's the only issue you can think about now."

From his coat pocket he drew several papers folded together. "I was going to talk to you about this later, but this is as a good a time as any." He unfolded the papers. In large curly script the heading said Power of Attorney. He handed it to her. "I've been thinking about what you said about needing help. I'm willing to put myself on the line for you, Sharon." He smiled gently into her eyes. "Whatever you need, I'm ready to stand up for you. You know that."

She scanned the pages. "What is this?"

"It's only a formality," he said, reaching into his pocket for a pen in a narrow leather case. "Sign that and I'll be able to take care of your business without having to bother you with every little detail. I'll give you reports once a month or once a quarter. You won't have to worry about anything at all."

She glanced at the closely written document. The words were flowery and so was the handwriting. She didn't have time to read it all now. She handed it back to him. "I can't sign anything today, Edward. It's Sunday. Besides, I've got too much on my mind to think about something like that."

He hesitated, then slowly took it from her. "How about if I call on you later in the week when you'll have time to read it over?" he asked.

She nodded. "That would be best, I think." She smiled up at him. "Thank you."

He took her hand and folded it over his bent elbow. "You are quite welcome."

She walked with him to the church door, then pulled away, imagining every female eye in the building turning to watch her come in late with Edward Kellerman.

The congregation was standing and singing when they arrived. With a nod, Edward returned to his seat on the left. Sharon found a seat with the McCormick family.

If only there were a chapter and verse in the Bible to give her the answer to her dilemma. Then again, maybe there was one, but she didn't know where to find it.

The preacher droned on and on. A fly buzzed around Sharon's pew. Roddy swatted at it until his mother jostled his arm. Would the message ever end? Sharon couldn't focus on a single word.

Later that afternoon, after leaving the McCormick family at their cabin, Jason said, "I'm not staying at my mother's place this afternoon. We have to deal with the water situation before sunset."

She nodded but didn't speak. What was she going to do?

Immediately after lunch, Sharon changed into riding clothes while Jason took the buckboard to the barn. When she came outside, Jason was in the saddle and leading Ginger toward the house. Wilson and Corky were mounted and waiting in the yard. When the bay mare saw Sharon, she nickered and picked up her pace. Sharon waited on the porch for an easier mount.

"Ginger! You good girl." She stroked the mare's face.

"You sure have won her over," Jason said. "No one cottoned much to Ginger before you came. She was too wild."

She sent him an arched look. "Ginger and I have a lot in common," she said and stepped into the stirrup.

The men had rifle scabbards on their horses, and they were wearing their gun belts. Sharon's hands were shaking, her heart thumping in her neck. She sent up a heartfelt prayer for safety. If only there was some way to settle this whole situation with no losers.

"Let's take it easy," Jason said as they set out. "It's too hot to get the horses lathered up."

Corky and Wilson moved ahead. Jason rode beside Sharon while she rambled on about Sophie eating the tail end of her apron string the last time she was in the pen. "One day soon, I'm going to tie a rope to her collar and take her riding with me. She had so much fun when we went to Chimney Rock."

When they all paused for a drink from their warm canteens, Jason said, "There must be some way to get through this drought without killing each other. If we think hard enough, we should be able to figure something out."

Sharon asked, "What about a well? We have a couple of them at the house. Could we drill for water out on the range and pump it for the cows?"

Corky let out a short laugh.

"It's not practical," Jason told her. "With the water table this low, we'd have a bad time drilling. Besides that, do you have any idea how much water one cow needs every day? And how much we'd have to pump? It would keep a man busy all day long."

They rode on in silence for a few minutes. There wasn't a bird, a rabbit, or even a lizard anywhere in sight. Every living creature was hiding from the glare of that broiling sun.

As they neared the water hole, a cowboy on a paint horse came into view. When he saw them, he whistled to someone out of sight.

A milling mass of about one hundred fifty cows were around and in the water hole. They were bawling as four cowboys tried to herd them south. When a handful moved away, a dozen more turned around and came back to the water.

"Whose cows are those?" Sharon asked. "All I see are Lazy H brands."

"They're all mixed up," Jason said, disgusted. "Getting them separated could be half a day's work the way things are going."

Luther Heinburg moved his mustang through the swirling herd and came near enough to shout, "We're trying to move them out!" he called. "We're not having much luck!" He took off his hat and rubbed his face with a grimy red bandanna, then urged his horse closer. The stallion fought the bit and edged around.

Finally, Heinburg was close enough for conversation. "Some mavericks busted down your fence. They must have smelled water. Once it was down, the rest of them followed." He took his hat off but still held it up to shade his eyes. "This weren't our doing, Miss Hastings," he said.

Both Wilson and Corky had their chins tucked down, disbelieving looks on their faces. Jason's arm stretched toward his rifle butt. Sharon reached out in a quelling gesture.

Jason stared at her. She held his eyes for a moment, then turned toward Heinburg.

"We both have a problem, Mr. Heinburg," she said. "So does everyone in this section of the territory. We want to work things out so everyone wins. I hope you'll help us do that." She gazed toward the water hole. "The trouble is, once the water gets so low and too many cows come around, they'll churn it into mud and make it useless. Then we'll both lose."

Heinburg replaced his hat. "I wish there were some easy answers. I truly do. Our groundwater is getting so low that the cows can hardly drink it. That's why they moved up here." He glared at the yellow sky. "Why doesn't it rain? Half a day would turn this whole thing around."

Jason scanned the jostling, bumping herd. "Looks like only about a third of them are ours. Don't worry about culling them out. Roundup is only six weeks away. We'll separate them then."

Heinburg relaxed a little. "I wish I could tell you we'd have the beeves off your land today, but they're giving the boys a bad time."

"Wilson and Corky will help you out," Jason said. He glanced toward the men, and they set off toward the herd.

Luther Heinburg wheeled his horse around and rejoined his men.

After a few minutes, Sharon voiced the question that had been on her mind for days. "What if the water hole dries up?"

"As far I as I know, that's never happened. But if it does, we'll round them up and head for the hills," Jason said shortly. "There's water farther north. Our source is the mountains. There's always water there."

In her heart Sharon cried out to the Lord. They needed help. Why didn't He answer? She couldn't understand it. There were so many things that she couldn't understand. Why had her parents died when she was so young? Why had she come into so much responsibility before she was ready? The trouble was, no one could really give her answers except to say, "God knows best," or "God never puts on us more than we can bear." To Sharon, those were no answers at all.

They were almost to the ranch when Sharon asked, "Jason, what is a power of attorney?"

"A what?" He moved closer to hear better.

"A document called a power of attorney. Edward Kellerman brought one to me and wanted me to sign it."

"Is that right?" His voice had a cynical edge. "I always knew there was something shady about that guy. He's trying to run a ringer on you."

Her mouth tightened. "Why do you say that? He's a nice guy—polite, refined. . ."

Jason spurred his horse ahead so she couldn't see his face.

It was a simple question. Why didn't he give her a simple answer?

Hot and weary and disgruntled, she didn't try to catch up with him. They rode into the ranch apart. Without a word, he took Ginger's reins from her and went into the barn. She didn't see him again for the rest of the day.

Chapter 13

The next morning over biscuits and pan gravy, Wilson drawled, "We worked on them beeves for nigh on four hours before we got them headed back to the Double O. Corky and I checked that fence, and Heinburg was telling the truth. It was knocked down this time, not cut."

Jason set his fork on his plate and leaned back in his chair to give Wilson his full attention.

The cowhand went on, "Once we broke the ice, Heinburg's men were decent hombres." He forked a bite of biscuit. "I'm glad we didn't draw down on 'em."

Jason picked up his fork. "Why don't we ride over to O'Bannon's place and have a talk with him?" he asked Sharon. "He's a fairly reasonable man. Maybe together we can come up with a compromise."

"That's a great idea," Sharon told him. "I'm ready to ride as soon as we finish here." She glanced at Max and winked. "Wrap up one of those dried apple pies you made Saturday."

Two hours later, Jason and Sharon arrived at the Double O spread, a place about the size of the Lazy H. The house was a little larger than Sharon's house, with two floors instead of one, but the rest of the place was about the same: a giant barn, several corrals, and a long, low bunkhouse. Somewhere toward the back of the property, a dog was barking loud and long.

Leaving their horses a short distance from the barn, Sharon and Jason took a few steps toward the open doors when a large red-haired man stepped outside. He wore a green-and-black checked shirt with the sleeves rolled up to the elbows and the collar open. His face was set.

His voice rumbled from deep in his chest. "Riordan," he said. "I was about to come and see you." He waved his meaty hand toward a couple of backless benches. "Have a seat. It's cooler out here than inside."

Jason shook the man's hand and said, "Jared O'Bannon, meet Sharon Hastings, Rudolph's niece. She's the new owner of the Lazy H."

With a bland expression, he faced Sharon.

Sharon smiled and offered her hand. He shook it and gave her a curt nod.

When they were seated, Jared O'Bannon found a place across from them and started right in. "Miss Hastings, I owe you an apology for my men cutting your fence." He looked her in the eyes. "It won't happen again."

He let out a heavy breath and rubbed his jaw. "My groundwater is about gone. When cattle get thirsty, they'll knock down the Rock of Gibraltar to get to water. I can't promise they'll never come on your land again."

"Your apology is accepted, Mr. O'Bannon," she said. "We came here today to try to come up with a solution to both our problems." She smiled. "I don't think neighbors should act like they're in a contest, with one winning and the other losing. I hope we can get through the drought with both of us coming out on top."

"We came to see if we could help each other out," chimed Jason.

O'Bannon said, "I don't know what to tell you, son. If we don't see rain soon, we're all gonna lose our shirts."

Jason leaned back and crossed his right ankle over his left knee. "There's still water northeast of here in the foothills. Most of it is government land. What would you think of driving our herds up thataway?"

O'Bannon shook his head. "I've got a bumper crop of new calves this year. They can travel a little ways, but you're talking twenty or thirty miles." He leaned back against a porch post, considering. "Of course, if the drought goes on we'll lose them anyway, and their mothers, too."

Sharon said, "The water hole is so low that it can't last much longer with the cattle milling around in it."

"I've got my hands watching that section of the fence to keep them from busting through," O'Bannon said. "But that's not to say some canny renegade won't find a place down the line to cross over."

"Maybe it'll rain before we have to do anything," Sharon said, standing. "We're praying that way."

As he stood, O'Bannon muttered, "I'm thinking of selling out. This water problem is making an old man out of me, and it's killing my wife."

Sharon said, "Would Mrs. O'Bannon mind if I stopped at the house for a few minutes? I'd very much like to meet her."

He nodded. "She'd like that. Go on around the house. She's washing clothes in the backyard." He turned to Jason. "I've got a sick mare. Would you mind taking a look at her?"

The men moved into the barn, and Sharon strode to Ginger to fetch the box tied behind the saddle. A few minutes later, she rounded the house and saw a tall, slim woman bent over a washboard. She wore no sunbonnet, and her face showed the effects of countless hours in the sun. Her hair was completely gray.

At Sharon's call, she straightened and rubbed suds from her arms. She waved, then moved to a pump nearby and worked the handle.

"Hello," Sharon said when she drew nearer. "I'm Sharon Hastings from the Lazy H."

Rinsing her arms, Mrs. O'Bannon nodded. "It's kind of you to stop by," she said wearily. "Would you like a drink while I've got the water running?" At Sharon's nod, she lifted the tin ladle hanging by the side of the pump and filled it.

Sharon handed her the pie and took the ladle. The water was cool. It must have come from far down.

"I'm Peggy," the older woman said. She opened the box lid. "Well, what do you know?" she said, brightening. "Jared is partial to apple pie. It's very kind of you to bring it."

They exchanged small talk for a few minutes, then Sharon excused herself and headed for the barn. What a depressing life, she thought. The Lazy H had a family atmosphere, a team spirit. Peggy was all alone, working from morning to night. How did she stand it?

When Sharon and Jason were on their way, she flexed her shoulders and looked straight up in a gesture of relief. "That went better than I'd hoped," she said.

Jason grinned at her. "I believe you won him over."

She told him about meeting Peggy O'Bannon. "What a depressing life! And she's a nice person, Jason, a really nice person. When I think that once she was young with hopes and dreams like Lucy and me. . ."

She rambled on for a few minutes, then sighed. "Ranching seems like such a hard way to make a living."

His expression grew serious. "You are right," he said. "It seems like there's always something—too much rain, not enough rain, hoof-and-mouth scares, low beef prices, or something else that no one ever heard of yet."

"Why do people stay here for years and years?"

His eyes scanned the horizon. "There's your answer. It's the life—open sky, room to ride, nobody breathing down your neck. Can you imagine Corky or Wilson wearing a white shirt with sleeve garters and saying, 'Would you like anything else, miss?' while they filled a grocery sack?" He chuckled. "Or Max slinging hash in a restaurant with people barking orders at him from morning 'til night?"

She shook her head. "Not in a million years."

"They'd make about the same amount of money, or maybe even more. But would they want to?" He paused to look at her. "Would I?"

At that moment, a rifle report echoed across the range. Sharon looked around to see where it came from. She felt a sudden burning in her left side and looked down. A deep red spot grew to the size of a quarter, then a silver dollar. She tried to touch it, but her arm wouldn't come up.

She tried to call Jason. Then the edges of her vision turned dark. . . .

Chapter 14

Jason heard the rifle report and saw the shock on Sharon's face. He didn't fully understand what had happened until he saw her slump and begin to slide from the saddle. Wheeling his horse nearer, he caught her as she collapsed.

He swung his leg in front of him over the saddle, grabbed her shoulders, and slipped to the ground. He laid her down as gently as he could to see where she was hurt. A spreading bloodstain on her left side told the story. There was a hole in her shirt, and he used that to tear an opening wide enough for him to stuff his handkerchief against the bullet wound.

Scanning the horizon, he tried to see who had fired that shot. Stark horror replaced the panic of the moment. Who would do such a fiendish thing? Was he still out there, waiting for a clearer target?

Jason had to get Sharon to safety. Whistling for his horse, he forced the animal to lie down until he could get Sharon across the saddle. After the horse stood up, Jason mounted, put his arms around her, and held her against him.

Traveling as fast as he could in that awkward position, he made a beeline for his mother's cabin and prayed that Sharon would live until he got there. Ginger whinnied and galloped after them.

The thing that scared him most was the growing slick spot on her dress. It spread across her middle and down her skirt. Her head bent back to rest against his shoulder, and she never stirred once.

Bellowing for help the moment he rode into the yard, he waited only seconds until Lucy ran outside.

When she saw Sharon, she drew up and her hands flew to her mouth. "What happened?" she squealed.

"Someone shot her," he rasped. "I didn't see who it was. Help me get her inside. I've got to get the doctor."

He eased Sharon's limp form down and Lucy lowered her to the ground. He lunged from the saddle to carry Sharon into the house. Blood had soaked the entire front of her dress. Her face had a greenish tinge, and her lips were white.

"Take her to my room!" Lucy called after him.

His mother was in the rocking chair when he stepped inside. She gasped when she saw him but didn't say a word.

Lucy dashed around him to open the door to the back bedroom. She tore back the covers, so Jason could lay Sharon on the sheet. Not stopping in to even wash his hands, he dashed past Lucy toward the front door. Outside, he grabbed Ginger's reins and leaped into the saddle.

Lucy ran for a basin of hot water, scissors, and a roll of bandages. As she moved, she called out to her mother what Jason had told her.

With her head against the back of the rocking chair, Mrs. Riordan gazed at the ceiling and called aloud, "Lord Jesus, keep Thy hand upon our girl. Give wings to Jason's horse. . . ." While Lucy worked over Sharon, Mrs. Riordan never stopped praying.

Lucy used the small tear Jason had made to finish tearing the dress off of the injured girl. She pressed a small pad against the wound until the bleeding was only an ooze. Cleansing around the wound, she applied a bandage and arranged one of her old nightgowns over Sharon's form. Then she covered Sharon with a faded quilt. In spite of the heat of the day, her skin felt cold to the touch.

After that, all Lucy could do was sit beside the bed and join in her mother's prayers.

The doctor was at his apartment over his office when Jason arrived. "Sharon's hurt!" he shouted as the doctor opened the door. "Someone shot her! You have to come right away!"

Dr. Lanchester hurried into his office, pulled open a drawer, and picked up several items to drop into his black Gladstone bag. The next minute he was following Jason outside.

"Let me ride your horse back," the doctor said. "Saddle my horse and bring him out."

Jason veered toward the stable and soon heard Ginger's pounding hoofbeats fading down the street. He paused to wash off his hands under the faucet near the stable.

Saddling the doctor's horse was no small matter with his hands trembling. His arms felt weak and he couldn't concentrate. The horse sensed Jason's distress and pranced around the stall. Finally, Jason stepped away. He leaned against the rail and closed his eyes for a full minute, then grabbed the cinch strap again.

Fifteen minutes later, Jason was in the saddle. As the ground moved under him, his mind was racing. Who would want Sharon dead? It made no sense. He was beginning to wonder if life ever made sense the way things had been going these past three months.

He kept the horse to a gallop until the cabin came into view.

Lucy threw herself into Jason's arms when he stepped inside. She was crying.

Holding his sister, Jason's breath stopped for moment. What had happened?

His mother said, "The doctor is taking out the bullet. He says it's only a flesh wound, but she's lost too much blood. She may not be able to stand the surgery."

Lucy lifted her apron and dried her eyes. "Who did this to her?" she demanded.

"It was a rifle shot from inside a stand of trees. I couldn't see anyone, and I was more worried about taking Sharon to safety than chasing the guy." He tore off his Stetson and raked his fingers through his hair.

"How could someone do this? Whoever he is, he won't be safe in the territory once he's caught." He flexed his fingers. "He won't be safe in the whole country as long as I'm alive."

For the next thirty minutes, they talked about possibilities and suspects but got nowhere. Jason paced in front of the fireplace, tearing at his hair and scowling.

Finally the doctor came out.

Jason lunged at him. "How is she?"

"She survived the surgery," he said, worried, "but she's terribly weak. I'm concerned that she hasn't regained consciousness. I poured whiskey into the wound to sterilize it, and she didn't react at all." He turned to Lucy and gave her a paper envelope. "Give her this when she wakes up. I wrote the dosages on it." He pulled out his pocket watch. "It's twenty past five. I'll be back in three hours."

Jason shook his hand. "Thanks, Doc."

"If you need me, come a-running" was his only good-bye.

Jason turned toward the bedroom door. "Lucy, check to be sure she's decent. I've got to see her."

With a questioning glance at her brother's intense expression, Lucy eased the door open and peered inside, then opened the door wider. Sharon lay with her head on the pillow, a quilt tucked up under her chin. Her French twist had fallen down, but the pins were still in her hair, popping up at odd angles. Wispy strands of blond hair clung to her face.

When Lucy stepped aside, Jason crept into the room. He felt a physical pain in his chest at seeing Sharon so still and white. What would he do without her? How could he go on?

He dropped to his knees beside the bed and gently clasped her hand. Why did they shoot her and not him? If only he had been the target. He held her hand to his lips and prayed like he hadn't prayed in years.

Finally, Lucy pressed her hand against his shoulder. "Better let her rest," she whispered.

Slowly, reluctantly, he stood and gently replaced Sharon's hand on the quilt. Three steps and he was back in the living room.

Lucy stared at his shirt. "We'll have to throw that out," she said. "There's no way I'll ever get it clean."

He glanced down and realized for the first time that his shirt was covered with blood.

Lucy gave him a hard look. "You've got it bad, haven't you, brother?"

He blinked at her as though looking through a dense fog. "What are you talking about?"

She unbuttoned his shirt and pulled it off of him while he stared at her.

Lucy leaned forward to whisper, "You're in love with her, you idiot. It's written all over you in giant letters."

Jason shook his head to clear it. He had to sit down somewhere. "Lucy," he said, "what am I going to do?"

She stepped away from him. "You're going to scrub from head to toe while I fetch you clean clothes. Then you're going to pray." Her voice faltered. Suddenly, she put her arms around him and squeezed hard. "What if she dies, Jason? How could we bear it?"

They clung to each other while Lucy cried. Their mother's voice, reedy and quavering, filled the room. " 'Oh, God, our help in ages past, our hope for years to come. . . .' "

Her children came to her, knelt beside her chair, and sang with her to the end of the verse.

With her hands on their shoulders, she prayed as though God were standing right there in the room with them. And He was.

Around seven that evening, Corky knocked at the cabin door. Jason answered and stepped outside to talk to him.

"Max has been worried sick because Sharon didn't come back to the house," Corky said. "I saw Ginger in your corral and wondered what had happened."

Jason thumped his fist against the porch post. "On the way back from O'Bannon's place somebody shot Sharon. It's a flesh wound in her side. The doc says she's lost too much blood. She may not pull through."

Corky sucked air between his teeth. "Where did it happen?"

Jason told him where they had been riding when it happened. "It seemed to come from the northeast," he finished. "Maybe from that big grove of desert willow."

Corky nodded. "Wilson and I will head out that way at first light. Maybe we can spot something, some sign of who was there."

"Look after things, will you, Corky? I'll stay here until I know something more about her condition."

Corky moved to his horse tied nearby. "I'll let the men know what's happened." He swung to the saddle and set out at a trot.

Jason stayed on the porch for a while. His feelings ran so deep that he couldn't express them. He could only cry out, "Please, help us!"

The first thing Sharon knew was a burning pain deep in her side. She tried to move to ease it and got a stab from the effort. She moaned and tried to open her eyes.

Cool fingers touched her forehead. "Sharon, you're okay. You are with me, and you're going to be all right." It was Jason. What was he doing in her room? Again blackness closed over her.

Sometime later, she swung back the cover. Too hot.

When she managed to open her eyes, Lucy was bending over her, wiping her face with a cool cloth.

"What happened?" Sharon mumbled. She felt so tired she could hardly breathe.

"You had an accident on the way back from the Double O Ranch. The doctor had to stitch your side. That's why you're in pain." She helped Sharon sit up enough to drink from a glass.

When she lay back, Sharon murmured, "Jason."

"He's outside. He's been here for two days, waiting for you wake up." She gave Sharon a gentle smile and hurried out.

The next moment, Jason rushed to her side. He didn't say anything, but the look on his face reached her deep inside. She tried to tell him, but she was too weak. A single tear slid down toward her ear.

He touched her face and wiped it away. "You're safe now. You're with me and you're going to be all right."

She nestled her cheek against his hand and closed her eyes.

Jason cradled Sharon's cheek until a cramp forced him to move his hand away. She hadn't cried until he came in. He wanted to fold her into his arms and never let go.

"It's ten o'clock," Lucy whispered from behind him. "You ought to get some rest. You've had a long day."

He nodded and stood. "I'll sleep a couple of hours, then come downstairs so you can sleep." He gazed down at Sharon's sleeping form. He hadn't been able to leave the house. Corky and Wilson had taken over Jason's chores for a few days. There was no way he could think of anything besides Sharon.

Lucy touched his arm and he came to himself. "There's some corn bread and buttermilk in the kitchen, if you need to eat," she whispered, then pressed him toward the door.

Eat? Would he ever eat again? He stumbled up the stairs and flung himself on the cot he'd slept in since he was a boy, and instantly fell into an exhausted sleep.

When the doctor arrived on the third day, Sharon was awake. He completed his examination and invited Jason and Lucy into the room. "She's going to be fine," he said, beaming at the patient. "You gave us a bad scare, young lady," he said. "I prescribe two weeks of complete rest before you can go home. Drink as much water as you can hold, and don't make any sudden moves."

He shook Jason's hand on his way out and grinned at Lucy.

When the door closed behind him, his mother said, "God be praised. Lucy, come and help me up, so I can see our girl."

With Lucy holding tightly around her middle, she tottered in and took the only chair in the room. "Child," she said, "God has His hand on you. He's spared your life twice now. You are blessed."

Sharon's eyes filled with tears. She couldn't speak.

With a pat on Sharon's hand, Mother stood and slowly made her way out. "You kids stop hovering over her now. Let her rest, or she'll never get better."

Jason waited until his mother crossed the threshold before he came into the room. "I won't stay long," he said. He pulled the chair closer and sat, bending close to Sharon's face.

She said, "Max?"

"He's coming over tomorrow when you're stronger. He was mighty worried about you—we all were." He smiled into her eyes, and she felt warm and safe.

That warm, safe feeling lasted for the rest of the time she stayed at the Riordan cabin. After the first week, Jason left at times to attend to ranch business, but he continued to sleep there. When she was strong enough, they'd sit on the porch in the evenings, listening to the cricket chorus, slowly rocking and talking until Lucy came to shoo Sharon to bed.

"Do you have any idea who did this to me?" she asked him on the eighth day.

His face grew grim. "I wish I could say we knew who it was, but I never got a look at him. All we know is that someone used a rifle with a scope. Otherwise, I'd have seen him." He stopped rocking and stretched out his legs. "Wilson couldn't spot any sign. He didn't halfway know where to look."

She shivered. "What if he's still out there? What if he comes back to try again?" She hugged herself and scanned the darkness.

"No one could see us sitting here. The light from the window is too dim."

"But what about later? Will I be able to ride Ginger again? Will I have to stay like a prisoner in the house?"

He came out of his seat and squatted beside her. He gazed into her eyes. "I'm going to take care of you, Sharon. I'll find out who did this if it's the last thing I ever do. I promise you."

Sharon forgot the danger. She forgot the crickets and the ache in her side.

He drew closer.

She tilted her face toward his.

"Sharon?" Lucy called as she opened the door. "It's eight o'clock, time for you to go to bed."

Quickly, Jason stood and stepped away. "I'll help her inside," he told his sister.

Lucy went inside, but didn't close the door.

Jason offered Sharon his arm and braced her with his hand, so she could stand. Any full-body movements still gave her pain. She grunted as she came to her feet.

They moved slowly through the living room and into Sharon's temporary room. She curled her fingers around his arm, and he covered her hand with his.

"Can I get you some water?" he asked when she eased herself down to the edge of the bed. When she nodded, he poured her a glass from a metal pitcher close to the bed. She drank it, handed him the glass, and lay back.

Jason closed the door and left her in the darkness.

Sharon let her body meld into the feather tick under her. Her eyes were closed, but she could see Jason clearly. She could feel his nearness and the warmth of his gaze. If only she didn't have to go back to the ranch. If only she could stay here like this, safe and cared for—with Jason—forever.

Chapter 15

Sharon's recovery was steady and without any infection. On the morning of the sixteenth day, she hugged Lucy and said good-bye. "There's no way I could ever thank you for all you've done for me," she said.

"I'm going to miss you," Lucy replied. "I should be thanking you for the company." She gave Sharon's hand a squeeze. "I'll come and see you before long."

Sharon said, "Tell Mother I said good-bye. I didn't want to wake her. She gets precious little sleep."

Jason set a box under the iron step on the surrey and helped her up. She gripped the edge of the seat as the surrey began to sway. With many anxious glances in her direction, Jason kept the horse to a slow pace. The journey seemed endless.

When they reached the ranch house, Jason lifted her off her feet and gently set her down. He held her for moment as she got her balance. Then Max burst out the door, and Jason turned her loose.

"I'd hoped you wouldn't come until after lunch," Max burst out. "I didn't want you to see the house like this. Someone broke in last night. Everything's a mess. I think they were looking for something."

Sharon's already pale face turned ashen when she saw the floor strewn with torn ledgers, broken tally books, and loose papers. The sofa cushions were ripped open, and the rocking chairs lay on their sides. Desk drawers lay upside down with their contents thrown across the floor.

Her steps faltered. Max came to support her other side, and they got her onto her bed in short order. In her room, her dresses lay in a heap on the floor, her toiletries dumped all over the dresser top.

"I want to change," she said weakly. "I had a gown in there." She pointed toward the overturned trunk at the end of her bed. "If you will find it for me, I can do the rest."

Jason found the clothing and laid it on the bed. When he closed the door, she was pushing herself to a standing position beside the bed.

"Max," Jason said, "did you hear anything last night?"

The little man's face was troubled. "The horses were restless, but that was all. We figured there was a coyote in the neighborhood."

"There was a coyote in the neighborhood, all right. He was in here." He scanned the room, disgusted. "All this is going to upset her to no end. We've got to get it cleaned up right away. I'd ask Lucy, but she's had all she can take with two invalids to care for these past two weeks." He bent over to gather papers into a stack.

Max started picking things up around the desk. "Whoever it was, he had to be looking for something," he repeated. "There's nothing in here worth stealing."

They worked for a good half hour and finally had the floor cleared, but the desk was still in shambles. Jason closed the lid on a jumbled mess. Sharon would have to sort things out when she felt better. As the owner, she was the only one who could decide what was important enough to keep.

Leaving Max to his kitchen work, Jason went out to the barn and didn't return until the triangle jangled for lunch. When he came in, Max had a tray made up for Sharon. Jason took it from him and carried it to her room. He knocked briefly, then entered when she called out.

Sitting up on the bed, she had a robe tied around her. She frowned at the food. Her stomach felt like lead. "I don't think I can eat anything."

"Max made chicken soup with egg noodles. Eat two small bites to make him happy. Can you do that?" He held up a dish towel. "He sent you this so you wouldn't spill on yourself."

She tried to smile. "I should have one of those even when I'm at the table." She finished half the bowl, then handed it to him. "Are you going to eat?" she asked.

He handed her a tall glass of water. "I can eat anytime." He stared at the pile on the floor. "Will it tire you too much if I straighten up in here?"

"Quite the opposite," she said wearily. "I've been scolding myself for being such a sissy. I should be picking things up instead of lying here."

"That's just what I *don't* want you to do: scold yourself or pick anything up. That's what I'm here for."

She wrinkled her nose. "It's not proper for you to be handling my things," she said.

"Who is going to know? Just Max. And he's not skittish." He set about hanging up her dresses and stuffed the rest into the trunk and the dresser. Closing the last drawer, he said, "That wasn't so bad, was it?" He touched her foot through the quilt. "I'm going out so you can get some rest."

He disappeared through the door. Pulling off her robe, Sharon lay down and closed her eyes. She wanted to cry, but she didn't have the strength. That ride home really took it out of her.

That night Max finished tidying up the kitchen shortly after supper, then left the house. Alone in her room, Sharon lay with her eyes wide open, hearing every creak in the house and every rustling limb outside her window.

What if that man came back? He was here last night. Did he find what he was looking for? Was he watching the house, knowing that she was home?

What if he came into the house? She was too weak to even scream. The triangle was outside. What would she do?

It was well past dark when the front door groaned as it opened. Footsteps sounded like gunshots on the plank flooring. A gentle tap at her door. "Sharon?" Max said. "Are you awake?"

Pulling the quilt to her chin, Sharon said, "Max! Come in." Her breathing was quick and shallow. "You scared the life out of me."

"Honey, I'm so sorry. I should have called out when I opened the door. I came to see if you are okay."

"Would you mind sleeping in the house for a few days? What if someone came back in the middle of the night? I would be trapped in here with no way to call for help."

He put his hand on the edge of the door. "I'd be glad to do that. I'll get my things from the bunkhouse." He glanced at her empty glass on the night table. "Let me refill that while I'm here." He took the glass and disappeared.

Her eyes drifted closed, and she never knew when he brought it back.

For the next two days, Sharon felt fussed over until she was thoroughly tired of it. On the third morning, she insisted on dressing and coming out to breakfast.

"So tell me what's been happening," she said as she spread butter on a pancake. "It hasn't rained yet. I know that. What about the water hole?" She glanced at Jason and waited for his answer.

He made a show of finishing his coffee and slowly set down the cup. "Last week the water hole sank to eight inches deep. O'Bannon is out of water. His cows have smashed our fence line for over two hundred yards. There's no chance of driving them back now. They're too crazy with thirst."

Wilson added, "I rode over there yesterday. We've less than six inches now. Soon it will be totally mud."

Sharon took in the news for a moment. "Since I've had so much time to think, I was wondering if we could do this: How about if we rounded up our herd and pushed them into the foothills? At least our cows would have access to good water. We can give O'Bannon free range on our place so his cows can get to the streams to the north and east."

"There is still water in the streams up toward the north end," Wilson said. "Much of our herd is already there."

Jason nodded. "That could work, if we get started right away before they get so weak that we can't drive them." He pushed back from the table. "We really need a few extra hands."

Corky said, "Roddy and Mike can help us out. I think we'd best leave Ian to tend to the stock here."

Jason nodded. "It'll be tough going, but once we get them to the fresh water we won't have to worry about them drifting back. We can make two or three sweeps and get most of them." He glanced at Max. "Can you pack us some grub? We'll camp on the range at least one night."

Before he finished speaking, heavy footsteps sounded on the front porch. Max hurried to open the door and Jared O'Bannon stepped inside. His face was haggard, and he hadn't shaved in at least a week.

When he saw Sharon, he removed his hat. "Miss Hastings, I need to speak to you. I'm sorry, but it can't wait."

"Mr. O'Bannon," she said, "please have a seat here at the table. Would you like some hotcakes and coffee?"

He took a step toward the table. Max hurried to the kitchen. He came back with a mug of steaming black brew and set it before O'Bannon with an empty enamel plate and a clean fork.

"I'm much obliged," the big man said. His shoulders slumped against the back of the chair. "You said you wanted to find a solution to our problem," he said. "I came to see what we could work out." He licked his dry lips and raised his coffee cup.

Sharon said, "We were discussing that. Jason?"

"Sharon had an idea that may work. How about if we play leapfrog? We'll drive our cows north, up beyond our boundary into the government land in the foothills. You drive your cows into the northeast section of the Lazy H. That way, your calves won't have to travel so far. Our calves can make it into the foothills with no problem." Jason leaned back, waiting for O'Bannon's response.

The rancher sat unmoving for a long moment. He slowly turned to Sharon. "You would do that?"

"It's the best idea we could come up with. But it's not a permanent solution. If it doesn't rain for another two weeks, our water will be gone, too."

"That's true," he said, "but that would give my calves time to rest between moves."

Another knock sounded at the door and Max exclaimed, "Who else?" He hurried to the door and the next moment Edward Kellerman stepped inside. He was wearing his black suit and carrying his black leather case. He had his hat in his hand and flipped it onto a peg as he walked in.

When he saw Jared O'Bannon, Kellerman's expression darkened. "Good morning, Sharon," he said. "I see you have company."

Sharon smiled, trying to ease the atmosphere. "Have you met Jared O'Bannon, Edward?"

"Only by reputation," he said shortly.

"Sit down and have some coffee," Sharon invited. "Have you had breakfast?"

Max got Kellerman a plate and a mug of coffee, then returned to his seat.

Jason stood. "We can work out the details," he told Sharon. To O'Bannon he said, "I'll walk with you to your horse." Wilson and Corky stood with them and the ranch hands left the house.

Max started stacking plates.

Edward picked up his dishes and moved closer to Sharon. "I hope that wasn't trouble," he said as Max began rattling dishes in the dishpan.

"Not at all," Sharon said. "I think we're going to get things worked out." She glanced at his leather case lying on the table. "What brings you here so early?"

He forked two hotcakes on to his plate. "Well, first of all I wanted to see how you are. I heard you had an accident." He poured syrup.

"As you can see, I'm doing fine. I'm a little tired, but otherwise I'm as good as new."

Between bites he said, "What's O'Bannon up to? Is he pushing you to share your water? If he is, you should send your hands to the fence line with rifles. You've got to protect your rights, Sharon. Once these men see you as weak, they'll take advantage of you. That's one reason that I came out here this morning." Pushing his empty plate aside, he opened the leather case and drew out the forms he had shown her outside the church, the power of attorney. He didn't hand them to her but set them on the table.

Sharon stood up. She didn't want to discuss business. She moved into the living room, intending to sit in the rocking chair.

Edward stepped in front of her, close enough for her to notice the perfect knot in his tie. He clasped her hands in both of his and pulled them toward his lips. "You don't know how worried I was when I heard what had happened to you. I found out only yesterday." He had a hurt expression. "I wish you had sent word. I would have been here every day."

"Edward. . ."

At that moment Jason burst through the door. He drew up, and his cheeks took on a reddish hue.

Sharon pulled her hands away. "Yes, Jason, what is it?"

He hesitated. "We're getting ready to ride. I came to fetch the grub."

"I've got it ready!" Max called from the kitchen.

Jason made a wide circle around Sharon and met Max halfway. Taking the lumpy bundle, he headed out the door without saying good-bye.

Disgruntled, Sharon sank into the rocking chair. Edward Kellerman was becoming a distinct nuisance.

Sitting on the very edge of the sofa, he reached toward her. Their knees almost met as he handed her the power of attorney papers. "If you'd like time to read this, I can take a walk for a few minutes. I hope you can understand how important this is for your protection."

She frowned. "Don't you know that I'm in the middle of a crisis? Why do you keep bothering me with this paperwork?"

He took the papers back. "I apologize. I guess I'm so worried about you that I'm not thinking straight." He folded the papers back into his case. Raising his perfectly manicured hand, he smoothed his right eyebrow. "I'm your attorney. That means I'm your friend and advisor. All this trouble is taking its toll on you, Sharon. There's no reason to put yourself in this kind of distress. I'm here to help you. I *want* to help you. But you have to let me."

He reached into his jacket and pulled a second set of papers from the inside pocket. "You'll be glad to know that your uncle's will has been recorded. And I have here an offer to buy the ranch for five thousand dollars. You might be wise to consider it."

She took the pages and read them. This was less than Rudolph had paid fifteen years before.

She shook her head and handed them back. "I can't do it."

"I think this party may double the money," he said.

She stared at him. "Why would anyone pay that much? We are having the worst drought in years."

He pursed his lips. "They probably have good reason. Cattle isn't the only thing this land could be used for."

Max stepped in from the kitchen. "I don't mean to butt in," he said, "but are you talking about the Cattlemen's Treasure?" He grinned. "You may as well be talking about gold at the end of a rainbow." He returned to the kitchen, chuckling.

Kellerman wasn't smiling.

When Sharon tried to hand the offer to him, he gently pushed it back. "You keep that," he said. "Sleep on it. You may think better of it in the morning."

She shook her head and pressed the offer toward him. "Maybe for ten thousand," she said. "But never for five thousand." She stood. "I'm awfully tired. This has been a long morning, and I need to rest now." She turned toward her room, then remembered her manners and paused to say, "Thank you for coming out, Edward."

Stuffing the papers into his pocket, he stood. "I'll check on you in a couple of days." He took his leather case, lifted his hat from its peg, and went out.

When Sharon woke up from her nap, Max was frying bacon in the kitchen. He poured her a cup of coffee without her even asking and set it on the table at her place. Pouring himself a cup, he pulled the skillet to the cold side of the stove and came to join her.

"Feeling better?" he asked.

She nodded. "I can feel my strength growing every day. Before long, I'll forget all about this weakness." She sipped her coffee.

Max rotated his cup by the handle. "I hope you don't think my nose is too long, but something about that lawyer doesn't sit right with me."

Sharon didn't reply for a moment. What was it about Edward that had irritated her this morning? "I don't exactly know what it is," she said, "but there's something wrong about him. I didn't feel it until this morning. Here I am, wounded by some unknown attacker, and all he can do is shove papers in my face." She turned toward Max with anxious eyes. "What should I do? There's no other lawyer in Farmington, is there?"

"You're right about that. But do you need one here? You could travel to Bloomfield to take care of your business if you had to."

"I'll talk to Jason about it when I get a chance."

"If all goes well, he'll be back tomorrow night." He stood and slid the skillet back into place. "I'm going to ride out to meet the hands later this afternoon with more grub. Do you feel up to pinching off some biscuits? I'll mix up the dough so you won't have to strain yourself with stirring."

"I'd be glad for something to do. Sitting still gives me cabin fever. It's bad enough in the winter but unbearable in the summer."

Max grabbed a bowl and dumped in flour, lard, and other ingredients. "Sophie's been going crazy in the nanny pen. She'll be all mighty glad to see you."

Sharon smiled softly. "I wish I could go out to see her, but I'd better wait a couple more days. She's so lively, she'll knock me down. I can't brace myself right now."

She dropped a soft lump of dough into a pan. "She may forget me by the time I'm well enough to go out."

Max snorted. "Not a chance of that. You've branded yourself all over this place, my dear, and not only in Sophie's mind."

Chapter 16

For nearly forty-eight hours Jason had brooded over catching Sharon and Kellerman with their heads together when he came upon them in the living room. But when Jason returned home the next afternoon, the last thing on his mind was Edward Kellerman.

Sharon was reading in the rocking chair and looked up, startled, when he burst in, his face flushed, his eyes wild. "Jason, what is it?" she cried.

Max trotted into the room to hear the news.

"We found Rudolph," Jason gasped. "Corky was riding a ridgeline about ten miles north of here and spotted Rudolph's red plaid shirt at the bottom of a gully. I've come to fetch the buckboard to bring him home. I'm going to take a door loose from the tack room to put the body on and hoist it up."

"Take an old quilt to wrap him in!" Max called over his shoulder as he hustled toward the spare room. He returned with the blanket in his arms. Jason grabbed it and rushed out.

Max sidled up to the sofa and sank down. "Now don't this beat all," he murmured. "How in the world did Rudolph get to be ten miles up in the foothills? He would have never ridden off our range without telling someone first."

"Somebody took a shot at *me*," Sharon said. "Who's to say they didn't shoot him first? If Jason hadn't been with me, who knows? You may have never found me, either."

Max rubbed his head. "I can't understand why anyone would do such a thing. Rudolph was a decent man. He always went the extra mile to help someone in trouble. He didn't care if a man had been in prison, he'd still help him."

"Well, someone had it in for him," Sharon said. "We need to figure out who. Mixed in there somewhere is a great big *why* running underground like a subterranean river." Her brows drew together. "Maybe we've been looking at it wrong. Instead of looking for enemies, maybe we should start thinking about people who should love Uncle Rudolph." Her eyes widened. "Maybe they *should* love him, but they resent him instead."

"You may have something there, missy," he said, getting to his feet and setting off toward the kitchen. "Let me study on that while I finish supper."

Several hours later, the men brought the body home and put it in the tack room. They couldn't bring it into the house because of the smell.

Soon after, the sheriff arrived on horseback, and the undertaker in a closed wagon. Put together, the two men had lived more than a hundred years in these parts. Their set faces showed that very little surprised them anymore.

After they examined Rudolph's body, Sheriff Quentin Feingold met with Sharon and the hands outside the barn. More than six feet tall, he was wide and thick from his neck to his belt buckle. "From what we can tell," he said in a deep, gravelly voice, "Rudolph was shot twice through the chest and then dumped into that ravine. He must have died almost instantly." He paused, then engulfed Sharon's hand in his. "My condolences, Miss Hastings," he said. "This is bad business."

"Thank you, Sheriff," she said. "We'll come into town tomorrow morning to make the arrangements."

"There's no hurry," he told her. "The doc will have to make a complete examination before we can let you bury him. But you can go ahead and see Darien," he said, jerking his neck toward the undertaker, Darien Michaels, who was busy at his wagon, "and the parson anytime you wish, to let them know your plans."

He turned to Jason. "Son, I'll need to meet with you and your men to get your statements about what happened the day Rudolph disappeared."

Jason nodded. "We'll come into town and get that taken care of."

The officials loaded the remains in the undertaker's wagon and left together, anxious to get back to town before dark.

As the hands ambled back into the barn, Jason walked with Sharon to the house.

"How horrible," Sharon said. "I can't imagine that someone we know did this to Uncle Rudolph." Suddenly, she sounded hopeful. "Maybe it was one of the Double O hands, or some stranger passing through."

"It would be nice to think it's someone without a face or a personality, someone who's like a paper doll cutout to us," Jason said, "but that's not likely, Sharon."

She told him about her conversation with Max that afternoon. "What if the gunman wasn't someone who hated Uncle Rudolph? What if it was someone that he had helped? Someone who should love him?"

They climbed the porch steps and sat together on the short bench to the right of the door.

Sharon went on, "Do you know who Uncle Rudolph has helped recently?"

Jason scanned her eager face. "Are you wearing yourself out with all this?" he asked with a worried note in his voice. "You mustn't get too worked up."

She grew impatient. "I'm trying to tell you something important."

"So am I," he replied, still gazing at her.

Meeting his eyes, Sharon's tone softened to almost a whisper. "I'm getting stronger every day."

He leaned closer.

With loud, clomping boots, Max stepped up and scraped a bench across the porch so he could sit across from them.

Jason said, "Max, we were about to list off the people Rudolph has helped. We're wondering if any of them may be his murderer."

Max nodded. "Sharon and I were talking about that earlier."

"Let's see. . ." Jason extended one finger at every name. "There's the Widow Braddock who ended up selling her place and moving to Santa Fe. Zach Ingles who owns the general store and is about the richest man in town, Rev. Nelson, Corky. . .and Sharon."

She gasped. "Me?"

He bent his little finger back toward his palm. "Just joshing you," he said, grinning. "As a matter of fact, I should put one finger up for me and Ma and Lucy. He sure did help us when Pa died." He stretched out his little finger again.

"Put up another finger for me," Max said. "He helped me out, and not only once, neither."

With that, Jason let his hand rest on his leg. "Looks like we're barking up the wrong tree," he told Sharon. "I can't imagine anyone on that list wanting to hurt Rudolph. It's got to be someone else."

"The Cattleman's Treasure," Max blurted out. "That's got to be it."

"That old saw?" Jason retorted. "That's pure hogwash. There is no treasure."

Max said, "We know that, but you know how rumors grow in small towns. There may be some folks who believe it."

"Even if the rumor were true," Sharon said, "why shoot Uncle Rudolph?"

Max held up his pudgy hand. "Because he wouldn't sell at any price. Maybe someone wanted to buy the ranch and they figured it'd be easier to buy his estate than convince him to sell."

"They didn't figure on him having an heir," Jason added. "That would answer for why they took a shot at Sharon, too."

She froze. "Edward just brought me an offer to buy the ranch. It was all drawn up and legal."

"Do you still have it?" Jason asked.

She shook her head. "I wouldn't take it from him."

"Too bad," Max said. "We could have checked to see who wanted to buy it."

"I read it," Sharon said. "It wasn't a person. It was a company." She leaned her head back and closed her eyes. "What was it? It was a funny name."

"How much did they offer?" Jason asked.

"Five thousand dollars, and he said the party would be willing to double it."

Jason whistled. "That's a lot of money for a ranch in the middle of the worst drought in years."

"He said. . ." Sharon hesitated, trying to remember the exact words. " 'Cattle isn't the only thing this land could be used for.' "

Max nodded. "That's when I came into the living room and told him that if he meant the Cattleman's Treasure, there was no such thing."

"I don't want to hurt you," Jason told Sharon, "but I'm afraid your friend Edward Kellerman has got something deep going on under all his pretty ways."

Max added, "It don't look good, and that's a fact."

Sharon let out an impatient gasp. "But how can we prove anything? Offering to buy the ranch isn't admitting guilt." She shifted in her seat. "Besides, his name wasn't on the offer."

Jason said, "He could have a partner, or he could own that company."

"Or he could get a cut for persuading you to sell," Max added.

Jason had another idea. "That could be what that power of attorney nonsense was about."

"When he was here, he tried to get me to sign that, too," Sharon said.

Jason scowled. "If you had signed that paper, he could have sold the place without asking for your permission."

Max leaned forward. "I wouldn't have let her do that," he declared. "I was listening to that oily rascal from the kitchen."

"After all that courting, he wasn't interested in me at all," Sharon announced. "He wanted my inheritance."

"He could have planned to get it by marriage—as a last resort," Jason drawled. He slanted a look at her. "As handsome as he is, that may still be an option."

She sent him a scorching look, which his expression showed he thoroughly enjoyed.

Max said, "I've got it! I've got it!"

Jason and Sharon stared at him, waiting.

"We set up a trap," the little man went on. "We bait it with information about the Cattleman's Treasure and see who bites."

Jason looked doubtful. "There could be a lot of people biting on that one. It's been a rumor for a long time. Anyone could try to cash in on it."

"Not if we're smart about who we tell," Max insisted.

Jason wasn't buying it. "Once the word gets out, it's any man's game. We could have the whole town down on us."

"That could happen," Max admitted. He massaged his face. "I guess we'll have to think about it some more."

Jason slapped his knees. "Meanwhile, we need to go to town in the morning." He turned to Sharon. "Are you feeling strong enough for the trip? I could visit the preacher and undertaker for you."

"I'd like to go," she said. "I think I'll be fine, riding in the surrey." She stood.

"If I'm going with you, I'd better say good night and get some rest."

The men said good night to her, but didn't move from their seats. Sharon heard the soothing sound of their husky voices droning on until she fell asleep.

When they set out for town after breakfast the next morning, Sharon scowled at the sky. "I'm beginning to hate the heat and the dust. If only there was some relief." Wedged between Jason and Max, she turned to Max. "Do you think the territory is going to end up like the Sahara? I've read *The Arabian Nights*, but I never wanted to live there."

"It's got to break sometime. Can't be much longer."

Jason let the reins hang loosely from his hands. "Corky and Wilson should be heading a bunch of cows toward the hills by this time. I hope the sheriff don't take it ill because they didn't come with us. We've got to get the herd moved. After we found the body, we didn't get a single thing done. Those beeves can't wait another day."

All around them the landscape was brown—the grass, the bushes, even the trees. They came to a stream that used to come up halfway to the buckboard's axle. It was completely dry, the streambed cracked and hard. The wagon jolted and rumbled across. The only things moving were several buzzards circling in the distance.

Sharon had nothing to report to the sheriff, so she went directly to the pastor's home, hoping that Rev. Nelson was there. His wife, a tiny, birdlike woman, let Sharon in.

"I came to see the pastor about funeral arrangements for my uncle," Sharon told her.

The woman's features showed concern. "He had a service at the ranch a few weeks ago," she said.

"We found his body yesterday," Sharon told her. "We want to bury him as soon as possible."

Trying unsuccessfully to hide her shock at the news, Mrs. Nelson's voice became soothing. "Of course. The pastor is in his study. He'll be glad to speak to you." She led the way through a narrow hall and opened the door. "Miss Hastings is here to see you, dear." She stood aside for Sharon to enter. "Would you like some coffee?"

"Water, please. We just drove from the ranch, and I'm thirsty. Thank you very much."

Leaving the door ajar, Mrs. Nelson scurried away.

The preacher rose to shake Sharon's hand. When she told him her errand, he frowned.

"It was foul play?" When Sharon nodded, he went on. "That's so hard to believe. Rudolph was a kind man, gruff at times but good deep down. I know of several people that he helped when they were in desperate straits."

Sharon came alert. "Would you mind telling me who they were?"

His face became pensive. "I'm not sure the parties involved would like it to be known."

"There's going to be a criminal investigation," she said urgently. "Since we can't seem to find any enemies, we were starting to think that someone he helped did this."

Steepling his fingers in front of his waistcoat, Rev. Nelson said, "There was the Widow Braddock and her four children. Rudolph found a buyer for their place, so they could move south to be near her relatives."

Sharon nodded. "I've heard about them. You know, he sold his share in the general store not long ago. I'm beginning to wonder if he didn't give away the money he made from that. There's no bank account, and nothing was recently paid on the mortgage."

"Right." He nodded. "Zach Ingles was another one. Fresh out of prison, no job, no money, and a family to feed. Rudolph took a chance on him, and it paid off. It's still paying off for Ingles."

"Was there anyone else?"

"He helped my wife and me numerous times. Fixed the roof on our house, brought us a milk cow, and a lot of other things, too many to list out." He smiled sadly. "The church is going to miss him." He drew in his lower lip, thinking. "There was a young fellow, a rascal that everyone considered a nuisance. Rudolph gave him a job, but the boy ended up stealing from him. This was three or four years back. Rudolph let him go, and we never heard from him again."

"His name?"

"Billy Gants. Wilson Gants' nephew."

Chapter 17

Forcing her mind back to the subject at hand, Sharon made arrangements for a funeral service at the church in two days. That should give the sheriff time to get what he needed from the doctor's examination.

Leaving the pastor and his wife shortly afterward, she hurried toward the sheriff's office and met Jason outside the door. She dove in before he could say anything. "Did you know about Uncle Rudolph firing Billy Gants?" she demanded.

He looked puzzled. "Of course. Billy and I practically grew up together."

"Do you think he may have come back for revenge?"

Taking her arm, Jason moved to a nearby bench in the shade. "Let's sit here. I can't take much more of that sun."

Staring at his face, Sharon wouldn't let her question die.

"Billy was trouble. There's no doubt about it," he told her. "I don't know if Wilson asked Rudolph to give Billy a job or not. One way or the other, Billy came to work with us. He only lasted about six months."

"He was caught stealing," she added.

He looked doubtful. "I wouldn't say that to anyone. Billy's got family here. Even if it were true, it would shame them, and they didn't do anything illegal."

Sharon glanced around. Five horses stood at the hitching rail in front of the general store, but no humans were in sight. She lowered her voice. "This is between us, Jason. I want to know if you think Billy could have come back for revenge."

Reluctantly, he said, "I suppose it's possible. From what his sister says, Billy hasn't been to Farmington since Rudolph let him go. It's a grief to that family. It probably is to Billy, too. He can't see his family because of what he did."

At that moment Max stepped out of the sheriff's office and headed toward them in the rolling gait common to sailors and people who are both short and wide.

"Don't you think we should tell the sheriff?" Sharon demanded in a whisper before Max reached them.

"That's your call," he said, shrugging. "I can't make it for you. I personally don't think it's that important."

Irritated by his nonchalant attitude, she stood and marched into the sheriff's office. One of these days when he put her off like that, she'd forget everything Mrs. Minniver had worked so hard to teach her.

Twenty minutes later, she stepped out and found Jason waiting for her on the same bench. He stood when he saw her.

"Max's at the general store," he told her. "We'll catch up to him."

"I haven't talked to the undertaker yet," she said primly.

"He's down at the end of the street." They paced six steps before Jason said, "So, what did the sheriff say?"

"He wrote it all down. That's all I know."

"Look, Sharon"—he tugged on her elbow, and she came around to face him—"I know you're anxious to get this behind us, but be careful. There are a lot of side issues in every question. Since you're new here, you could do a lot of damage without meaning to."

Finally, her shoulders relaxed and her chin came down. "I'm sorry, Jason. Patience has never been one of my virtues."

"Don't apologize," he said, his voice low. "It's understandable that you're upset. Just remember"—he leaned closer—"I'm on your side."

The undertaker's office was a small structure that resembled a smokehouse or a potting shed. Jason knocked and the undertaker, Darien Michaels, came to the door wearing a leather apron. His brand of cologne wouldn't have brought much on the open market. When he saw Jason and Sharon, his stoic expression never changed. "Good morning, Miss Hastings, Riordan."

"I just came from speaking to the preacher," Sharon said. "We'd like to have the funeral service the day after tomorrow at ten o'clock. Will that be convenient for you?"

He nodded once. "The doctor and I have already finished with Mr. Hastings. I'll build the coffin this afternoon." He paused. "Normally, the family brings clothes, but with the condition of the body it would be best to leave it as it is. We'll have a closed casket, of course."

Working hard at breathing as little as possible, Sharon gulped and said, "That will be fine, Mr. Michaels. Thank you."

As they walked away, Sharon turned to Jason and demanded, "Do you send him a quarter of a beef every spring, too? Or do I need to pay the man?"

Jason burst out laughing. He laughed until they reached the general store.

Max turned, a question in his eyes when they stepped inside the store. Still grinning, Jason stopped to look at the leather goods while Sharon went farther inside.

"Hello, Timothy," she said, smiling sweetly at the clerk.

"Sharon!" His face it up. "How are you doing? I've been wondering how the water hole is holding up."

Max glanced from Sharon to Timothy, then moved down the counter to look at a mound of cabbages piled on a table.

Timothy stepped closer. "How about another ride to Chimney Rock? I'm off tomorrow."

"I'd love to," Sharon said, "but we'd better wait at least two more weeks. I'm not completely back to full strength yet."

He came to stand directly across from her at the counter. "Have you been sick?" he asked.

She shook her head. "I had an accident, but I'm doing much better. When I'm ready, we'll go back up there. Believe me"—she smiled broadly—"I'd go today if I could."

Jason stepped up. Glancing at him, Timothy hurried to wrap Max's purchases.

"Do you feel strong enough to stay around for a meal?" Jason asked her. "Or would you like me to fetch a box lunch from the restaurant and stop somewhere along the way for a picnic?"

Sharon sighed. "Max and I went to the restaurant the last time we were here. It was scorching hot and packed with people. I vote for a picnic."

"I second the motion," Jason said. "Since there are only three of us, the ayes have it." He called to Timothy, "Add five cans of peaches to that order, will you please?"

The clerk waved at him.

Jason looked down at Sharon. "I know a perfect spot in the shade where you can wait until we finish our business. You really ought to sit down and rest before we take off."

They strolled down the boardwalk to the stage station where a large awning blocked the sun from a smoothly carved bench with a sloping back and wide arms.

"There's no stage due for a couple of hours," he said. "You'll be comfortable here. I'll be back in a few minutes." With that, he hurried away.

Even with the shade, Sharon felt sticky and miserable. She thought about Billy Gants hiding in the trees or behind some rocks with a rifle.

Or maybe it wasn't Billy. Maybe it was some member of the Gant family who was sore. One never could tell with situations like that.

On the ride home, the horses were anxious and leaning into the harness. "They're as miserable as we are," Jason commented as the wagon bounced down the trail. "Why not let them go? We can eat while we're riding."

"Hand me that box," Max groaned. "My belly button is about to kiss my backbone. I'm that hungry."

At that pace, the breeze cooled Sharon's burning face. She took off her bonnet and held it carefully in her lap.

Jason grinned at her. "Hand me a piece o' chicken" is all he said.

Wilson was waiting for them on the porch when they got back to the house. He came down the steps and grabbed the bridle. "Heinburg was just here. He said they're going to drive their herd to the northeast corner of our property. The water hole's dry. He said that O'Bannon doesn't want to, but his cattle are desperate."

Sharon gazed up at Jason.

He squeezed her hand. "There's enough water in that sector to last another couple of days. Meanwhile, we'll ride out that way and see how far up the main stream is dry. If it doesn't rain for a while yet, we may have to move our herd farther up into the mountains."

He spoke to Wilson. "Remind Corky that no one leaves the ranch yard without his sidearm and a rifle."

"Guns?" Sharon gasped. Her hands trembled as she grasped Jason's shoulders to step down from the buckboard. When she reached the ground, Wilson led the horses toward the barn, and Max headed into the house.

"It's going to be all right," he murmured, gazing into her eyes. "You'd better get some rest now. I'll take care of things, so don't worry."

"But what if someone comes here while you're gone? We still don't know who wants me out of the way."

Turning toward the house, Jason said, "Let me show you something." He led the way into the house with Sharon close behind him. He lifted the shotgun from over the mantel and brought it to her. It had SHARPS engraved on its side.

"Have you ever used a gun?" he asked.

When she shook her head, he said, "You press this release here." He showed her a knob near the end of the barrel. "That allows it to open." He pressed on the ends of the weapon and it came apart as it bent in the center. "This one holds two cartridges. See, it's loaded." He snapped the ends together with one quick motion.

He swung the barrel toward the ceiling and a rolled-up paper flew out. It landed on the floor in front of the rocking chair.

"What is that?" Sharon asked, hurrying to pick it up. She unrolled it, and Jason came to see. "It looks like a page from a ledger." She scanned down the closely written columns. Pacing to the table, she tried to spread it out, but it kept rolling up. Jason held two corners, and she held two.

"What have you got there?" Max asked, joining them.

"It looks like a business ledger," Jason said. "But there's no name on it."

"Let's see what's listed," Sharon said, peering at the tiny writing. "What are they buying and selling?" She read out, "Twenty-five pounds cornmeal, a hundred pounds molasses"—her finger slid down the page—"two coffee grinders, one keg of nails, six cases of paper, a hundred fountain pens. . ."

"It's Ingles' store," Max announced. "I'd stake my new stove on it."

"Wait a minute," Jason said. "What's so special about this page? Why was it hidden in the shotgun?" He pulled out a chair to sit down. Sharon and Max did the same.

"Read those off again, Sharon," Max said, "slower this time."

He closed his eyes, listening. Suddenly, he blinked and said to Jason, "Did you ever hear of Ingles selling paper and pens?"

Jason shook his head. "Old Starky at the newspaper office sells that kind of stuff. I asked about some when Lucy was still in school. Ingles said he wouldn't give the old man any competition because Mrs. Starky was so sick and he needed the money."

"I've heard about this kind of thing," Sharon said. "Sometimes when people want to cover up for missing money, they list purchases that never happened. It's called embezzling," she said, still staring at the page. "And the dates are shortly before Uncle Rudolph disappeared."

Max massaged his face. "You think that's why Rudolph sold out to Ingles?"

"Why would he sell out if the other man was wrong?" Jason asked. "Why not force Ingles to give up his half and take it all?" He stood. "Put that paper somewhere safe," he told Sharon. "I'm going to ride back into town and face Ingles."

She grabbed his sleeve. "Tell the sheriff," she said, coming to her feet. "Let him take care of it."

Jason's face was rigid. She held on to him, determined that he would listen. Finally, he relaxed. "You're right. I'll get the sheriff." He backed away. "But I've got to do it right away." He strode to the door. "With a fresh horse, I should be back in just a few hours." With a lingering look at her, he turned and rushed out.

Sharon rolled the paper into a tiny tube. "Where should I put it?" she asked Max.

"We might need the shotgun," he said. "Don't put it back in the barrel."

Moving slowly, she walked to the back door, looking all around to find a hiding place. She kept going down the steps and looked around the lean-to kitchen.

Sophie came to the fence and bawled for her. Sharon forgot about the page in her hands and hurried to pet her. "Sophie! You didn't forget me, did you, baby?"

Looking up, she spotted a crack in a beam under the roof of the goat's hut. It was a perfect fit. She slid the roll of paper into the crack and it loosened enough to fill the spot, invisible under the tin covering.

She drew the milking stool close to the fence and sat down. "Sophie, girl. You've grown so big."

Chapter 18

When Jason reached Farmington, the sheriff was already at home for the evening. He listened to Jason's story, then reached for his Stetson and went with him to the Ingles' home next to the store.

With a sinking feeling in his stomach, Jason stood to the side as Sheriff Feingold rapped on the door.

Timothy was the one to open it. "What can I do for you, Sheriff?" the young man asked, opening the door wider. "Would you like to come in? We're closed, but if you need something—"

"We're here to see your pa," Feingold said.

"He's in Albuquerque on a buying trip. He left yesterday, and he won't be back until later this week." He turned to Jason, puzzled. "Is there something I can do for you?"

"We'll wait until he gets back," the sheriff said. "Good evening."

Timothy nodded, said, "Good evening," and closed the door.

Jason and the sheriff returned to the street.

"I'll check on Zach when he gets back to town," Feingold said, shifting a toothpick in his teeth.

"Thanks, Sheriff. Much obliged." With no further conversation, Jason climbed into the saddle and turned the horse toward home. Let the law take care of things. He had a drought to worry about.

Sharon was dressed and ready to go before breakfast the next morning.

When Jason saw Sharon in the living room, his eyes narrowed. "Where are you going?" he asked.

She looked him straight in the eyes. "I'm going with you."

"Sharon. . ." His mouth set into a firm line.

"I'll be all right," she insisted. "It's better for me to be out there with you than to stay here and worry myself into a frazzled knot by the time you get back. If I get tired, I'll find a tree and take a break in the shade." She touched his arm. "Please, Jason."

He traced her face with his eyes, and his expression grew tender. "What if we end up camping on the range, or what if there's a problem with the Double O hands?" He lifted his hands as though to rest them on her shoulders, then dropped them to his sides. "I—we almost lost you once. I don't want to take any chances on a second time."

"It's so much cooler in the foothills," she said. "This heat is unbearable. Think of what it will be like for me if I stay here."

Wilson came in at that point, and Sharon moved into the dining area to sit at the table. Jason sat across the corner from her.

"I'd like to come along this time," Max said.

"Good idea," Jason replied. "Corky and Wilson could use an extra man."

When the meal was over, Sharon simply walked out of the house with the men. Wilson saddled Ginger, and they set off. If they spotted any stray Lazy H cattle along the way, the men would gather them up and push them north.

The sun was directly overhead when they crossed the fence line at the northern boundary of the Lazy H. The streambed was parched and dry as far as they could see.

"We may have to go up a ways before the water starts," Jason said, riding near Sharon. He peered at her face. "Are you feeling all right? Do you need to stop for a while?"

"I'm fine," she said. "I'm not anxious to stop in this heat. Let's get up where the temperature drops a little. Then I'll rest."

They spread out with Corky, Max, and Wilson far afield. Sharon followed the dry streambed with Jason fifty feet behind her. They rode that way for the better part of an hour. In the distance, the mountains stretched toward the sky. They seemed so close, but they were actually miles away.

Another two hours passed, and still not a trickle came down the depression that had once been rushing with water.

"I'm getting really thirsty," Sharon said when Jason rode up beside her. "I can imagine Ginger feels the same way." She took a long drink from her canteen and slid down to the ground. Wetting her bandanna, she swabbed out Ginger's nose and poured some water on the horse's long tongue. "Sorry, girl. That's the best I can do for now."

"I can't understand it," Jason said. "It was this dry back in '86, and we never lost the water hole."

"Maybe it's because of O'Bannon's cattle coming onto our land," Sharon said. "Twice as many cows. Or maybe more depending on how many Rudolph had back then."

Suddenly, a whistle reached them. One of the men waved his hat.

Jason said, "Looks like they've found something." He urged his gelding to a trot. After Sharon remounted Ginger, the horse took off running. Sharon let her go. There had to be water up ahead.

When they reached the hands, Corky said, "Some crazy hombre dammed up the stream. Look there!"

A pile of stones, sawed-off tree limbs, and dirt filled the streambed. Moving beyond it, Sharon drew up, shocked to see a wide, cool pond filled with clear water. "Who would do such a criminal thing?" she cried. "Why?"

Ginger walked into the center of the pond for a long drink.

Sharon pulled off her shoes and tied them together to hang them from the pommel and looped the strings of her bonnet over it as well. Laughing, she slid off the horse and into four feet of water. She let herself sink until the cooling liquid met her chin. "This is like heaven!" she cried. "Come on in!"

"I thought you hated to be wet!" Jason said, laughing at her.

"Do I?" she replied, scooping a handful of water at him. "That must have been some other girl."

Four pairs of boots hit the dust; four gun belts soon followed. Then the pond was filled with fully clothed people. They soaked and splashed and laughed and joked.

An hour passed before Jason said, "We've got to blast that blockade out of there."

Looking like a rain-soaked puppy, Wilson nodded. "I've got some shotgun cartridges. We can take the powder from them and make a big enough bang to blow out a hole. The water will do the rest."

Sharon was the last one out of the water. She plodded to the bank, dragging Ginger's reins behind her, and spent the next ten minutes wringing out her split skirt. Surprisingly, she felt good. She'd expected to be miserable in wet clothes, but she only felt cool.

Wilson shouted, "Everybody, get back! Way back!"

Sharon guided Ginger a hundred yards up the stream. She found a shady spot nearby to stretch out on the grass.

She took her cotton bonnet, folded it flat, and laid it under her head, then closed her eyes.

Suddenly, someone grabbed her arms and hauled her to her feet.

She screamed and thrashed around, but his strong fingers dug into her flesh, bruising her. "Settle down, Sharon," he snarled into her ear. "You'll only hurt yourself doing that."

She immediately froze. "Timothy!" she gasped. "What are you doing?"

"I'm saving my life," he said, dragging her downstream.

"No! They're going to blast the dam! We can't go down there."

His voice was harsh. "That's exactly why we're going there. Now stop struggling. I don't want to hit you, but I will if I have to."

Trembling, she decided to bide her time and do what he asked.

"Put your hands behind your back," he said. When she did, he tied her hands together and used her elbow as a handhold to drag her closer to the men. A few yards later, they stopped behind a large cottonwood tree at the very edge of the pond. Timothy pulled out his revolver.

"Riordan!" he shouted. "Stop!" He shot into the air. "Stop! If you blast that dam, Sharon's dead. Do you hear me? Dead!"

Think, Sharon, she told herself. *Stop panicking and think.* She watched her captor and marveled at the change in him. His face was grim, his eyes hard. He seemed like a totally different person from the smiling young man she thought she knew.

"Who is that?" Jason's voice boomed. "What do you want?"

"Stop trying to blast the dam, or I'll blast Sharon. And this time I'll finish the job!"

"Why are you doing this?" she asked Timothy. "What do you want from me?"

He grinned in her direction. His chilling smile stopped her breath. "I used to want you to leave Farmington," he said. "I wanted you to sell the ranch and leave." His smile faded. "I tried to make things so tough you'd give up ranching and no one would question it or blame you. Thirsty cattle, trouble with the neighbors, you name it. But you're too stubborn for that." He glanced in the direction of the ranch.

Sharon followed Timothy's line of sight. A pillar of black smoke rose into the sky and billowed out like a giant storm cloud.

"My house!" She let out a sob. "Timothy, why?"

"Evidence," he said. "You've got it, and I couldn't find it. One way or the other, it'll be gone now. Even if your men took off running, by the time they get home, it'll be too late. Everything's dry as tinder."

Peering around the tree, he went on, "Your uncle tore a page from the store ledger. He said it was to keep me honest. Actually, it was to hold me hostage. I had to watch every move I made for fear he'd turn me in."

"You were stealing from your own father?"

He glared at her. "He never paid me a dime. All I took was my rightful wages. That's all I took." He peeked around the tree. "Rudolph said he'd give me a second chance. Every six months he checked out the books to make sure they were all right." Holding his pistol high, he glanced at her. "I took it as long as I could. Then I knew I had to get rid of him."

She felt a weight on her chest that made it hard to breathe. He was talking too much. He had no intention of letting her go.

She tried to look around the tree. Where was Jason? Why hadn't he answered?

Ingles yanked her back. "Stay right there, missy," he ground out. "I'm not playing around, you hear me? You'll get yourself killed."

"How can you imagine you'll get away with this?" she demanded. "Someone will know what you've done. You'll go to prison."

He shook his head. "O'Bannon is going to take the blame for this one. At least his ranch hands will. Everybody in town knows how desperate the Double O is for water. They know crossing a fence line means trouble between ranchers."

"Ingles!" Jason boomed from close behind them. A shot split the air.

Timothy jerked around.

Sharon lowered her shoulder and hit him under the rib cage with all the force she could muster. He lost his balance and tumbled into the pond.

Jason and Wilson plunged into the water and overcame him before he could come up for air.

"The house!" Sharon screamed. "He's burning down the house!"

Tossing his head to fling his wet hair from his eyes, Jason called, "We saw the smoke a few minutes ago! Max's already headed for home!"

Corky arrived and cut the ropes to set Sharon free as Wilson tied Timothy hand and foot with rawhide pigging strings. A nonstop string of profanity spewed from the young man until Jason pulled out a handkerchief and stuffed it into Timothy's mouth.

"He was stealing from his father," Sharon said. "Uncle Rudolph tore out that ledger page to keep him honest, so Timothy killed him."

Jason said, "Corky, take this *outlaw* to the sheriff. Sharon and I will go to town later and tell him what we know." Looking at Sharon, his mouth quirked in. "We lost the evidence," he said. "That's not good."

"No, we didn't. I hid it in the nanny pen," Sharon replied with a glint in her eye. "Did you hear that, Timothy?"

He mumbled something around the cloth in his mouth and glared at her. Corky yanked him toward the horses.

Wilson said, "You folks had better stand back. I'm going to blast that dam before anything else happens." He trudged away.

Hiking upstream, Jason and Sharon stopped in the middle of a grove of trees. Shaking so badly that she could hardly stand, Sharon said, "What am I going to do? The house is gone. Where am I going to live?"

Jason drew her into his arms and held her until her sobs subsided.

A deep, rumbling *boom* shook the ground beneath them. Sharon cringed and he drew her close again.

In a few minutes, he said, "We'd better check on Wilson. I don't like leaving a man when there's a dangerous job like this. Then we'll head back to the ranch yard."

He whistled and got an answering, "Yeah! I'm all right!"

The explosion had indeed blasted a gap in the dam. Water gushed out, carrying sticks and debris with it. The three of them stood on the banks, watching as the hole widened and the sides of the dam caved in.

"That's good enough for now," Jason said. "We'll come back later and clean it out."

Wilson nodded. "I wonder how much that will affect the water hole," he said. "Should be at least eight or ten inches."

"Enough to get us through until it rains," Jason agreed.

"How despicable to stop up the water when it's so low!" Sharon exclaimed. "And he seemed so nice."

Jason helped her mount Ginger, and she immediately set off for home. A few minutes later, Jason and Wilson caught up with her. No one talked on the ride home. The black cloud had thinned out across the horizon. Not much smoke was rising from the ground now.

When they reached the yard, there were twenty men in a bucket brigade leading from the horse trough to the house. At first glance, it appeared that the fire had started at the front porch, now a charred and smoking skeleton. The roof was burnt halfway up the front, but no flames were visible.

Max waved and stepped out of the line to meet them. His clothes and face were black. Only his eyes showed white around the edges. "O'Bannon's men saw the first smoke and came a-running," he said. "They were too late to save the porch or the living room, but the rest of the house is intact." He smeared more soot over his cheeks as he massaged his jaw. "But the smoke. . ." He turned toward Sharon. "I'm afraid everything inside that was cloth or paper is ruined, honey. I'm so sorry."

Sharon stared at the smoldering house, numb from her eyes to her toes. Jason came to help her down. She slid into his waiting arms and hid her face in his shirt.

"Where can I go?" she asked.

"You're not going anywhere," he murmured. "You're going to stay here with me."

"But the house—"

"Is only boards and windows," he finished. He put his arm around her and led her toward the barn. "Let's get you out of the sun," he said. "You're all in."

They sat on the bench outside in the shade, watching the flurry of activity like spectators at a horse race. "Why don't you sell half of the land?" Jason asked her.

"What? Give up now?"

"Not all of it. Sell the lower half to O'Bannon, from the water hole south. That would give him the water he needs, and you could build a house on the north side where it isn't so hot and dry. We could dig out a new water hole where the small stream forks off the big one. It would be perfect for cattle, much better than here. As things are now, we don't use a third of the land we can lay claim to."

She considered that. "You may have something there."

"He may give you five thousand for half of it, and consider it a bargain," Jason went on. "It'll make all the difference to him, Sharon. I don't see how he could refuse. Then you could pay off the mortgage and have plenty left to build a nice house."

"But where will I live in the meantime?"

"Lucy and Ma will be delighted to have you." He stood. "Come here." Taking her hand, he led her into the barn. When they reached the comforting dimness inside, he pulled her into his arms like he'd never let her go. "I love you, Sharon," he whispered. "I want you to marry me."

"How could you?" she asked. "I'm stubborn and opinionated. I've ignored your advice and—"

He stilled her lips with a warm and tender kiss that came from deep within. When he finally released her, he murmured into her hair, "You're feisty and funny and as beautiful as the morning sun."

"I love you, Jason," she said and he kissed her again.

Entwined in his arms, Sharon forgot about the ruined house. She forgot about the hardships and sorrows of that endless summer. Sharon had just come home.

Epilogue

On the second day of September, the Riordan cabin glowed from the stones on the fireplace to the windows on the porch. Platters stacked high with flaky pastries and tiny pies covered every surface in the kitchen. Max had an apron over his white shirt and black tie. He was wiping counters and cabinet fronts while Mrs. Riordan sat at the table, happily talking of her girlhood days and the winsome ways of her only beau, a handsome man named Daniel Riordan.

In the back bedroom, Sharon giggled. "I can't believe it, Lucy! I can't believe it's today. My wedding day!"

Beaming, Lucy hugged her, then gently pushed Sharon into a chair. "If you don't sit still, how can I finish your hair?"

Sharon patted Lucy's hand. "I'm glad you're going to be my sister, Lucy girl."

"Going to be?" she asked around pins in her mouth. "I already am, you goose."

"Who would have ever dreamed when I gave you that trunk full of clothes that I'd have to take some of them back?"

"If you weren't so generous, you would have lost *everything*." Lucy hugged her from behind. "Except Jason. You could have never lost him."

Sharon's smile was dazzling.

The front yard had been swept clean. Pots of flowers lined a wide aisle between two banks of benches. At the front stood more flowers and Rev. Nelson in his black suit, reading his notes for the service.

The ceremony began at noon. Jason stood before the preacher as Mrs. Nelson sang "O Promise Me" and Lucy strolled down the aisle. Then Sharon stepped out holding Max's arm and pacing toward the man she loved.

" 'Marriage is an institution of divine appointment,' " the pastor read from his little black book. " 'It is the most important step in life and should not, therefore, be entered into lightly, but soberly and discreetly.' " A few minutes later, he said, "Sharon, do you take this man to be your lawful husband. . . ?"

Gazing into Jason's eyes, she said, "I do."

Soon after, Jason also said, "I do."

A deep rumbling from overhead drowned out the pastor's next words.

A second rumble sounded when he said, "You may kiss your bride."

As Jason lifted Sharon's veil, she melted into his arms while the first fat raindrops fell. As he pulled her to him, the sky opened up.

Gasps went up from the guests. Benches overturned as they raced for the shelter of the porch.

Jason lifted his head to say, "You're getting wet, Mrs. Riordan."

She laughed aloud and leaned her face back to catch the spray on her cheeks. "Yes!" She closed her eyes, savoring the coolness. And he kissed her again.

Rosey Dow

Rosey has thirteen novels in print with more than half a million copies sold. Winner of a Christy Award for *Reaping the Whirlwind*, Rosey is director of ChristianFictionMentors.com and CEO of Experts in Focus: an online book promotion company. A former missionary to the Caribbean, her husband pastors a small church in a tiny town in Delaware. Visit her Web site www.RoseyDow.com.

TO TRUST AN OUTLAW

Dedication

This book is dedicated to the men in my life. Marty McConnell, my brother, this book is for you. Lance Gibson, my son, a would-be outlaw, who is a mighty man of God—I'm proud of you. Nathan Baron, God knew we needed another son; I'm glad He gave us you. James Gibson, my best friend and loving husband, my writing wouldn't happen without you. I love you, honey.

A special thanks goes to my good friend Debbie Doggett for her endless hours of answering my questions about the history of New Mexico and for her forever friendship. Also, a special thanks to the staff members at the Farmington Museum; they welcome all who enter their doors and reveal history like no other place on earth.

Chapter 1

New Mexico, 1900

A cruel wind whipped the buckboard along the flat, dusty road. Elizabeth Winterspoon held her breath, clamped her eyes shut, and gripped the edge of the wagon while praying for deliverance.

"Yah!" The wagon driver snapped his whip, motivating the team of horses to run faster.

Elizabeth's hair lashed her face. She shoved it back, opened her eyes a crack, and turned to glance at the four bandits who were quickly closing the gap behind her.

Bullets whizzed and popped around the wagon. Several times she felt one fly by her. An explosion jolted the mail wagon. Her body trembled as she clutched the seat. Her bag, containing the few belongings she'd brought with her, skidded to the back of the wagon toward her trunk, and she threw herself after it, her midsection slamming into the driver's restraining arm. The bag teetered, then dropped to the ground and rolled to the side of the road.

The driver screamed beside her, and she chanced a look toward him. Clutching the reins in one hand and wielding the whip with the other, he swayed, his wide eyes focused on the dusty path before them. He screamed again and clutched the side of his head, dropping the whip and the reins. Blood spread out from his fingers. He slumped to the side.

"Samson!" Elizabeth grabbed the rough material of his shirt, but it slipped through her fingers as he went over the side of the wagon.

Elizabeth flopped like a rag doll against the seat. The animals' hooves beat the hard-packed ground, hammering in time with her heart. Despair welled in her soul. Dust boiled up through the floorboards and settled on her. Her sweat-drenched hands slipped on the splintered wood of the seat.

Two men with bandannas over their faces caught up to the wagon and jumped from their horses onto the backs of the team.

"Whoa!" one of the men yelled.

The animals gradually slowed and finally came to a stop, sides heaving.

Elizabeth's pulse beat in her neck like the war drums she'd read about in dime novels. Two more horses raced toward the mail wagon. Each animal held a rider bent low.

As they jerked their mounts to a stop, choking dust swirled around the wagon. She covered her nose and mouth with the sleeve of her dress. *Please don't let them hurt me*, she silently prayed.

"You gave us a merry chase, lassie." A hulking man with dirty red hair, a scraggly beard, and cold green eyes pulled even with her.

Shock held her immobile for what seemed an eternity. She pushed up from the wagon seat and clambered over the side. As soon as her feet hit the hard ground, she took off in a run. She willed her legs to move faster, but they refused. Her lungs ached as she fought to breathe.

Elizabeth stumbled over a rock. She flailed for balance, regained it, and kept running. Boots pounded the ground behind her. She glanced over her shoulder and saw a wiry young man with brown hair closing in on her. "Please don't let him catch me." The prayer stumbled from her lips as sobs threatened to break free.

He tackled her from behind. The full force of his weight slammed into her, then the ground rushed up to meet her. Rocks and gravel bit into her palms. Air rushed from her lungs.

The man pushed up from the ground and hauled her up to face him. He captured her wrists and pinioned them firmly in front of her. The roughness of his calloused palms scraped against her injured hands.

Twenty-year-old Elizabeth looked into the face of a man near her own age. She kicked out with her foot. Her boot connected with his shin in a satisfying *thump*.

"Be still, you little wildcat," he hissed. "If you want to continue breathing, you'll do as I say." His blue eyes dared her to defy him. He jerked on her wrists, pulling her closer to him.

"I won't be still!" She twisted and pulled on their hands, trying to break loose.

Elizabeth suddenly sank to her knees, hoping the movement would surprise him and allow her time to regain her freedom. He used the move against her, whipping her arms behind her back and forcing her to stand once more. Unable to move anything but her legs, she thrashed at his shins with her booted feet.

Her captor's hearty laughter filled the hot afternoon air as he pulled her back to the wagon.

Elizabeth glared at the three remaining horsemen. She hoped the look conveyed to them she would continue to fight. They returned her stare. Fear threatened to turn her into a weakling. She refused to give in to it and focused instead on her anger. How dare they treat her this way?

The man with the red hair pulled two mailbags from the wagon. He turned his horse toward Elizabeth. "Leave the lassie be, boy."

The young man known as "boy" dropped her hands.

She dusted herself off, thanking the Lord above that her carpetbag seemed to have been overlooked. What would Claire do in her situation? Elizabeth wished she were still home with her friend and housekeeper. The scrappy old lady would have faced her attackers head-on.

Lifting her chin, Elizabeth did just that. Her hands trembled. She clutched them together. Outnumbered and with no way to escape, she considered her circumstances and what they implied. These were no gentlemen. What did they have in mind for her? Could she continue this farce of courage?

The leader shifted his hefty weight in the saddle and pushed his hat back, revealing a wide forehead.

A small, dark-skinned man sat to his left, two guns strapped around his hips. In his gloved hands, he held the reins of a black horse. He grinned down at her. She shuddered and looked away.

On the leader's right, a blond man sat tall in the saddle, his unruly hair sticking out under a black hat. A long scar over his left cheek marred his otherwise handsome features. He held her horse's reins in his hand.

Why did they untie Ginger from the back of the wagon? She noted that he also held the reins of the two horses that had been hitched to the mail wagon. Elizabeth marched toward the blond man. "I'll take my horse, sir." She tried to sound commanding as she pulled on the reins.

He sneered. "Lady, I ain't no sir. Name's Porter, and I'd be honored if you'd whisper it in my ear tonight." Porter leaned against the saddle horn and winked down at her.

She felt her cheeks flame and decided no comment would be better than giving him the satisfaction of continuing that line of conversation. She turned back to the leader. "Sir, I demand you return my horse. I need to get my driver back to Durango. He needs medical attention."

The dark-skinned man said something to the leader she couldn't hear.

Elizabeth trembled. *Oh, Lord, please make them leave. I've got to help Samson to town before he dies. . .if he isn't dead already.*

The leader studied her for several long seconds. His cold green eyes reminded her of a snake's. Narrow and dangerous. "You have a name, lassie?"

She squared her shoulders. "I'm Elizabeth—"

Before she could finish, the small man chuckled. "*Sí*, Elizabeth Hamilton. Her father is the banker in Durango. I heard the banker say to the clerk, 'Go to the general store for my daughter, Elizabeth, and tell her I need her.' I followed this man, and when he entered the store he called her name, and this girl answered. The door closed, and I do not know what else she said, but she is the one. Sí."

Elizabeth started to deny it. Her father was the general store owner, not a banker. But something in the men's eyes held her back. She looked to the young man who stood beside her. He studied his boots, avoiding her gaze.

"Her *padre* will pay big money for her, boss." The dark-skinned bandit rubbed his gloved hands together.

The leader returned his attention to the boy. "What do you think, Harry? Should we kill her or see if her old man will pay for her return?"

Elizabeth shivered with cold even in the blazing heat. Her heart pounded so violently, she thought it might explode. *My life depends on what he says!*

When Harry didn't respond, the leader prompted him. "Hmm?"

Elizabeth looked at Harry. Kind blue eyes returned her stare. She could see now that she'd been wrong to think him her age. She now guessed him to be a few years younger. And her fate rested in his hands. The thought sent new fear tumbling through her mind and heart.

"I think her pa will pay a lot of money to have her back." He stepped around her and took the reins of the black horse from the dark-skinned man.

"I'm guessing you're right, boy. Well, lassie, looks like you're going to be spending a few days with me and the boys." The big man's voice left no room for argument. He moved his horse forward. "Harry, help the lassie onto her horse, and you ride with her."

The younger man handed his reins back to the dark-skinned man. He stepped into the stirrup of Elizabeth's horse and hauled himself onto Ginger's back. He extended his hand down to her.

What could she do? Elizabeth looked from one impassive face to another. *How am I going to get out of this, Lord?*

Harry inched the horse closer to Elizabeth. She backed up until her body bumped against the warm animal behind her.

Her captors laughed loudly. Elizabeth looked up at Harry. He wasn't laughing. He kicked his boot out of the stirrup, then scooted off the saddle and onto the rump of the horse. "Come on. I'll help you up."

Elizabeth reluctantly placed her hand in his rough palm. He hoisted her up. Sitting sidesaddle, she grabbed the sun-heated saddle horn.

Keeping her gaze averted from the men, she noticed Samson. He lay thirty feet away in the dirt, a dark pool of blood oozing from under his body and soaking the parched ground.

The boss and his horse moved closer, blocking her view of her driver. "Give me your bandanna, Harry."

Elizabeth caught her breath. The scent of tobacco and sweat assaulted her sense of smell as the leader leaned toward her. His green gaze bored into her.

She felt Harry shift on the horse behind her. "Here you go, boss."

The older man snatched the cloth from Harry's fingers. He folded it into a thick band, then handed it back. "Cover her eyes," he barked.

Harry did as he was told. The cloth felt soft against her closed eyelids. He fumbled with the knot, giving her a moment to open her eyes and see a faint line of daylight at the bottom of the bandanna.

Elizabeth trembled as rough hands tied something else around her head. The sliver of light disappeared, leaving only darkness. A coarse rope bit into the flesh of her wrists as they were tied tightly against the saddle horn. She flinched against the pain.

The sound of retreating horses filled her ears.

"Hang on to her, boy."

Harry's strong arm came around her. She felt him slide forward into the saddle, crowding her against the horn. He pulled her back against him and whispered, "You're going to be all right. Jonathan will know what to do."

She wondered who Jonathan was. Surely not the burly red-haired leader they all called "boss." The name didn't seem to fit the dark-skinned man with the Spanish accent, either.

"Hang on," Harry said.

The horse's muscles bunched against her legs as the beast lurched forward. Hot air whipped her hair out behind her. Fear swelled in her chest. *Oh, Lord, please help me.*

Jonathan Russell stood in the doorway of the old ranch house, looking out over the yard that faced the opening of the outlaws' hideout. Trees shaded the dirt yard, where five men cleaned their weapons and relaxed in the afternoon shade. He lowered his voice. "Where did they take off to this time?"

His partner, Edward Concord, sat behind him, playing a game of solitaire. He slapped another card on the table. "Red said they were gonna stop the mail wagon today. That's all I know."

On days like this Jonathan hated being an undercover lawman. A crime was being committed, and all he could do was stand by and wait to see what the extent of the corruption would be this time. So far the outlaws' criminal acts had been small. But Red was a loose cannon and possibly a killer.

His thoughts went to Red's room and the chest that might or might not hold evidence Jonathan desperately needed. "Is the room locked?"

"Tighter than the bank vault in Durango."

Disappointed, Jonathan wondered if Red would ever slip up and leave the room open. All the men knew Red kept a chest in his bedroom. But they also knew that if any man ever stepped foot in there without the boss's permission he would soon depart this world—or wish he had. Still, Jonathan's thoughts went to the bedroom window.

As if reading his mind, Edward said, "I checked the window, too. Still nailed shut from the inside."

Jonathan looked over his shoulder. "Who went out?"

"Red took Porter, José, and Harry." Edward shuffled the cards and dealt out a new hand.

Jonathan walked to the small woodstove that stood in the corner against the back wall. He picked up the tin pot sitting on it and poured some coffee into his cup. "Why do you suppose he took Harry?"

"Same as always. Training."

Jonathan made his way to the window. In the shelter of the trees, a cool breeze fluttered into the house. "I wish he'd leave the boy alone." The sweet scent of lilacs filled his nostrils. He enjoyed the view from the window. While the front door revealed the entry to the hideout, the window faced the mountain.

"Yeah, me, too. He keeps taking him on bigger jobs. You know, ole buddy, we already have enough evidence to take Red and most of these guys in." Edwards paused. "They'd be put away for life."

"I don't want to put Red away. I want to see him hang." Jonathan had been a lawman for four years, but the job wasn't what he loved, nor the thrill of hunting down killers. He'd sold his farm in Texas and taken on the badge to find the man who had murdered his sixteen-year-old sister. Jonathan felt sure that her killer was Red Marshall, but he didn't have proof. So for the past year, he'd stayed in the outlaw camp undercover, searching for something, anything, that would prove the leader of this motley bunch was a murderer. To his way of thinking, it was taking way too long. If only he or Edward could get into that room.

Jonathan drank deeply of the lukewarm, bitter brew. It reminded him of his own bitterness. If he hadn't gone hunting that day, maybe Sarah would still be alive. She hadn't wanted him to go. But since their parents had died of pneumonia and his brothers lived in Missouri, it was his job to run the farm and hunt for food. Being responsible for his younger sister had weighed heavily on him. That day he'd told her to stay home and do the laundry because he'd wanted a little time alone, to think and plan their futures. Sarah had been begging him to move into town, but he loved the farm and hadn't wanted to leave it. Now he wished he hadn't been so self-centered.

The sound of cantering horses announced the return of the bandits. Jonathan plodded to the door. He heard the soft *swish* of Edward's boots as the other lawman moved up behind him.

"Looks like trouble." Edward's words echoed Jonathan's thoughts.

Harry pulled up at the rear. In front of him sat a blindfolded woman in a blue calico dress. Her strawberry blond hair cascaded down, curls touching her shoulders, and she held her head high.

Oh, Lord, now what? Jonathan cautiously stepped out onto the porch. He knew Edward had slunk back into the shadows. His partner always protected his back until they were both assured that their covers hadn't been blown while the other outlaws had been away from camp.

"Hey, Johnny boy! Come see what I fetched home." Red's saddle creaked as he slid down, and his horse stepped sideways. He turned to face Harry and the woman who sat in front of him. "Miz Elizabeth Hamilton," Red announced as if presenting royalty. "The banker's daughter from Durango."

Jonathan stepped off the porch. As he passed the outlaw boss, his first instinct was to wipe the smirk off Red's face. Instead he planted a stupid grin on his own lips and sauntered over to Harry and the woman.

"Nice." He made his voice sound warm, throaty, and crude. Just the way these men seemed to think women liked it. He appraised her from head to toe. Jonathan hated this part of his job. God's Word made it clear that this type of behavior was not the Lord's will. But as part of the job, what choice did he have?

"I'll say." Porter climbed down from his horse, walked over to the woman, and rested a hand on her thigh.

She kicked at him. The toe of her boot caught Porter under the chin and sent him flying backward. The tall, skinny man thudded to the ground.

Red's booming laugh echoed off the rock cliff behind them. The other men joined in on the merriment.

"Why, you. . ." Porter jumped to his feet and stumbled to the horse. He reached up to pull her down.

Jonathan jerked the horse around and pushed Porter away. "You deserved it. Can't you tell this is a lady?"

Once more Red's amusement filled the air. "Even blindfolded, the woman got the best of you!" he roared.

A grin tugged at Jonathan's lips. It was nice to see Porter get what he deserved for a change. The handsome blond was too cocky for his own good. Unfortunately, now that the young woman had shamed him in front of the whole gang, Porter would be looking for a way to exact revenge on her.

"Go tie up the horses, Porter," the burly leader ordered, then he slapped Jonathan on the back. "I'm glad you like her, Johnny boy. She's yours."

Saddles creaked as the other men dismounted and handed their reins to Porter. The angry outlaw stomped toward a hitching post several hundred yards away from the house.

The last thing Jonathan needed was a woman—especially one Porter had his eye on. Instead of protesting, he grinned.

"I belong to no man." The woman's voice sounded muffled through the layers of cloth bound over her face. She and Harry still sat atop her horse. "When my father. . ." Uncertainty filled her voice, and she blindly kicked out again.

Red stopped laughing. "She's right, for now." He raised his voice to a near shout. "Let all the men know, this woman ain't to be touched."

Jonathan's skin prickled. What did Red have in mind for the lady? "If she's not mine to do with as I want, then what am I supposed to do with her?"

"Aw, don't look so downhearted, Johnny. As soon as her old man pays our ransom, you can do whatever you like with her. But until then. . .I want her kept safe. I expect you to guard her as well as you do this hideout. Got it?" Red punched a finger into Jonathan's chest.

Jonathan felt his jaw harden. He focused on relaxing his face. "Sure, boss, I got it."

"Good." Red looked up at the young man squeezed into the saddle with the lady. "Harry, hand that woman over to Johnny boy."

Harry nodded. "Sure, boss."

Red turned his attention to Bowman, one of the outlaws who'd remained at the hideout today and had moseyed over to check out the excitement.

The short, fat outlaw straightened his shoulders in an effort to appear taller under the boss's gaze. Like the other men, Bowman had been watching the scene unfold in front of him. "Bowman, you're taking a trip to Durango. Go to the bank and wait there until closing time. Once you get that banker off alone, tell him we have his pretty little girl and we expect him to pay five thousand dollars if he wants to see her alive again."

He gave the lady a brief, regretful look. "Okay, boss."

"I expect you back here in a week."

"You got it." Bowman hurried off.

Edward came into view around the corner of the house. He tilted his head toward the boss in greeting. Porter returned to the group, as well. Jonathan watched as the two men sized each other up, like they did every time they came into the same area as each other. They reminded him of two starving dogs after the same soup bone. Dangerous.

"The rest of you, come inside. Harry, join us when you're done out here. It shouldn't take long, so don't keep us waitin' while you put away that horse. We have plans to make and mail to go through." Red pulled the mailbags from his saddle and led the way toward the house.

Eight men paraded into the house behind Red—the five Jonathan had been watching, plus Edward, José, and Porter. Jonathan watched them go, then he turned to Harry and the woman. He studied the stiff way she held her body. His lawman instincts told him this was a lady, not some country bumpkin. Her poise and bravery told him she wasn't going to stay here without a fight, and she wasn't going to make this easy for any of them.

Harry slid off the horse. "If you promise not to kick me, I'll untie your hands and help you down."

Jonathan wished he could see her eyes, but the blindfold blocked them from view. Elizabeth looked as wilted as a flower under the hot New Mexico sun.

"All right." Her voice sounded weak.

Harry tugged at the rope binding her hands to the saddle horn, but it wouldn't budge. She flinched slightly as she endured his clumsy efforts. Jonathan moved to Harry's side. "Let me try," he mouthed.

Harry stepped back and Jonathan moved in, avoiding her foot in case she decided to kick out. Her hands were ice cold and the cord had eaten into her flesh. Anger raced through his veins. Whoever had tied her this tightly deserved a good beating. He'd ask Harry later who was responsible.

She stiffened at his touch, but didn't make a sound. Jonathan knew he was hurting her, so he worked as quickly as he could. It took several attempts, but finally the knot gave, and he freed her bleeding wrists.

"May I take off the blindfold now?" she asked as she massaged her hands and fingers.

"Go ahead," Jonathan answered.

She fumbled with the material at the back of her head. "My hands don't seem to be working properly." Her voice shook.

Harry spoke softly, as if talking to an injured animal. "If you give me your hand, I'll help you off the horse."

She lowered her hands and felt for Harry. The boy seemed at a loss as to how to get her down. Jonathan stepped forward, put his hands around her tiny waist, and gently lowered her to the ground.

Her breathing quickened, and her nostrils flared, sniffing the air as if trying to catch his scent.

"Harry, take the blindfold off the lady." Jonathan continued to face her. They stood inches apart.

Harry moved behind the young woman. As the cloth lowered, beautiful green eyes shadowed by sooty lashes appeared. She blinked several times. Then her gaze focused on him. "You must be Johnny boy."

The mocking tone made him feel relieved. If she could still show spunk, she must not be hurt too badly. "Just to Red. To everyone else, I'm Jonathan."

She nodded, took a step back, and looked at her wrists. Her mouth quivered for a moment.

"I'm real sorry about that, ma'am." Harry shifted from one booted foot to the other.

She gave the boy a slight smile. "It's all right. I know you were only following orders."

"You did that?" Jonathan pointed at her bleeding hands. When he saw both Harry and the woman flinch, he realized his voice had come out harsh and dangerous.

Harry shook his head. "No. I'd never do that to a lady."

"Then who did?"

"Red."

Jonathan spit on the ground. Loathing for the leader of the gang of criminals threatened to overpower his normally calm resolve. With each cruel act the outlaw performed, Jonathan's emotions became more violent. If he weren't looking for his sister's murderer, he wouldn't have to deal with the likes of this man. *Lord, I don't know how much longer I can fight these feelings of hatred.*

Harry looked pointedly at Elizabeth's rope-burned wrists. The cord had eaten into the soft flesh, leaving it raw and bleeding. "Do you think we should take her to Millie? I bet she could fix her wrists."

"You're right. Let's pay Millie a visit."

Harry tied the mare's reins around a small tree.

"Who's Millie?"

Both men looked at her. Harry answered first. "She's our cook. You'll like her. Millie lives in the shed behind the kitchen. See?" He pointed at two buildings, standing off to the right of the house, that served as the outlaws' hideout.

Jonathan followed them to the kitchen. The thought of her sleeping in the house with him and the other men crashed through his mind. He'd have to fight all night long just to keep her safe. Elizabeth would need a safe place to sleep.

How would Millie respond to having a roommate? *Lord, please don't allow Millie to mind. I can't bring myself to force Elizabeth on her.*

As he watched the captive woman hold her head high, he realized he now had another ward to protect. First Millie, then Harry, and now Elizabeth. New fear threatened to choke him. He forced it down and leaned on the Lord for assurance that everything would be all right. But he couldn't stop his raging thoughts.

How did I go from not wanting to protect anyone to protecting everyone?

Chapter 2

Elizabeth studied the layout of the camp as she followed Harry. It didn't look like an outlaw hideout at all, at least not like the ones she'd read about in the dime novels. An old house loomed nearby. The kitchen they were headed toward sat several feet to the right of the house. She noticed five horses tied to a hitching post that stood beyond the kitchen. Her gaze moved back to her own horse. The desire to run to the little mare and flee pulled strongly at her. Only the sound of Jonathan's boots crunching on the dirt behind her held her in place. He'd catch her before she'd run ten feet. *Time, Elizabeth. Wait for the right time.*

Fear gripped her as she realized she had only a week. Bowman would be back by then with news that she wasn't the banker's daughter and there would be no ransom money. Elizabeth forced back the fear and tried to focus on anger instead.

She ground her teeth harder with each step. *Who do these men think they are? Don't they know God hates liars and thieves?* She doubted they cared.

They cheated and took whatever they wanted. Just like her father.

Stop it, Elizabeth, she chided herself. *You've forgiven your father.* She reminded herself that she had more important things to focus on than childhood hurts.

"Here we are." Harry pointed toward the small building made of raw boards and rusted nails that stood beside the big house. An old screen door hung a little off its hinges.

"Millie?" Jonathan called. "Can you step outside, please?"

The aroma of apple and cinnamon wafting through the open door soothed Elizabeth's frayed nerves somewhat. She inhaled deeply. If she concentrated enough on the heavenly scent, perhaps she'd forget the stinging pain in her wrists.

The irritating man behind her clamped a large hand over her aching shoulder. She shrugged her arm in an unsuccessful attempt to dislodge the outlaw's hand.

Unlike the other men, this one didn't send off offensive odors of sweat and tobacco. He sounded different from the others, too. His voice carried a definite southern drawl. Elizabeth noted his nose had been broken at some point.

Probably while robbing some innocent soul.

The screen door squeaked open. A tall, thin woman stood in the gap. Her light brown hair, streaked with gray, was pulled back, making the woman's face appear thin and pointed. Elizabeth guessed her age to be close to sixty years. But a smile broke across chapped lips, softening Millie's features, and she couldn't be sure.

"Millie," Jonathan said, "this is Miss Elizabeth Hamilton."

Elizabeth winced at the use of the last name. *God hates liars. But I have to lie to save my life.* The thought sent shimmers of fear into her heart and a silent prayer for forgiveness heavenward.

"Do come in, Miss Hamilton." Millie's clear blue eyes gazed at Jonathan with questions in their depths. She wiped her flour-coated hands on a stained apron and led them inside.

When Jonathan finally released his hold on her shoulder, relief washed over Elizabeth. But then his hand moved to the small of her back, and she stiffened. He gave her a gentle push forward. Then he turned to Harry.

"You'd best go to the meeting with Red. I'm sure he'll be looking for you."

"Good idea."

The screen door slammed behind Harry. Elizabeth couldn't help but wonder if the boy was glad to be rid of her. But with him gone, what would Jonathan do with her? She trembled, thankful Millie was there.

Her gaze moved about the kitchen. A long rectangular table with two benches sat against the right wall. The fireplace and stove stood at the back of the large square room. Makeshift shelves lined the walls. Open cans filled with kitchen utensils stood among battered bowls and cookware. The floor appeared clean. Several chopped tree stumps sat about the room, apparently the only chairs in the place.

"Please, sit down." Millie pointed to the table. Her gaze moved to Elizabeth's bleeding wrists. "Looks like your hands could use some tending to. Mind if I see what I can do?"

Elizabeth settled on one of the benches, happy to put some distance between herself and Jonathan. She looked down and wondered if the cuts were deep enough to scar. "That would be nice, thank you."

"Happy to do it." Millie moved to the back of the room and pulled several rags from one shelf and a bowl from another.

Jonathan sniffed the air. "Are those fresh pies I smell?"

"Sure are." She dipped water from a bucket and put it into the bowl. "Soon as we get Miss Hamilton's wrists cleaned up, I'll dish up the pie."

"Please, call me Elizabeth."

"All right. I'll just get the things we'll need to clean up your wounds." Millie walked toward the fireplace and stove.

Jonathan sat across from Elizabeth and stared at her for several moments. "You put up a good fight, didn't you?"

"Not good enough." Elizabeth scooted over, making room for Millie to sit beside her.

"This will sting a mite," Millie said, taking Elizabeth's left hand into hers.

Elizabeth focused on the roughness of Millie's skin instead of the pain that the cleaning inflicted. Millie's hands felt rough and calloused. She fought the tears that sprang forward when Millie opened her palm, scraped at the dirt and rocks embedded in her skin, and cleaned her bleeding wrist.

She turned her eyes to Jonathan. He sat watching her face as if he could read her every thought. Elizabeth jerked her gaze away and focused on Millie once more. Millie dropped the dirty cloth back into the bowl of water.

Then the older woman tore one of the clean rags into strips and wrapped Elizabeth's left wrist. "I know that hurts, but you don't want infection to set into those cuts." She tied it off and reached for Elizabeth's right hand.

"Thank you."

Millie took the wet cloth out of the water and wrung it out over the bowl. "Don't thank me just yet. We still have this hand to do, too." She began scrubbing at the dirt on Elizabeth's hand with the wet cloth.

Elizabeth closed her eyes and focused on thoughts of escape. She wanted to get as far away from this camp as she could as soon as she could. The banker in Durango would think the outlaws were crazy, asking him for money to save her. When Bowman found out her father was the store owner, what would he do? Probably ask him for the money. Would her father pay it? No. Five thousand dollars was a fortune, and even if he could pay it, his new bride would stop him. Panic filled her. *I have to escape. But how? Lord, please supply a way.*

"All done," Millie announced. She picked up the bowl of dirty water, walked to the door, and tossed it out.

Elizabeth looked down at her hands. They were clean and her wrists were bandaged with fresh cloths. "Thank you."

Jonathan stood. "Would you like a slice of pie, Elizabeth?"

When had she given him permission to be so forward? Didn't he know it wasn't proper for him to address her by her first name? She opened her mouth to protest, but then realized that as an outlaw, he probably didn't know or care what was proper. She felt too tired to fight over which name he used for her.

"Yes, please." Her thoughts moved to the early breakfast she'd rushed through. Had it only been this morning when she and Samson had talked about going to Farmington, where she'd been offered a teaching job? They would have arrived there by this time tomorrow if the outlaws hadn't ambushed them.

Millie turned toward the fireplace, above which several pies lined yet another shelf.

Jonathan followed the older woman. They spoke in hushed tones. Elizabeth strained to hear what they said, but their words were muffled.

As her thoughts ran wild, her breath became shallow. Jonathan and Millie continued to talk at the fireplace. Her eyes darted to the open door. *Escape!* Elizabeth stood quietly and crept toward the door.

"Going somewhere?"

Disappointment filled her as she stopped and turned to face Jonathan.

Millie made a *tsk, tsk* sound, then returned to the table with a fragrant, golden-crusted pie.

The desire to make a run for the door tore at Elizabeth, but common sense told her she wouldn't get far. She walked back and sat down.

Millie placed the pie on the table. She pulled three plates from a nearby shelf and set them on the table, then selected a knife from a tin can bristling with kitchen utensils and cut a huge slice. The smell of cinnamon filled the warm kitchen. Millie retrieved a fork from the same can and scooped out the slice.

Jonathan licked his lips as apples and pale yellow syrup pooled in the pan.

Millie handed Elizabeth the first piece. "Here you go. I hope you enjoy it."

"Thank you. I'm sure I will." Elizabeth bowed her head and prayed silently. *Thank You, Lord, for my safety. Thank You for the food that's been supplied for my needs. Father, I ask that You keep watch over Samson. Please send him the help he needs. In Jesus' name. Amen.* The prayer seemed strained and unnatural. She decided to offer a more heartfelt prayer later.

Jonathan sat down. He pulled the second plate toward him and forked a good-sized bite of pie into his mouth. Millie moved to the stove and returned with a steaming mug for each of them, then served a slice of the pastry to herself and took her seat.

Jonathan sipped his coffee. "You'll stay here with Millie," he announced.

She hadn't thought about her sleeping arrangements. She'd hoped to be gone before nightfall. Her gaze moved to Millie. The kind woman smiled at her. Was that what they'd been whispering about?

"I have a small room behind the kitchen. Well, really it's the shed and it's not much, but we can share it." Millie's welcoming words lightened Elizabeth's heart.

Relief filled her at knowing she wouldn't have to spend the night anywhere near the men. "Thank you, Millie." The sweet flavor of sugary apples coated Elizabeth's tongue as she took her first bite. Hot tears slipped down her cheeks. She hated weakness, especially in herself. But Millie's kindness, compounded with the scare she'd just experienced, sent her emotions reeling.

Jonathan pushed his empty plate back and cleared his throat. "I warn you not to attempt an escape. Red and his men won't be so nice if they have to capture you all over again. They have no qualms about raping, beating, or even killing a woman."

Elizabeth gasped.

"He's right," Millie added. "They're not a bunch you want to cross."

Elizabeth stared from one face to the other. She knew they were serious. But she would not give up. She would do everything in her power to escape, regardless of their warnings.

Jonathan braced his elbows on the table and stared into her eyes. "I promise I'll protect you, but you have to follow my orders. Stay with Millie. You've already made an enemy in this camp. Given half a chance, Porter might kill you and make it look like an accident. But not before he's made you pay for embarrassing him in front of the other men."

A shiver of fear ran down her back. She wondered why he was offering to protect her and what his orders might be. It really didn't matter. If the opportunity presented itself, she'd get away and no longer be his concern.

Needles of pain in her lower back woke Elizabeth. Her first conscious thought was that the sun was shining. She could see its faint light through the cracked, dirty window. The night before, she and Millie had talked for several minutes before sleep had claimed her. Millie's bed now sat neatly made and empty.

Elizabeth groaned as she sat up. Her bandaged wrists throbbed. *Lord, thank You for keeping me safe during the night.*

She glanced around her sparse surroundings. The one-room shed had a potbellied stove, a rough wooden table, two log stools, and two single cots. Against the opposite wall a simple shelf held a dented washbasin and a chipped, light blue enamel pitcher with yellow flowers painted on the side. A tarnished mirror hung above it and a writing desk sat beside that.

Even though the shed was separate from the kitchen, it was close enough for the smell of fried bacon to filter through the window, awakening her appetite. Elizabeth forced her bruised body off the cot and shuffled to her carpetbag by the door. *How did that get here?* Yesterday, she'd arrived with nothing but the clothes on her back.

She bent to pick up the bag, and her spine popped, reminding her of the rough ride she'd had the day before. She returned to her bed. The stiffness in her fingers made it difficult to open the bag. A quick inventory revealed her two clean dresses, stockings, Bible, lotion, a bar of soap, hairbrush, and hairpins. She prayed that her trunk, which held more clothes and another pair of shoes, would somehow make it to Farmington. For a brief moment she allowed herself to wonder if anyone might be looking for her. Would the people of Farmington and Durango send out a search party? Surely they would. She held on to that hope as she asked the Lord for protection.

After several minutes she managed to get dressed. The thought of running away came and went swiftly. She wasn't in any shape to make a speedy escape; her body protested with each movement she made.

Cool air blanketed her as she opened the door and stepped outside.

"Good morning." Jonathan stood propped against the wall of the shed, a stem of straw between his teeth.

She should have realized he'd be standing guard. Elizabeth felt a blush rise from her neck and settle into her cheeks. What was it about the outlaw that sent her pulse to racing? "Good morning," she mumbled.

He pushed away from the building. "Did you sleep well?"

"A gentleman does not ask a lady how she slept." She raised her chin. The muscles in her neck protested, and pain ricocheted down her spine and into her hips, but she held her head high.

"I'll try to remember that." He moved to her side. "Now, where are you going?"

"I smell breakfast."

"In the future, wait for me before you leave this shed."

"And why would I have to do that?" Elizabeth bridled at having to explain herself.

"I don't want you out here alone. The men here aren't exactly honorable. Remember?"

She nodded but thought, *And you are?* Elizabeth doubted this man was any better, but she chose not to voice her opinion. Instead, she took short steps toward the kitchen, the muscles in her legs screaming with each stride. He kept pace alongside her.

When they arrived at the kitchen, Jonathan opened the screen door, waiting for her to enter.

Manners dictated she acknowledge the gesture. "Thank you."

As she crossed the threshold, with Jonathan directly behind her, the smells of bacon and biscuits filled her senses. Millie stood beside the stove, stirring a pot of something. Eight men sat at the long table, eating breakfast. They stared in her direction. None of them were the men who'd abducted her the day before.

"Hey, Jonathan," one burly outlaw called after spitting tobacco juice onto the floor, "let me know when ya get tired of playing mama. I'd be glad to entertain the little lady." His eyes ran over her suggestively.

The offer prompted lewd grins and laughter from the others. Elizabeth shuddered with disgust and fear.

Jonathan jerked the man to his feet by his shirtfront. "Frank, you come near her and you won't be able to see another pretty woman," he growled. "If you so much as look at or speak about her again, I'll have your eyes gouged out and your tongue ripped from your mouth."

The man nodded. His eyes remained focused on Jonathan's sneering face.

Jonathan pushed the offender away from him, then eyed each of the remaining men. "That goes for the rest of you, too."

Apprehension raced through Elizabeth. Her body ached all over as she forced her way toward Millie.

The woman turned from the fireplace. In her hands she held a steaming pot of oatmeal, which she placed on top of the stove. "Don't let their squabbling get to you. Sit down there." She indicated a large tree stump. "I'll bring you a plate as soon as I get these men fed and out of here. 'Course, it might be a while before I get back to you. They come and go for about an hour." She looked at the men waiting to be served. "There are always a few stragglers. Go ahead and sit. That stump's pretty comfortable once you get used to it." Elizabeth sank onto the oversized log. She saw Jonathan standing beside the table, talking in a low voice with one of the other outlaws. Easing from side to side, she tried to find a less painful position on the smooth surface of the stump. Millie moved about the room, filling mugs of coffee and dishing up plates of bacon, eggs, fried potatoes with green chillies, and oatmeal.

Jonathan pulled a mug from one of the shelves beside the fireplace and poured coffee into it, then handed it to Elizabeth. "Here. This might make you feel better."

"Thank you." Her voice quavered as she accepted the cup from him. He had just threatened to rip a man's eyes out of his face. She didn't doubt for a moment that he would do it.

He knelt in front of her, keeping a close watch on the men from the corner of his eye. "Harry and I went out last night to check on your wagon driver," he said in a low voice. "He wasn't where Harry said the gang left him. I'm sorry."

Elizabeth swallowed. Was Samson alive? Not knowing brought tears to her eyes. *I won't cry. I won't.*

She placed a trembling hand on his arm, holding him in place and drawing his warm brown gaze to hers. "Are you the one who brought back my carpetbag?"

He nodded.

"What about my trunk?"

"Whoever took the driver must have taken it, too."

She hoped he was right. She'd need all her belongings once she was back in Farmington. Elizabeth pulled her hand away from his arm, uncomfortable with the contact. "Thank you."

"You're welcome." He stood.

Sipping her coffee, she watched Millie dish up food for the men at the table. The older woman made several trips back to the fire for coffee and more food. The men talked and laughed loudly among themselves. Elizabeth felt their eyes move to her from time to time and was aware that Jonathan's standing beside her, quietly observing everyone in the room, was the only thing keeping the outlaws at bay.

Four of the men finished their breakfast and left the kitchen. Jonathan seemed to relax somewhat. He drained the last of his coffee from the cup in his hand, then turned to her. "Elizabeth, darling, I have work to do. I want your word you'll stay with Millie."

Darling? What was he thinking? She wanted to shout that she wasn't his darling, but the dangerous glint had reentered his eyes, and she decided it would be better to stay on this man's good side.

"I will." What other choice did she have? Thanks to the roughness of the day before, her body hurt all over. She'd need all her strength to successfully escape the camp—and Jonathan.

"Good. I'll see you this evening." He dropped his cup into a tub of hot water that sat beside the stove and left the room.

Elizabeth assumed he found the remaining men harmless or he wouldn't have left her and Millie alone with them. Two of the men, having completed their meals, piled dishes in the tub of water and exited. She stood slowly. While Millie continued to serve breakfast, Elizabeth rolled up her sleeves and sank her bruised hands into the water. Her wrists and palms stung from the heat, but her pain faded as the pile of dirty dishes shrank. A sense of satisfaction drifted over her tired mind and body.

The door slammed behind the last man as he exited the kitchen. Millie set the coffeepot on the stove. "You didn't have to do those." She nodded at the stack of clean dishes.

"I enjoyed it. It gave me something to think about besides my situation." Elizabeth dried her hands on a tea towel. " 'Whatsoever thy hand findeth to do, do it with thy might.' " Claire, her friend and housekeeper back home, had drilled this Bible verse into her when she was small and complained about doing chores. "If you don't mind, I'd like to help out while I'm here." *At least until I feel well enough to escape.*

Millie studied her. "I've not heard that scripture in years." For a moment she seemed lost within her own thoughts. Then she smiled. "I'll enjoy having another woman to share the chores."

Jonathan waited for Edward on a rock beside the San Juan River. The river sat a good half mile from camp and was a favorite spot for him and his partner to meet. The water flowing over the rocky bottom normally soothed his soul, but not tonight. Elizabeth Hamilton rested heavily on his mind. He'd insinuated in front of the men that Elizabeth was more than just his captive. Thankfully, she'd gone along with him this morning. For a moment, he'd been worried she'd blow the farce. He thanked the Lord that she hadn't. But what was he going to do with the woman for a week until Bowman returned?

A soft whistle alerted him to Edward's approach. He turned to face his friend.

"How is she?" Edward knelt on the ground and selected several smooth stones.

"Tired but safe for the night. I left Harry on guard."

Edward chose a pebble and skipped it across the river's surface. "Bowman's not coming back." He spoke low.

"How do you reckon?" Jonathan watched the last of the ripples the stone created in the water.

"He took everything he owed."

"That doesn't mean he's not coming back."

Another stone bounced on the water. Edward grinned as it skipped across. "He also mumbled something about no woman being worth risking his hide."

Crickets filled the silence between them.

"So he ran." Red would surely send another man when Bowman didn't return. That meant Jonathan had to try to safeguard Miss Elizabeth Hamilton from the rowdy outlaws for at least two weeks. Two weeks in which her mere presence would keep him from the evidence he needed to prove the identity of his sister's killer. Jonathan felt the heavy weight of responsibility settle on his shoulders, and he sighed.

Chapter 3

Elizabeth laid down the Bible she'd been reading in the first glow of daylight and scooted off the cot. She pulled a bottle of vanilla-scented lotion from her bag and rubbed the cream into her skin. For the last three days, she'd worked hard in the kitchen to gain Jonathan's and Millie's trust while she planned her escape. But now it was time to go. Her muscles were feeling stronger, and the scrapes and bruises were healing. Besides, the man Red had sent out the day of her capture would return soon. Then he'd alert the camp to the fact that she was not the banker's daughter and they would not be getting their ransom.

She put the lotion back in her bag, dressed, and hurried to the door. Expecting to see Jonathan or Harry standing against the wall, she was surprised to find the space empty. No one waited to walk her to the kitchen.

Chance or fortuitous coincidence? She had no time to waste wondering. She had to move while the window of opportunity remained opened.

What would Jonathan do when he found her gone? Chase after her? What if Porter or one of the other men caught her leaving? Elizabeth trembled in fear. Porter watched her every move with hate in his eyes.

I can't think about that. Now's my chance. I have to take it.

If she was careful, she could be gone before the men awakened. Fear turned to joy at the prospect of freedom. Elizabeth rushed back inside. She grabbed her bag and slid the Bible into it, then slung the strap over her shoulder, the reassuring weight of the bag at her side. She slipped out the door, closed it quietly behind her, and rested against it for a moment, looking around. Still no sign of the men.

Her boots made crunching sounds as she worked her way across the front yard. *Please don't let me get caught.*

She sneaked around the side of the main dwelling. Five horses stood tied to the hitching post some distance from the house. She paused and listened. Nothing moved. Elizabeth ran across the clearing and ducked between the horses, looking for Ginger.

Disappointment filled her when she realized none of the animals was hers. She laid her head against the last mare. "I can't leave without Ginger," she whispered.

How foolish is that? Of course she could. She could ride any of these horses to Durango, contact the San Juan County sheriff, and return with him when he came to arrest this bunch of thieves. He would help her get her horse back.

The back door slammed open against the house.

Elizabeth ducked behind the nearest horse, then peeked out from under its neck. The dark-skinned man, José, ambled across the porch. His presence set her heart to pounding in fear. Something in his dark eyes always screamed danger. He set a steaming mug on the porch rail, then ambled down the steps and into the woods.

Unable to move, Elizabeth held her breath as she waited for him to come back into view. Blood pounded in her head. Perspiration ran down her back.

Why hadn't she taken the horse and left when she'd had the chance? Maybe there was still time. She pulled the reins from the hitching post.

José returned. Elizabeth dropped the reins, crouched down, and eased back. She waited while he collected his mug and walked to the side of the cabin. He leaned against the building, cradling the cup in his hands.

Hints of orange and pink rose over the ridge as the sun climbed farther into the sky. Soon it would be full daylight. And then what?

If she moved, José would see her and call the others. *Please, Lord*, Elizabeth prayed silently. *Let him finish his drink and leave.*

She hunkered closer to the ground, wondering whether darkness would conceal her if she crawled to the trees. Elizabeth pressed her stomach to the dirt and inched across the hard earth, peeking over her shoulder to see if she'd been spotted.

The outlaw rocked the mug between his palms. His eyes looked closed, though Elizabeth couldn't be sure.

Dirt and gravel scratched her sensitive hands as her fingers grasped the undergrowth of the bushes. Thankfully, she'd reached the tree line.

The back door made a creaking sound as it opened. She looked back to the cabin and saw Jonathan leaning against the porch railing. He scanned the perimeter, staring in Elizabeth's direction. She shrank behind a tree trunk, half expecting him to come crashing into the woods and drag her back.

Instead he eased down the stairs and walked toward the side of the house. She released a pent-up breath.

José, who was still leaning against the wall of the dwelling, pulled himself up to his full height. "Mornin', *amigo*."

Jonathan faced him. "José." He nodded, then turned his attention back to the tree line.

José pulled a gun from the holster on his hip. "You see somethin' out there?"

"Put that thing away," Jonathan growled. "I'm just being cautious."

Elizabeth sighed into her hands when José dropped the weapon back into its holster. What if he'd shot into the trees?

"No need to worry, *amigo*," José said. "Amos and Sam, they been doin' watch duty. No one gets past ole Amos."

Jonathan moved toward the horses. "See you at breakfast."

"Ah, the little *señorita* waits, no?" Crude laughter filled the morning air.

Jonathan turned with the speed of a rattlesnake. "She's none of your business. You'd be smart to remember that."

José's laughter died as quickly as it had taken life. His hand inched toward the holster.

"Touch that gun and we'll be feeding your carcass to the dogs for breakfast." The warning came deep and low.

José raised the cup to his lips and took a sip. He tossed the dregs of his coffee to the ground, then turned swiftly on his booted heel.

Elizabeth watched him go back inside the cabin. Then she turned her gaze back to Jonathan. He was headed toward the horses. Panic closed her throat. *What if he sees where I pulled my body across the ground toward the trees, or worse, sees that I untied one of the horses?*

She whirled and ran wildly through the woods.

Her feet slipped on the wet grass. She fell heavily, tumbling downhill. Rocks tore at exposed skin as she slid. Blinding pain shot through her right leg. She landed with a thud.

Elizabeth fought to get air back into her lungs. A fiery sensation pooled around her knee. She turned onto her stomach, trying to blend in with the ground. For several moments, the only sound she heard was her own gasping.

Slowly, she turned onto her back and realized she'd fallen into a narrow valley. Horses of all shapes and colors filled the ravine. *Horses?* She looked around and realized that she'd landed in a natural corral. Rocks surrounded it on three sides; she'd fallen down the back wall. Elizabeth searched for the guard.

After several long minutes she realized she was alone. She took a deep breath and forced herself to stand in spite of the pain. She searched the area for the most suitable mount. She blinked when she saw Ginger standing a few feet away, next to a beautiful black gelding. Elizabeth limped toward the animals.

The gelding snorted and moved away when she approached. But Ginger nosed Elizabeth's hand. She rubbed the little mare's velvety nose. Ginger pressed her head into Elizabeth's chest and neighed softly.

Elizabeth looked about the quiet enclosure. She heard no boots pounding against the hard-packed ground. She sighed. Satisfied they were alone, she hugged the horse's neck. "Oh, Ginger, we have to get out of here fast."

"You aren't going anywhere."

Chapter 4

I should've known she'd try to escape. Anger poured through Jonathan's veins as he stared at the woman cowering before him.

Tears slipped down Elizabeth's cheeks and dripped from her quivering chin. Fear radiated from the watery green depths of her eyes. "I just want to go home. Let me go, please."

His heart softened, he took a step toward her. "You know I can't."

Elizabeth bowed her head. "You won't get your ransom. And even if you do, you're probably going to kill me anyway." She swiped at the moisture on her cheeks.

He sighed. He had hardened his heart against a woman's tears a long time ago. And his stubbornness had cost him everything dear to him. He would not make that mistake again. "Whether you believe it or not, Elizabeth, I'm trying to protect you."

A sob broke from her lips.

I hate this. He wished he could just let her go. But he couldn't blow his cover with the other men. He'd worked too hard to earn their trust. *Lord, please make a way for her to return to her family soon.*

"Come on," he said as softly as he could. "I've got to get you back before the others realize you tried to escape." He reached for her hand, but she jerked away.

Frustrated, Jonathan grabbed her and pulled. She dug her heels into the soft dirt. Worry and irritation caused him to yank harder on her arm.

Elizabeth fought back.

He dragged her, kicking and screaming, through the gate and back toward the main house. Elizabeth struggled with the uphill climb, crying out every so often. Jonathan wished she'd accept the fact that she couldn't get away from him.

As they approached the house, he saw Porter, Doc, and Jones coming out the back door of the kitchen.

"Looks like the lady don't like your company no more," Porter blurted.

Doc spat on the ground. "Give her to me, Jonathan. I'll tame the little filly for ya." His tobacco-stained grin sickened Jonathan. Doc wasn't known for his bedside manner. Quite the opposite. Jonathan suspected Doc had joined the gang because too many of his patients turned up dead, and no one in his right mind would go to him for care.

Porter cursed. "What's the matter, Jonathan? The little lady decided she'd rather be with a real man?"

From the corner of his eye, Jonathan saw Elizabeth's cheeks flush and her gaze move to the ground. He dropped her arm and took a step toward the group of men. Anger pulsed through his body. "Watch your mouth, Porter," he warned.

Porter leered at Elizabeth. Ignoring Jonathan, he stepped closer. "Tell him, honey. Tell Johnny boy you want a man who'll keep you warm at night. Like me."

Snickers filled the air.

Jonathan moved closer to the vile man, fury boiling in his veins.

Red came out of the house. He pushed his way through the three outlaws and stood between them and Jonathan. With his back to them, he addressed the men while keeping his eyes on Jonathan. "That's no way to be talkin' to the lassie, boys."

A hush fell over the men.

Jonathan knew Red had only delayed a battle between himself and Porter. He'd have to watch Elizabeth—and himself—more closely in the future.

"I have to go feed my horse," Jones said, moving away from the group.

"Yeah," Doc muttered, following Jones.

"I have to relieve the guard from watch duty." Porter licked his lips and winked at Elizabeth suggestively, then started to walk away.

Jonathan felt his blood pressure rise. He clenched his jaw and his fists.

"Porter," said Red, "I'll see you in my room in ten minutes. Don't be late."

Porter nodded as he continued walking away.

Jonathan grabbed Elizabeth by the arm and drilled his gaze into hers. He prayed she'd heed his unspoken demand to keep silent.

"This little lassie givin' you trouble, Johnny boy?"

"Nothin' I can't handle." Jonathan tightened his grip on her arm.

Red ran his index finger down Elizabeth's cheek. Her head jerked back, and she twisted her face to the side. He put his hand back in his pocket and rocked on his heels. "I'll see you at lunch, lassie." He headed toward the back door of the house, calling over his shoulder, "Keep her out of trouble, Johnny boy!"

Jonathan sighed and released his hold on Elizabeth's arm. She slowly walked toward the porch, where she sank down and dropped her head onto her knees.

Finding her gone that morning had almost caused his heart to give out on him. When he'd run into Harry, the boy had sworn he thought Jonathan was going to walk her to breakfast.

Obviously, she hadn't given up her plan to escape. And he couldn't blame her. He'd have done the same if their circumstances were reversed.

He'd have to check with Millie about taking Elizabeth with her to the kitchen in the mornings from now on. He would assign Harry to watch the horses, in case she attempted to escape again. He'd also need to ask Edward to help him keep an eye on her. Jonathan didn't trust any of the rest of the men with Elizabeth's well-being.

She stood and started walking back to the kitchen. He caught up to her and took her by the arm, shepherding her toward the shed as though she were a troublesome toddler.

Elizabeth glared at him, pulling against his grip. "I need to help Millie with breakfast."

"Sorry, ma'am," he said, opening the door to Millie's place. "But you gave up your freedom this morning. You'll be staying right here until I decide to let you out."

Elizabeth's shocked gaze darted from him to the doorway. Jonathan noticed her limbs trembling. *Good. She needs to realize what kind of danger she's in.*

"My father isn't going to like this."

"Maybe not. But I suspect he'll be so glad to have his daughter back, this little inconvenience won't bother him near as much as it does you."

She opened her mouth to protest further. He cut her off. "And I wouldn't try to escape again if I were you. If you do, and one of the other men finds you, your safety will no longer be in my hands."

A harsh laugh erupted from her throat. "You just don't want any trouble with Red. Men like you don't care about the safety of decent people."

Her boldness surprised him. "I'm sorry you feel that way, ma'am." He closed the door.

Jonathan leaned against the wood. He wished he could tell her the truth, but he didn't believe that would convince her not to try to escape again. *I can't watch her every minute! How can I keep her from running as soon as my back is turned?* Millie was in the middle of serving breakfast, so he couldn't approach her yet. The solution was simple yet bitter. For now, he'd have to lock her in.

Elizabeth limped to the cot. It squeaked when she sat on the edge. Grass stains marred her brown calico dress. She pulled up the hem to examine her knee. Heat and pain throbbed through it. Warily, she touched the swelling flesh and flinched.

"Oh, Lord," she said aloud in the empty room, "I really made a mess of things today. Why didn't You let me escape? What am I going to do?" When Bowman came back and reported that her father was a poor general store owner and not a rich banker, there was no telling what these men would do with her. Fresh tears slipped down her cheeks.

A knock sounded at the door.

Elizabeth dropped her skirt back over her legs and wiped the moisture from her cheeks. "Yes?"

The door swung open. Jonathan stepped into the room, holding a plate filled with ham and eggs. "Millie says you might be a prisoner, but we're not going to starve you to death." He walked over to the cot and handed her the dish.

She took the plate and fork, breathing in the pleasant aroma. "Please tell Millie I said thanks." Elizabeth scooped a mound of scrambled eggs onto the fork.

"Look, I hate to do this, but I'm going to put a board across the door. If you need anything, just tap on the wood. Edward or I will be standing guard outside."

Elizabeth viciously tore off a piece of the ham. "You trust this Edward?"

Jonathan nodded. "With my life."

Obviously with mine, too.

Chapter 5

Elizabeth winced as Millie pushed a pillow under her swollen leg. The stuffing was so thin that it had to be doubled to do the job of supporting her knee. She glanced about the bedroom, hating having to spend the day in bed.

"I'm sorry. I know that hurt. But this knee has to be elevated."

"That's fine. But what about my head?" Elizabeth tried to sound lighthearted but knew she'd failed miserably.

"Does it hurt, too?" Millie picked up the pillow from her own cot and handed it to Elizabeth. "Here. You can use mine."

"No, my head doesn't hurt. I can't take your pillow." Elizabeth pushed it away. "I've already taken too much from you."

Millie's soft laughter filled the room. "Nonsense. You've given me more than you'll ever know." She fluffed the pillow, and then pushed it behind Elizabeth's head. She stood and smiled.

Elizabeth rested against the cushion. "I don't know how I could have given you anything. Seems to me all I've done is add to your chores."

Millie pulled a small crate to the side of the bed and sat on it. "Before you came, I felt all alone here."

"How long have you been in this camp?" Elizabeth leaned up on one elbow.

Millie picked at the dried bread dough on her apron. "Four years."

Elizabeth sighed. Would she end up here for years, too? She pushed the scary thought away. "Why do you stay?"

"I'm a prisoner here, same as you."

"Why haven't you escaped?" Dread filled her at what Millie might answer. She couldn't imagine anyone staying in a camp of outlaws and not trying to get out. Had the men hurt her? Threatened to kill her?

"Where would I go?"

"Wherever you lived before you came here." Elizabeth couldn't imagine not attempting to escape, yet here Millie sat saying she had no place to go so why bother.

"I'm not sure anyone from home would want me back."

"Why wouldn't they?" She chewed on a broken fingernail. Wouldn't her father accept her if she escaped? Wouldn't the good people of Farmington still allow her to teach their children?

Millie clasped her hands together. "Would you like to hear my story?"

"Only if you want to tell me." Elizabeth offered what she hoped was an encouraging smile.

Millie's gaze moved to the window. "I have a daughter. Christine. She's beautiful. Her hair is brown, and her eyes are the purest blue."

"How old is she?"

"She turned twenty-three last May."

Three years older than I am.

"When she got married, she let me stay with her and her new husband, Mark. They have a lovely home with a garden behind the house. I was grateful to have a place to live and to be able to stay with my little girl. But I knew the newlyweds needed some quiet time to themselves. So I spent a lot of my time weeding the tomatoes in the cool of the evening." Her voice faded, a faraway look entered her eyes, and for a moment she looked happy. Then sadness drifted across her face as gentle as a summer rain.

"You don't have to tell me this." Elizabeth's voice pulled the woman from whatever thoughts had held her captive.

Millie turned from the window. "It's all right. I like having someone to talk to about her."

"And I like hearing it."

"Christine and Mark had been married two months, and I was fixin' to tell them it was time for me to move on. I'd decided to work in town as a seamstress. As I weeded the tomatoes, I tried to figure out how to tell her. I was so focused on my thoughts, I didn't hear the outlaws approaching until they rode up just a few feet behind me."

Elizabeth gasped. "Was it Red and his gang?"

Millie nodded. "Red weighed a lot less back then and could move a lot faster. He was off that horse and on me faster than I could scream. He covered my mouth and threatened to hurt my family if I didn't come along quietly. I couldn't let that happen." Tears filled Millie's eyes. "I've been here ever since."

Elizabeth pushed herself into an upright position, biting her lip so she wouldn't cry out at the pain in her knee. "Did you ever try to escape?"

"A few times, in the beginning."

"Why didn't you keep trying? Surely they don't watch you all the time."

"Not like they used to." Millie shook her head. "But they know I can't return home."

"Why not?"

"Red knows where my kids live. He'd kill them if I ever left."

"Well, I'm going to get away from here. And when I do, I'll tell the San Juan

County sheriff where this place is. He'll catch Red and his gang. And then we can both go home."

Sorrow filled Millie's face. "Please don't do that." Millie hung her head.

"Why not?"

Millie clasped her hands together, her knuckles white and her cheeks flushed. "Because of Jonathan."

Confusion washed over Elizabeth. "What's so special about him? Are you two. . ." She felt heat fill her cheeks.

Millie's mouth opened and closed like a fish out of water. "It's not like that. He's young enough to be my son."

"Then what does he have to do with all this?"

Millie stood. She moved to the window and stared outside. "Jonathan is a good man. His job is to keep the camp secure. He's captain over all the outlaws and responsible for everyone's safety."

"Was he with Red and the others when they kidnapped you?"

"No. He arrived last year." Millie chuckled. "He talks a lot about God being loving and kind. You know, I almost believe him."

Elizabeth found this hard to swallow. *Could an outlaw be a Christian? Maybe he's one of those people who just talks about God but doesn't mean a word of it.*

Millie smiled over her shoulder. "I owe Jonathan a lot." The smile slipped from her features. "He put a stop to the horrible treatment I'd been receiving. He convinced Red that I'd make a better cook than a. . ."

Shock like ice water hit Elizabeth in the face. Had Red really used Millie like a prostitute? Would she face the same fate herself? How would she handle such shame? She didn't know. At least for now, Elizabeth was thankful that God was protecting her.

"I'm sorry. I've embarrassed you." Millie dropped her forehead to the window frame. "But you understand now why I can't go home. Even if Jonathan could convince Red not to follow through on his threats against my family, they would ask questions. If they found out what happened to me, they wouldn't want me around them. Especially if they have children by now." Her voice cracked.

Elizabeth sat up. When she dropped her feet to the floor, her knee throbbed. But she stood slowly and moved to stand beside Millie. "You have nothing to be ashamed of. I'm sure your daughter would understand." She wrapped her arm around the older woman's shoulder. Still, the jarring reality of how her friends and her father might view her told her otherwise.

Millie patted her hand. "Thank you. I'd like to believe what you say is true. But people can't control how they think and feel."

If that's true, then I'm doomed to live a life of loneliness, too. No man will ever believe I wasn't raped or that I didn't give myself to these men willingly to save myself.

Jonathan ducked his head as the black horse he was riding pranced under a low bough of a cottonwood tree. He casually watched the road below. Night guard duty didn't bother him. But the mosquitoes did. He slapped the back of his neck, and then looked up into the sky, seeking the peace the view offered.

In New Mexico the stars felt close enough to touch. Half of the heavens glistened with twinkling lights; the other half shone with moonbeams. Texas had open plains, too, but New Mexico had mountains and mesas. *Maybe I'll stay in New Mexico when this mess is cleaned up.* He'd promised himself he'd get out of the lawman business and get back to farming as soon as this job was done. After four long years, he needed to get back to the land, back to a simpler life.

He heard the *clip-clop* of a horse's hooves. Jonathan looked over his shoulder and saw Porter arrive on his buckskin mount.

"All clear?" Porter asked as he pulled his horse next to Jonathan's.

"All clear." Jonathan tipped his hat and turned his horse toward the hideout.

"Hey, what's this I hear about you locking Lizzy up in her room?"

Jonathan turned his horse back around. "That's none of your business."

"Maybe I'd like to make it my business." He rubbed his chin. "Seems I owe her. She almost knocked my jaw out of its socket."

Jonathan urged his horse closer, stopping directly in front of the blond outlaw. "You go near her, and I'll consider that reason to shoot you."

Porter backed his horse up. "I'll keep that in mind."

"See that you do." Jonathan watched Porter take his place on the knoll. Then he turned his mount back toward camp.

That had been too easy. What was Porter up to? Maybe Red had enlightened him a little at their meeting this morning. Jonathan decided to check on Elizabeth before putting his horse away.

A lone figure stood in the shadow of the shed. Jonathan eased off his horse. As he moved in closer, he saw that it was Millie who waited for him. "Evening, ma'am. Where's Edward?"

Millie stood with her feet braced apart and a deep scowl on her face. "What did you do to Elizabeth today?"

He leaned against the side of the building. "Let's see. I hunted her down and kept her from escaping. Then I brought her back here."

"You hurt her."

Jonathan pushed away from the wall. "I didn't mean to hurt her feelings. I'm just trying to keep her safe from the likes of Porter." He shoved his hat back on his forehead.

"Not her feelings, Jonathan. You hurt her leg." Millie drew a circle in the dirt with her boot tip.

"How?" Jonathan's thoughts raced over the day. The only time he'd touched her was that morning. And he'd only grabbed her arm to keep her from running off.

"I don't know, but her knee is the size of a small pumpkin, and it pains her something awful. I've made her as comfortable as I can, but she'll need to stay off of it for a few days."

"I didn't know." He leaned one arm against the building.

"Well, you know now." Millie turned away from him and slipped quietly into the shed.

Lord, You know I never meant to hurt Elizabeth. She'd fought like a wildcat. He'd never realized she was in pain.

The desire to protect her swelled. Jonathan pushed it down. He shook his head to clear it. He'd decided long ago that his life would be less complicated without a woman in it.

He grabbed his horse's reins and marched back to the corral. *I don't want to be responsible for anyone but myself.*

Chapter 6

For three days, Elizabeth had been locked up in the room she shared with Millie. Harry and Edward had kept a constant watch on her and the shed, but she'd not seen Jonathan once.

"I wish I could work in the kitchen with you again." The desire to escape was foremost in her mind, but she couldn't tell Millie her real thoughts. Fear of what was to come once Bowman returned caused her voice to sound shaky. "My knee feels much better."

Millie laid down the dress she'd been mending and walked to the door. "You'll have to ask Jonathan." She opened the door and smiled over her shoulder. "Here he comes now." Millie strode out to meet him.

Elizabeth limped to the doorway. She enjoyed the warmth of sunshine on her face. Her body craved the fresh air.

Would Jonathan allow her more freedom if she asked? Millie had claimed he was a good man. So far, she hadn't seen that side of him. She wasn't sure she ever would.

⁂

"Millie, could I impose on you for a picnic lunch today?" Jonathan asked in full voice, glimpsing Elizabeth lingering in the doorway of the shed. Then he whispered, "How is she today?"

"Antsy, bored, tired of being cooped up."

Jonathan took off his hat and ran his fingers through his hair. He'd been so tied up with guard duty and making sure the men were kept busy with odd jobs that he'd neglected looking in on Elizabeth.

"Any news from Bowman?"

Jonathan studied the ground. He flicked an ant with the toe of his boot. "He hasn't returned yet." He replaced his hat. "Millie, the picnic lunch?" he reminded her.

"What do you want with a picnic lunch?" Millie asked, placing both hands on her hips.

Jonathan returned to his normal voice, which he knew would carry to the shed. "Red gave me a day off to head into town and relax. I thought I'd take Elizabeth down by the river instead. Let her get out of that stuffy room for a change."

Millie's face beamed. "I'll go fix it right now. And you can give her the good news yourself." Millie hurried off to the kitchen.

Jonathan turned toward the shed. When Elizabeth saw him looking her way, she stepped back, leaving the door open.

He followed her inside and found her sitting at the small table. The sad expression on her face pulled at his heartstrings. "How are you feeling today?"

She frowned. "Like I'm a prisoner. I'm not an animal. I need fresh air."

"I agree." Jonathan leaned against the door frame. "How would you like to go to the river today?"

Her eyes narrowed. "There's a river around here?"

"The San Juan runs about half a mile from camp."

"And why do you want to take me there?"

The suspicion in her voice made him cringe. Did she think he wanted to drown her? "Millie told me she thought you'd like to get away from here for a while. But if you'd rather not. . ." He pushed away from the door.

"Wait!" She stood so fast she knocked the chair over.

Jonathan placed a hand on each side of the door frame, grinning. "Changed your mind?"

She chewed on her bottom lip. "Maybe. What did you have planned?"

"Lunch. A little fresh air. Nothing more."

Elizabeth eyed him. "May I take a couple of dresses and wash them in the river?"

"Sure."

Elizabeth limped to the end of her cot and pulled a small box out from under it. Taking out two dresses, she folded them over her arm and then returned to him.

Millie hurried up to the door behind Jonathan. "Here you go." She handed the basket to him.

"Thanks." Jonathan took the food.

"You're welcome." Millie stepped past him into the room. "Elizabeth, you ought to soak that knee in the cool water. It'll help with the swelling."

"I will. Jonathan says I can wash out my dresses. Do you have anything you'd like me to wash out for you?"

Millie patted her arm. "Bless you, child." She pulled a box out from under her bed and selected a few items. She dropped them into a flour bag and held it open. Elizabeth stuffed her two dresses inside.

"About ready?" Jonathan asked.

"Definitely," Elizabeth answered.

"I've got to get lunch ready for the men. You two have fun."

As Millie scurried back to the kitchen, Jonathan offered his arm to Elizabeth.

She declined with a shake of her head. He couldn't really blame her. After all, he'd kept her locked up for three days. Still, when she stepped outside, he grasped her elbow and walked with her out into the yard.

Edward approached with the black stallion. "Here you go, my friend." He handed the reins to Jonathan. The horse pranced sideways.

"Easy, Shadow." Jonathan handed Edward the basket of food.

Edward chuckled. "I had a hard time getting that horse of yours to leave the corral." He winked. "The big guy didn't want to leave this young woman's mare behind."

Jonathan knew how Shadow felt. He pulled himself up into the saddle.

Elizabeth eyed the large horse. "I don't know if I can get up there. My knee is still a little stiff."

"Let Edward lift you up."

Edward set the basket down and smiled at her. "Ma'am?"

She clung to the flour sack and nodded. Edward grasped her around the waist and lifted her with ease, setting her in front of Jonathan. "There you go. That wasn't so bad, was it?"

She shook her head. "Thank you."

Edward tipped his hat. "You're welcome, ma'am." He passed the basket up to Jonathan.

Jonathan breathed in the scent of vanilla that seemed to cling to Elizabeth. With one arm around her waist, he helped her situate the clothes bag on her lap. Then he set the basket on top of the sack, wrapping the handle over the saddle horn. "Can't let our lunch spill out on the ground, now, can we?" Slipping both arms around her, he took the reins.

Her hair tickled his face as she shook her head in response.

Edward moved away from the horse. "What time do you think you'll be back?"

"We should be in before supper."

"See you then."

Elizabeth sat straight and rigid all the way to the river. Jonathan wondered what had happened to the spitfire he'd left a few days ago. The woman in front of him kept her eyes downcast as she clung to the saddle horn. She held her body stiff against his chest.

His thoughts turned to his sister. For the past year, he'd been living with these outlaws, hoping one of them would say something that would shed some light on the day Sarah was attacked. Jones had once mentioned an incident that had happened during the month of June five years ago. He said Red had picked him up in an alley, drunker than a cowhand on a Saturday night. They'd ridden all night and into the next day until they found themselves on a farm in the middle of nowhere. He said he'd had a real headache that morning and that Red had insisted they stop at a farm to water their horses. Jones seemed to have grown sad and became a little more tight-lipped but did confess that a girl died that day. But none of the other men seemed to know anything about the death of a young girl on a farm. Or if they did, they refused to tell him or Edward about it.

"It's beautiful out here." Elizabeth's voice pulled him from his troubled thoughts. He felt her back relax and her sides move as she inhaled the clean fall air.

"Yes, it is."

"I heard you tell Millie you could have gone to town. Why didn't you?"

He shifted in the saddle. "I prefer to be outdoors where the air is fresh, the only noise is the sound of birds in the trees, and peace seems to fill the world."

She gazed at the trees and shrubs they passed. A light breeze lifted her hair, and her green eyes shone with delight. It amazed and shamed him that she could take such joy from a simple outing.

When they arrived at the river, Jonathan slid off the horse, took the basket and flour sack from her, and set them on the ground. Then he reached up for her.

She came willingly into his arms.

For a brief moment, he thought he saw trust in her eyes. Jonathan gently lowered her to the ground. He stared into her pretty green eyes. "This is one of my favorite spots."

A hint of pink entered her cheeks. Elizabeth stepped out of his arms and gazed about. "I can see why. It's lovely."

She turned, her green skirt swishing as she made her way through the tall grass. She stopped under a large cottonwood tree.

Jonathan secured his horse, picked up the flour sack and picnic basket, and followed her to the tree. "How's this for a place to picnic?"

A sincere smile touched her lips. "Perfect."

He set the flour sack off to the side and pulled a blanket from the basket. Elizabeth took one end of it and helped him spread it out on the ground. Keenly aware that she was watching him, Jonathan pulled cheese, ham, tomatoes, pickles, and bread from the basket.

Birds sang in the trees. Water gurgled and splashed over the river rocks. The world seemed just right at the moment.

Elizabeth moved to the river's edge, lowered herself to the ground, and dipped her fingers into the cool water. She closed her eyes and pretended to absorb the sunshine. Why had Jonathan really brought her down here? Had Bowman returned? Had her father refused to pay the ransom? And was he supposed to get rid of her? Drown her? She wanted to ask Jonathan what was going on but the fear of knowing held her tongue. She'd wait and let him tell her what he knew.

Jonathan moved to stand beside her, rocks shifting under his weight. "Millie tells me the last few days have been hard on you. I'm sorry." He sounded sincere.

Elizabeth opened her eyes and gazed out over the shimmering river. "It's true." She sighed. "But I take the blame for part of it. If I hadn't been so clumsy, I wouldn't have fallen down that embankment and twisted my knee."

He knelt down and picked up a stone. It skipped across the smooth surface of the water. "I'm not so sure you fell because you're clumsy. You were in a hurry to escape."

His gaze followed another pebble as it bounced across the water. Elizabeth focused on his profile. "Why did you bring me here?"

Jonathan looked at her. "I thought you could use the fresh air."

So he was sticking to his original answer. "I do love being outdoors."

A smile touched his lips. "Would you like to eat now?"

"I'd like to wait awhile if you don't mind."

"All right." Jonathan stood. "See that rock?"

She noticed a large rock in the center of the river, water sloshing against its mossy sides. "Yes."

"It looks like a perfect place for you to sit and let your legs hang into the water. To soak your knee."

Elizabeth wondered what he was up to. Had Red told him to take her out here? Bowman could easily have returned by now. Perhaps he'd told Red that her father wasn't the banker and they wouldn't be getting the ransom after all. Her heartbeat picked up. *Maybe Jonathan intends to take me to the middle of the river and drown me!*

She tried to control the fear building in her chest. He didn't look as if he had murder in mind. But if he did, Jonathan would not find her easy to kill. "If that's what you want."

"It's up to you." His chocolate-colored eyes searched hers.

Elizabeth nibbled on her bottom lip. "Would it be all right if I washed out my dresses first?" She rushed on before he could answer. "Then when I finish soaking my knee, I can change into fresh, dry clothes."

"Sure." He stood. "I'll make a fishing pole while you do your washing."

Would a killer be patient enough to make a fishing pole before murdering his victim? *Maybe I've read too many dime novels. Then again, maybe it's a ruse. Maybe Jonathan thinks to catch me off my guard so I'll be easier to deal with.*

"Would you like me to bring your dresses to you?"

She'd forgotten about the dresses. They'd only been brought to make him think she'd given up all thoughts of escape. "No, thanks. I'll get them." Elizabeth rolled over and pushed herself up off the ground. The injured knee protested. She took a deep breath and forced herself to stand.

Jonathan watched her every move. *Do I look as weak and awkward as I feel?* Elizabeth tried not to limp as she walked to the blanket where the flour sack lay. She repacked the food into the basket.

"I'm going to find a limb to make the fishing pole. I'll be right back." Jonathan turned and strolled into the woods.

She looked over her shoulder and saw that he hadn't moved very far into the woods. If he looked up, he could see her. With the injured knee she wouldn't be able to get far before he noticed. She took a deep breath and bent to pick up the clothes.

Maybe he really is a nice man. Hadn't Millie said Jonathan talked about God? She pushed the thoughts away. *No. He's an outlaw, a man who breaks the law and hurts innocent people.* Elizabeth picked up the sack and walked back to the river.

Her knee protested as she tried to kneel beside the water. She sat on a rock, where she wet the dress and rubbed the stains. "What I wouldn't give for a nice slice of lye soap." She sighed. *A real bath would be heavenly, too.*

A minnow swam by. Its silver back reflected light up at her. It flickered in the water close to her hands, unaware of how quickly its freedom could be snatched away. *Like mine.*

The sound of Jonathan's whistling filled the warm air. She recognized the tune to "Amazing Grace." Her favorite hymn.

Jonathan stepped through the trees, holding a branch in one hand and a large knife in the other. It hadn't occurred to her that he might stab her and then toss her body into the water. With a knife that size, he could pierce her through the heart and be done with her. Would she die instantly? Or would she simply suffer from the knife injury as she drowned? She shivered.

A smile touched his lips as he glanced in her direction. Then he headed for his horse, where he pulled string and a piece of wire out of the saddlebags. He also took out a slim piece of rope.

The rope brought on fresh thoughts of death. With the rope he could choke her to death and still throw her into the river. Not without a fight! If Jonathan planned on killing her, she'd fight. Elizabeth stood, using her good leg, and gradually put weight on her bad one.

Act natural, she commanded herself. The wet garments hung from her arms. She searched for a rock or tree to hang them on and kept Jonathan in her sight at the same time. She chose a small bush and draped the fabric over its branches, fully aware of Jonathan sitting on a rock not far from her.

"What do you think?" Jonathan held up his fishing pole. His brown eyes twinkled, and a grin spread across his face, making him look like a little boy seeking her approval.

"Very nice." Elizabeth returned his smile.

"Thanks. Want to help me dig for worms?"

She wrinkled her nose. "I don't think so."

"It's fun."

"It's disgusting."

Jonathan laughed.

"Have you ever been fishing?"

"No."

"My dad and I went fishing every afternoon when I was a kid. What did you do for fun?" Jonathan asked, shaping the wire into a hook.

Elizabeth watched with interest. "I read books." She still didn't trust him but it wouldn't do for him to sense her true emotions.

He looked up. "I guess a banker's daughter would have access to a lot of books."

She cringed at his mention of her being a banker's daughter. But his reference to it meant he didn't know any different. Apparently Bowman hadn't returned yet—at least not before they'd left. Or had he? She felt as if she were living one of her dime novel mysteries. Not knowing and feeling uncertain of Jonathan's motives. "Did you have any books?"

Jonathan tied the hook onto the string. "Not many. I grew up on a farm in Texas. We didn't have much time to read." He focused on the knot.

"That's too bad. Books can open up whole new worlds." She clasped her hands together to throw him off her real motive for what she was about to say. "You know. . .I've read mysteries that put me on the edge of my seat. The killer would bait his victim until the last moment, and then he'd kill her." She watched his face to see if he'd react to her words. Would he give himself away?

He continued to concentrate on the hook. "Sounds interesting. I prefer westerns myself." If he had any plans of killing her, they didn't show.

"All done." He walked to the river's edge and knelt down. "Sure you don't want to help?"

"I'm sure."

He stood. "Then how about I help you get onto that rock?"

A flicker of fear quickened her pulse. He stood before her. His face looked relaxed, but she couldn't help remembering the times he'd threatened the other outlaws. This was a dangerous man. Someone to fear. She managed to say, "I can do it."

Jonathan lay down his pole. "Those rocks are slick. With your bad knee, I'm afraid you'll slip."

Sure you are. You'll drown me the first chance you get, Johnny boy. She sat on the rocky shore, her heart hammering against her ribs. "I have to take off my boots and stockings. Go dig up your worms. I'll call if I need help." Her voice quivered.

A puzzled look crossed his features. "If you're sure. . ."

"I'm sure." Elizabeth let out pent-up air as he walked back to his fishing pole.

The first boot came off easily. Elizabeth looked over to where Jonathan knelt, digging at the damp soil. *Maybe I can swim to the other side of the river and escape.*

She turned her attention to the other boot. She bent her knee as much as she could and tugged. The boot didn't budge. But her knee throbbed.

"Having trouble?" Jonathan stood over her once more.

She frowned up at him. "I can't seem to get it off."

"Here." He moved to her feet and bent over. He grasped the boot and gave it a gentle tug. It slipped free of her foot.

Elizabeth sucked in air as pain shot up her leg. It subsided. She tried to ignore the ache that remained and reached for her stocking.

"I'm sorry. I didn't mean to hurt you." He pushed her hands away. "Let me get that for you." His big hands surrounded her calf.

Shocked, Elizabeth slapped his hands away. "No. It wouldn't be decent." Heat filled her cheeks.

"I'm sorry. I've lived with men so long, I've forgotten what is respectable." Jonathan stood and turned his back to her.

Elizabeth took off both stockings. She shoved them into her boots and pushed herself up from the ground. The earth felt warm under her feet. She dug her toes into the moist soil.

She stepped into the cool water. Rocks and gravel hurt her bare soles. Jonathan still stood with his back to her. She pushed through the water as fast as her injured leg and the slippery rocks would allow. She heard him splash into the water behind her.

"Please let me help you." Jonathan grabbed her elbow and pressed her against his side.

Elizabeth fought the panic that tore through her. "Really, this isn't necessary." She pulled away from him. The water came up to meet her as she pushed farther into the river. Walking upright in the current proved more difficult than she'd anticipated, and she held out her arms to keep her balance.

She looked over her shoulder. He stood a few steps behind her, looking thoroughly confused. Taking advantage of his confusion, she continued on. She'd almost made it to the rock when he overtook her.

His arm snaked around her waist, and his hand tightened on her arm. He propelled her toward the center of the river.

She struggled against him, trying to get away.

"Stop wiggling." Jonathan tightened his hold on her.

"No!" she shrieked. "I don't want to die."

He stopped pushing forward. "You're not going to die. I'm a good swimmer. Besides, the water's not that deep." The seriousness in his voice penetrated her frightened mind. She stopped thrashing against him.

His brown eyes expressed concern. Then understanding. His jaw tightened. "Come on."

Elizabeth's foot slipped on a rock. She plunged into the chilly water.

He caught her into his arms and held on, frowning at her. "It might be easier if I carried you." He picked her up and slung her wet body over his shoulder.

Hot tears streaked down her cheeks. Her emotions were raw, and her knee was burning. She had no more energy to fight. This beautiful river would soon be her grave.

He deposited her onto the stone with a plop. Jonathan stood in water up to his hips. The water ran swiftly here, much faster than near the shore, and the currents splashed against him and foamed against the rock. She hadn't realized the river would be this dangerous. She stared into his eyes. Why hadn't he drowned her when he had the chance?

"Why did you choose this rock instead of the one I was pointing at?" he asked.

She followed the path his finger pointed. A large boulder sat a little away from the shoreline, calm water lapping at its sides. He hadn't meant to kill her after all. "I misunderstood," she sputtered.

"Dangle your feet off the boulder," he demanded as he moved away from her and trudged toward shore.

She watched him shove his way through the water. *He seems angry.* Perhaps it was because he couldn't drown her after all, as Red had undoubtedly ordered him to.

She was still his prisoner. If she tried to get off this rock, she'd drown in the current without his help.

Elizabeth scooted down the rock and did as Jonathan had ordered. She pulled the pins from her hair and set them on the hard surface. Using her fingers, she combed out the tangles.

After a few moments, the cold water did make her knee feel better. Too bad it held her prisoner just as completely as Jonathan did.

Chapter 7

Jonathan sloshed back to shore. What was it about this woman that caused him to think and act irrationally? *Not good for a lawman. Not good at all.*

He plopped onto the ground, jerked off his boots and his socks, then wrung the water from the socks onto the ground. He stared across the river at the object of his frustration. She'd scooted to the edge of the rock and was dangling both legs in the water. Her hair spread out behind her. He'd only seen her with her hair down when she was first brought to camp. The sight stirred emotions he'd never experienced.

Had she really thought he would drown her? Bitterness coated his thoughts. She had. He hated this job and the way it portrayed him.

Still, it shouldn't bother him what Elizabeth Hamilton thought of him. She was a spoiled little rich girl who would soon be returned to her family. The thought that Red wouldn't release her troubled him. He vowed to himself that Elizabeth would be reunited with her family. One way or another, he intended to make it happen.

Careful, Jonathan, ole boy. Keep her at a distance. It's safer.

At least with her on the rock in the middle of the river, she wouldn't be running off anytime soon. He focused his attention on the unbaited fishing pole lying on the bank a few feet away.

Since he hadn't found worms near the shore, he returned to the edge of the woods, moved a large rock, and dug into the rich soil. Within moments he pulled a wiggling worm from the moist dirt. Elizabeth's wrinkled nose came to mind, and a smile tugged at his lips.

He carried the worm to the pole and threaded it onto the hook. He cast his line into the water. A slight breeze picked up.

Jonathan turned his eyes toward heaven. In a quiet voice he prayed, "Lord, thank You for my safety. I know I don't say it enough, but I love You and I respect You. My life is nothing without You in it. Please continue to keep me safe as I do the job before me." He lowered his gaze and found himself looking in Elizabeth's direction.

He dug his toes into the moist soil. *She's quite a woman, Lord. Please keep her safe. I already let down my sister. I couldn't bear to go through that again. And, Lord, while Elizabeth is in my care, please help me keep my distance from her.*

"For God hath not given us the spirit of fear." The scripture verse worked its way through Jonathan's mind. He knew that his fear of failing another person he cared about wasn't God's will.

He picked up the thin rope he'd brought to the bank and tied one end to a sturdy-looking rock, creating a stringer for the fish he hoped to catch. He lay the rope down and waited for the fish to bite.

Jonathan felt a tug on his line. He jerked the pole just hard enough to set the hook. The line tightened as the fish ran with the bait. He raised the tip of the pole, dragging the fish closer to the shore. It darted away, but the line held fast.

He gradually worked the fish in close enough to reach out and grab it, holding it firmly so the spiked fins wouldn't puncture his hand.

The catfish's lips moved in a gasping motion as it fought for air. He held it with one hand, careful not to let the top fin stick him, while he took the hook in the other hand and gently worked it loose.

He pushed the rope through the fish's gills and out its mouth, then released the fish back into the water. He looped the other end of the rope around a large rock. That cat wasn't going anywhere until he was ready to leave with it.

Jonathan checked to make sure his bait still clung to the hook. Casting his line out once more, he squatted back down. His thoughts turned again to Elizabeth. What was he going to do about her? For now she was safe. But what would happen when Red got the ransom money? Would the outlaw really let her go? He didn't think so. She'd already seen the hideout. What am I going to do, Lord?

His gaze was drawn to Elizabeth. She now lay on the rock on her side, apparently oblivious to his epic internal struggle. From this distance he couldn't tell for sure, but he figured the warmth of the sun and the rush of the water had lulled her to sleep.

Jonathan sighed. He couldn't fight the protective feelings welling up inside him. He knew he could never allow any harm to come to Elizabeth. Even if it meant blowing his cover.

Elizabeth yawned and stretched. The hard rock felt warm under her. The desire to continue sleeping pulled at her until she heard Jonathan's rich voice.

"Wake up, Sleeping Beauty."

Feeling the warmth of sleep slowly subside, she opened her eyes. As the fog of slumber lifted further, she realized Jonathan sat atop his horse, staring down at her. The river slapped and eddied around the animal's legs. "Oh!" She sat up, careful not to fall off the slippery rock.

"I didn't mean to startle you." Jonathan leaned on the saddle horn and smiled into her eyes.

Jonathan had rolled up his pant legs to keep them from getting wet again.

Elizabeth forced herself to look away from his hairy calves and bare feet hanging free of the stirrups.

She attempted to pin her hair back up, but the tangled tresses slipped from her fingers.

Jonathan tugged the horse up close to the rock and motioned for her to move forward. "It's all right. Shadow is reliable."

Elizabeth's gaze focused on the extended hand before her. She looked up into eyes that pleaded for her trust.

"I won't let you fall," he promised.

Before she could lose her courage, Elizabeth placed her hand into his calloused palm and set one foot in the stirrup. He lifted her gently and smoothly. Once she was securely in the saddle, he released her. She grabbed the saddle horn.

His warm breath tickled her ear as he leaned forward and grasped the reins. A chill ran down her spine. "I'm not Sleeping Beauty, by the way."

With one arm firmly around her waist, Jonathan turned the horse back toward shore. "No, I guess not. I didn't have a chance to awaken you with a kiss."

She tilted her head to the side and saw the teasing in his gaze. She decided to play along. "And are you a prince?"

A grin tilted his lips. "Want to kiss me and see if I turn into a frog?"

Elizabeth laughed. She wasn't sure what made her feel so daring. "Since I'm not a princess and you're not a frog, I'll have to pass."

Shadow's hooves slid on the uneven riverbed, and he lurched, sending Elizabeth sliding sideways on the saddle. Jonathan slung both arms around her, holding her tight, and gave the animal free rein.

Finally, the horse regained his footing and clattered onto dry ground, tossing his head. Jonathan slid off, then reached up and pulled her down. His hands stayed on her waist for several moments. He leaned close. "Too bad I'm not a frog."

The urge to kiss him almost overwhelmed her. She stepped out of his grasp and searched for something that would distract him. Her gaze landed on the picnic basket. "I'm famished. Shall we eat?"

He chuckled. "Sure. Let me tether the horse, and then we'll feast on ham-and-cheese sandwiches."

Elizabeth appreciated his warm, quiet laughter. It wasn't mocking or scornful, just pure pleasure. She gathered her boots and moved to the blanket. Jonathan had done her no harm. She'd let her overactive imagination convince her that Red had ordered her death.

But could she trust him to tell her the truth when she asked whether Bowman was back? Elizabeth hoped that she could.

As she lowered herself to the ground, her knee didn't protest as much as it had earlier. Millie had been right. The soak had helped with the swelling. She pulled out the sandwiches and asked, "What else is in this basket?"

"You tell me, princess." Jonathan finished tying the stallion to a tree, then made his way to her. He scooped up his socks and boots on the way.

"I told you I'm not a princess." Hoping he didn't notice the heat coursing into her cheeks, Elizabeth looked inside at a medium-sized dish. She pulled it from the basket and lifted the cover. The aroma of cinnamon and sugar rose to tease her senses. "Apple pie?"

"I don't think so. Look again." He knelt on the blanket across from her.

Elizabeth lowered her gaze to the pie. Thick chunks of peaches poked out through the flaky crust.

"Peach pie!" She smiled at him. "I stand corrected."

Jonathan picked up a sandwich. "If you eat all of your sandwich, I'll let you have the biggest piece."

Elizabeth decided to take advantage of his good mood. Her leg felt better, and at the first opportunity she was going to escape. That plan depended on his answer. "If you let me work in the kitchen again, you can have the big slice." She held her breath as he chewed, then swallowed.

"All right." The playful tone left his voice and eyes. "As long as you promise not to attempt another escape."

Eager to change the subject, she said, "Tell me how you became an outlaw."

Jonathan's face turned hard. "There are some things you don't need to know."

Elizabeth felt the sting of his words but pressed on. "But there are some things I do need to know. Like has Bowman returned?"

He stared deeply into her eyes before answering. "I have word that Bowman isn't returning, but Red doesn't know that yet. I expect when he hears he'll send out a new man to collect the ransom."

"Oh." Her heart picked up a beat as she realized her identity was safe for at least another week. It also meant Jonathan would have to continue watching her during that time. If only she knew how he felt about that. Would he consider helping her escape? She didn't think so. Elizabeth finished her meal in silence. Even the peach pie couldn't lighten the mood between them. She served the largest wedge to Jonathan.

He ignored the dessert and walked to the shore. He pulled a rope out of the water. A catfish dangled on the end of the line. She opened her mouth to praise him but stopped at the anger reflected in his eyes.

He carried it back to the blanket and let it fall to the ground. It flopped on the grass. "As soon as you're done with your dessert, we'll return to camp." He pulled on his dry socks and his boots. Then he stood, picked up his fish, and walked past her without another glance.

Chapter 8

Jonathan leaned against the wall of the living room in the big house as Red paced the wood floor. The *tick* of the clock seemed to mock each step he took. "Bowman has been gone for nine days." Red snaked his hand out and knocked the annoying clock off the side table.

Percy and Hugh jumped at the sudden show of anger. They stood behind Red, awaiting instructions. As the leader paced, the clock continued ticking on the floor. Jones used a pocketknife to pick dirt out from under his fingernails. Porter and Frank silently studied a checkerboard that sat between them on a short-legged table. José stood by the door. Edward stared out the window. To the untrained eye his stance would have seemed relaxed, but Jonathan knew better.

Amos and Sam were on guard duty, watching the only entry passage into their little valley. Jonathan was glad he'd assigned Harry corral duty. He felt sure Red would have singled out the kid to go find Bowman. The rest of the men were either out hunting for fresh meat or on a fishing trip to the river. Millie was keeping an eye on Elizabeth in the kitchen.

Red spun to face Percy. "Find Bowman!" he bellowed. "Bring him back, dead or alive. No, alive. I have a few questions I want answered." He pounded his fist into his open hand. "No one in this outfit abandons his post."

"Yes, sir," Percy stuttered, staring at the dust-covered floor. "I'll bring him back."

"You better," Red warned. He turned to the man next to Percy. "Hugh, you find Hamilton. Tell him we have his daughter, and if he wants her back alive, he'll pay that ransom." He resumed his pacing.

Both men glanced uneasily at Jonathan. Jonathan inclined his head. They moved toward the door, their boots stirring up dust.

"You have one week." Red's boots thumped against the hardwood floor. "Don't make me come after you, too."

The men hurried from the house.

"The rest of you get back to work." Red marched off down the hallway toward his bedroom.

Any other time, Jonathan might have trailed after Red in hopes of seeing into the room where he was sure evidence lay that would prove Red had killed Sarah, but not today. Red wasn't in the mood, and Jonathan didn't need the outlaw's wrath to fall upon him now. Instead he followed everyone out the door. He turned toward the kitchen to check on Elizabeth.

∞

Elizabeth hauled an old washtub from the shed into the kitchen. "Millie, I need a bath." She placed her hands on her back and stretched the kinks out. "Goodness, that tub is heavy." Her knee still felt tight, but she'd managed to use her back instead of her leg to get the old washtub inside.

Millie turned from the stove, where she'd been stirring a large pot of beans. "You took one at the river three days ago." She placed the spoon onto an old lid.

"Soaking my legs in the water isn't a bath. I want a real bath with hot water. Don't you?"

Millie picked up a dishrag and dunked it into the bucket of dishwater. She wiped off the board that served as a counter, then rinsed out the cloth. "Sure I do, but one of us will have to haul water in from the well."

With Millie's confession that she'd like a bath, a grin touched Elizabeth's lips. Millie needed the bath more than she did. It would be nice to have them both smelling fresh again. "Maybe you could persuade Jonathan and Harry to help us. I just saw them outside."

"So the meeting is over then," Millie said as she wiped off the table.

Elizabeth pushed a strand of hair from her eyes. "What meeting?"

Millie laid the rag down and sat at the table. "Red called the men together. Bowman hasn't come back yet."

Fear and understanding came at Elizabeth at the same time. So he was sending another man out like Jonathan said he would. She eased onto the bench across from Millie. "Did all the men go?"

Millie paused. "No, only the core group of men that Red trusts. There are other men in this camp that he doesn't trust as much; they fish, hunt, and help with guard duty. They are also the men that he takes out on big jobs, like cattle rustling and stuff like that."

Elizabeth stood slowly. "Why didn't you tell me about this meeting? I could have escaped." She slapped her hands onto the table.

"I didn't tell you because Red has guards at the entrance to the hideout, and I knew you'd want to escape. I didn't want you to get caught again." Millie picked at a splinter on the tabletop.

Tears filled Elizabeth's eyes. What decision had been made at that meeting? She began to tremble. Grabbing two water pails, she headed out the door. She tried to focus on the task of getting water and taking a bath. Anything to fight off the growing terror that threatened to consume her. *If I hold on to the faith that I will get out of here alive, then fear can't control me.*

Elizabeth hadn't spoken with Jonathan privately in three days, not since they returned from the picnic. She wanted to try to understand who he was. But each time she'd worked up the nerve to talk to him, something or someone got in the way. Now she needed answers. What had been said in that meeting?

She stepped outside and looked about. Moments earlier, Jonathan and Harry had been standing beside the well talking, but now they seemed to be gone. Her pulse quickened. Fearful joy soared through Elizabeth. *This is my chance to escape.* She dropped the buckets, picked up her skirts, and decided to run to the corral to get Ginger. "Hello, princess," Jonathan said, stepping from the shadows.

She jumped. "Jonathan." The hope of escape died as quickly as it had flared to life.

"What are you doing?" His eyes locked on her hands, which still held her skirt up. She moved toward the buckets she'd dropped on the ground and scooped them up. "Just getting water."

He stepped in front of her, blocking the way. "How much do you need?"

"Enough to fill a washtub," Elizabeth countered and walked around him.

"It's too late to be doin' laundry," he muttered, falling into step beside her. "What are you really up to?"

"It is not. But if you must know, Millie and I are going to take baths. Is that all right with you?" She hated telling him the intimate details of her life. Why was it she could have no secrets and he seemed to have several? *But even you have a secret.* She pushed the still, small voice away.

At the well, Elizabeth lowered the bucket. She needed to find out what had been said at the meeting. Elizabeth pulled on the rope connected to the now full and heavy bucket of water.

"Let me pull that up for you." Jonathan took hold of the rope, and with one mighty pull, the bucket rose to the top of the well, water sloshing over its rim. After pouring water into the first pail, he lowered the bucket again. "Red sent another man out to collect the ransom."

So, she still had time to escape. Relief bathed the turmoil in her body. She wondered what had happened to Bowman but didn't dare ask. "What happens to me?"

"You stay in my care. I'll keep you safe." His arm muscles bulged as he pulled the bucket up a second time.

Had she heard real concern in his voice? She tilted her head and studied his profile. His jawline was firm, with a shadow of a beard. Jonathan was a handsome man. If she didn't know better, she'd think him kind and decent, someone she could see herself becoming attracted to.

He looked at her, and she realized she'd been staring. She ducked her head. It wasn't proper for her to gawk at him. "Thanks." Warmth consumed her as she picked up one of the full pails with both hands and started back.

Elizabeth heard the legs of his chaps brushing against each other as he caught up with her, carrying the second pail. "Let me take that."

Their hands touched briefly as Jonathan took the pail from her. His chocolate eyes turned black, and the scent of aspen tickled her nose. She loved the clean smell. Elizabeth jerked her gaze away and hurried to the kitchen.

When they arrived at the door, she held it open as he carried the buckets inside. He set the pails by the tub. Elizabeth looked around. Millie was nowhere to be seen.

"When you're done, the boys and I will empty the water for you," Jonathan offered.

"Thank you. But you don't have to do that." Elizabeth stared into his warm eyes. Why did she feel so nervous every time their eyes met?

A soft grin curved his lips. "It's nothing, princess."

The screen door slammed behind them. Elizabeth turned. Millie stood there with her arms full of clothes. She held them out to Elizabeth. "I hope you don't mind, but I got your yellow dress for you to slip into once you're done with your bath."

Jonathan poured the water into the tub and took the pails back outside.

"Oh, that's wonderful, thank you." Elizabeth laid the dress across the back of one of the benches. She'd been sharp with her friend but couldn't stay mad at her. Millie lived with fear the same as she did—only Millie didn't see a way out.

Millie held out her hands. "I also took the liberty of getting you these." In her palms lay the cake of vanilla soap and the jar of lotion Elizabeth had packed in her carpetbag.

She smiled. "We'll both use them tonight."

Jonathan returned with more water. He dumped it into the tub, then turned to leave again.

"Where did you get these?" Millie asked as she inhaled the fragrance of the soap.

Jonathan stopped at the door and turned to hear her answer. She couldn't admit that she'd ordered the soap for her father's store. "I bought it from the general store in Durango. The store owner's daughter ordered them for me from the catalogue." It was the truth, mostly.

Jonathan cleared his throat. "If you ladies don't need anything else, I'll be going for more water now." He headed for the door.

Jones stood in the entryway. He held two more buckets of water. Jonathan stopped in front of him and took the pails.

Elizabeth realized that the men must be watching her and Jonathan's every move. A shiver crept up her spine. How often had they been watching her and she wasn't even aware of them doing so?

"Me and the boys were wondering if there's any more coffee." The outlaw's eyes went to the washtub and the two women standing beside it. For a moment he leered at Elizabeth with a cold look of lust. She felt the color drain from her face.

Millie pulled the coffeepot off the stove. She crossed the room and handed it to Jones. "That's all that's left for tonight. Tell the men to make their own if they want more."

Jones continued to stare at Elizabeth.

Jonathan shoved Jones out the door, then faced the women. "Sorry about that." He turned to leave. "I'll be standing guard."

Elizabeth hated being a prisoner. Yet she was grateful Jonathan was her guard. Otherwise she might have been raped or killed by now.

Still, when the outlaws found out the ransom money wasn't coming, she felt sure that even Jonathan wouldn't be able to protect her.

From his post outside the kitchen, Jonathan heard Elizabeth splashing in the tub. It wasn't his intention to listen, but he didn't want to get too far from the door. He'd already had to threaten Jones and Frank.

"What are you going to do once you're free from this place?" Millie's muffled voice floated through the cracks of the closed door.

Jonathan leaned against the door to hear better.

"I'm going to Farmington."

"Why?"

Water gently sloshed in the metal tub. "They hired me to be the new schoolteacher there. I was expecting to teach this fall. Of course, they may have hired someone else since I didn't show up."

Jonathan chewed on a piece of straw. He should have known she was a teacher. Hadn't he seen intelligence in her eyes? Plus, she wore bossiness like a piece of clothing.

A dreamy quality came into her voice. "I've always wanted to be a teacher. But before my mother died, I felt like I had to help out with the family business." She paused. "Then last year, Dad announced he was remarrying. So when Mr. Allen came into the store and said he was visiting Durango and looking to hire a schoolteacher for Farmington, I told him I was qualified and that I could start in the fall. A couple of weeks later, he returned to the store and offered me the position. It was a dream come true."

Jonathan stood up straighter. *Why was she at the store both times this Allen fellow came to town?*

"You were at the store both times?" Millie asked.

"Oh. Well, yes. I spent a lot of time there."

Her voice sounded faint. Jonathan leaned back to hear better.

"Oh, that's right. You were good friends with the storekeeper's daughter. Right?"

"Yes." Elizabeth's voice came through a little louder and clearer. "I'm so looking forward to teaching."

"Oh, honey. I'm sorry."

"Whatever for?" Elizabeth's words echoed Jonathan's thoughts.

"Even if you manage to escape from here. . .or if your ransom gets paid and Red lets you leave—which is doubtful—those parents in Farmington aren't going to allow you to teach their children. Not after they find out you've been living in an outlaw camp with all these men."

"Why not? I've done nothing wrong!"

The sound of wet feet hitting the wooden floor told Jonathan that Elizabeth was out of the tub.

"Folks tend to judge based on what others tell them."

"What do you think they'll say?" Sorrow filled Elizabeth's voice.

"That you chose to stay here." Millie's voice dropped lower. "Or that you were forced into prostitution."

At lunch the next day, Millie's words still ate at Elizabeth. She'd been so concerned about getting out of this place alive, she'd given little thought to her future once she was free.

She wiped the sweat off her brow with her apron. The heat in the kitchen became stifling at mealtimes.

Jones, Frank, Sam, Harry, and Edward were the last of the men who had filed through the busy kitchen. While she handed Edward a slice of fresh bread with one hand, Millie poured the men fresh cups of coffee with the other. Elizabeth returned to the stove to dish up the last bowl of green chili stew.

"Princess." The whispered endearment made Elizabeth jump, sloshing stew over the side of the bowl.

"You scared the daylights out of me," Elizabeth scolded Jonathan as she wiped the thick broth from the side of her bowl. She licked the gravy from her fingers.

Millie joined them. "What are you two whispering about?" She picked up a fresh loaf of bread from the top of the stove.

"I was just about to ask her if she'd like to eat lunch with me today."

"Go on, then," Millie said. She turned around to take the bread to the men. "I have everything under control here."

Millie's face turned red when she saw Sam leaning against the wall with his muddy boots on the table. "Sam!" she yelled. "Get your feet off of there."

"Aw, Millie, they ain't hurting nothing." He grinned and winked.

"I'll not have them on my table. Now get them off." She shoved him.

Jones laughed and jabbed Sam with his spoon. "Better do it, Sam. She might just hit you with that loaf of bread."

Sam grabbed Millie around the waist and jerked her down.

Jones and Frank hooted.

The sound of a gun's hammer being clicked back brought the room to silence.

"Dinner's over for you three." Jonathan waved his gun at Frank, Jones, and Sam. "Let go of her, Sam."

The old outlaw frowned, released Millie, and dropped his boots back to the floor. "We were just having a little fun."

"Was that fun for you, Millie?"

She glared at Sam. "I should say not."

"I should say not," Jones mimicked. He dropped his spoon to the table. "Sounds like she's been hanging around the little rich girl for too long. I'll be glad when Hugh gets back with that money."

Sam shoved back the stump he'd been sitting on and stood. "Come on, boys. It's getting too rich in here for my blood." He spat on the floor. The door slammed behind the men as they left.

Elizabeth trembled.

"Thanks, Jonathan." Millie pushed the stump back to the end of the table.

He grinned at her and tipped his hat. "My pleasure."

Elizabeth didn't like that Millie always sided with Jonathan. But she thanked the Lord that she knew the woman did. Otherwise, when the time came to escape, Elizabeth might have told Millie, and her plans of escape would be ruined.

"Let's get out of here." Jonathan led Elizabeth out of the kitchen. She still held her bowl of stew.

Jonathan stopped beside a large cottonwood tree, where a thin red blanket covered the ground. Four stones held the corners down. A loaf of bread, two spoons, and a bowl of stew sat in the center of the blanket. He'd obviously planned this little picnic.

A crooked smile touched his lips. His neck turned red. "I was hoping you'd say yes."

"What choice did I have?" She knelt on the cover.

He sighed and sat beside her. "You could have said no." Jonathan lifted the bowl and spooned stew into his mouth. His eyes searched hers over the bowl.

Elizabeth saw the sincerity in his gaze. He would never force her to spend time with him, unless it was necessary to his job.

A light breeze blew the leaves in the tree, creating a whimsical sound as Jonathan and Elizabeth ate. It felt good to be out of the hot kitchen. The green chili stew soon had her tongue stinging. "This is nice, but we forgot drinks. I'll go get some water."

"Wait." Jonathan set his bowl aside and reached behind the trunk of the tree. He pulled out two tin cups and handed one to Elizabeth.

She took it and looked down into the pale yellow liquid. She lifted the cup to her lips and sipped. Cool sweetness coated her tongue. "It's apple cider!"

His deep chuckle warmed her insides almost as much as the stew had.

"I hope you like it."

"I do. Thank you." She drank again.

He leaned against the trunk of the tree. His gaze followed her every move as she ate and drank. Her hands shook and her palms began to sweat. "What?"

"Princess, things aren't always as they seem."

What's that supposed to mean? She picked up the cup and finished drinking.

"Take this camp, for instance. Most of these men are petty thieves. Only a few are truly criminals. The rest joined the gang, and then Red wouldn't let them out." His gaze searched hers. "Have you ever been in a situation where you thought things were one way and then found out they're different?"

Elizabeth thought about Harry. When she'd first met him, she'd thought him a stupid kid trying to prove himself to be a big, bad outlaw. Now she saw him as a young man attempting to figure out the difference between right and wrong. "I guess so."

"That's the way it is here. As strange as it sounds, I'm both your warden and your protector. So please, don't do anything foolish."

So that was it. He simply wanted to remind her of their roles. She nodded. "I'll try not to do anything stupid."

Chapter 9

That night Elizabeth stared at the ceiling above her cot. Jonathan's words had caused her to think about the difference between appearance and reality. As a little girl, she had always believed her father to be an honest man. But after working in the store for a few months, she realized that he weighted the scales for certain customers. People who didn't have math skills ended up paying double for their flour, sugar, and salt.

She blinked tears away. How could someone she loved and trusted be so deceitful? Jonathan's words echoed in her mind. *"Things aren't always as they seem."*

When she had confronted her father, he apologized. *"I didn't realize I was hurting anyone. I'll fix the scales and charge the correct amount."* She kept a close eye on him after that, and he seemed to fulfill his promise.

Then Elizabeth learned an even darker secret. Her father had a mistress.

Margaret Dooley pranced into the store one bright sunny morning and looked her square in the eye. "It's time you move on, Lizzy. Your pa and I have had to hide our love for years. Now that your ma's gone, I intend to take what's mine."

When Elizabeth looked to her father for understanding, he said, "I'm sorry, Elizabeth. I didn't mean for you to find out like this."

"How could you do this to Mama?" she wailed, realizing for the first time that her father had been unfaithful.

"It was your mother's fault. She refused to be a good wife."

His whining voice still haunted Elizabeth. She'd always thought her parents were happily married. Her mother had been a kind, sweet woman who catered to her father's every whim. How could he say she wasn't a good wife?

Elizabeth forced her thoughts to the present. She'd forgiven her father long ago. So there was no reason to continue reliving the past and the hurt. She wiped her tears with the back of her hand. Why had Jonathan told her things aren't always as they seemed? Was he trying to scare her, warning her that he was more dangerous than she thought?

She punched her pillow. She still didn't trust Jonathan. Something about him just didn't feel right.

Shortly after midnight, Jonathan stood at Red's bedroom door. The big house was still and quiet. Red and the gang had left the hideout half an hour earlier to rustle a few head of cattle from a neighboring ranch. Most of the men, including Edward, had gone with them.

The only ones left at camp were Amos and Sam, who'd been assigned to watch the entrance of the hideout. Since stealing cattle and then selling them was a full day's work, he knew this might be the opportunity he'd been waiting for. It was risky to leave Elizabeth unguarded, but he hadn't heard a sound from the shed behind the kitchen for well over an hour. She and Millie had gone to sleep long ago.

Jonathan turned the knob. *Locked.* He considered breaking it, but quickly rejected the thought. If he didn't find anything in the room to incriminate Red in the death of his sister, how would he explain the broken lock?

He walked back down the hall and out the front door, turned left at the corner of the house, and moved to the window he knew was Red's. Boards, nailed from the inside, blocked his view. Short of breaking the window and using an ax to cut the boards, he was locked out that way, too. Jonathan sighed. He'd hoped Red had taken down the boards in search of a cool breeze.

In five days, Red would know that Hugh wasn't coming back with the ransom.

He wondered if Millie would help him get the key. Could he ask her to do that? She'd have to put herself in a position in which Red would trust her. He shook his head. No, he'd deliberately not asked her before and he still felt he couldn't ask her to do such a thing now.

The poor woman had been raped by Red for several years. But during a holdup the year before, Red had been shot in the groin. Since that time he'd steered clear of Millie, and she'd done the same of him. And Jonathan had made sure the men knew she was still off limits to them. Thankfully, being the eyes and the ears of the boss had its perks when it came to protecting the older woman. No, he wouldn't ask Millie for help. He'd just have to think of another way to get inside that room. A way that wouldn't lead Red to suspect him.

The next morning, Jonathan made his way to the shed. The soft, sweet scent from the wildflowers he'd picked along the way from the main house tickled his nose. Thoughts of Elizabeth had haunted him all night.

"Who is it?" Millie asked.

"Jonathan."

She opened the door. Her gaze raced over the flowers in his hand. "For me?"

"No—I mean yes," Jonathan stammered.

"Well, which is it?" Millie leaned against the doorframe. Her lips twitched as she evidently fought off a smile.

Jonathan grinned. "They're for both you and Elizabeth. I thought they might brighten up your room." He tried to see around her and get a glimpse of Elizabeth.

"In that case, thanks." Millie reached for the flowers. "Elizabeth is getting dressed." She shut the door in his face.

He waited a few minutes and knocked again.

Elizabeth opened it this time. Her hair hung around her waist. His hands itched to feel it, to see if it was as silky as it appeared.

"Forget something?" she asked.

"Red and his boys are gone for the day."

Millie materialized behind Elizabeth. "All of them?"

"They left Amos and Sam to stand guard."

"Then we have the day off." Millie relaxed her shoulders and sighed.

"Yes, and I thought you might want to go down to the river with me." He smiled. He turned his full attention onto Elizabeth. "I could teach you how to fish."

Elizabeth looked to Millie.

"We'd love to," Millie answered for both of them.

Elizabeth laughed. "As long as I don't have to touch a worm."

"Deal. I'll go round up the horses." Jonathan hurried to the corral. He returned half an hour later, riding his stallion and leading a small brown mare.

Millie emerged from the kitchen. "I left ham, cheese, and apples for the men and packed the same for our lunch."

"Sounds good to me." He dismounted from his horse.

Jonathan pulled on the mare's reins, bringing her forward. "This one's for you, Millie." He held the horse while Millie stuck her foot in the stirrup and hauled herself up onto its back.

He turned to Elizabeth, who'd plaited her hair in demure braids. "You're riding with me, princess."

"No, I'm not." Elizabeth planted both hands on her hips. "Why didn't you bring me Ginger?"

He leaned on the saddle horn and looked at her. "Give you a horse you're familiar with so you can more easily escape? I don't think so."

Elizabeth met his gaze. "If I decide to escape today, it won't matter which horse I'm on."

Her green eyes flashed. Jonathan wanted to pull her into his arms and kiss away her anger. But he knew she wouldn't take kindly to the affectionate gesture.

"How long is this going to take?" Millie huffed. The saddle leather squeaked under her weight.

He swung up on his stallion and reached down for Elizabeth's hand.

Elizabeth stepped up to Millie's horse and placed a boot into the stirrup. "Help me up."

He smiled as Millie struggled to pull Elizabeth onto the rump of her horse, their skirts tangling under their legs.

As he led the way, Jonathan glanced over his shoulder. Strands of Elizabeth's hair caught the sunlight and shimmered around her heart-shaped face. He turned back around.

Laughter and pounding horse hooves sped past him. Elizabeth's braided hair flew out behind her. The smile on her face expressed pure pleasure and happiness.

How I'd love to see that look all the time.

Jonathan urged his horse into a canter. But he allowed the women to stay a little ahead of him.

They stopped on the shore of the river.

Jonathan closed the distance between them, and then jumped from his horse. He swept Elizabeth down from Millie's. He briefly kissed her mouth. Her lips felt soft and moist against his. As he released her, confused emerald green eyes searched his.

Jonathan smiled, then turned to help Millie. He puckered his lips and urged her toward him.

"Don't you go kissin' me," Millie protested as he lifted her from the horse. Before he set her feet on the ground, Jonathan planted a swift kiss on her weathered cheek.

~

What was she supposed to make of the kiss? Elizabeth watched Millie playfully swat Jonathan on the shoulder.

Deciding to pretend the kiss meant nothing to her, she laughed along with Millie.

Her gaze caught Jonathan's, and her heart clutched. *No matter how hard I may try to pretend it didn't happen, it did.*

"Ready to learn how to fish?" He pulled two poles from behind a tree.

She eyed the crude-looking sticks. "I guess so."

Millie took the basket and blanket to the nearest shaded area. "I'm going to enjoy the quietness of this place." She spread out the blanket.

"We'll be digging up a couple of worms." Jonathan placed the poles on the bank beside the rushing water.

Elizabeth shrugged at Millie and headed into the woods behind Jonathan. She admired his wide shoulders as he moved. He seemed relaxed, yet alert to his surroundings.

He knelt under a shady bush and dug with a wicked-looking hunting knife.

"The soil here is pretty wet. I bet we'll have two juicy worms in no time." He scooped up a handful of mud and dumped it near her feet.

Then he looked up and grinned. "This is more fun when two people dig. It doesn't take as long, either." He winked at her.

Elizabeth laughed. She knelt down and dug her hands into the moist soil. "If I find a worm, you'll have to pick it up."

When she leaned forward, a tendril of hair fell forward. Before she could push it back, Jonathan reached over and tucked it behind her ear. His finger lingered on the side of her face.

"Hey, what are you two doing here?" Harry pushed through the trees.

Jonathan pulled his hand away and wiped it on his pant leg. "You're back."

"Red sent me back to camp. Said to tell you that he and the boys will be gone another day or two." He took off his hat and wiped sweat from his brow. "He also said that Amos and Sam are getting too old to be guarding the entryway for that long a time and wanted me to relieve them. I went on out there, but Sam sent me to you. Said you'd have better use for me than they do."

Jonathan's eyes bore into Harry's. "I don't need any help."

"Sam also said that if Hugh or Percy shows up, I should come get him."

Elizabeth listened carefully, hoping one of the men would let slip some useful tidbit.

Jonathan cleared his throat. "Did you and Millie leave enough food in the kitchen for three men?"

"There's enough for ten."

Jonathan looped his arm over the younger man's shoulder and led him away. He spoke in low tones that Elizabeth couldn't make out, and she grabbed a fistful of mud and squeezed it as though she could wring information from it. Harry nodded and took off.

"Did you get your worm?" Jonathan asked, coming back to her.

Her thoughts hadn't been on catching worms, they'd been on forming a plan of escape. With someone watching her at all times, the chances had been slim to none of getting away in the past. She still wasn't sure how she was going to do it. Elizabeth crinkled her nose. "No."

A smile touched his lips. "We can't have that, now, can we?" Jonathan knelt beside her again. He dug in the muck and pulled out several wiggling worms.

She shivered. "Those are disgusting." She stood, wiping dirt and grime on her skirt.

Jonathan laughed. "They aren't that bad." He pulled two of the larger ones out of the mix, dropped the rest back into the mud, and rose to his feet. "Come on. If we're lucky, these two little fellas will catch a couple of big fish."

Elizabeth walked back with him. "Jonathan, are you expecting Hugh and

Percy to return soon?" Her voice shook, revealing her fear.

"No. I think Red just hopes that they will."

"But he sent Harry back."

Jonathan stopped walking and turned to face her. "Hugh and Percy aren't coming back for a while. You'll just have to trust me on this."

"How can you he be so sure?"

He studied her face for several moments. He opened his mouth, and then shut it again. Pulling her close, he cupped her chin in his hand and leaned his forehead against hers. "There are some things I can't share with you, princess. Please trust me."

Elizabeth felt as if he wanted to share something important with her, but she knew he wouldn't. Her voice caught in her throat as she choked out with disappointment, "All right."

He let his hand fall to his side and started walking back to the river.

As she followed, Elizabeth fretted. *If he won't answer my questions, why should I trust him? Red may know more than he's told Jonathan. Plus, Jonathan is an outlaw, just like the rest of the gang. First chance I get, I'm running.*

Elizabeth asked, "What's it like to live on a farm?"

His pace slowed. "It's hard work but it's honest. I used to fish for hours in the summer."

They reached the bank. Elizabeth waved to Millie. "We got two worms."

Millie yawned. "Good for you." She stretched out on the blanket and closed her eyes.

Jonathan threaded a worm on Elizabeth's hook. "What was your childhood like?"

She met his warm gaze and took the pole he offered. "It was quiet. I went to school, read books, and did a few chores. Mother made my days fun, even though she and Daddy were so busy with the st—the business."

If he noticed her slipup, he gave no indication of it. He moved behind her. "Hold the rod like this." He positioned her hands toward the bottom of the stick.

Her heart pounded at his nearness. His scent washed over her as he breathed against her ear. Shivers tingled up her arms.

"Now bring it back."

Elizabeth did as he said.

"Good." He stepped away and demonstrated. "Bring your arms forward." He ducked and laughed as the string flew high over their heads, then plopped into the water a few feet from the shore.

Elizabeth jumped up and down. "I did it."

"Yes, you did. Now watch me." The muscles along his arms worked easily with the pole as he cast his line into the middle of the river, steady and even. Everything about the man seemed controlled.

"See?" He smiled. "Easy as falling off a log." He lowered himself to the ground.

Elizabeth frowned. "Well, sure. If you've been doing it all your life." She sat near him.

"You'll get better with practice." Jonathan propped one knee up and rested his arm against it.

Elizabeth looked out over the clear water. "What kind of farm did you have?"

"We raised cotton, but we also had our own vegetable garden. We raised tomatoes, peppers, okra, corn, and beans."

"It must have been big."

He nodded. "That garden fed us most winters. Did you have a garden, princess?"

Elizabeth felt as if she could drown in his rich chocolate eyes. She focused on the bobbing line of her fishing pole. "We did, but I doubt it was as grand as yours." What would it be like to live on a farm where you could fish or swim at the stream every day and raise a garden big enough to gather enough vegetables to last the winter?

Her line jerked.

"Oh! Is it supposed to do that?" She scrambled to her feet, clutching the pole.

Jonathan laughed. "Only if a fish is on the other end."

Elizabeth squealed as the line dunked again. "What do I do?"

"Pull it out," Jonathan instructed as he stood.

How? Elizabeth decided the best way would be to run backward. She ran. The fish flew up on shore and flopped about.

"I caught it!" Elizabeth did a little jig on the shore. "Look, Millie! I caught one!"

Millie had already started down. "I can see that." She laughed as she helped Jonathan hold the line still.

Elizabeth's heart pounded in her chest. She'd never had so much fun in her life.

Jonathan smiled, hooked a finger in the gill, and held it up. "Look at the size of him."

She clapped her hands and panted. "I can't believe I really caught a fish."

"Want to hold him?" Jonathan held it out to her.

"No!" Elizabeth squealed and backed up.

Jonathan and Millie chuckled. As Millie headed back to the blanket,

Jonathan put the fish on a string, tied the other end of the line around a large rock on the bank, and tossed the fish into the shallow water.

"Why'd you do that?" she asked.

Jonathan washed his hands in the river. "To keep it fresh until we're ready to fillet him." He stood. "Ready to cast your line back in?"

She nodded.

Jonathan came behind her. His hands moved hers to the right position on the pole. "You're lucky we didn't lose your worm or we'd be digging in the mud again." He wrapped his arms around hers.

All thoughts of the fish vanished. She tried to focus on casting the line and not on the warmth of the arms that surrounded her or the rough, calloused hands. Leaning against him felt natural. She turned her face and found his inches away.

His breath caressed her lips. "Elizabeth?"

The sound of her name in that southern drawl melted whatever reserve she'd had. "Yes?"

"I'm going to let you go."

Chapter 10

Jonathan smiled as Elizabeth's big green eyes stared at him in wonder. "You're going to let me go?"

"That's right." He slowly backed away from her. "Go ahead and cast on your own."

She dropped the fishing rod and sank to the ground. Tears filled her beautiful eyes.

"What's wrong?"

"When you said you were going to let me go, I thought. . ." Her whisper was barely loud enough for him to hear.

Understanding dawned, and he felt like a worm. He moved closer to her. "I wish I could. I really do. But too much rides on keeping you captive."

"But the men are all gone. I could escape, and no one would blame you."

"It's not that easy, princess."

"Stop calling me that." Elizabeth spat the words out.

"I know you don't believe me. But I'm not going to let anything bad happen to you."

"I believe you will *try* not to let anything bad happen to me." Her words came out soft. "Only God knows what will really happen." Her chin quivered, and tears threatened to spill from her eyes.

Jonathan wanted to assure her, but she was right. His sister had trusted him to take care of her and she was dead. The thought of letting Elizabeth escape pulled at him. If he let her go, Red would never trust him again. That meant he might never get the proof he needed to convict Red.

Elizabeth drew a circle in the dirt beside her. "How long have you been an outlaw?"

Jonathan sighed. "Too long."

"When I was a little girl, the only thing I wanted to do was be a teacher. Now all I want is to be free. What about you? What do you want?" She turned her clear gaze on him.

"I want to buy a farm and live in peace." He pulled at his fishing line. It tugged back. Just like Elizabeth was tugging at his heart right now.

Elizabeth couldn't believe the ease with which Jonathan landed his fish.

He took the fish off the hook. "I have to go dig up another worm. That fish ate my bait." Jonathan headed for the woods.

Elizabeth sat on the shore and listened to the birds in the trees. The river appeared peaceful, even as its waters gurgled noisily over the rocks. Despite its powerful currents, it seemed tranquil, as if it knew it belonged here.

Unlike her.

Movement across the river caught her attention. A mother deer and her fawn approached the water's edge. The doe stood watch while the baby drank deeply. She looked across the river at Elizabeth. They stared at each other. The mother nodded as if to say hello. Elizabeth smiled.

"Looks like a late birth," Jonathan whispered close to her ear.

She felt his warmth at her back as he knelt behind her. "How do you know?"

"The fawn is very young." He rested his hands on her shoulders. "See its spots?"

She nodded, afraid to speak as the little deer raised its head and looked to its mother. The doe lowered her head and drank.

"Only young fawns have spots."

The mother raised her head and looked both ways. She bounded back into the woods with the baby by her side.

"They were beautiful."

Jonathan dropped his hands from her shoulders and moved back. "All of nature is beautiful." He fed a large worm onto his hook.

"Is that why you enjoy farming so much?" Elizabeth pulled her knees to her chest and hugged them close.

He cast out his line. "It's one of the reasons."

"Please tell me about it." As long as they talked about him, she felt sure he wouldn't ask about her. Or her father.

"My family started each day with prayer, chores, breakfast, more chores, and lunch. During the summer months we fished, swam in the stream, and sometimes hunted. Then we'd return for more chores and supper." A smile touched his lips as he stared across the water. "After the sun set we cleaned up, sat on the front porch, and enjoyed the cool evening breezes." A far-off expression remained in his eyes.

"Sounds like a lot of hard work."

Jonathan laughed. "It was. But there were good times, too."

She smiled.

"This has to be boring to you."

"Not at all." Elizabeth stretched out her legs. "Tell me more."

"I will. As soon as you pull in your fish."

Elizabeth felt the tug on her line about the same time he informed her it was there. She squealed and jerked on the pole. The fish went flying over their heads. She jumped up and ran to watch it flop on the ground.

Jonathan picked it up. "This one's frying size." After putting it on the string, he turned to her. "Ready to go get another worm?"

She wrinkled her nose. "I guess so."

His laugh sounded youthful and carefree.

"Isn't there some way we can get more than two worms at a time?"

"There is, but I forgot to bring a container. At least this way, we're not wasting them." Jonathan chuckled. He shoved back a tree limb and held it for her to pass through.

"Thanks."

They stopped by the tree where they'd been digging up earthworms. Jonathan knelt in the dirt. "In the winter we had barn dances and church socials. When the weather was really bad, I liked to catch up on my reading."

"I thought you said you didn't have time to read when you were young."

"Guess I exaggerated a little." He dug his hands deeper into the mud. "Got one." He showed her the wiggly worm he'd unearthed.

"That ought to do the trick."

"Enough about farm life," he said as she followed him back to the river. "What was it like growing up as a banker's daughter?"

Elizabeth caught her lower lip between her teeth. She had no idea what life as a banker's daughter was like. "Everyone in town has pretty much the same routine. We get up, have breakfast, do chores, eat lunch, then do more chores."

"Hey, you two, ready for lunch?" Millie called as they stepped into the clearing.

"I am," Elizabeth said eagerly, thankful for the interruption.

Chapter 11

As they washed the supper dishes, Elizabeth whispered to Millie, "What do you think they're up to?"

The older woman glanced to the table, where José, Frank, Sam, and Amos discussed something in low tones.

"I don't know."

Tension hung in the air.

"I'm going to see what they're talking about." Elizabeth pulled the dishrag from the soapy water and walked to the table. She wiped the end opposite of where the men sat, trying not to look obvious.

"There may be a payroll on that train," Frank said. He looked over his shoulder at Elizabeth and winked.

She shuddered with uneasiness. A dark smudge under his right eye gave him a more menacing look than usual.

José punched Frank's arm to get his attention. "Of course there's a payroll. Why else would Red want to hit it?"

"I don't like the idea of going all the way to Durango," Amos grumbled. "These old bones can't take that many days in the saddle."

Durango? Elizabeth scrubbed at a spot on the wood. Would they pass Hugh on the way there and discover the truth about her?

"Jonathan's talkin' to the boss about it right now," José said. "Maybe he'll get you assigned to the camp while the rest of us have our fun. He has a soft spot for old men."

The group laughed and slapped the old-timer on the back.

Frank nodded in Elizabeth's direction. "Careful. His sweetie might hear us."

Elizabeth pretended not to hear them.

Edward entered the kitchen and walked over to Millie. "Sorry I'm late. Boss had me watchin' the horses tonight."

"I saved you a plate." Millie pulled his supper from the back of the stove.

Edward took it and joined the men at the table. "What are you three jawin' about?"

Sam nodded in Elizabeth's direction. "Nothin' important."

"You scared of a slip of a girl?" Edward winked at Elizabeth, then cut a slice of the beef on his plate.

Elizabeth headed back to the dishpan.

"I wouldn't be sportin' with Jonathan's woman if I were you, Ed," Sam warned.

She cringed and felt her face warm.

"That so?" Edward bellowed.

"Jonathan took his frustrations out on Frank the other night," Sam grumbled. "When the ladies were taking a bath." He whispered the last part, as if saying it aloud would bring Jonathan's wrath upon his head.

Elizabeth handed Millie the dishrag and put away the dry plates. Her cheeks burned with embarrassment. Her gaze moved to Frank. She'd noticed a dark bruise earlier; now she wondered if Jonathan had put it there.

Millie poured Edward a cup of coffee and set it in front of him.

"I don't understand why you cower to him." Edward gulped the hot coffee. "He doesn't seem that tough to me. Seems kinda like a sissy boy. Stays in camp, won't do the hard work."

"You weren't here the day Jonathan rode into camp." Millie refilled Sam's mug.

Edward set his cup down. "So?"

"So I was." Millie walked back to the stove. "He came in about a year ago, guns blazing. Took one look at three of the men and killed them where they stood. I ain't never seen a man so possessed."

Elizabeth lay down her dish towel and listened.

"When Red got back from selling off that herd of cattle they'd stolen, I told him about Jonathan. He was madder than all get-out. When Jonathan walked into the house like he owned it, he stormed right into Red's bedroom. They were in there yelling for a good ten minutes. But when they came out, Red told everyone Jonathan was the protector of this camp. Only person above him is Red."

Sam nodded. "I came in with Red that day. Couldn't believe Jonathan had taken out the Sullivan brothers and Campbell."

Edward mopped up his gravy with a slice of bread. "The Sullivan brothers? I've heard of them."

"Everyone in these parts has heard of Ike and Eb. They were the fastest guns around until Jonathan came along."

Elizabeth walked to the table. She sat on a stump a few feet away from the men. "How long have you been in this camp?" she asked Edward.

He turned gray eyes upon her. "Not long." He finished his coffee, carried his plate to the dishwater, and dropped it in. "Thanks for the grub and the warning, Millie. I'll be sure and walk softly around Jonathan from now on." He winked.

The benches scraped back as the other four stood. "Thanks, Millie," the men mumbled. Their boots pounded on the hardwood floor, and the screen door slammed as they left.

"I thought Edward and Jonathan were close friends," Elizabeth mumbled.

Millie grinned. "They are. Every so often, Edward and I do that little bit to keep the rest of the men from forcing their hands and challenging Jonathan."

"That works?" Elizabeth rinsed her dishrag out in the tub of water.

"Seems to." Millie smiled. "Did you happen to catch what they were whispering about?" She picked up the coffee mugs and carried them to the dishpan.

"Yes." And it was more important than ever that she leave this place before Red crossed paths with Hugh. "Red is planning to rob a train in Durango."

Jonathan stood beside the front door in the main house.

Harry came bolting out of Red's room at the back of the house. "Why'd you do that?" the youth demanded.

Jonathan had known the boy would be angry at being left behind, but it was for his own good. A train robbery was no place for a kid.

"I'm not used to having my decisions questioned." He kept his voice low and his movements subtle, not wanting the men playing cards at the table to hear him.

Harry lowered his gaze. "It's not fair," he muttered.

Jonathan jerked his head in the direction of the door. "Let's take a walk."

Once outside and away from listening ears, Jonathan sat on one of the large rocks that littered the base of a low-hanging cliff. The sun had just begun its descent. "Red needs experienced men for this job. And I need a few good men to stay here and look after things."

The boy sighed. "I appreciate what you're trying to do. But I'm almost a man. I don't need your protection."

"No?"

Harry sat on a rock facing Jonathan and rested on his forearms. "Red says there's a lot of money on that train. If I could get even a piece of it, I could leave this place and start a new life." His eyes pleaded with Jonathan for understanding.

"Do you really think Red's going to let you keep any of that money?" Jonathan leaned forward.

"I wasn't going to ask him if I could take it." Harry rubbed his temples.

"If Red thinks you want out of the gang, he'll kill you."

Harry's head shot up. His eyes widened.

"So far you haven't done anything that will land you in jail for longer than a few months. But if you go off with Red for that holdup and someone gets killed, you'll be facing the end of a looped rope."

Harry hung his head. "I may already be."

Jonathan sat up straight. "How do you figure?"

"That driver with Miss Hamilton. . .we shot him." Harry ran dirty fingers through his blond hair. "We left him lying in the road. There was a lot of blood."

Jonathan laid a hand on Harry's shoulder. "He isn't dead."

Harry's head jerked up. "How do you know?"

Jonathan wasn't about to tell Harry that he'd contacted his friend, Charles Nelson, in Farmington and found out the man was alive and doing well. He still wasn't sure how much he could trust the young man. "Do you really want to get out of here?"

Harry nodded.

"Then stop asking questions and do as I say." He squeezed the young man's thin shoulder. "I can get you out of here, but I have to know I can trust you."

Harry's Adam's apple bobbed. "You can."

"If you betray me, you betray yourself, because you will die." The threat hung in the air between them. Fear wasn't a device Jonathan enjoyed using, but to save the kid's life, he had to. "Understand?"

"He may not, but I sure do." Porter stepped from around a boulder, his gun trained on Jonathan. "Red is going to love this."

Harry stood. "You got it all wrong, Porter."

The outlaw scratched his chin. "Sounds to me like Johnny here plans on double-crossin' Red by helping his youngest recruit leave the business. That about sums it up, wouldn't you say?"

Jonathan gazed about the camp. No one else seemed to be about. "It's my word against yours, Porter. Who do you think Red will believe?" Jonathan prayed he looked as relaxed as he tried to portray himself.

"If I kill you, he'll have no choice but to believe me." Porter raised the gun and aimed at Jonathan's chest.

Harry stepped between them. At the same time, Edward moved out from behind a tree, gun in hand. He used the butt to hit Porter from behind. The outlaw crumpled to the ground.

Edward holstered his gun and looked to Jonathan. "What are we gonna do?"

"Let's get him away from camp. The last thing we need is for one of the men to find him like this." Jonathan picked up Porter's feet while Edward grabbed his shoulders. The two men hauled him deeper into the woods and dropped Porter on the ground.

"You could have been killed back there," Jonathan growled at Harry.

Harry looked at his feet. "I just thought—"

"You're lucky I came along when I did," Edward interrupted.

Harry looked at Porter's still body. "You gonna kill 'im?"

"Not today." Edward looked at Jonathan. "I'll take Porter to the sheriff in Farmington."

"See if you can get him taken to Santa Fe. We can't have one of the men finding him and telling Red what happened," Jonathan said.

Edward nodded.

Harry looked at Edward. "You ain't afraid the sheriff will arrest you?"

"Stop asking questions." Jonathan snarled. "Go get Porter's horse from the corral. Take the back way. If anyone asks what you're doing, tell 'em Porter sent you."

Harry nodded and took off through the woods.

"Think we can trust him?" Edward asked.

Jonathan sighed. "Looks like we'll have to."

Edward knelt and pulled up a blade of grass near Porter's unconscious body. "Red's gonna ask about Porter."

Jonathan recognized his partner's nervous habit even before Edward stuck the end of the blade of grass in his mouth. "Red will believe whatever I tell him."

"And what will that be?"

The criminal groaned.

Jonathan grabbed Porter's bandanna from the inside of his vest and stuffed it into his mouth. Edward pulled out his own bandanna and tied it around the outlaw's head to secure the cloth inside Porter's mouth.

"I'll tell Red that Porter went out to check on the men, Hugh, Hamilton, and Percy." Jonathan stood.

"Won't work. Red sent Frank out yesterday to check on them."

Jonathan stared at his friend. "He didn't tell me that."

Edward stood. "It was while Red, Frank, and I were scouting out information on the train."

Jonathan rethought his plan. "Then I'll tell Red that Porter slipped out, muttering something about beating the gang to the train so he could have all the money to himself."

Edward chuckled. "That'll set him off."

Harry arrived, leading Porter's big roan. The horse snorted and tossed his head, sidestepping the limp form on the ground. Harry held out a length of rope to Jonathan.

"Tie his feet and hands, Harry. Edward, while you're talking to the sheriff, why don't you mention the train robbery, too?

Harry finished tying Porter up and stood. "What?"

Edward pulled Porter's unconscious body to an upright position. "Help me get him on the horse." Together he and Harry shoved the man onto the roan's back. Then Edward swung into the saddle.

"Be careful," Jonathan warned.

"I'll be back in the morning." Edward turned the horse and sped away into the night.

"What's going on?" Harry asked, his eyes wide.

"Take a walk with me, son," Jonathan said. "I want to share a few things with you." Jonathan was confident that sending Porter to the local sheriff would end his quest to prove whether Red had killed Sarah. The bank robbery, along with other crimes he knew of that the outlaws had committed, would put most of the men away for life.

It would take some time to explain that he and Edward were undercover lawmen looking for evidence that Red was a killer. So he directed Harry toward the river, where they could talk in private. Jonathan only hoped the young man would help him keep the secret just a little longer. He also wished that he could tell Elizabeth but didn't feel now was the time. She was still in danger, and he couldn't risk her getting hurt because of him.

Elizabeth looked at Millie. The older woman was almost asleep on her cot. "Millie?"

"Hmm?"

"I need to go to the outhouse."

Millie cracked one eye. "Make it quick." She closed her eyes again.

Elizabeth slipped her carpetbag over her shoulder, praying the older woman wouldn't open her eyes and ask why she was taking her bag to the outhouse. She hated deceiving Millie but had no choice. Red had been meaner than two bears at dinner. She knew that waiting for Hugh and Percy to return was getting on the outlaw's nerves. For her own safety, she had to escape.

Slipping out the door, she sighed with relief. The moon was nestled behind a cluster of clouds. *Thank You, Lord.* Elizabeth hurried around the house toward the river. Once she got there, she'd cross to the other side, and then travel in the direction she hoped Farmington rested. If she didn't come into Farmington, then hopefully she'd arrive back in Durango.

She wished she could take Ginger. But someone would be guarding the horses, and the corral was the first place Jonathan and Millie would look when they discovered she was missing. She didn't want to get caught this time.

Her heart pounded as she hit the woods running. Darkness and the heavy bag slowed her movements. She focused on not stumbling in the darkness.

She looped the handles of her bag over her head and one arm. Its contents—apples, jerky, and cheese—would keep her fed for a few days. Elizabeth prayed she'd find a town or a farmer quickly.

The sound of running water reached her ears. She hurried toward the bank. The half moon shifted from behind the clouds, giving her light. Still, she couldn't tell how deep the water ran in the center of the river—or how much more swiftly it ran there. The knowledge that the outlaws would follow her footsteps until they caught her gave her the courage to step into the current.

The rocks felt slippery under the soles of her boots. Cool water lapped at the hem of her dress and weighed it down as she eased farther into the river. *Lord, please don't let there be a deep spot. And don't let me slip.*

When the water rose to her chest, she pulled the bag up over her head and continued to inch across the depths. With the water wrestling with her legs, snatching at her skirt, each step was a leap of faith. The thought of snakes crossed her mind, and she felt her heart lurch in her chest. She shoved the fearful thought back.

Slowly the water level receded as she made her way toward the opposite shore.

She felt the ground begin to climb upward. Elizabeth raised her gaze and gasped with a start.

Jonathan stood between her and the shore, with one hand outstretched toward her. Harry stood behind him.

"No!" Elizabeth jerked back into the river. She lost her footing. The water went over her head. Sputtering, she came up for air.

Harry helped her stand. "Aw, Miss Hamilton, why'd you go and do that for? Now you're all wet."

She clamped her lips closed and jerked her arm away from him. Jonathan grabbed her hand.

Anger in his eyes kept her silent as Jonathan pulled her out of the water and walked her downriver to a natural rocky bridge. They crossed in silence, back to the shore closest to the outlaw hideout. Jonathan dragged her back to the shed, Harry following close behind.

The next morning, Elizabeth and Millie fed the men and washed the dishes in silence. They hadn't said a word about the night before, in spite of the fact that Jonathan had practically thrown her back into the shed and then barred the door, locking them both inside until breakfast.

"Did you hear about Porter?" Millie asked.

"What about him?" Elizabeth asked as she dried the last dish, grateful that her friend was speaking to her again.

Millie sipped her coffee at the table. "Seems he decided to get a head start on meetin' that train out of Durango."

"Really?" Elizabeth took her coffee to the table, too.

Millie set her cup down. "Red is madder than a bull with a burr in its tail."

"What do you think he'll do?"

"Porter is a dead man if Red catches up to him."

Elizabeth rotated the cup in her hands. Would Red have killed her last night if he had been the one to capture her?

She raised her eyes and looked at Millie. "Why aren't you angry with me?"

Millie laughed. "I don't blame you for trying to escape. I've made my attempts, too."

"Do you know when the men are leaving to meet the train?"

"They're getting ready to leave now." Millie carried her cup to the dishpan and dipped it inside.

Elizabeth stood, too. She moved to a box filled with potatoes, picked it up, and carried it back to the table. "So, how many are going to be here for lunch?"

Millie went to the bin of pinto beans. "Not sure. Why don't you go find Jonathan and ask him?"

"Aren't you afraid I'll try to sneak off again?"

"The camp is full of men right now. You wouldn't get far." Millie took the bin to the table and began sorting through the beans, picking out small black rocks and discarding them. Elizabeth took off her apron and hung it by the back door.

"Just remember, Red is on edge. If you do anything to get on his nerves, he'll slit your throat and worry about the ransom later."

The visual picture set Elizabeth's pulse to racing. "Any idea where Jonathan might be?"

Millie dumped a pile of beans into the pot. "Check the corral."

She dreaded facing Jonathan. He hadn't come in for breakfast this morning. At daybreak he'd sent Harry to open the door to the shed with the message to Millie that she was in charge of watching over *the prisoner*.

Elizabeth stepped out the back door and made her way across the yard, where the men were preparing their packs. From the looks of things, they'd be gone for a few days.

Edward acknowledged her presence with the raising of his chin. She didn't indicate that she'd noticed him. She held her head high, ignoring the whistles and crude calls from the men.

She continued along the path around the house toward the horse corral. The sound of male voices coming from down the trail caught her attention. Elizabeth ducked behind a large yucca plant. The last thing she needed was to run into Red. Fear snaked up into her hair at the thought of what he would do to her.

"Have you given any more thought to what I told you about the Lord?" Elizabeth recognized Jonathan's southern drawl as the men passed her hiding place.

She heard Harry's muffled answer, but couldn't make out his words.

A hand clamped around her arm. "Is there a reason you're hiding in the bushes, Miss Hamilton?"

Chapter 12

Jonathan and Harry spun around at the sound of Elizabeth's squeal. Jonathan's gaze fell on Elizabeth as Edward pulled her up by the arm from behind a yucca plant.

She jerked and lashed out at him. "Get your hands off me." She aimed a kick at his shin. Her hair flew out of its pins and cascaded to her waist.

Edward's hat was knocked to the ground in his attempt to subdue her.

Jonathan decided he'd better intervene before Elizabeth hurt herself or his partner. "Let her go."

Edward released her so suddenly, Elizabeth fell to the ground. She scrambled up. With her hands on her hips, she glared at Edward. "Why were you following me?"

Jonathan admired her spunk. He turned his attention to Edward. "Why *were* you following her?"

The undercover lawman picked up his hat. "Shouldn't you be asking her why she was hiding in the bushes?" Edward cocked an eyebrow. He slapped the dirt from the rim of his Stetson.

"He has a point." Jonathan pushed his own black hat back and waited for her answer.

Her green eyes sparked with anger. "I didn't want to get ambushed by some overzealous cowboy."

Harry snickered.

But the fear in her eyes and the way her voice shook made Jonathan realize how scared Elizabeth felt.

"Why did you wait in hiding until after Jonathan and Harry passed you?" Edward demanded. "You could have called out to them."

A deep flush moved up her neck and into her cheeks. "I was going to." She frowned at Edward. "Until you grabbed me."

"I don't believe you. I think you were trying to escape." Edward crossed his arms and stared down at her.

She looked like a naughty child under his accusing gaze. "Millie sent me to ask Jonathan how many men are going to remain in camp so we'll know how much food to cook."

"Enough, you two," Jonathan said. "Let's go."

Edward motioned for her to precede him. She held her head high as she joined Jonathan and Harry on the path to the house.

"Take her to the kitchen," Jonathan ordered Harry, "but go through the woods. I don't want the others to see her."

Elizabeth squared her shoulders. "How many should we expect for lunch?" Her lips trembled, and tears threatened to slip down her cheeks.

The desire to pull her to him and offer the comfort of his arms pulled strongly at Jonathan. "Five."

Elizabeth walked off with Harry. Her hair danced about her waist with each step.

"She's getting under your skin, isn't she?" Edward asked, coming to stand beside him.

Jonathan focused on the path. "Elizabeth is just part of the job."

They walked in silence. As they approached the house, Edward said, "When we're done with our job here, I'm going to see if she'll let me court her."

The thought of Edward courting Elizabeth caused Jonathan to feel sick. "Do you think she'll want to step out with you once she learns we've been lying to her?"

Edward studied Jonathan's face. "Maybe not. But unless I ask her, I'll never know."

For a brief moment, anger consumed Jonathan. Then he saw the teasing gleam in his friend's eyes and knew Edward was only joking and would never ask Elizabeth out. He should have realized Edward knew his true feelings for their prisoner.

They entered the yard. Edward joined the rest of the men as they saddled up to meet the train.

"Johnny boy, I'm leaving the place in your hands. You hang on to that little gal. Her daddy should be paying up any day now." Red's saddle creaked as he pulled himself astride his horse. He nodded toward the house, and then raced out of camp. The other outlaws followed. Jonathan turned to see who Red had nodded to.

Millie stood in the doorway. Her dress hung sloppily on her shoulders. Without being told, he knew Red had spent the last few minutes with her.

He walked toward her. Tears filled her eyes, but she smiled at him as she led him into the empty living room.

"Are you all right?"

"I'm as well as can be expected. The train robbery is more important to him right now, but he promised we'd really celebrate when he gets back." She moved to the window and looked out.

Millie had that same frightened look in her eyes that had been there a year ago when he'd first arrived. His heart ached for the woman.

"I did it."

He took a step toward her. In a gentle voice he asked, "Did what?"

She faced him and extended her right hand.

Jonathan watched as she uncurled her fingers. A key lay in her palm. His eyes moved from her hand to her face.

"It's the key to his room. I got it when he kissed me good-bye. Take it, Jonathan. Prove that he killed your sister." Millie put the key in his hand. "Don't let him hurt anyone else."

Jonathan wanted to hug her, but knew she wouldn't allow him to touch her right now. "No matter what's in that room, Red will never hurt you again. I promise."

She nodded. "I'm going to the river. I need a bath." Millie walked out the door. She lumbered across the porch and headed to the shed.

Jonathan prayed that Millie would heal from the abuse of the outlaws. If all went well, Red and the rest of the gang would be caught attempting to rob the train. He sighed and looked at the key in his hand. Jonathan prayed it was worth the hurt Millie had suffered.

The sound of a horse galloping into the yard pulled his attention. Frank jumped from the animal's back and ran past him into the house.

Jonathan followed him inside. "What's your hurry?" he asked as Frank slid to a stop in the center of the room.

"Where's Red?" Frank demanded, turning to face him.

"He and the boys rode out about half an hour ago." Jonathan unobtrusively dropped the key into his pocket. Thankfully there was more than one path to Durango, or Red and Frank might have crossed each other's paths.

"I have news he's gonna want to hear." Frank started back toward the door.

Jonathan stepped in front of him. "What news?"

Frank eyed Jonathan for a few moments. "I guess there's no rush. Maybe I'll pay our guest a visit before I go. I'm sure Red won't mind now."

Jonathan felt anger boil within. "Red put me in charge of this camp and her, and you're not going to touch her. Now, what's the news?" He bit the question out with venom.

"I'll tell ya. But then I'm gonna find Red. We'll see who his favorite is after I tell him what I found out." Frank snorted.

"Get on with it."

The outlaw flopped into a chair. "The banker says he doesn't have a daughter named Elizabeth."

Jonathan paced in front of Frank. She wasn't Elizabeth Hamilton? She'd lied about who she was. But why? "Then who do we have here?"

"The storekeeper's daughter. But the storekeeper ain't gonna pay her ransom. He said she got herself into this mess, she could get herself out."

How could a man treat his daughter that way? Didn't he know what danger Elizabeth was in? Did he simply not care? "Did you explain what would happen to her if he doesn't pay?"

"Yep. He said he don't have that kind of money." Frank yawned. "You know, I might get a little shut-eye before going after Red and the boys. I've been in the saddle for days."

"Did you find out what happened to Hugh and Percy?"

"Don't know about Percy, but some men in the saloon told me Hugh got himself killed just outside of Durango. A kid and his pa recognized him as part of the gang, and the kid shot him in the back."

Jonathan stared at Frank. "What kid?"

"I don't know. He and his pa told the sheriff that Hugh had stolen some cattle off their place a while back. That's what I heard, anyway." Frank stretched his legs out in front of him, tilted his hat over his eyes, and folded his hands over his chest.

Fear for Elizabeth and anger at Frank consumed him. When Red got this information, he would kill Elizabeth—or turn her over to the men.

Soft snores filled the room. Jonathan crept closer to Frank, careful not to wake the sleeping man. Then he whacked him over the head with the butt of his gun.

Frank slumped to the floor. Jonathan hurried to another room of the house and retrieved rope to tie him up. Within minutes he had Frank bound and gagged.

He dug in his pocket and pulled out the key Millie had given him. He hurried down the hall, praying silently. *Thank You, Lord. Your timing is always the best. I pray I can find the evidence I need to put these men away.*

At the door, Jonathan inserted the key and turned the handle. It opened. He slipped inside.

A massive unmade bed dominated the room. The only other piece of furniture was a large trunk. Jonathan pulled on the lid. It lifted so fast he almost dropped it. He knelt in front of it and searched its contents.

A couple of shirts and a pair of pants rested on top. Jonathan picked them up and set them on the hardwood floor beside him. He looked back inside and found a big book. The word *Bible* on the cover surprised him. Jonathan opened it and read the inscription. *"To our beloved son, Randolph Marshall. Christmas, 1884."*

Even criminals have parents who try to direct them on the right track. Jonathan wondered if Red ever read it. He closed the Book, laid it on top of the pants, and reached inside the trunk again. He pulled out several more items before his fingers brushed a small velvet box. He pulled it out. An angel's face graced the top of the box. His breath caught in his chest. Could this be something Sarah had owned?

Taking a deep breath, Jonathan raised the lid. A pink cameo nestled against a soft velvet cushion. The air rushed from Jonathan's lungs.

Sarah's cameo. The one he'd given to her for her sixteenth birthday.

The gold, rope-patterned edge encircled the meticulously carved, intricate profile of a beautiful lady. Jonathan flipped the pin over. The back of the pink shell glistened. He flipped open the clasp and saw the initials S. B. R. *Sarah Beth Russell.*

Jonathan rubbed his thumb over the face of the jewelry, then placed it back in its velvet box and closed the lid. He wondered where Red had gotten the jewelry box and why he'd taken such good care of the cameo. *Probably planned to sell it someday.*

A desire to destroy everything in the room welled within him, but he couldn't indulge himself. He replaced everything in the order he'd taken the items out. Rage built in his chest. He'd been right. Red had killed his sister. And he finally had the proof he needed. But the jewelry wouldn't be enough to convict Red of murder. He needed a confession.

The sound of a woman weeping pulled him from the violence of his thoughts.

After dragging the still-unconscious Frank to a cave not far from camp, Jonathan headed for the kitchen, hoping to spend some time alone with Elizabeth, see if she'd open up to him and tell him who she was and why her father refused to pay her ransom. He paused at the doorway. How could he tell the woman he was beginning to love that her family wasn't willing to pay for her return?

Jonathan opened the kitchen door and found Harry and Elizabeth sitting at the table. She held a cup in her hands. Her eyes were red and swollen.

"This is about the best peach pie I've ever tasted." Harry dug into the slice of pastry with a crooked fork. He stuffed the midmorning snack into his mouth.

"Thank you." Elizabeth sipped at the steaming brew.

Harry licked the sweet syrup from his lips. "Jonathan, you should try this."

"I will. But first I'd like a word with Elizabeth."

She stared into the cup.

"Outside."

The sound of the bench scraping against the wood floor as she stood grated on his nerves. She clutched her hands in front of her apron.

Harry stood. "Take it easy on her, Jonathan. She's had a rough morning."

The desire to tell Harry she wasn't the only one having a hard day pressed upon Jonathan, but he ignored the impulse. "I'm only going to talk to her."

Harry eased back onto the bench.

Head held high, Elizabeth marched past him. He was glad to see she hadn't lost her stubbornness. The screen door slammed behind her. Jonathan reopened it and followed.

Elizabeth stopped beside the well.

He moved to the opposite side and searched her tearstained face. "I'm sorry Edward scared you this morning."

Silence hung between them. A flock of geese honked overhead. A light breeze lifted a small ringlet of hair from her temple. Time seemed to stand still.

"Why don't you let me go?" Elizabeth stared at him.

"Nothing would give me more pleasure. But I can't. Please, trust me." He wanted to tell her they were close to being done with this whole scenario. If all worked out right, Elizabeth would be free to go home.

Home to a father who didn't want her? And didn't seem to care about her?

Chapter 13

Elizabeth searched Jonathan's brown eyes. "What did you want to talk to me about?"

"Would you like to go apple picking with me?"

That was the last request she'd expected. "Apple picking?"

"There's a small grove of trees about a mile from here. Interested?"

Was he offering her an opportunity to get away? Probably not, but should the opportunity present itself, Elizabeth planned on escaping. "I'd love to."

"Go tell Millie. I'll get the horses."

She hurried off. He'd said *horses*. Could she hope that she'd have her own mount? She didn't dare hope he'd choose Ginger. Her thoughts turned to gathering her things, but she stopped herself short—Jonathan would think it strange if she took her carpetbag or any other belongings. If she did find some time when she was alone, she'd escape, and later, after the sheriff arrested the outlaws, come back for her things.

When Elizabeth entered the shed, she found Millie sitting on her cot, reading Elizabeth's Bible. Her hair hung wet about her shoulders. "I hope you don't mind that I borrowed your Bible."

Elizabeth dropped onto the other bed. She wondered why Millie's hair was wet and her clothing damp, but didn't ask. "Of course not."

The older woman ran her hand over the open page. "When I was a kid and learning how to read, my parents and teachers taught the Ten Commandments. We didn't actually get to read the Book. I had no idea there were so many stories in here."

"Which one are you reading now?" she asked, eager to encourage her friend to share her study of the Word.

"Noah and the flood."

Elizabeth sat up straighter. "I love that story." *Lord, please give me the right words to say.* "Can you imagine how Noah's wife must have felt? After God opened the door and they stepped out of the boat, she had to start all over again."

Millie caressed the page. "She did, didn't she?"

"Life must have been hard."

"I'm sure she was scared," Millie whispered.

"Maybe. But I think she probably also felt relieved. She didn't have to help clean up after filthy animals anymore. And she was free to go wherever she wanted instead of being confined to the ark."

Millie smiled. "I think I'd like to read that story again."

"I'd love for you to study the Bible as much as you want." Elizabeth sat beside Millie. "There are lots of stories in there you'll enjoy."

She hugged Elizabeth. "Thanks."

"You're welcome." Elizabeth returned the hug.

A knock sounded at the door, and she pulled away.

"That's Jonathan. We're going to pick apples. What will you do while we're gone?" For a moment Elizabeth thought about asking her friend to come along but realized if she did that, there would definitely be no chance of escape.

"I think I'll take the Bible to the kitchen, make a pot of coffee, and read there. You have fun."

"Thanks." She started to leave. Sorrow filled her at the knowledge this might be the last time she saw Millie.

"Elizabeth?"

She turned to face her. "Yes?"

"Guard your heart."

Elizabeth's thoughts pounded to the *clip-clop* of the horses' hooves. Why would Millie warn her to guard her heart? This trip didn't mean anything except a chance to escape.

"You're awful quiet." Jonathan rode his horse alongside hers. "Still angry from this morning?"

"No. I was just thinking about something Millie said before we left." Elizabeth's horse topped the ridge. Below lay the winding river. Trees with leaves in gold and crimson lined the bank.

Jonathan had indeed brought two horses. As he'd helped her onto Ginger, he warned her not to try to escape. His eyes had looked deep into hers, and for a brief moment she felt she'd promise him anything he wanted. But if the opportunity presented itself for escape, she'd take it.

"Will we be picking tart apples or sweet ones?"

"Both. They're Jonathan apples." He grinned over his shoulder at her.

Tart but sweet. That pretty much sums up Jonathan. Elizabeth pushed the thought away as the horses picked their way down the steep incline. She kept her gaze on Jonathan's back as he swayed in the saddle in front of her. A light breeze carried his clean scent back to her. She realized that after she escaped, she would miss his smell. The thought sent her heart to her throat.

Jonathan had never taken another soul to this place. Bringing Elizabeth here had been a spur-of-the moment idea. He smiled. Lately, he'd found himself doing a lot of things at a moment's notice, and most of them because of her. Today he didn't have to worry about Red and the gang. Most of them were miles away. And if his plan worked, Elizabeth would be free shortly after the men returned. When Edward came back with the Farmington sheriff, Red would be put away for murder, and the rest of the gang members would do their time for their crimes, as well. For the first time in years, Jonathan felt he could relax. At least for the day.

A cozy little cabin, nestled against the mesa, seemed to welcome them. Honeysuckle and buttercups thrived along the front of the house. His gaze moved to the side of the building, where apple and peach trees grew. An assortment of red, green, and yellow apples colored the branches of the trees.

The farm reminded him of home. Someday he'd have a place like this, but for now he'd make use of these trees. Whoever had built the cabin and planted the orchard had abandoned it long ago. Jonathan wondered if Elizabeth saw it as unkempt and overgrown. Or did she see the beauty of the place as he did?

He turned his horse and looked at her. "Well, what do you think?"

Elizabeth looked at the cabin with soft, dreamy eyes. "It's lovely. Who owns it?"

He swung from the saddle. "I don't know. Since I've been coming here, no one has been in the house."

She allowed him to pull her down from Ginger's back. "Have you ever been inside?"

The smell of vanilla teased his nose. "I wouldn't want to break into someone's home."

"Really?"

Surprise laced her voice. She still thought of him as an outlaw. And why wouldn't she?

"Really."

Her eyes were focused on the cabin. "Those are beautiful." Elizabeth pointed at the yellow buttercups close to the porch.

He stopped and picked one, then inserted the flower into her hair. "So are you."

A pink blush filled her cheeks. Elizabeth moved on to the porch. "Is this what your farmhouse looked like?"

He followed and leaned against the porch rails. "Ours was smaller, but we had a loft. My brothers and I slept upstairs, and our parents slept downstairs. Pa built a small room for my sister off his and Ma's bedroom."

"How many brothers do you have?" Elizabeth asked as she wiped at the dirt on the window.

He frowned. "Two." *Please don't ask about my sister.* "What about you? Any brothers or sisters?" He stepped off the porch and watched two chipmunks playing around the base of an old oak tree.

Sorrow filled her voice. "My mother was sickly. She didn't have any more children after me."

"I'm sure she must be worried about you."

"She died last year."

"I'm so sorry."

Elizabeth studied Jonathan's expression. Genuine concern rested in the gentle creases of his tanned face. "Thank you."

"At least your pa will be happy to have you back." He gestured to the horses, where they'd left two pillowcases they planned to fill with apples.

"If he can afford to pay the ransom, I'm sure he will." Elizabeth followed him to the horses. She wished her father loved her enough to pay for her return. She wished with all her heart that Jonathan wasn't an outlaw who was holding her against her will. And she wished she could allow herself to enjoy the growing feelings of affection she had for him.

Jonathan pulled the pillowcases from his saddlebag. "Bankers are wealthy men. He'll pay." He tossed one of the pillowcases to her and moved toward the orchard.

They began picking the ripe fruit, and as they moved deeper into the orchard, the heavier the scent of apples grew. She wanted to confess to him, tell him who her father really was, but Elizabeth knew the danger she'd be placing herself in if she did.

Her gaze moved to Jonathan. He pulled another apple off the tree and dropped it into his sack. What if she told him? Would he tell the other outlaws? Would he allow her to be raped or killed?

As if reading her thoughts, he asked, "Why don't you tell me the truth, princess?"

Chapter 14

Elizabeth stood, paralyzed.

Jonathan set his full pillowcase on the ground at their feet. "I need you to be honest with me." His brown gaze blazed into hers.

She nodded. "All right."

"Are you really the banker's daughter?"

She shook her head. "No," came out a whisper.

"Who is your father?"

"George Winterspoon, the general store owner." Her body trembled.

He pulled her to him. His hand rubbed her back as she quivered in his arms. "It's all right," he murmered.

"What are you going to do?" She closed her eyes, dreading to hear his next words.

"Nothing."

"Nothing?" Elizabeth leaned her head back and looked up at him. She read sincerity in his eyes.

"Your secret is safe with me. The men will never know."

She swallowed the lump in her throat. "What about Red?"

He released her and picked up the sacks. "Let me worry about him. Just don't tell anyone else. I'm working on something. You will be free soon. I promise."

That night, Elizabeth hurriedly slipped her nightgown over her head. She knew Millie would be returning from the outhouse soon.

The sound of voices outside the door drew her attention. She tiptoed to the window and peeked out. Jonathan and Millie stood by a small tree at the corner of the shed. Elizabeth strained against the wall to catch their words.

Jonathan's deep voice drifted on the evening air. "Her father isn't the banker. He's the general store owner and he refuses to pay the ransom."

"What are we going to do?

"I'm working on a plan. As soon as I have it mapped out, I'll fill you in."

Millie's voice quivered. "When Red finds out she's not worth anything, you know as well as I do he'll give her to the men."

The words sent a cold sweat over Elizabeth's body. Hearing someone actually voice her thoughts frightened her even more than she realized. Her throat closed, and she fought to breathe. *I must stay calm. And remember that God will protect me.*

"I'll die before I let Red turn her over to this lot."

Though Elizabeth feared for Jonathan's safety, her heart melted at the thought of what he seemed willing to give up for her.

"Millie, you and Elizabeth get packed and be ready to ride at a moment's notice."

Chapter 15

Jonathan watched Red, José, and Edward ride into camp at high speed. A bloody shirt was wrapped around Red's thigh. He wondered where the rest of the men were. "What happened?"

"The sheriff and a posse were waiting for us." Pain laced Red's features.

Jonathan helped the leader down. The big man leaned heavily on his shoulders and grunted as they inched toward the house.

Edward held the door open. As soon as they were inside, Edward pulled a chair close to the window.

Jonathan helped Red into it. "Let me look at that."

"I need a drink." Red grunted.

"I'll get it." José hurried out of the room.

Jonathan untied the knot in the material and pulled the cloth free from the flesh. Red gave a sharp intake of breath. Torn flesh surrounded the hole in his leg. Blood flowed from the wound.

José returned. "Here you go, boss." He handed him a full bottle of whisky.

Red gripped the cork between his teeth and pulled. He spit the plug across the room and drank deeply.

"I'll get something to clean this up," Jonathan said.

"You do that." Red downed another long swig.

Edward followed Jonathan to the kitchen. The scent of meat and fresh bread filled the warm room. But neither of the women were there. Jonathan guessed that as soon as Millie heard the men coming in, she'd hurried to lock herself in the shed with Elizabeth. "How did it happen?"

"The minute Red gave the signal to attack the train, Sheriff Dodson and his men hit us hard. I'm lucky they didn't shoot me."

Jonathan grabbed a washbasin. "How many men did Red lose?"

"All of them, except me and José." Edward pulled off his hat and wiped the sweat from his brow. "Good thing you kept Harry here with you."

Jonathan dropped a dishrag into the pan. He poured water from the kettle over the rag, and then set the kettle on the burner and tucked a clean dish towel into his back pocket.

"Dodson hauled seven men off sitting upright and six over the saddle."

Jonathan hated that six men had died. Even though they were outlaws, he hadn't wished them dead. Except Red. "I found Sarah's brooch in Red's trunk."

Edward whistled low. "Finally! I was beginning to think we'd never find proof. But that's not enough, is it?"

"Nope. We can't do anything without a confession."

Edward rubbed the back of his neck. "If we can keep Red drinking, maybe he'll start talking."

Jonathan took the half-full pan of water and started toward the house. "I've talked to Harry. He wants out of this mess. He agreed to try to get Red to confess to the killing."

"If he testifies against Red, that could lessen his jail time."

"That's what I told him."

"Where is he now?"

"Down at the river, fishing."

"I'll go get him."

"After you get Harry, head for the horse corral and wait for me there."

Edward headed toward the river while Jonathan took the washbasin into the house.

When he entered, Red called, "Johnny boy, come sit by me!"

Jonathan set down the washbasin, grabbed a wooden crate, and pulled it in front of Red's legs. He gazed at the half-empty bottle. "You might want to drink a little more of that. This is gonna hurt."

Red tilted the bottle back and gulped.

"What's for supper tonight?" José asked. He bit off a hunk of beef jerky and chewed. "I hope it's not beans. I could use a good steak." His dark complexion seemed a bit pale as he slumped against the wall.

Jonathan noticed the Mexican's right hand resting on the gun at his hip. "You doin' all right?"

"Sí."

Jonathan focused on cleaning the gunshot wound.

Red winced and straightened in his chair. "Who's on watch duty?" he asked through gritted teeth.

"Sam and Amos."

"Any news from the boys I sent to look for that gal's pa?"

"Not yet."

"Should've been back by now," Red grumbled. He slanted the bottle back and took another gulp.

Harry entered the room and set another bottle of liquor on the table. He walked behind Red and opened the window halfway. He nodded at Jonathan.

Jonathan finished cleaning the wound. He dropped the bloody cloth back into the water, and then pulled the dish towel from his back pocket. "Looks like the bullet is in the bone. It'll have to stay." He knotted the material around Red's thigh and jerked on the ends.

Red gasped and his face lost all color. He gripped the arm of the chair with one hand. The knuckles of his other hand turned white around the neck of the bottle.

"Sorry," Jonathan mumbled as he tied it off. He had thought he would be happy to see the outlaw in pain. But Jonathan found himself feeling sorry for the man. The thought that he might hang before turning from his evil ways and die without knowing Christ made him sad.

He picked up the pan filled with pink water. "I'll get rid of this and then check in with Millie. Maybe she'll serve supper a little early tonight."

Red drank from his near-empty bottle with a faraway look on his face.

Jonathan stepped out the front door. As he closed it, he heard Harry ask, "How'd the robbery go?"

Jonathan slipped to the side of the house and crouched behind a lilac bush near the open living room window.

"We didn't have time to rob the train." Red grunted. "We were ambushed. Someone warned the sheriff." Glass shattered. It sounded like the empty bottle had been thrown across the room and busted as it hit the wall.

"Here you go, boss." Jonathan assumed Harry handed him the new bottle.

"Soon as I find out who ratted us out, I'll kill him," Red muttered.

"How many people have you killed, boss?" Harry asked.

"Plenty. But only when I had to. And after what happened today, the dirty dog who spoiled our plans will die with my hands around his cowardly throat."

Jonathan saw Harry lean against the window. "Must have been Porter who betrayed us."

"I should have taken care of him years ago." Red's voice began to slur.

"Boss, I'm going to the kitchen and see if I can round us up some grub," José announced.

Boots clomped across the floor. The sound of the door closing alerted Jonathan to the fact that had José had left the house.

"I bet Porter never killed anyone," Harry muttered. Silence followed his words for several moments.

"There was one little gal," Red said. "About three years ago."

Had Jonathan been wrong? Was it Porter who'd killed Sarah?

Harry pushed away from the window frame. "Porter killed a girl?"

"Depends on how you look at it. I was the cause, but he pulled the trigger."

Jonathan had expected to feel vindication at having finally learned about his sister, but the only emotion he felt was sadness.

"You know, boss, if you had proof that Porter killed her, maybe the law would take care of him for you. That way he'll never be able to rat us out again. I'm sure he'd hang for killing the girl," Harry suggested.

Knowing Red's back was to the window and Harry was the only person inside, Jonathan chanced standing. The lilac bush concealed him as he looked through the window.

Red dropped his arm and rested the bottle of liquor on his uninjured thigh. "And if I had this proof, how would I get it to the sheriff?"

Harry hunkered down in front of Red. "I could take it for you. So far the law has no idea I'm a part of this group."

"Now you're thinking like an outlaw!" Red leaned forward and slapped Harry on the shoulder. "Boy, go in my room and drag my trunk out here."

Jonathan ducked back down, just in case Red decided to turn toward the window while Harry was out of the room. The sound of boots drifted out the window. After a couple of minutes, the scrape of wood across the floor alerted Jonathan to Harry's return.

"Here you go, boss." Harry puffed.

"Get that lid open and look for a little velvet box."

Jonathan rose cautiously and peeked inside the room. Red still faced the opposite wall. Harry knelt in front of him, looking inside the big chest. He dug around for several long moments before asking, "This one?" He pulled out the velvet jewelry box.

"That's it." Red took the box and opened it. Reverently he pulled out the cameo.

"That's mighty pretty," Harry said.

"Yes, it is. She was pretty, too." Red took another swig from the bottle.

"Who?"

"I don't know her name."

Harry shut the lid on the trunk and sat on top of it.

Red swirled the liquid around in the bottle. "She was a pretty young girl, brown hair, brown eyes, and pretty lips, full and sweet like ripe peaches." He paused in memory.

Jonathan wanted to shut his eyes and ears to keep them from seeing and hearing the man who spoke of his sister this way. But he knew he had to hear it all.

Red drank from the bottle, and then continued. "Me and the boys saw this farm. It was in the middle of nowhere, so we rode into the yard to water our horses. She came out the door and told us to leave." He paused. "Said her brother would be home anytime."

Jonathan eased down the wall. He sat on the ground, reliving that fatal day.

"I didn't mean to get her killed. All I wanted was a kiss. But she acted all uppity and told me not to touch her. I grabbed her and she got hold of my gun.

We wrestled with it. Then Porter shot her. This tore from her dress as she fell."

So Porter had killed Sarah. *How could I have been so stupid? No wonder Porter never wanted to talk about his early years with Red. To do so, he might have slipped and told of the murder.* Jonathan was thankful that Porter was being held in Santa Fe. At least now, he wouldn't have to chase Porter down.

After several long minutes of silence, Red's garbled voice said, "Here. You take it."

Jonathan pulled himself upright. He watched through the window as Red leaned his head back and closed his eyes. Snores filled the room. Harry stood there, holding the open jewelry box.

Jonathan motioned for Harry to join him at the window. He leaned inside and whispered in Harry's ear, "Stay a few minutes and make sure he's really asleep. Then come to the corral."

Harry nodded.

Jonathan felt his eyes burning with tears. He fought the desire to grieve for his sister and headed for the horse corral where he'd asked Edward to wait for him.

"Porter did it," Jonathan told Edward at the corral.

Edward stared. "It wasn't Red?"

"No. He was there, but he didn't actually shoot her."

At the sound of running boots, the two men turned.

Harry rushed up to them, clutching the jewelry box. He handed it to Jonathan.

Edward clasped Harry's shoulder. "You did well."

"Harry," Jonathan said, "I want you to go with Edward." He returned the brooch to him. "Take this and Frank to the San Juan County sheriff. You'll find Frank at the hidden cave."

"I know the one." Edward moved toward the horses. "I'll go get him."

Jonathan turned his attention to Harry. "Go get your things, then stop by the kitchen. Ask Millie to put together enough provisions for the three of you. And don't let Red or any of the other men see you leave."

"I'll be careful." Harry tucked the jewelry box into his inside vest pocket and took off.

Jonathan saddled Harry's horse, praying for the young man's safety. He silently thanked the Lord for showing him the truth of what happened to Sarah.

Edward rode up on his saddled horse. "Don't worry about Harry. I'll take good care of him."

Jonathan cinched Harry's saddle into place. "Thanks."

"What are you going to tell Red when he finds out we're gone?"

"That I sent you in search of Frank."

Edward nodded. "We'll be back as soon as possible with the sheriff and his men." Then he turned his mount toward the cave.

Two days later, Elizabeth paced in the small shed. Millie and Jonathan had told her she needed to stay locked up for her own protection. But two days was a long time to be left alone with no companionship other than Millie's.

She sighed. *I miss Jonathan.*

The front door creaked open. Elizabeth realized with a start that she'd forgotten to lock it when Millie left after lunch. Her knees shook. When she saw Jonathan fill the entryway, she released a pent-up breath.

Her heart leaped at the sight of him. His windblown hair made her long to run her fingers through it.

He held out his hand to her. "I thought you might like to get out for a while. The fresh air will do you good."

She slipped her hand into his. "Where are we going?"

"For a walk through the woods." He glanced over his shoulder and pulled her outside.

She hurried to match her pace with his long strides. Once within the trees, he slowed down. His fingers tightened around hers. Elizabeth inhaled the musky scent of the oak, cottonwood, and pine trees.

"I'm sorry it's been so long since you've been out." Jonathan smiled at her. "With guard duty, taking care of Red, and keeping José busy with chores, I've been preoccupied. But everything should be wrapped up soon, and you'll be free."

Elizabeth frowned. "What do you mean? Has the ransom been paid?"

"I'm sorry. I can't give you any details. If José were to get his hands on you, you might talk, even though you don't want to."

A shiver of fear ran over her at the thought of José touching her.

Jonathan lifted her face. Elizabeth felt his coffee-scented breath upon her lips. His mouth eased closer. She closed her eyes. Warm lips lingered on hers.

He broke the kiss and tucked her against his side. She knew José was still out there, but in that moment, with Jonathan beside her, Elizabeth felt safe and secure for the first time in her adult life.

"I'd give my life before I let any harm come to you, princess." He clasped her hand and pulled it against his chest.

She wanted to believe him.

They stood under the trees for several moments. "I need to get back."

Holding hands, they started toward camp. Elizabeth decided to give Jonathan something she'd withheld for a long time.

Her trust.

Chapter 16

Every muscle in Jonathan's body knotted with tension. He lifted his gaze from the domino game he was playing with Amos and cocked his head to the side. Everything was still. Even the birds had stopped singing.

From his chair by the stove, Red opened his eyes. "What's going on?" He raised his head.

Amos laid down a domino. "I didn't hear anything."

"That's just it." Red's eyes, now alert, bore into Jonathan's. "Can you sense it, Johnny boy?"

It's about time they got here. Jonathan stood and pulled his gun from its holster. "I'll go check it out."

Red rubbed his thigh. "No. I want you with me." He pointed to Amos. "You go."

Jonathan moved to the door and stood off to one side. "Check on the horses first."

The old outlaw nodded and slipped out. Jonathan watched him press his body to the side of the house. His gaze searched Jonathan's.

Jonathan nodded.

The old man slipped around the house and toward the back.

"Get my gun." Red moved to the window, dragging his injured leg. He sank to the floor and leaned against the wall.

Jonathan crouched low, hurried past the window, and headed down the hallway to Red's bedroom. Edward stood outside the open window.

"Is he armed?" Edward whispered.

"No. What's going on out there?" Jonathan saw Red's pistol lying on top of the trunk. He picked it and emptied all the bullets from its chamber.

"The sheriff and his men are here. We have Amos, Sam, and José. Don't forget Red carries that knife in his boot." Edward ducked below the windowsill and out of sight.

Jonathan returned to the living room. "There you go, boss." He handed Red his gun.

Red flipped open the chamber and saw that there were no bullets. His green eyes narrowed as Jonathan drew his weapon.

"You're under arrest, Red."

Red stared up at him. "You a lawman, Johnny boy?"

Jonathan nodded.

"I kinda been thinkin' you were. Just didn't want to trust my instincts." He reached for his boot.

Before Red could get to the concealed knife, Jonathan grabbed his hand and pinned the big man's arms to the dirty floor.

Despite his injury, Red fought back with brutal strength. Jonathan grappled with him, muscles straining, breath whistling between his teeth as he tried to lever the much larger man's weight off him. Red bellowed and shoved his arm against Jonathan's throat and bore down with his full weight. Jonathan's vision blackened.

Edward shoved the door open and rushed into the room. He slammed his knee into Red's injured thigh. The outlaw screamed in pain. Edward jerked the weapon from Red's boot.

"'Bout time you got here," Jonathan huffed as he pinned the struggling outlaw's arms behind him.

"That's gratitude for you."

Edward reared his fist back. Jonathan moved his head out of the way, and Edward delivered a blow to Red's jaw. The big man slumped the rest of the way to the floor. Edward rubbed his knuckles and winked.

Together they lifted the unconscious man and half carried, half dragged him outside. José, Sam, and Amos glared at them from the backs of their horses. Their hands and feet were bound, and bandannas covered their mouths.

The San Juan County sheriff, J. C. Dodson, motioned for two of his men to seize Red. The deputies moved forward and took Jonathan's and Edward's places by the outlaw's sides. They hauled Red toward another lawman, who helped them get him mounted on a horse.

Jonathan watched as the men tied the still-unconscious outlaw leader's hands and feet under the horse's belly. Red was going to jail tied to the horse on his belly. Jonathan knew the outlaw was going to be angrier than a wet skunk when he woke up.

"Good work, Jonathan."

"Thanks, J. C. I couldn't have done it without Edward."

J. C. laughed. "That's what he tells me."

Edward grinned.

"You boys ready to saddle up? We're taking these men on into Santa Fe." J. C. pulled himself up on his horse.

"Not me." Jonathan patted the sheriff's mount on the shoulder. "I promised a certain young lady I'd escort her to Farmington. I'll catch up with you as soon as I get her there safely."

Edward stepped into the stirrup of his horse and swung into the saddle. "I'll meet up with you in Santa Fe."

"Keep an eye on Harry for me."

"Why else would I be going to Santa Fe?"

Edward joined the other men. Dust filled the air as they rode out of camp. Jonathan waited until the last man disappeared from sight before turning back to the shed.

He couldn't wait to tell Elizabeth he was a U.S. Marshal and not an outlaw. As he walked, he allowed himself to dream. On the way to Farmington, he'd tell Elizabeth he loved her and wanted her to be his wife. He'd let her know about his plans to buy an apple orchard in Farmington. Jonathan imagined her saying she loved him, too, and that she'd always wanted to live on a farm.

He hurried to the shed and the woman he loved.

Elizabeth and Millie hid under Millie's cot. Edward had stopped by half an hour earlier and told Millie to barricade the door.

Silence now filled the room. What if the new outlaws took over the camp? What would happen to her and Millie? Where was Jonathan? Was he safe?

Elizabeth hated waiting and not knowing. Fear ate at her insides, causing her stomach to cramp. "What do you think is happening?"

"Shh. Someone's coming." Millie pressed her back even closer against the wall.

Elizabeth laid her head on her arms, closed her eyes tightly, and prayed, *Lord, please keep us safe.*

A knock sounded at the door. Both women jerked. Elizabeth pushed as close to Millie as she could.

"It's me. Jonathan. Open the door."

Elizabeth and Millie scrambled out from under the bed. They pulled away the furniture as fast as they could, then flung open the door. "Is it safe?" Millie asked breathlessly.

"Yes." Jonathan stepped into the room.

"What happened?" Elizabeth asked.

Millie shut the door and sat on her cot.

He took Elizabeth's hand and pulled her toward the cot. They sat on the edge of the mattress. "All the outlaws have been arrested."

Her heart leaped with joy. "So we're free?"

He smiled. "Yes."

She jumped from the bed and grabbed her friend's hands. They laughed and danced about the room.

Jonathan's warm laughter filled the room.

Elizabeth stopped dancing and studied his face. "How come you weren't arrested, too?"

He stood and walked to her. "I'm not an outlaw, Elizabeth."

"You're not?"

"No. I'm a U.S. Marshal. So is Edward. He and I have been trying to catch Red for three years for murdering a woman in Texas." He stared off at the wall for a moment, his emotions veiled. "We weren't sure if he was the right man until a few days ago. Only it wasn't Red who shot her. It was Porter."

The news hit Elizabeth hard. The man she'd decided to trust had lied to her. She realized he'd possibly done it to keep them both safe. But when she'd told him the truth about her, why hadn't he told her about himself?

"I'm not surprised Porter is a murderer." Millie's words were sharp.

Elizabeth met Jonathan's guarded gaze. "Does this mean I can go on to Farmington now?"

"I'll take you as soon as you're ready."

"And Millie, too?"

"Of course."

Elizabeth turned to her new friend. "I'm ready to leave now."

"Nothing keeping me here," Millie replied.

Elizabeth held the door open for Jonathan. She couldn't control the sound of anger in her voice as she said, "We'll be ready in a few minutes."

She saw confusion in his eyes as he stood to leave. What had he expected? For her to jump for joy that he'd lied to her?

After he walked out, Millie said, "I'm not sure if my family is still in Farmington, but you've convinced me I should try to find them."

Elizabeth hugged her. "I think that is a great idea." She grabbed her bag and began throwing her things inside.

"You don't think Jonathan will mind my tagging along?" Millie asked as she walked to her cot.

"Why should he?"

"I just thought you two might want to be alone." Millie pulled the pillowcase off her pillow and dropped her personal items inside it.

Elizabeth picked up her Bible and clutched it to her chest. "We're not a couple, Millie."

"Why not?"

"He lied to me." Her voice cracked. "My father lied to me and my mother." Elizabeth put the Bible into her bag.

Jonathan had placed his life on the line to protect her. But he'd also hurt her. And no matter how foolish it seemed, she felt justified in being angry.

Millie tied a knot in the end of the pillowcase. "You weren't entirely honest with him, either."

"True. But my life depended on my keeping my identity a secret."

"Obviously his did, too. Why don't you talk to him?" A smile touched the older woman's lips.

Elizabeth sighed. "I guess you're right." She snapped her carpetbag closed and looked at her friend. "Ready?"

Right or wrong, she still felt anger radiate from her like fog from a river.

Chapter 17

If he lived to be a hundred, Jonathan felt sure he'd never understand women. *She should be happy I wasn't carted off to jail with the rest of the gang.* Instead her eyes flashed at him every time she looked in his direction. Which wasn't often.

As he finished saddling Ginger, he peeked at the two women waiting beside the barn. Elizabeth studied the bag in her hands while Millie shifted nervously from one foot to the other. He moved to the other horse. *She doesn't have any reason to be angry with me.*

"You sure you don't mind my coming along?" Millie asked.

He finished saddling the small black mare and grinned. "Of course not."

"Thanks. I'm not even sure why I'm going back to Farmington. My family may tell me to get right back on that horse and keep riding. I might be better off to go to Durango and start fresh. But I have to hear my family say they don't want me before I move on. I must be crazy as a loon."

Jonathan lowered his linked hands, and Millie placed her booted foot into them. With a gentle push, he helped her into the saddle. "No, you aren't crazy, and if they do reject you, at least you'll know you tried and can move on with your life."

"True."

"And in the meantime, we'll pray."

"I appreciate that."

He turned to help Elizabeth mount, but she was already on Ginger. His gaze searched out hers, but she refused to look at him. He mounted his own stallion.

As he led the way, Jonathan tried to figure out what had made Elizabeth angry with him.

Millie rode up beside him. "Thank you for bringing me with you." She smiled. "I appreciate everything you've done for me over the past year. I wouldn't have survived if it weren't for you."

"You're welcome. I just wish Elizabeth were as pleased as you are."

"Oh, she's happy to be free. She just has a lot on her mind right now."

Jonathan nodded. "I don't understand why she's angry with me."

Millie shifted in the saddle. "Elizabeth is hurt that you didn't tell her who you really are. Her father hurt her, too, and she's trying to sort out her emotions right now."

Of course, he'd never meant to hurt her. But if he had it all to do over, he'd do everything the same way if it meant protecting her and capturing Sarah's killer.

Millie pressed on. "She hasn't told me so, but I know she's also concerned about how the people of Farmington are going to accept her. And if they don't, what is she going to do? Her future is just as uncertain as mine is right now."

I should have realized she'd be worried about that. He glanced over his shoulder.

Elizabeth rode with her head bowed, as if deep in thought or prayer.

Jonathan faced front. "I'll take care of her."

"What if she won't let you?"

The question hung between them. "I've vowed to protect her."

"You're a good man. I just hope Elizabeth realizes it." Millie smiled and eased her mare back beside her friend's.

What had she meant by that? Did the woman expect him to quit caring for Elizabeth just because she was being stubborn? Never! He'd give her time to sort things out. But he intended to fight for this new love he'd discovered.

Elizabeth dropped from her horse. In her haste to get down unassisted, she jarred every bone in her body. She gazed about the spot Jonathan had chosen to camp for the night.

They were close to a river, with ancient oak trees and stands of cottonwoods nearby. Rocks surrounded them on three sides, which would make it difficult for anyone to approach their camp without notice. The echoes of the rambling river soothed her tired nerves.

Jonathan pulled his saddlebags from the stallion and handed them to Millie. "I packed a few things. Use what you can for supper."

"I brought a few things, too. We'll eat well tonight."

Elizabeth moved to Ginger's side and began taking off her saddle. She hadn't even thought about where her next meal was coming from. Had she started to expect Jonathan to take care of her so much that she'd never given a thought to her own needs?

When she'd left Durango, Elizabeth had been a bitter young woman out to make a new start for herself, depend on herself, and not expect others to take care of her. What had happened to that person? Had she merely transfered her bitterness from one man to another?

"Here, let me take care of that." Jonathan gently brushed her hands away from the saddle.

"No, thanks. I need to do it myself."

"Why?"

Elizabeth looked into his eyes. "You won't always be here, Jonathan."

He stepped back.

She continued to pull at the saddle. Its weight slid from the horse and knocked her backward. Strong arms wrapped around her, holding her upright.

His warm scent enveloped her. A quiver ran down her back. The desire to stay in his arms tempted her to give up the anger that ate at her, but stubbornness overruled. She forced herself to step out of his embrace. "Thanks." She stumbled to the closest tree and dropped the weight.

When she turned around, she saw Jonathan slip Millie's saddle from her horse and set it easily on the ground near hers.

"I'll gather some wood for the fire," he said.

Millie dug inside the saddlebags. "Thanks, Jonathan."

He strolled into the woods. Elizabeth walked to the riverbank. Tired of fighting her emotions, she sat on a large rock to think.

How could she feel this way about a man who had lied to her? Led her to believe he really cared about her? He'd betrayed her trust. Why, he was a lawman. He could have taken her from the outlaw camp anytime. But apparently, bringing Red and his gang to justice was more important.

Her gaze moved to the heavens. Geese honked overhead. *Lord, help me to overcome this feeling of bitterness.*

Clouds floated peacefully in the sky, but no word from God touched Elizabeth's heart. She heard Jonathan drop the gathered wood on the ground. Pushing up from the rock, she walked back to Millie and squatted beside her.

"Can I help?"

Millie smiled. "Sure. Let's fix supper. We can have coffee, biscuits, bacon, cheese, apples, and canned peaches. How does that sound?"

She couldn't help but feel the joy her friend radiated. "Wonderful."

They worked in comfortable silence. She pulled food from the bag while Jonathan started the fire and Millie pulled out a small frying pan.

Jonathan stood and stretched. He picked up a tin coffeepot, and then walked to the water's edge, where he washed his hands and filled the container with water.

"I can't believe we're finally free. It seems like a dream come true." Millie laid the slab of bacon in the skillet. "I am so thankful for Jonathan and Edward. Without them, we'd still be in the camp with a bunch of outlaws."

"I know." Elizabeth had been so focused on the fact that Jonathan had lied to her, she'd never given a thought to the reality that he'd helped get them out of the camp. *Oh, Lord, I'm so sorry. I never thanked You or Jonathan.*

Millie sat back. The smoky smell of bacon filled the evening air. "Jonathan told me that he and Edward had been on Red's trail for years. I always figured it was Red who killed that girl, not Porter."

"What girl?" Elizabeth pulled her gaze from Jonathan and focused on Millie.

"Jonathan's sister, Sarah. She was killed one day while he was out hunting. He and Edward weren't sure Red was the one who had murdered her until Harry got the confession out of him. She was the reason Jonathan became a marshal." Millie split a cold biscuit in half and forked bacon into it. She handed it to Elizabeth.

Red killed Jonathan's sister. No wonder he didn't want Red to find out who he really is.

"We're lucky Jonathan took an interest in us." Millie continued stuffing biscuits with bacon.

Elizabeth stared into the flames as they leaped and crackled. How awful it must have been for Jonathan, having to obey commands from a man who might have killed his sister. Her heart ached for the man.

She looked up and realized Millie was watching her. Disapproval laced the woman's eyes. "Jonathan never meant to hurt you. Why don't you think about the good he did instead of the bad you *think* he did?"

Her mind spun in several directions. What could she say? She'd behaved like a child.

Millie set the skillet to the side, picked up several bacon-filled biscuits, and joined Jonathan by the river before Elizabeth could form an answer.

Elizabeth stared at the biscuit in her hand. She set it with the others and went in search of her carpetbag. She found it with Millie's pillowcase.

Her Bible rested on top. She pulled it out and returned to the fire. She allowed the Book to fall open on her lap. "*When you don't know what to search for, let the Spirit lead you,*" Claire had advised years ago. Not sure where to search for answers, Elizabeth decided to simply read where it had opened. She looked down at 1 Corinthians 13:4: "*Charity suffereth long, and is kind; charity envieth not; charity vaunteth not itself, is not puffed up.*"

Her gaze moved to where Jonathan and Millie sat, eating in the dimming light. She wanted to join them. But there was much she needed to work out within herself.

She read the verse again. *"Charity suffereth long."* Jonathan had shown her patience. Even when she'd behaved badly. Did that mean he loved her?

She continued with the next phrase. *"And is kind."* He'd shown her kindness even when she'd been rude and hateful. *"Charity envieth not; charity vaunteth not itself."* Jonathan hadn't boasted that he was a lawman. *"Is not puffed up."* Since the day she'd met him, Jonathan had never behaved pridefully.

Had she judged him falsely? *I've been fighting my feelings for him because I'm afraid of getting hurt again. This has to stop.*

She raised her head and looked at Jonathan. She wanted to tell him how she felt and why. Was it too late?

Peace settled over her. She bowed her head and whispered, "Thank You, Lord, for showing me the extent of my feelings for Jonathan. Help me to be patient and kind, not to envy or be prideful. I want to be the kind of Christian I know You want me to be. In Your Son's name. Amen."

Chapter 18

The next morning, Jonathan rose early. He saddled the horses and made coffee, then sat on a log near the fire. He gazed at Elizabeth, lying on her side, both hands resting under her cheek. Her long hair curled about her body, and the soft firelight created a halo around her head, giving her an angelic look.

He smiled when her eyes opened. Her smile in return warmed his heart. Gone was the look of anger and distrust in her eyes. She sat up and yawned. Then she wrapped the blanket about her shoulders and walked to his side.

He scooted over and patted the log.

She sat beside him. "I'm sorry about the way I behaved yesterday."

Jonathan handed her a cup of coffee. "I'm sure you had your reasons."

"Not good enough ones to justify the way I acted." She held up her hand when he started to interrupt her. "You hurt me, even though you didn't mean to, and I had to work through that. But I am truly sorry for my rudeness." She sipped the hot brew and looked at him over the rim of the cup.

"I meant only to protect you."

"I know." She smiled.

He laughed softly. "I think I like you best early in the mornings."

She stifled another yawn. "Good."

After several moments of comfortable silence, Jonathan spoke. "We should reach Farmington this evening. Have you given any thought as to where you will be staying?"

"No. When I was offered the teaching position, I was assured there would be proper housing when I arrived." She hugged the blanket closer. "But I don't know whether that offer still stands."

"Last year's schoolteacher moved from one home to the next. Each family who had children in the school housed her for a week or so." He watched her face in the flickering light.

Disappointment crossed her features.

"I have a friend named Charles Nelson. He and his wife, Abby, are God-fearing people. They have four children, and Abby is expecting their fifth. She could use some help with the children. Would you be interested in staying with them?"

"That sounds wonderful."

He put an arm around her waist and pulled her close. It felt good to know he'd been forgiven. Jonathan kissed the top of her head. Her hair felt silky smooth under his lips.

Over Elizabeth's head he saw Millie yawn and sit up. She stared across the fire at them for a moment, then smiled. "I'm glad you two are getting along this morning."

Elizabeth eased away from his side, her cheeks flushed with a rosy glow.

~

At dusk, they pulled their horses to a stop on a hill that overlooked Millie's daughter and son-in-law's farmhouse. Smoke curled out of the chimney. "My daughter and her family may not even live here anymore." Millie's voice sounded strained.

Jonathan moved his horse to one side of her, and Elizabeth drew Ginger up on the other. Elizabeth stretched and touched her friend's shoulder. "If things don't go the way you hope, we can get a place together." Elizabeth wasn't sure about her own future, but Millie had shown her kindness in a time when all seemed lost. She wanted Millie to know she would always have a home with her. If not in an actual house, at least in her heart.

"Thank you." Millie patted her hand.

Jonathan shifted in his saddle. "Want me to lead the way?"

Millie nodded.

He inched Shadow down the hill, Millie moved her horse behind his, and Elizabeth trailed them both.

The path down the hill took them to the front yard. A big black dog ran out from under the porch. Its barks filled the air.

Over the frenzied barking, a male voice, coming from within the house, demanded, "Who is it? What do you want?"

Jonathan looked over his shoulder at Millie. She shrugged.

He turned his attention back to the house. "Jonathan Russell, U.S. Marshal."

The door crept open. A young man stepped out onto the porch, pulling the door closed behind him. He held a rifle in his hands. "What's your business here, Marshal?"

A curtain covering a window at the front of the house fluttered. Elizabeth wondered who might be watching. Could it be Millie's daughter, Christine?

Millie moved her mount up beside Jonathan. "Mark?" she called out to the man on the porch.

"Millie?"

The front door flew open and hit the wall with a *bang*. A young woman with brown hair ran across the porch. Her skirts flew out behind her as she raced across the yard. "Ma! Ma! Is it really you?" Tears streamed down her face.

"Christine!" Millie scrambled from her horse. Dust rose under her feet as she ran to meet her daughter.

The two women held each other and cried. The dog pranced and whined at their feet.

Elizabeth looked at Jonathan. She offered him a wobbly smile and wiped the moisture from her eyes.

"Jonathan, Elizabeth, I'd like you to meet my family." Millie pulled away from her daughter and waved them forward.

He swung from the saddle and walked to where Millie stood with her family. Elizabeth slipped off her horse and joined them.

"This is my daughter, Christine, and my son-in-law, Mark."

"Nice to meet you." Jonathan and Mark shook hands.

"Ma?" A child's sleepy voice called from behind them.

They all turned and looked to the house. A little girl with her mother's hair stood in the doorway. "The baby is crying."

"All right, Glory, I'm coming," Christine called.

As they walked toward the house, Millie asked, "Glory?"

Christine smiled, her blue eyes brimming with emotion. "We named her Gloria Jean, after Grandma."

Tears formed in Millie's eyes. "Ma would have liked that."

"Marshal, let's get these horses into the barn." Mark took Ginger's reins and pulled her toward a large building that sat to the right of the house.

Jonathan gathered his and Millie's horses' reins and followed. "Please, call me Jonathan."

Elizabeth trailed behind the ladies into the house. Millie and Christine hurried to the bedroom behind the kitchen. The sound of a baby crying and its mother cooing made the small house feel like a home.

Her gaze moved around the kitchen. The counters and stove were clean; nothing littered the surface like at the camp. Here everything seemed to be put away, out of viewing.

She walked into the living room. A couch, chair, coffee table, and bassinet surrounded the fireplace. The fire added comfortable warmth to the room.

The muffled sound of Millie's and Christine's voices made her smile. Millie had made it home. Her family loved her and had welcomed her with open arms.

Elizabeth wondered if the Nelsons would accept her as readily. Jonathan seemed to think they would. Would the people of Farmington still want her as their new teacher? Or would they have offered the job to someone else by now?

The sound of laughter came from the bedroom. Millie came out, carrying the little girl. The child looked to be about four years old. Her brown hair was a mass of curls, and her wide eyes were the shade of blue that seemed to run in her family. She stuck her thumb into her mouth and laid her head on Millie's shoulder. "I'm sorry, Elizabeth. I didn't mean to leave you alone."

She smiled. "No need to apologize. I'm happy for you."

"Thanks." She smiled. "This is my granddaughter, Gloria Jean." Millie ran her hand over the little girl's curls.

"Hello, Gloria Jean."

"Hello," Gloria Jean mumbled around her thumb.

"I figured I might be a grandmother by now. But seeing the children and holding them. . ." Millie kissed the top of the girl's head. "I can't even describe the love."

Christine entered the room, carrying a little boy who looked to be about three months old. "Have you eaten yet?" she asked, tucking a blanket tighter around the baby's body.

Boots scraped on the front porch. Mark came through the door, followed by Jonathan. He hugged his wife. "Honey, would you mind pulling out the ham we had for dinner? Jonathan is leaving in a few minutes, and I'd like to have him go on a full stomach."

Christine gave her husband the baby. "I'll have supper on the table in a few minutes."

Mark sat in one of the chairs.

Elizabeth started to follow Millie and Christine into the kitchen.

"Would it be all right if I borrowed Elizabeth?" Jonathan asked.

Millie smiled. "Of course."

Jonathan took her hand in his. His palm felt warm against her cold hand. She allowed him to draw her across the room and outside. He closed the door behind them.

"I'm going to the Nelsons' tonight to make arrangements for you to stay with them." They walked across the yard toward the corral.

"Do you still think they'll take me?" She clung to his hand. Now that she realized she loved him, she didn't want to let him go.

He smiled at her. "I'm sure they will."

"What if the citizens of Farmington don't want me to be their schoolteacher?"

"I talked to Mark about that. Turns out he's on the school board. He says they haven't replaced you. The driver told them you'd been attacked. The mother of one of the students has been teaching until they could find you. Mark said he'd let the board know you're here and will be available to start school next month."

She smiled. "You mean I still have my job?"

"Sure do."

Elizabeth hugged him. "Oh, thank you!"

He wrapped his arms around her, kissed her softly on the lips, and placed his chin on her head.

Elizabeth rested her head on his chest. For the first time in a long time, she felt truly safe.

"Hey, supper's ready!" Mark called from the doorway.

He released her. Elizabeth immediately felt the chill of the night air. His hand grasped hers as they walked to the house.

"Will you be back in the morning?" she asked.

"I'll try to be here before noon." He opened the door and held it open for her.

She smiled at him. "Good. I'm going to miss you."

Elizabeth perched on the edge of a chair in the Nelsons' sitting room. It was a comfortable room with a large sofa, an overstuffed chair, and two end tables, one at the end of the sofa, one beside the chair. A large fireplace graced the end of the room. A thick rug covered most of the floor. A box of wood sat on one side of the fireplace, the box on the other side had toys spilling over its rim.

"Miss Winterspoon, we are so glad you have agreed to stay with us." Abby Nelson handed Elizabeth a cup of tea.

"I'm the one who should be thanking you for allowing me to stay." She took a sip of the hot, honey-laced beverage. She admired the stylish dress Abby wore. The woman looked fresh, happy, and wealthy. Her light brown hair was pinned in a fashionable roll on top of her head, but wayward ringlets drifted down around her face.

Abby poured a cup for herself, then set the teapot back on the coffee table in front of the couch. "You may decide you want to move after spending a few days in this noisy house."

"I'm sure I'll enjoy my stay, Mrs. Nelson." Elizabeth prayed her words were true.

"Please call me Abby."

"Only if you'll call me Elizabeth."

"Agreed." Abby sipped her tea. "The children can be a handful. Patricia Louise is the oldest at six and tends to boss the other children. Molly, who is five, rebels against Patricia Louise every chance she gets. The two of them fuss at each other a lot."

"Isn't that what sisters do?" she asked with a grin, wishing she had a sister.

Abby's tinkling laughter filled the room. "Those two sure do. I never had a sister, only brothers."

"I think we'll get along fine." Elizabeth set her cup down and folded her hands.

"Yes, I believe we will."

"Jonathan says you have two boys, also."

Abby poured more tea into Elizabeth's cup. "Dennis is three, and Linn just turned a year old. The boys are much quieter than the girls. So far."

Elizabeth picked up her cup. "Thank you."

"You're welcome." She smiled. "As you can see, I'm expecting our next child in a few months. So I really appreciate your staying with us and helping me out. It will be great to have a new friend."

Elizabeth wasn't sure what to say. She was glad when the sound of giggling drifted into the room. Abby stood. "Please excuse me."

"Of course." Elizabeth sipped her tea and thanked the Lord for this nice home and the family who had taken her in. She prayed she'd be happy here.

Movement caught her eye. She saw a little girl with light auburn hair and green eyes standing inside the door. Abby's description of the children led her to conclude that this was Patricia Louise.

She set down her tea and motioned for her to come closer. The little girl approached shyly. "What's your name?"

"Patricia Louise."

"I'm Elizabeth. How old are you?"

"Six."

"It's nice to meet you. I'm going to be the new schoolteacher. Do you think it would be all right if I lived here with you and your family?"

Patricia Louise nodded.

"I'm so glad. I think I'm going to have fun here."

Abby entered the room with two children, holding an infant in her left arm. "I see you've met Patricia Louise." She pushed two children forward. "These are Molly and Dennis." She pressed her finger against the baby's nose. "And this little fella is Linn."

Molly sucked her thumb. She looked just like her mother, with light brown hair and brown eyes. Dennis had darker hair and green eyes. Linn had auburn hair and blue eyes. They were all adorable. "Hello, children."

Patricia Louise jerked Molly's thumb from her mouth. "Say hello."

"No." The little girl glared at her sister, then returned her thumb to her lips.

Patricia Louise shook her head and returned to Elizabeth's side. "She's not 'posed to do that. Papa don't like it."

"I see."

"Your pa also doesn't like it when you act bossy, does he, Patricia Louise?" Abby gently reminded her daughter.

The little girl's lips pursed together. "No."

Abby gave her daughter a one-armed hug. "Why don't you take Molly and go get a cookie. And bring one back for Dennis. One of the hard ones."

"All right, Ma."

The little girls hurried from the room.

"When's your baby due?"

Abby patted her rounded belly. "Three months."

Elizabeth heard the front door open. Jonathan and Abby's husband, Charles, entered.

"It's time for me to go, princess," Jonathan announced.

At the familiar nickname, a delicious shiver traveled up her arms. She set her teacup on a small table by the couch and stood. "I'll walk you out."

A smile touched his lips. "I was hoping you'd say that."

"It was nice to see you again, Jonathan." Abby smiled. "Do come back soon."

"I plan on it." Jonathan held the door open for Elizabeth. They walked across the yard to the barn, where Shadow stood waiting for him. He checked his saddle, and then turned to face her.

Elizabeth fought tears. She knew he had to get to Santa Fe for Porter's trial. Still, it hurt to see him go. "I'll miss you," she choked out.

"I'm gonna miss you, too." He pulled her forward and kissed her soundly.

She inhaled the clean scent of him and squeezed her eyes shut. He said he was coming back, but he hadn't told her he loved her. *Lord, please let him confess his love for me.*

Jonathan pulled away and hauled himself into the saddle. "Charles says the doctor's been storing your trunk. I'll stop by his office on my way out and ask him to send it over."

"Thank you." Elizabeth barely managed to get the words out as she looked up into his chocolate-colored eyes.

He nodded once, and then turned his horse to go.

Elizabeth's heart ached. How many times on the trail had she wanted to tell him of her love? But it would have been improper to do so before he confessed his for her. She wondered if he really did love her. Had she just imagined the emotions in his eyes?

Her throat tightened, and tears burned her eyes. She stood in the afternoon sun, watching the man she loved ride out of the yard.

The desire to turn his mount around and tell Elizabeth how much he loved her threatened to choke Jonathan. But now wasn't the time. He had to take care of Porter and Harry first. Then he could cast off his badge and create a life for Elizabeth and himself.

Chapter 19

Elizabeth tucked Patricia Louise under the covers. She smiled at the little girl with lopsided pigtails. Naptime was always hard. Patricia Louise used any excuse to keep from going to sleep.

"I get to go to school with you next week." Patricia Louise squirmed on the bed she shared with Molly.

"Yes, I know. Come on, now, settle down so Molly can take her nap." She knew that once Patricia Louise settled down, both little girls would be asleep in no time.

Her green eyes sparkled with excitement. "Papa says tomorrow we'll go into town and get me some shoes."

"I'm not sleepy," Molly complained from her side of the bed. She yawned and her eyelids drooped.

"If you both lie really still so your ma can rest, I'll buy you each a piece of candy tomorrow at the general store."

"Yea!" they cried.

Elizabeth slipped the rose-patterned quilt under their chins. "Shh. You'll wake the boys." Elizabeth looked to the boys' beds. Both slept soundly.

She returned her gaze to the girls. They were as different as two sisters could be. Patricia resembled her dad, with auburn hair and green eyes. Molly's hair was light brown and her eyes the color of coffee, a miniature image of her mama. Patricia Louise had more energy than five children, and Molly moved with the speed of a snail.

During the last three weeks, Elizabeth had fallen in love with all four children. "You two stay very quiet and don't wake the boys or your ma. All right?" They nodded. She bent over and kissed each of them on the forehead.

"Can I get lemon drops at the store?" Patricia Louise whispered.

She smiled. "Yes, but only if you're very quiet."

"I will be."

"Me, too," Molly added.

Elizabeth closed the door behind her as she left the bedroom. She walked across the hall into her room, where her Bible lay on the bedside table. The bed looked inviting with its log-cabin quilt, but Elizabeth wanted more than a nap. She wanted some time alone with God and nature. She swept up the

Bible and headed downstairs.

"Did they give you a hard time today?" Abby sat at the kitchen table, shelling peas.

"No. They're just excited about the trip to town tomorrow." Elizabeth laid the Bible down on the entryway table just inside the living room. "I thought you were going to go rest, too."

"I was, but then I remembered these peas and decided to get them shelled first." She dropped more peas into her bowl.

"Why don't you let me finish that and go relax while you can?" Elizabeth sank into the chair beside her new friend.

"I'm almost done, but thank you. You've been such a blessing these last few weeks."

"I love being here." She had enjoyed her time with the Nelson family, too, but she missed Jonathan and Millie terribly. The two women worked in comfortable silence.

As soon as the peas were shelled, Elizabeth took them to the sink. "We can wash and put these up later. Now, off with you. Get some rest."

Abby stretched and braced her hands against her back. "You may be right. A short nap with the children might be nice." She yawned.

Relief washed over Elizabeth as Abby shut the door to her bedroom. She moved to the small living area and grabbed her Bible. Easing outside, she shut the front door as quietly as she could and walked across the yard and into the woods.

The coolness of the shade made her wish she'd grabbed a wrap. She thought about going back to the house and getting one, but her time alone would be shortened by the action. Elizabeth pressed deeper into the trees.

The smell of autumn lingered in the shadows. Her boots crunched the fallen leaves. She stopped at the sound of something in the underbrush. A small brown rabbit leaped into her path. Elizabeth pressed on.

She stepped out onto a meadow. With lighter steps, she continued across the browning grass that came up to her thighs. A quail burst from the bushes and into the air. Elizabeth laughed. Her skirts swished as she continued into the woods. New Mexico amazed her with its versatile countryside.

Charles would have a fit if he knew she wandered this far from the house every day. He seemed to care for her almost as much as for his own family. Abby and the kids were lucky to have such a devoted husband and father. She felt blessed to call him her friend.

The sound of bubbling water reached her ears. She smiled and hurried forward. The big old apple tree greeted her. It was her favorite one in the orchard. Its limbs stretched in all directions. She dropped at the base of the tree and sighed with contentment. The river extended out in front of her. The rest of the apple orchard spread out behind her. She stared at the water. She couldn't look at a river without thinking of Jonathan. His memory would forever be connected with the water and the way it churned across the rocks.

He'd been gone for three long weeks. Had he forgotten her?

She pushed him from her mind and focused on the Bible. She found the last passage she'd been reading and concentrated on it. She'd been studying a chapter a day since she'd found this spot. Today she read Genesis 13.

She laid the Bible down and dreamed about the new school year. She would begin work next week. She'd already planned out the lessons. Her first objective would be to find out from their current teacher where all the children were in their studies and then build on them.

Over the last three weeks, she'd attended church services with the Nelsons and met many of the families in the area. Her life would be complete if only Jonathan would return. She loved him and prayed daily that he loved her as much as she did him.

Would Jonathan be back by next week? Did he ever plan on coming back? She sighed and pushed up from the ground.

Elizabeth picked up her Bible and headed back to the house. She thought of Millie. She'd hoped her old friend would attend the same church as the Nelsons, but she didn't.

She crossed the yard and slipped inside the two-story house. All remained quiet. She moved to the kitchen sink and began rinsing the peas.

Life with Charles and Abby had been different from anything she'd experienced. With four children there was always work to be done. There were also a lot of hugs and kisses from the children. She went to bed every night exhausted. And truth be told, she loved it.

The sound of a wagon pulling into the front yard drew her to the window. *Millie!* Elizabeth wiped the water from her hands and hurried to the front door.

Millie jumped from the wagon.

Elizabeth ran to meet her. She grabbed her friend and hugged her close, the familiar scent of cinnamon and sugar wafting from the older woman. "I have missed you something awful." She released Millie and stared at her shining face.

"I've missed you, too. You look really good."

"Thanks. I've been getting plenty to eat and lots of exercise."

Millie laughed. "Me, too."

Christine stepped down from the wagon. Gloria Jean scrambled over the back of the bed. Christine caught Gloria Jean just in time to prevent her from falling to the ground.

Millie grinned. She reached into the wagon, picked Mark Junior up off the seat, and cradled the sleeping baby close.

Elizabeth and Millie stared at each other. The pleasure of having Millie with her again brought an even bigger smile to Elizabeth's face.

"Oh, where are my manners? Please come inside." She led them into the house, hoping the visitors wouldn't wake the children.

Abby came out of the bedroom, looking refreshed.

Elizabeth introduced them.

Abby smiled. "Millie, I'm so glad you came for a visit."

"Thank you. I missed Elizabeth and wanted to check on her. I hope it's not a problem that we brought the little ones."

"Oh, not at all."

"This is my daughter, Christine, and her children, Gloria Jean and Junior."

Elizabeth ushered everyone into the living room. "You all have a seat, and I'll get refreshments."

A smile touched Abby's lips. "That would be wonderful. Thank you." She sat on the couch and encouraged Millie to join her by patting the cushion. "Elizabeth has told me so much about you, I feel as if I know you already."

"I hope it was all good."

Abby laughed. "Of course it was."

Christine turned toward Elizabeth. "I'll come with you." Setting Gloria Jean down beside Millie, she followed Elizabeth into the kitchen. "Elizabeth, I'd like to thank you."

"Whatever for?" Elizabeth set about making a pot of coffee.

Christine sat at the table. "Mom told me how you talked her into coming home and how you helped her understand that God didn't judge her based on what other people had done to her. For that I will be eternally grateful."

"You're welcome. But Millie helped me, too. I would have never made it in that camp without her guidance and friendship."

"Mom says Jonathan Russell saved both of you." Elizabeth's heart leaped at the thought of him. "Have you heard from him?"

"No." Elizabeth walked to the cookie jar, put fresh-baked sugar cookies onto a plate, and set it on the table.

"He came out to the house yesterday. I thought he'd come here next." Christine picked up a cookie and nibbled at it.

Pain shot through Elizabeth as she realized he hadn't bothered to come see her. She turned her back to Christine to compose herself, then pulled down a tray to carry the snacks to the living room.

She took a deep breath as she placed the coffee, mugs, and cookies onto the tray. "I'm sure he's busy getting on with his life." Elizabeth hoped she didn't sound as bitter as she felt.

Chapter 20

Jonathan and Charles rode out to the Nelson farm. He'd been in town for a week. Two days before, he'd gone out to check on Millie. He'd told her the plans he had for himself and Elizabeth. She'd been thrilled for them.

"Elizabeth doesn't know I'm here, right?" Jonathan searched his friend's face.

"Didn't say a word to her this morning. Knew you wanted to tell her yourself."

"Thanks. It's been hard making myself stay away, but I wanted to have a future to offer her. She deserves that."

Charles nodded. "I felt the same way when I met my Abigail."

They continued on in silence. The brisk air whipped at Jonathan's cheeks. A small voice taunted him. *After what happened to your sister, are you really ready to take on the responsibility of another woman? What if something happens to her? Are you sure you can protect the woman you love?*

He'd made peace with himself, thanks to the Lord, and he refused to let the destructive thoughts tear into him again. He fought the inner voice with scripture. "*I will strengthen thee; yea, I will help thee. . . . It is God that girdeth me with strength. . . . I can do all things through Christ which strengtheneth me.*"

The mental torment ended as quickly as it had begun.

As Charles and Jonathan pulled their horses up beside the barn, Jonathan felt his heartbeat pick up. In just a few moments he'd be with the woman he loved. The woman who'd helped him see that it wasn't his strength he needed to rely on, but God's.

"She's not here." Charles's words pulled him from his thoughts.

"What do you mean?"

Charles looked up at the sky. "This is the time of day when she sneaks off to the orchard by the river. More than likely, she's down there absorbing a little peace and quiet." A smile touched his face. "Can't say I blame her. Our house gets pretty noisy."

Jonathan tied his horse to the rail of the fence. "How can I find her?"

He pointed. "Just go though the woods there, cross the meadow, and follow the sound of the river. She'll be down by the big apple tree."

Jonathan took off at a run, not caring if he looked like a lovesick boy. He'd thought he'd have to talk to her in front of the whole family, but God had granted him a chance to be alone with her. His heart expanded with each step that brought him closer to Elizabeth.

The meadow extended before him. He found the small path Elizabeth must have taken and rushed through the tall grass. Birds scattered in his wake. He felt wild and free, running through the grass and laughing.

When he entered the woods, Jonathan slowed down. The sound of the river met his ears. What was he going to say? How would he go about asking her? His heart hammered against his ribs. He'd gone over it a hundred times and still didn't know.

Over the river's gurgle, Jonathan heard soft sobs. He pulled his gun and ducked down. This was her place of solitude; why would she be sobbing unless something was wrong?

He ducked behind trees as he made his way toward the sound. Elizabeth sat under a massive apple tree. Her Bible lay open in her lap but trembling hands covered her beautiful face. Her shoulders shook.

"Princess?" he whispered.

Elizabeth stilled. Could it be him? Or was she just imagining what she wanted more than anything? Without looking up she said, "Jonathan?"

"What's wrong?"

It was him! Elizabeth wiped at the tears on her face. "Nothing. I'm fine." The lie tasted bitter, but she couldn't bring herself to say she'd been crying over him.

He holstered his gun and sank down in front of her. "You scared me to death."

"I'm sorry." *I must look a sight.* Puffy eyes, red nose. She almost wished he couldn't see her.

Jonathan wiped a tear off her cheek with his thumb. "I've missed you." His voice sounded husky.

"I've missed you, too."

He stood and extended a hand down to her.

She set her Bible aside, placed her palm in his, and allowed him to pull her up. She wasn't sure what he had in mind, but she knew she could trust him. He'd already proven he was a man of God.

She searched his eyes. "What are you doing here?" The question popped from her lips. *Please say you came to see me.*

His eyes twinkled with joy. "I bought part of Charles's land. It's not a big place, just a few acres."

Disappointment filled her. He hadn't come for her. She refused to let the sorrow show. "That's wonderful. But when will you have time to work it?

Lawmen don't have a lot of time for farming, do they?"

"I'm not a lawman anymore, princess. I gave it up. My plans are to work the farm and the apple orchard. I want to spend my free time fishing, reading, and going on picnics. And I need to do all those things with you."

Elizabeth's heart jumped in her chest. She felt as if she couldn't breathe. Was he saying what she thought he was?

His eyes sparkled down at her. He encircled her waist with his arms. "Will you go fishing with me? Read books with me and spend Sunday afternoons picnicking with me?"

She caressed his rough cheek. "I would love to do all those things with you." *And more.*

His arms tightened around her waist, and he pulled her even closer. He rested his head on hers. "Elizabeth, I love you. I can't imagine life without you."

She felt him inhale deeply before he released his hold on her.

He stepped back, knelt in front of her, and looked up. "Princess, will you marry me?"

She looked deeply into his eyes. "Yes." Her voice cracked. "I will marry you. I've loved you for what seems like an eternity."

Jonathan stood and gathered her in his arms again. She felt his body tremble against hers. "I was afraid I'd waited too long."

She pulled away and looked up into his face. His brown eyes swam in moisture.

Elizabeth placed a hand on each of his cheeks. "I could never love anyone the way I love you."

His kiss came soft and slow. Elizabeth enjoyed the warmth and trust she felt for this man. When he released her lips, she laid her head against his chest and listened to his steady heartbeat.

Thank You, Lord. Without Your love and understanding I would not be marrying the man I love. Be with us always.

Epilogue

Thanksgiving morning, 1900

Elizabeth stood just outside the sanctuary and took a deep breath. The light, sweet scent of honeysuckle and buttercups quieted her nerves. She held the bouquet tightly in one hand and placed the other on Charles Nelson's muscular arm.

"Please hold the flowers for a moment." She handed the bouquet to Charles and fidgeted with her hair below the tulle veil. The ringlets had to be just right. *I want to look perfect for Jonathan.*

Charles passed the flowers back, tucked her free hand into the crook of his arm, and gave it a fatherly pat. "Relax. You look beautiful. Jonathan is one lucky man."

"Thanks. I appreciate your giving me away." For a moment she wished her father could see her wedding day. Give her away. But he'd refused when she and Jonathan had asked him. His new wife couldn't travel since she was expecting their first child. He'd wished them luck and given his blessing for their union.

Charles pulled her from her thoughts. "Ready?"

Was she ready to marry Jonathan? To trust him to take care of her? To love her? To be her best friend for all time?

Yes!

"I'm ready."

They stepped forward.

Jonathan stood at the front of the church with the preacher. His heart beat swiftly as the beautiful strains of Mendelssohn's "Wedding March" filled the small church.

Millie and Claire, the matrons of honor, began the wedding procession. They wore matching mauve gowns of silk and burgundy. Wide-brimmed, cream-colored hats covered their heads.

Next, Patricia Louise and Molly Nelson came down the aisle. They wore identical yellow dresses. Jonathan smiled as the little girls tossed white flower petals made from crepe paper in the air and at the guests.

Then a vision of beauty in a white silk gown proceeded down the aisle. Lace and white pearls lined her collar and sleeves. A pearl headband crowned her veil. *His princess. His bride. His love.*

Jonathan couldn't pull his gaze from Elizabeth's sparkling green eyes.

She smiled.

He relaxed.

The wedding party turned to face the preacher. Edward and Harry stood to Jonathan's right as his best man and groomsman. He felt proud to have them both standing beside him as he pledged his life to Elizabeth.

They stood before the preacher and repeated their vows. Jonathan stared into her face during the whole ceremony. He silently thanked the Lord for this woman who grew more beautiful to him by the moment. His heart swelled to the point of taking his breath away.

When he heard the words, "You may now kiss the bride," Jonathan pulled her into his arms, lifted the transparent veil, and did just that. He'd been waiting months to be able to call her his wife.

The preacher cleared his throat. Reluctantly, Jonathan released Elizabeth's lips. He gave her a quick hug before turning to the sea of faces. Jonathan whispered, "I love you, princess, and I thank God for you."

She pulled back and smiled at him. "I love you, too."

They turned together to greet their friends.

"Ladies and gentlemen, I am proud to present to you Mr. and Mrs. Jonathan Russell."

Rhonda Gibson

Rhonda resides in New Mexico with her husband, James—her best friend and greatest supporter. She is thrilled that God is using the talents He gave her to entertain and share her love for Him. Her novel, *To Trust an Outlaw*, was awarded favorite historical romance of the year in 2007 by readers of Barbour's Heartsong Presents line. She feels blessed to have achieved such an honorary award. When not sitting in front of her computer writing, Rhonda enjoys making cards and jewelry for her family and friends. She loves hearing from her readers, too, so please feel free to write to her at P.O. Box 835, Kirtland, NM 87417. No time to write a letter? Visit her Web site at www.rhondagibson.com or read her blog at www.rhondagibson.blogspot.com.

A Letter to Our Readers

Dear Readers:

In order that we might better contribute to your reading enjoyment, we would appreciate your taking a few minutes to respond to the following questions. When completed, please return to the following: Fiction Editor, Barbour Publishing, Inc., P.O. Box 719, Uhrichsville, OH 44683.

1. Did you enjoy reading *Desert Roses*?
   - ❑ Very much—I would like to see more books like this.
   - ❑ Moderately—I would have enjoyed it more if ______________

____

____

2. What influenced your decision to purchase this book? (Check those that apply.)
   - ❑ Cover ❑ Back cover copy ❑ Title ❑ Price
   - ❑ Friends ❑ Publicity ❑ Other

3. Which story was your favorite?
   - ❑ *Stirring Up Romance* ❑ *Sharon Takes a Hand*
   - ❑ *To Trust an Outlaw*

4. Please check your age range:
   - ❑ Under 18 ❑ 18–24 ❑ 25–34
   - ❑ 35–45 ❑ 46–55 ❑ Over 55

5. How many hours per week do you read? ______________

Name ____

Occupation ____

Address ____

City ______________ State ______________ Zip ______________

E-mail ____